THE RED BARON LIV

THE RED BARON LIVES!

Brian Innes

NEW ENGLISH LIBRARY

For Eunice, Simon, Andrew and Jamey

First published in Great Britain in 1981 by New English Library

First NEL Paperback Edition November 1982

NEL Books are published by
New English Library,
Mill Road, Dunton Green,
Sevenoaks, Kent
Editorial office: 47 Bedford Square, London WC1B 3DP

Typeset by Fleet Graphics, Enfield, Middlesex

Printed and bound in Great Britain by Cox & Wyman Ltd, Reading

British Library C.I.P.

Innes, Brian
  The Red Baron lives.
  I. Title
  823'.914[F]   PR6066.0/

ISBN 0-450-05401-2

FOREWORD

I MUST confess that this is strictly a work of fiction since, in the absence of any diaries or personal correspondence, I have been compelled to construct not only imaginary dialogue but also a considerable portion of subsidiary details. However, the reader may discover for himself (as I did) that all the facts are true. He need only go, as I did, to the Public Record Office and apply for all those papers released under the fifty-year rule that relate to the tortuous negotiations of the Versailles Peace Conference. And perhaps, as I did, he will have delivered by mistake to his desk a file whose reference code differs by one small digit from the correct one. It bears on its cover (apart from the usual minuted acknowledgements and a swarm of initials) only the single word 'Baron' in an elegant Civil Service hand, and it contains, not the recommendations of a Treasury SEO on optimum levels of consumption of rubber bands and pencil sharpeners that I expected, but the astounding papers that form the basis of the current narrative.

What I read with mounting excitement that day in the PRO was of course but the beginning: the select bibliography attached as an appendix to this work is evidence of not more than a fraction of the research that I carried out in the succeeding months. Indeed, the pages that follow are only the first part of an astounding story that it is my intention, in due course, to reveal in full. It is a story spanning forty years that have changed the lives of every one of us, and its protagonist is a man who, through no fault of his own, was compelled to live out his life unacknowledged and unknown. Whether he was a traitor or a hero is for the reader to decide.

Such a story would never have seen the light of day without the invaluable help (generally unwitting) of a great many people. I would like to acknowledge, in particular, the assistance and unfailing courtesy of the staffs of the Public Record Office, the Royal United Services Institution, the RAF Museum, Hendon, the British Library, the Imperial War Museum; and above all that haven of desperate writers, the London Library.

CHAPTER 1

21 April 1918: Cappy

EVEN ON Sundays, the growl of the dawn barrage could be heard at the airfield, nearly twelve miles behind the lines. The prevailing west wind brought it, gently and insidiously, over the devastated fields of the Somme Valley, and with it a whisper of death: the sickly sweetness of decomposition, the musty hay smell of phosgene, the spent fumes of lyddite. But this morning the sound of the barrage had sunk to a desultory grumble, felt more than heard, like the promise of a summer storm far away. The mist and the smoke of battle still lay on the land like an old and filthy blanket, but the last spasms of the 'Michael' offensive had spent themselves against the flanks of the Morlancourt ridge; and the wind was blowing from the east.

The drogue, which the British fliers facetiously called a wind-sock, still hung listlessly from its mast at the bottom end of the field, but every time it stirred it stretched more positively toward the west, toward the front line. There would be no dawn patrol on either side this morning, because the spring mist clung wetly to everything, but each strengthening puff of breeze moved it in grey strands, revealing, now and then, a pale blue sky above it.

Captain Manfred liked to sleep late when he could, and this morning, exercising his renowed self-discipline, he had managed to keep himself deeply and calmly asleep until after eight

7

o'clock. Waking, he immediately sat up in his cot and swung his feet round and onto the floor; but he remained sitting in this position for several minutes, taking stock of the day and of his emotions. Roughly pinned to the grey wooden wall before him were two pieces of torn aircraft fabric. They were painted a light brown, both badly scorched, and each bore the registration number of a Sopwith Camel – they were the trophies of his previous evening's sport, his seventy-ninth and eightieth kills. His square but handsome face was expressionless, his pale blue eyes cold, as he stared at them, and almost unconsciously his fingers felt his skull above his right ear, along a four-inch furrow in the bone. Only a few weeks before, he had had more splinters removed from the wound that was scarcely hidden beneath the close-cropped hair.

Since the opening of the last offensive he had been filled with thoughts of death, of being shot down in flames, trapped in his cockpit as the liquid fire poured over him, and the triplane corkscrewed crazily from the sky to flatten itself in the two-dimensional world of the trenches. He remembered the day of his wound, how the Albatros D5 had seemed to tumble down the air, the veil of blood in his eyes, how he had torn his goggles from his head and still been unable to see – and how by willpower and sheer skill he had managed to bring the triplane onto an even keel and land her, eventually, near Wervicq. But had it been skill, or little more than good luck? He angrily brushed the thought aside, and stood up.

His orderly, Corporal Menzke, hearing the movement from behind the door of the hut, tapped gently, entered with a click of heels, and poured hot water into the tin basin balanced on the washing stand. Manfred stripped, washed, and shaved, seeing in the mirror how every day his eyes sank deeper in the hollows of his face, and then – and only then – walked slowly to the window as he towelled himself and looked out, almost apprehensively, at the weather. The drogue, visible only momentarily through the slowly thinning mist, was still hanging heavily: there would be no flying for at least two hours. Still pensive, he dressed slowly, putting on first a pyjama suit of fine grey silk, buttoning on the right shoulder and with his monogram embroidered on the left breast in a darker grey, then dark grey leather breeches and gleaming black boots lacing to

8

the knee. He shrugged into his uniform jacket, meticulously tugging it into shape as he fastened each button, and then carefully hung below his collar the *Pour le Mérite,* his coveted 'Blue Max'. Bareheaded, he opened the door between his bedroom and the squadron office.

There were no telegrams, and no movement orders. Lieutenant Karl Bodenschatz, his adjutant, had left a brief handwritten note to report that two of the aircraft were out of action: mechanics were unable to get the 220hp Mercedes engine of one of the Albatroses to fire evenly, and the upper planes of a Fokker would have to be stripped and strengthened again. Manfred turned his attention to his breakfast: a tall glass of hot tea with sliced apple in place of the unobtainable lemon, and two dry rolls. There was no butter, even for officers, and the bread, which his orderly had travelled to Peronne to bully from a Frenchwoman who had managed to set up a bakery among the ruins, was hard and bitter-tasting. He hated Cappy; he hated the gaunt ruins of the village, the shattered stumps of trees, the mud that crept everywhere, and the dank air of the Somme. Yet he was thankful that the offensive had for the moment exhausted itself, and that they would not be ordered to move forward yet again. Already they had moved twice within the month, from Avesnes-le-sec to Lechelle, and then to Cappy, and each time it involved many hours of paper work, of planning and organisation. Many of the planes could be flown, of course, from one field to another, but the rest had to be transported on limbers, with all the tents and the knock-down huts – more like a travelling circus than a *Jagdgeschwader* of Battle Fliers. Happily the British had retreated so rapidly over the ground at Cappy that they had left the flying field intact, together with one of their round-roofed huts of 'elephant iron'. Even the artillery – dear God, how he hated the gunners! – had done little damage, and the few shell-holes were soon filled and levelled. And in two days' time he would be going on leave; the passes were on Bodenschatz's desk, and by Thursday he and Hans Wolff would be flushing woodcock in the Black Forest. For the first time that morning he felt cheerful and optimistic.

Leaving one of the rolls uneaten, Manfred returned to his bedroom, where he swilled his teeth with a glass of water before shouting for Menzke to come and brush a few crumbs from his

9

jacket. Then he was helped into a short leather over-jacket, settled the soft-topped cap on his head at the jaunty angle known to buyers of patriotic picture postcards all over Germany, picked up his hand-carved walking-stick (souvenir of another shooting holiday in the Black Forest), and stepped out onto the narrow verandah of the hut.

The noise struck him the moment that he opened the hut door, before his eyes had focused on the scene before him. In brightly buttoned tunics and stiff caps that contrasted oddly with the studied nonchalance of a group of fliers standing by, and even more incongruously with the battle-stained field grey and jerrypot helmets of the infantrymen they had been intended by von Moltke to lead gloriously to victory, a small military band was brought rigidily to attention in front of the hut. None could be described as able-bodied; despite the efforts of their conductor, and of their regimental colonel, a music-lover who still subscribed his season-ticket at the Bayreuth *Festspielhaus,* every fit bandsman had been taken to strengthen the attack in the recent *Kaiserschlacht.* Several of the players were little more than schoolboys, others were veterans of the peacetime army; some had been wounded, and had escaped a return to the front line by revealing some musical ability; the lead euphonium player had only one leg, and balanced precariously on a crutch as he performed.

Manfred, recognising after some seconds that they were playing the national anthem, came stiffly to attention, and remained, upright but almost teetering on the top step, until the music changed into Mozart's 'Turkish March'. Scowling, he stepped down to the ground, nodded curtly to the conductor, and began to walk across the thin grass of the flying field. Bodenschatz fell into step at his left shoulder.

'What an unholy din, Karl! Dear God, what does it mean?'

Bodenschatz grinned briefly. 'A little serenade, Rittmeister. The commander of 9th Division sent them over at dawn this morning, to congratulate you on your eightieth kill last night.'

'They ought to be in the front line,' grunted Manfred. 'They'd frighten the Britishers so much, the war would be over tomorrow.' The noise of the band died away over the grass as the two men reached the far side of the field. Here stood a long line of tents, opening up into a canopy at the front, like refreshment marquees at the military manoeuvres. Each held two aircraft, and standing now out front was a short line of Fokker triplanes, each with its attendant mechanics. Manfred thought to himself how strange it was that, even after many months, he still missed the ghostly sound, like the spirit of a piano-tuner, as the riggers checked the flying wires. The Fokker, with its solid struts and cabane, and its tubular steel fuselage, is built more like a bicycle than a bird.

The predominant colour of every plane in the flight was a bright red, although each pilot was allowed to make modifications as he wished. Manfred's own plane was all red, as was that of his cousin Wolfram, who would be flying in his first combat patrol this morning. One plane had a bright blue rudder and tailplane, another's fuselage was white, and one pilot, in imitation of the late beloved Werner Voss, had painted the cowling of his Oberursel engine with a fierce face and two bristling moustaches.

Manfred's own sergeant mechanics, Pickel and Lange, came briefly to attention beside his triplane, but returned to their endless tinkering as soon as he acknowledged their salute. Although he had now been flying for nearly three years, Manfred took little interest in technical details: he left the care of his plane and its engine to the riggers and mechanics, and even its twin Spandaus were solely the responsibility of the armourer. It's your job to get me into the air, he would tell his men, and my job to hunt down the enemy; if anything goes wrong, the fault is yours, and it will be my responsibility to get out of trouble. So now he passed on down the line to speak with the fliers who were to join him on patrol.

His flight leader, Lieutenant Hans Weiss, gave him an informal but respectful salute; even Emil Karjus, whose Fokker had had to be specially modified for his single hand, managed a suitable gesture; but Richard Wenzl, who had been in the squadron only a month, stayed stretched out in a canvas deck-chair, apparently dozing in the spring sun that was beginning to break through the mist. Manfred took two brisk steps forward and kicked out the staybar of the chair, so that Wenzl bumped to the ground: 'What is the matter that you don't salute your commanding officer?' he demanded with a tense smile. 'You must be more awake than this, or you'll find an

English lord on your tail.' Ruefully rubbing his behind, Wenzl rose with a frown and walked away: none of the bystanders could be sure that Wenzl was truly angry. As Bodenschatz, always the peacemaker, hurried up, Hans Wolff decided to resolve the tension in his own way. Clown-like, he picked up the deck chair, juggled it into temporary stability, and lay down in it in an exaggeration of Wenzl's sleeping pose. Manfred, obviously smiling now, kicked out the bar again; Wolff rose and, acting injured dignity, stalked off after Wenzl.

Inwardly, Manfred was seething. This morning he had meant to hide his nervousness, suppress his brooding, and be once more the boyishly enthusiastic, single-minded hunter of the skies. God be thanked! Hans had saved the situation, and now all he had to do was smile until the flight was airborne. But there were still too many minor irritations to be suffered: a mechanic saluted him nervously and, holding out a postcard, asked for his autograph: 'For my boy, sir.'

Manfred signed, but again he could not entirely subdue his concern. 'Couldn't this wait? Or don't you think I'm coming back this morning?' Then, seeing puzzlement in the man's eyes, he added more kindly: 'Has any of you seen my dog this morning?' and turned his head and whistled sharply, shouting 'Moritz! Moritz!'

His answer was a strangled sound, half bark and half whimper, and a few seconds later, from between the triplanes, the giant brindled Great Dane struggled, desperately towing from his tail a huge wooden wheel chock: Wenzl had taken his revenge. Apprehensively, the fliers watched to see how their commanding officer would take this; but he laughed, and stooped to untie the cord that fastened the baulk of wood to the dog's tail. Then as Moritz stood on his hind legs, his front paws on Manfred's shoulders to lick his face, the mood changed momentarily again, for out of the corner of his eye Manfred saw the mechanic taking a photograph. Damn it! Didn't they know Boelcke had been photographed only minutes before his last flight? Was everyone determined to remind him of being shot down, of death in the sky, of the ultimate horror of falling in flames?

The mist was clearing quickly now. The sky was streaked thickly with cloud, but the sun shone in the patches of blue.

12

Manfred strolled back to his triplane, where one of his men was already preparing to dress him. Over the clothes that he already wore he put on a flying suit thickly lined with fur, and was helped into a pair of thigh-length fur boots. He took his gauntlets, leather flying helmet and goggles, and handed his uniform cap and walking-stick to Bodenschatz, who already had his hand about Moritz's collar. One bundle still lay on the ground beside the Fokker, and Manfred eyed it thoughtfully; then remembering again the British planes that had plunged below him in flames so many times during the past few weeks, he signalled to his mechanics to put the straps of the Heinecke parachute harness around him.

Similarly dressed – although most were without parachutes, which they found restricted their already limited movements in the cockpit, and which they, in any case, distrusted – the other fliers gathered round, as a small figure could be seen to emerge from the distant squadron office and begin to run across the field.

'Gentlemen,' began Manfred, 'we must certainly bag ourselves a few milords today. Like me, I expect, you would rather be north from here, on the Lys; but remember that our offensive against Amiens is only temporarily halted, and the Britishers will be up in their usual way to observe our preparations. Notice' – he glanced at the drogue which now stood out stiffly toward the west – 'the wind is from the east today. So far we have fought almost always with a westerly wind, which blows the English over our lines, and keeps us from drifting over theirs. So, gentlemen, remember: don't get too far downwind. The hunter should always stalk into the wind, not with the wind at his back, but today we have little choice.' Bodenschatz handed him the telegraph form that the runner had brought: 'So, friends, the milords are up, and waiting for us. *Gott mit uns!*'

As the ground crew trundled the triplanes forward and turned them into line facing into the wind, Manfred called his cousin Wolfram over for last instructions. How he disliked the over-confident, self-satisfied fool! But there was no doubt that he was a good flier, and the ties of family were stronger than personal antipathy. 'This is an order,' he said brusquely. 'On no account are you to get into a dogfight today. Stay with us until

13

we meet the milords, then maintain height, keep circling above us, watch everything we do, but don't get involved. Good luck.' He slapped him lightly on the shoulder with a gauntleted hand.

When Manfred put one foot on the step of the Fokker, and the other on the point where the wing joined the fuselage, the whole structure creaked gently, and Pickel hurriedly took part of his weight as he swung his bulkily-dressed body into the cockpit. The parachute was an added encumbrance, both raising his body a little higher in the bucket seat and pushing him annoyingly close to the controls, but he soon wriggled himself into a comfortable position and began to run through the routine sequence of tests before take-off.

First he kicked the rudder bar one way and the other, looking over his shoulder to watch the rudder wag from side to side behind him. The fuselage of the triplane, although of the usual hexagonal Fokker section, ends in a vertical sternpost rather than the customary horizontal bar. Pivoted on this sternpost is the large, comma-shaped, balanced rudder.

Satisfied, Manfred took hold of the control stick and moved it gently forward and back. The control wires to the elevator are crossed behind and below the pilot's seat, so that a backward movement of the stick lifts the elevator, causing the plane to rise in flight, while a forward movement lowers it – and it has been known for a careless rigger to forget to cross them when re-connecting them. He glanced back at the broad triangular tailplane, very different from that of the Fokker biplane but not unlike that of the Albatros he had flown until last autumn, and watched with pleasure the elevator sections move up and down like the tail of a courting blackcock.

He looked up at the big balanced ailerons, hinged from the trailing-edge of the top plane but extending well beyond the wing-tips. Moving the stick to the left raised the left aileron and depressed the right; shifting it the other way reversed the movement. All was in order so far.

Manfred nodded, and Lange moved to his position beside the propeller. 'Switch off!' shouted Manfred, putting his hand deliberately on the switch to check.

Lange took hold of the propeller tip, moving it through a small arc to draw the mixture into the cylinders and, feeling compression begin, shouted 'Contact!' The switch went down,

14

Manfred's hand rose into the air. Lange bumped the engine over compression and stepped quickly back; the engine gave a single polite cough and the propeller stopped with a jerk. Behind him, Manfred could already hear two or three engines in full throat, and impatiently he and Lange went through the complete procedure once more. This time the Oberursel fired. Manfred let it run for a few seconds, feeling the wind screwing past his head and the throbbing of the wheels against the chocks, before he eased the hand throttle and looked back once more at his flight.

Everyone had his engine running except Hans Wolff; his mechanics still tried desperately to swing it, but now he lifted both hands above his head in a comic gesture of despair, and the triplane was trundled quickly out of the line with Wolff still in the cockpit. He seemed to be trying to shout something above the rumble of the engines, then with another gesture he signalled that he would follow the flight as soon as possible.

Manfred waved to his crew to drag away the chocks, and gently opened the throttle. The propeller, screwing to the left, tries to turn the machine over to the right, thus putting more weight onto the right-hand wheel. It is important to give the machine coarse left rudder to correct this, at the same time moving the stick slightly to the right. As soon as the plane is moving in a straight line across the grass, the stick is pushed forward to get the tail up, after which it must be eased back before the machine falls forward onto its nose. As air speed increases, the rudder is centralised and the stick brought back to centre position. The air speed indicator is a small Pitot tube fastened to the leading edge of the upper plane, and connected by rubber tube to a meter on the control panel of the aircraft. When it flickered into movement, the needle creeping slowly past the sixty mark, Manfred brought the stick back, and felt the triplane almost leap into the air. He opened up the throttle, flicked the stick to the right to hoick his left wingtip upward, and began a fast right-handed climb. Behind him, one by one, Weiss, Wenzl, Karjus, Sergeant-major Scholz and his cousin Wolfram rose quickly to follow him.

21 April: Bertangles

Captain Roy Brown was on the can. It was the third time this morning that he had made his unsteady way to the latrine, avoiding the solicitous eyes of his fellow pilots in case he saw in them the ghost of a contemptuous smile. He was sick: a dose of trench-fever picked up from the filthy Australian infantry who had retreated below him too often during the past weeks, a recurrent bout of dysentery, or just his war-shattered nerves – whatever it was, he had lived for the past month on little but brandy and milk. Brandy from the looted cellars of the Château du Bois l'Abbé, milk from a tin; and sometimes he had a little of the hard, dry bread that the orderlies brought in daily from Amiens. He had asked for leave, but it had been refused: fliers who had learned to stay alive were worth more than any raw replacement.

Brown had drawn the dawn patrol this Sunday morning for the second time in three days. He had slept only a few hours, twisting in pain on his cot for long after he left the mess, then falling into a sour, nightmarish doze that seemed to have lasted only a few minutes before the operations officer lifted the dew-drenched flap of the bell tent that he shared with 'Wop' May and Frank Mellersh, shook each man by the shoulder, and, leaving a bottle of Scotch on the folding table, silently withdrew. The bottle had remained unopened – Brown kept to his brandy and milk, and neither of the two lieutenants had yet picked up the habit of dawn drinking. May had been tempted; he was flying his first offensive mission that morning with Brown and, although he was looking forward to it with enthusiasm, he had been shocked by the deterioration he found in the Roy Brown he had known four or five years before in Alberta. There was little sign of the cheerfully extrovert athlete who had set out confidently for the Wright flying school at Dayton in Ohio. Here was a prematurely middle-aged man who carried himself in a tense stoop, his bloodshot eyes hollow in his haggard face.

Apart from the agony of dragging oneself out of bed in the cold and clammy dark, pulling on damp flying suits and boots, and staggering, unshaven, to the line of aircraft where the sergeants poured great mugs of tea, too hot to drink, too sweet to taste, and too weak to crawl up the spout of the pot – apart from these horrors, the dawn patrol was less of a nightmare than those later in the day. All British fliers, unlike their German counterparts, were under orders to carry the fight over the enemy's lines; but at dawn the Hun fighters were not always up, and the targets of the allies were the AEG bombers, droning back at less than ninety miles an hour after dropping their loads on the factories, railway yards and ammunition dumps of the rear areas. From 10,000 or 12,000 feet the scouts would see the bombers silhouetted, an easy target, against the spreading glow of the eastern horizon; then, screaming down at more than 120mph out of the sunlight and into the earth's shadow, they would try to steady themselves against the raking fire of the AEG's rear Parabellum, long enough to put in a seven-second burst that, with luck, might hit a feedline, the fuel tank, or even the pilot himself.

But this morning artillery observation posts up and down the line had reported a low and clinging mist, and Major Butler, after the met officer had consulted his barometer, whirled his humidity meter like a football rattle, and finally stood with his nose raised to the east for some minutes like a scenting foxhound, had announced that there would be no flying for at least two hours. The pilots had dispersed, some to shave, some to eat bacon and eggs in the mess hut; Brown had made his first visit to the latrine, and Simpson, the engineering officer, had gone into a huddle with the mechanics over the magneto of one of the Sopwith Camels.

Now, nearly three hours later, Brown heard through the thin latrine walls the sudden break in distant chatter, followed by brisker conversation, that warned him he would soon be needed. Painfully dragging up his breeches, he emerged from the little cabin to find the mist clearing, sunlight catching the elms at the end of the field, and patches of luminous blue showing beyond them. The pilots of A flight, which he was to lead, stood talking together: Wop May, Mellersh, Mackenzie, and Lomas. 'Wind's easterly,' Mackenzie was explaining to May, eager relief in his voice: 'that's an advantage we don't often have. Jerry likes to fight with a westerly wind that keeps him behind his own lines and makes it harder for us to get home. Make a long dive with the west wind behind you, and you'll find yourself having to hedgehop back with every little Hun private taking a pot at you, and Archie trying to blow you out of the sky like a farmer after a crow.'

Brown nodded: 'I've only one order for you, Wop – stay out of it. Maintain altitude. Our job is to escort a couple of Harry Tates from Poulainville next door. If we get into a fight, which we're almost bound to, keep circling, watch your tail, take a look at what's going on below you, you'll maybe learn a thing or two.' He smiled wearily, briefly. 'That way, perhaps you'll get back here for lunch.'

Pilots were clambering heavily into their Camels, checking their ailerons and elevators, wagging their rudders; one by one they went through their starting routines, until all fifteen engines were throbbing, the chocks dragged away, and the mechanics straining at the wingtips. Brown was the first into the air, and within three minutes the rest of his flight were up behind him, jockeying into the regulation V pattern as they climbed steadily up through the clouds over Amiens. Very soon, however, Mellersh's engine began to pop and stutter, and defying all that the instructors had tried to drum into him at Chingford, he swung back toward Bertangles. 'In case of engine failure, *don't turn back*' the manuals all insisted. 'Pilot decides to turn back and, endeavouring not to lose height, stalls engine . . . machine out of control, spin commencing . . . spinning nose dive . . . crash.' But Mellersh was too experienced a flier: he brought the Camel with its protesting engine safely back to the airfield, and, less than half an hour after his flight had taken off, was once more in the air.

Meanwhile, Brown's flight had been followed by C flight, led by Lieutenant Redgate at the apex of a V made up of Lieutenants Edwards, Siddal, Aird and Drake. A few minutes behind them came the American 'Boots' Boutillier, leading Lieutenants Brock, Harker, Foster and Taylor.

Although the mist had cleared at ground level, there was still extensive cloud at about 9,000 feet. Over Amiens and still climbing, the flights were able to orientate themselves through the gaps in the cloud by the straight roads that radiated below them: north-east, straight as an arrow, to Albert and Bapaume; due east, through Villers-Bretonneux and undeviatingly on, almost to St Quentin; south-east to Roye and

Noyon. They followed the south-eastern direction, levelling out at 12,000 feet somewhere over Le Quesnel, about six miles behind the German lines, and turning northward from there began their patrol. B flight came up with A flight, but soon Lomas and Edwards, their engines firing only intermittently, swung off again toward Amiens, and Brown was left with only six companions until Mellersh suddenly reappeared somewhere over Bayonvillers, droning out of a cloud to take up station close behind Brown.

At about this moment the two RE8 reconnaissance aircraft, from 3 Squadron of the Australian Flying Corps at Poulainville, were in position at 7,000 feet over Hamel, north-west of Brown's Camels. And, at 10,000 feet, racing westward from Cappy to intercept them, came nearly twenty Albatros scouts and Fokker triplanes. They flew almost parallel with the Morlancourt ridge, where the Australians held the high ground between the Ancre and the Somme. Below them, the fingers of the ridge protruded southward, like those of a stubby hand, forcing the Somme to wind sinuously around them. In the hazy sunlight, the flood waters of the valley gleamed a flat silver.

From somewhere on the ridge near Sailly-le-sec, anti-aircraft guns began firing at the approaching German planes. The gunners had ranged the cloud ceiling at about 10,000 feet, and just below it the puffs of smoke burst white, distinct from the occasional black burst to the west, where the German Archie was firing at the RE8s as they plodded on their photographic patrol. Closing fast, with a height advantage of nearly half a mile, Brown spotted first the white shell-bursts, and then the brilliant colours of the German circus. With a last wave of the arm to Wop May, signalling him to stay out of the fight, he led his two depleted flights down. But even as he pushed the joystick forward to put the Camel into a fighting dive, and eased his thumbs over the trigger releases of the twin Vickers, Aird pulled away to the left, the spluttering of his engine betraying yet another magneto failure, and began the long, swooping glide toward the lines that would, he hoped, put him quickly out of reach of the Hun and safely down on the grass at Bertangles.

For the first few seconds of the dogfight, the two sides were evenly matched: Brown's remaining six against one *kette* of

19

Jasta 11, led by Hans Weiss in his all-white Fokker – while Manfred, still half a mile behind, urgently signalled to his cousin Wolfram to climb above the fight. Then two *ketten* of *Jasta* 5, from far to the east at Neuvilly, came racketing into the fray, and Brown found himself hard-pressed. For several minutes, as he twisted desperately to shake two Fokkers from his tail, he was unaware that Boots Boutillier's flight – minus Brock, another victim of a refractory magneto – was also in the battle.

The Camel is a fine fighting machine, but the excellent lift of the Fokker, combined with its short wingspan, gives it a considerable advantage in manoeuvre: each time Brown banked or put his aircraft into a tight climbing spiral, he found one of his adversaries coming in closer from the side and behind, as the two Fokkers followed a figure-of-eight path that effectively enclosed his own. In desperation he put the Camel into a long, screaming dive away from the fight, and cut out the engine with the spring-loaded ignition button on his joystick. Then, when the two triplanes, deceived by the ruse, had turned back toward the dogfight, he released the button, brought his engine once more to life, and, easing back the joystick and swinging it to the left, began a steady climb in a large circle that would bring him above the fight, now more than a mile away, where Wop May should still be hovering. He stared up through the transparent 'window' in the upper wing, through the air quivering in the heat above his guns, but Wop was not in sight. Then, a little below and half a mile to his left, he saw a frantically twisting Camel. Behind, and gaining fast, came an all-red Fokker triplane, tracer flickering suddenly against a shadow on the trenches below, as a cloud passed before the sun.

Wop had forgotten his orders. Keeping his high, easy circle above the dogfight, watching Mellersh score against Wenzl's blue-tailed triplane, and seeing Mackenzie, wounded, spin away down to 3,000 feet before levelling off toward the Allied lines, he had suddenly found himself above an all-red triplane. It was Wolfram, obeying orders and leaning half out of his cockpit to watch the action below. To May at that moment it seemed a chance too good to miss; with an hysterical college yell he tipped his nose downward and jammed both thumbs on his gun releases. He saw the arcing tracer bullets, one in three, sweep close to Wolfram, but not close enough; and the German, with a quick, startled glance over his shoulder, threw his plane into a steep, twisting dive, with May close on his tail. Within seconds both novices realised that they had dived straight into the heart of the dogfight: Wolfram swung east for Cappy like a scalded cat, while Wop, firing his guns blindly against any aircraft that might cross his sights, dragged back the joystick and climbed for the clearer air above.

To reduce weight, the feed belts for the Vickers arming the Camels are made of aluminium instead of the usual brass, and jamming is a continual problem. When May found that both his guns had stopped firing, and, standing up in the cockpit and hammering at the breeches with his fist, had been unable to clear them, he knew that his only course was to follow Wolfram's example and get away as quickly as possible. Dodging and spinning downward again, he levelled out at only a few hundred feet, swung until he had the sun, high in the noonday sky, on his port beam, and, praying that he was too high to be hit by ground fire and too low to be a target for Archie, set out for home. It was then that the first bullets struck splinters from the wing strut close forward of his head; instinctively he kicked the rudder bar and jerked the joystick back and to the right, and, as he swerved violently to one side, he caught a glimpse of the all-red Fokker close upon his tail.

The Sopwith Camel is a snub-nosed hornet, the 130hp Clerget rotary engine protruding only a little forward of the leading edge of the wings, so that the mass of engine, fuel, pilot, and guns is concentrated very close to the centre of gravity. As a result, the torque reaction of the engine and propellor can convert a turn into a spin with very little warning – as Wop's predecessor in the squadron had discovered. May had been trained on Camels, and had already put this disconcerting characteristic to good use in spinning his way out of the dogfight, but at only a few hundred feet above ground he could not take the risk. For the same reason, he could not dive out of trouble, and a climb, with the enemy so close upon his tail, was also out of the question. His only chance lay in sudden, banking zigzags to left and right, giving his pursuer little opportunity to take steady aim. They were in the valley of the Somme, fast approaching the positions of 52 Battalion of the 3rd Australian Division, where the thinly wooded slopes rose above Sailly-le-sec to the crest of the Morlancourt ridge; and as May, lower than the top of the ridge, jinked his way above the spring flood waters that lay either side of the Somme canal, he thought of the jacksnipe, zigzagging out of gunshot, among the Winnipeg swamps.

But Manfred was a hunter, wise in the ways of snipe. As May turned he turned with him, but always on a larger curve, so that as May changed direction he found himself crossing his enemy's line of fire. And each time Manfred was a little closer. He was saving his fire now: the twin Spandaus were hot, and he was running low on ammunition. He meant to make this his eighty-first kill before he took his leave to hunt a more appetising quarry. He did not realise that he had crossed the Australian lines, he did not realise how low his chase had taken him, and he did not realise – until a burst of fire riddled the Fokker's fuse-lage, splitting large splinters from the struts and singing off the tubular steel framework – that Brown had dived on him from out of the sun, pulled up in a steep curve below his tail, and very nearly brought him down. Brown was now climbing southward again; May, at a point where a shell-scarred stone windmill rose above the bluff, followed the curve of the river around a wooded spur; and Manfred, with a thin-lipped smile of triumph, eased back his joystick and took the triplane straight over the spur, banking sharply to clear the screen of trees.

Looking back, Brown saw May buzzing alone along the river in front of Vaux; he could not see the triplane, and thought he might have brought it down. But one matter above all else dominated his consciousness at that moment: the last dive, turn and sudden climb, the inexorable pull of gravity, and the relief after the terrors of the past few minutes, had made great demands upon his bowel control. Very doubtful whether he could make base without an intensely embarrassing incident, he turned away for Bertangles as fast as he could go.

But Fortune still smiled on Wop May. As Manfred cleared the trees and came at May from almost abeam, both his Spandaus jammed, and, as they did so, he heard for the first time the ground fire that was being directed against him. He recognised the distinctive note of two or three Lewis guns, and bullets ripped through the plywood section forward of the cockpit. Half standing, he reached forward and thumped grimly at the breeches of the two guns, hoping to dislodge a stuck firing pin, or whatever it was that had caused the stoppage. Then he threw himself back in his seat, and, as he came over the end of the ridge above the town of Corbie, banked sharply to the right. When the bullet smashed in below his right armpit, pierced his lung at its lowest tip, miraculously missed his gall bladder, and emerged again, ripping cartilage and some small muscles around the sternum, he had just time instinctively to reach forward and switch off the ignition, and then tear his goggles from his eyes, before the seesawing blackness swept up and over him.

21 April: Corbie

On the reverse slope of the ridge, a mile or so outside the town of Corbie, 53 Battery of the 14th Australian Field Artillery Brigade had built their dugouts and lined their six 18-pounders, out of sight of the Huns but with a range over the battlefield of four to five miles. The road from Corbie to Bray, unmetalled and now a deeply muddy track, ran in a slight depression behind the artillery position, and here were the horse lines and the limbers that brought the ammunition from the railway station in Amiens.

The men of the battery had been standing to since dawn. The previous evening, from the old stone windmill above Vaux, observers had reported that they could see great activity in the German lines. Work parties had been clearing wire between the forward and support trenches, and bobbing lines of heads in the communication trenches showed that supplies were being brought forward. It seemed likely that a morning attack was being mounted, and, as the light faded, the battery had put down nearly 300 shells in a concentrated twenty-minute barrage. Other batteries along the Australian front had followed suit, and – whether the bombardment had succeeded, or whether no attack had been planned – the morning so far had been quiet. The mist still lay over the lines, and since stand-to the gunners had been busy wiping down the breeches and dials with cotton waste, and rearranging their camouflage netting. Among the leafless trees around them chaffinches chattered, and somewhere above the mist a skylark could be heard, scribbling on the sky.

Outside the dugout of Major Les Beavis, which was also the battery HQ, a Lewis gun had been mounted on swivels on a post to afford some protection against aircraft attack; another was positioned at the northern end of the line of guns. Bombardier Joe Seccull and Gunner Bob Buie stood by the first Lewis, extra drums of ammunition stacked on an empty box by their feet, and Gunner Snowy Evans manned the second. This morning, despite the clinging damp, the churned mud that came halfway up their kneeboots, and the knowledge that at any moment a German whizzbang could blow them to bits, they were almost content. This morning the field-kitchens had rumbled up from Bonnay and brought them, as it was Sunday, not only the usual ration of a quarter-loaf, plum and apple jam, and dixies of scalding hot SM's tea, but a couple of thick rashers apiece, hard and salty, but infinitely satisfying.

Slowly the mist cleared. Westward, below in the valley, the little town of Corbie, with its huge, cathedral-like church, came into view. To the north-east, the chimney of the brickworks of Ste Colette was poking its way through the haze: it had given good ranging practice to the gunners of the 1st Battery of the 16th Field Artillery Regiment, holding the German lines across the valley near Hamel, and the stack was so full of holes that the diggers had nicknamed it 'the whistler'. Two Harry Tates from 3 Squadron at Poulainville came droning over Villers-Bretonneux to the south and began their slow photographic reconnaissance up either side of the front line. And away in the east came three flights of German planes, Albatroses and Fokker tripes, the sun sidelighting them in flashes of red and white, silver and purple.

The dogfight over Cerizy was too far off for much to be seen from the Australian lines. The planes tumbled in a confused swarm like gnats on a summer evening, and the distant stutter of their machine-guns was more like the sound of a corporal's typewriter in a headquarters office than the scything roar that the men in the trenches knew at close quarters. All along the front between Hamel and Morlancourt faces were turned upward, field-glasses scanned the skies, Vickers, Lewis, and 3-inch anti-aircraft guns were manned in case the chance of a lucky

24

potshot came; but there was little excitement. To the men in the front line, their own aircraft were a very mixed blessing. Sometimes, unable to tell from a mile or so high exactly where they were, they dropped bombs on the Allied trenches; sometimes, on a photographic recce, they demanded that troops should give away their positions by firing off Very lights until every Hun battery for miles had the range and distance. So the men watched, relaxed in the spring sunshine and the fleeting knowledge that it was Sunday, but felt no involvement in the battle.

Suddenly the atmosphere changed. 'Cripes! Here comes one of our blokes, and a Jerry right behind him!' Men in the trenches scrambled up onto firesteps, working the bolts of their Lee-Enfields; men in shallow shell craters, risking being picked off by a German sniper, stood up to get a better view; and Buie and Evans, hands grasping the butts of their Lewis guns, and fingers slipping instinctively inside the trigger guards, swung their sights onto the approaching aircraft and began their traverse. The two machines disappeared below the edge of the ridge. All that could be heard were the bursts of fire from the twin Spandaus of the pursuing Fokker, and the irregular popping of innumerable rifles. Then, with a howl from their two full-out engines, the aircraft came into sight round the trees, only forty or fifty feet away from the ridge, and almost level with the battery.

Neither Lewis gunner could fire for fear of hitting the Camel in front. Bullets from Jerry's guns were splatting into the mud and sandbags all around. There was a roar of a Vickers from a position lower in the valley. The Camel, twisting and bobbing, shot past. Snowy Evans, on open sights, pressed his trigger and swung in traverse with the Fokker. Buie followed his example. The triplane banked steeply to the right, its guns silent; its engine coughed once or twice and then stopped. While the Vickers and Lewis continued to fire, while Wop May sped on in his hedgehopping course until the shooting had died behind him, the Fokker held its downward glide, wobbling slightly, until it came to earth, slid forward on its splintering under-carriage, and stopped with its nose in a pile of mangel-wurzels beside the road, two hundred yards from the brickworks whistler.

For perhaps five seconds there was silence. Then, from 53 Battery, from the HQ of 8th Brigade Field Artillery, from 108 Howitzer Battery, men and officers broke cover and began to run, cheering, toward the shattered triplane lying on the open hillside. Lieutenant Don Fraser, intelligence officer at 11th Brigade Infantry HQ, sprinted from the door of his dugout across the muddied grass of the downland. He found a dozen diggers, cheerfully ripping pieces of fabric from the plane, quarreling over splintered fragments of propeller, levering instruments away from the panel with their pocket knives and bayonets. Manfred lay slumped over the controls, with his head against the cockpit rim; his eyes were open, and they were very blue. Blood flowed slowly from his mouth and trickled into a spreading stain across the front of his flying suit.

Fraser reached into the cockpit and fumbled with the release of the Heinecke harness. Then, with the help of three or four diggers, he dragged and lifted until the lifeless body came free and could be lowered to the ground. Even as he opened the airman's flying suit, eager hands were pulling off the fur boots and leather gauntlets. Inside his flying suit, the pilot wore the uniform jacket of a cavalry captain, and beneath this a grey silk pyjama suit. On the left breast the initials MvR were embroidered in a darker grey. Fraser whistled quietly, slowly, and seizing the torn edge of silk where the bullet had emerged from the middle of the breast, quickly tore out a piece with the monogram; then he slipped his hand inside the uniform jacket, took out the pilot's wallet and papers, whistled again, and said in an unsteady voice: 'Do you know who this is? It's Manfred von Richthofen.'

There was a moment's silence. Then an awed voice in the crowd said 'Christ boys, we only got the bloody Red Baron.'

21 April: Aftermath

Two minutes after Manfred had crashed on the exposed slope of the ridge above Corbie, the gunners of the 1st Battery of the 16th Field Artillery Regiment began to put down a box barrage around the aircraft. Observers in the German lines had seen the Fokker glide easily to earth, apparently with engine failure, and they had watched with horror as the Australians appeared to be attacking the defenceless pilot. In an attempt to save Richthofen's life and disperse the diggers, they laid their guns to surround the site with explosions of shrapnel and showers of mud and splintered chalk. Within a few seconds the hillside was empty, except for Manfred's body and the ransacked triplane, while from every dugout and declivity men watched and waited. Between the explosions, the foolhardier ones rushed out to snatch another souvenir. The afternoon sun shone warmly, and in those moments of silence there came the most disturbing sound of all: the faint crack of the first buds bursting on the shell-shot trees.

Within half an hour, the distinctive grind of a Crossley tender in low gear could be heard on the sunken road from Corbie. The recovery truck from 3 Squadron had arrived in the charge of Lieutenant Warneford, the squadron's assistant equipment officer; with him came a detail of eight men headed by Sergeant Dick Foale. They parked close by the ammunition limbers, where the bank of the road rose high on their right, and a short distance from where Major Beavis stood at the door of his dugout. The recovery detail were not unused to the sound of shellfire, and it was not the first time they had come into the forward areas, although until now their job had been to salvage downed British aircraft; but as they crouched against the brief cover of the bank and heard the howling and huffing of shells close above their heads, they looked at each other with dismay.

Major Beavis had his watch out, and was counting seconds. 'They're firing fairly slowly,' he told Warneford. 'We can fire as quick as twenty rounds a minute when we're really laying it down, but Jerry's taking it very easy. I reckon they've six guns laid on a diamond pattern, and they're only firing each every two minutes. That's twenty seconds between each round. So if one of your blokes wants to go out and take a look, he's got nearly half a minute to get there. They won't be firing at him, remember,' he added, seeing the look on Warneford's face, 'they've got the range pretty well, and nothing's fallen close to the plane in the last ten minutes. In fact, they seem to be getting a bit tired already, the firing's slowing up.' He cocked his head: 'Here's another' – and with a noise like an express train suddenly entering a cutting a shell passed overhead and

27

exploded in a fountain of mud on the far side of the road. One of the horses, grazed by a splinter, squealed and reared; the aircraftmen rolled into the ditch, and Beavis laughed. 'Bloody useless,' he said scornfully, 'them Huns', as Warneford recovered himself and began to wipe the dirt from his jacket.

It was Air Mechanic Colin Collins who volunteered to crawl out to the triplane. Accompanied by enthusiastic diggers, the detail made their way a couple of hundred yards up the road, and Collins, after a quick peep over the edge of the bank, made a frantic scramble, on all fours, across the open ground to the plane. In a minute he was back: 'We can put a rope round the fuselage, and drag it back here from cover, sir. Blimey, I thought a bit of shrapnel had got me, sir, but it was only a chunk of those bleeding mangel-wurzels!'

Warneford suggested that they should get Richthofen's body first, the squadron commander had been very insistent about that, and one of the Aussies offered to fetch the stretcher from HQ dugout. By the time he returned the airman's body was being inched cautiously across the mud on the end of a long rope. Laid on the stretcher, it was carried back and rested on two empty ammunition boxes in the dugout. It was just two o'clock.

Warneford was surprised to see a battered Crossley staff car parked behind his tender. Inside the dugout, resplendent in the grey-blue uniform of the newly-created Royal Air Force, he found Lieutenant-Colonel Cairnes from 22 Wing, Major Butler from the Canadian 209 Squadron, and a pale, uneasy pilot who was introduced as Captain Roy Brown. Beavis was excitedly describing the morning's incident as the officers stood in a half-circle, staring at Manfred's body in the gloom. Brown stood slightly to the rear, nearest the dugout entrance, and a small crowd of diggers had gathered outside, craning to see what was going on.

'I suppose we can put him in the back of the car, eh Butler?' Cairnes said quietly.

Warneford came stiffly to attention. 'Begging your pardon, sir. The machine's down in our recce sector, and I've had strict orders to bring it and the pilot back to Poulainville. After all, sir,' he added apologetically 'we're right next door to you, and I'm sure you're welcome to come across and see him any time

28

you want.' Cairnes shrugged, and spoke in an undertone to Butler. Warneford caught only the words 'claim' and 'tomorrow'. Beavis bristled, but said nothing.

Cairnes said, brusquely, 'Very well,' and ducked his head to walk through the dugout door. Butler and Beavis followed, and Warneford bustled away to organise bearers to carry the stretcher to the tender.

Brown stood still in the half-light, staring at the body. This was what it was like to be shot down: to be dead, and dragged through the mud, and lie here suffering the brief respect of men you did not know. He moved closer, bending forward to study the features of the most famous of Germany's air aces. Manfred's face, and the parts of his chest exposed by the ripping open of his uniform, were caked with dried blood. His skin was almost translucent in its paleness, and the sightless blue eyes were still wide open. From the nostrils the blood still flowed, slowly but liquidly.

Brown turned quickly, staggered slightly as he emerged from the gloom of the dugout into the bright light of the April afternoon, and saw Cairnes and Butler standing alone a few yards away. His few whispered words were enough: Cairnes strode across to Beavis, urgently requested the use of his telephone, and disappeared with him into the dugout. Butler, without a word, turned a puzzled frown on Brown and then took up a position in front of the entrance so that no one else could enter.

But Brown stayed where he was, deeply breathing in the Sunday air; even among the stench of gangrene and horse manure, the bitterness of ruptured earth and explosive, there was the scent of spring, reminding him of the days when the snow began to melt in the Manitoba woods. The nightingales had sung last evening in the woods around the airfield. In his stomach brandy and milk, and the few spoonsful of Maconochie he had downed at lunch, stirred sluggishly. He felt lightheaded; the earth moved beneath his feet even when it was not shaken by another German shell. He stared uncomprehendingly at Warneford in the road below him, organising the turn-round of the Crossley tender: the lorry, and the figures around it, were two-dimensional against the afternoon light, flat in perspective like the photographs in his mother's stereoscope.

Cairnes and Beavis emerged silently from the dugout, and stood apart from one another, staring dazedly like Brown. No one seemed to hear the continuing German bombardment, the shouts of the men, the drone of a single Bristol scout overhead. When Warneford brought two bearers up the slope with him, and superintended the transfer of the stretcher with Manfred's body to the open back of the tender, only Brown took a quick hesitant step forward and then, with a glance at his commanding officer, an equally hesitant one back again. Only after Mick Worsley, with Corporal Bigum sitting beside him, had started up the Crossley and begun the slow rumbling trip back toward Poulainville did the three RAF officers seem to awake, as from a dream; they shook Beavis briefly by the hand in turn, nodded silently to Warneford, and climbed into the back seat of their staff car, whose driver had been sitting motionless for the best part of an hour.

The car caught up with the tender in the outskirts of Corbie, and followed close behind on the road to Pont Noyelles and Querrieu. Between Querrieu and Allonville the trees grow close to the road, and here, as they rounded a wooded corner, they found a Wolseley staff car stopped broadside on and barring their way. The driver wore a sergeant's stripes, and the passenger was sitting half out of the door, with his feet on the ground, smoking a short-stemmed polished briar pipe. From his gleaming boots to his red tabs and major's crowns he was the typical staff officer, but the effect was spoilt by the battered field cap on his head and by his darkly-tinted spectacles. He was short and broadly built, and the spectacles gave him the look of a predatory beetle. He came to his feet, tapped out the pipe, strolled past the ticking tender with a nod to the driver, and introduced himself: 'Colonel Cairnes? Major Despard. I believe you need my assistance?' Then he turned, calling to his driver: 'Sar'nt, I believe I noticed a little estaminet a few hundred yards back along the road. Why don't you take the corp and these two drivers there for a spot of light refreshment?'

As soon as the men were out of sight round the bend in the road, Despard's nonchalant air vanished. 'Right,' he said, 'let's have a look at him,' and swung himself up over the tailboard of the tender. Butler and Brown moved to get out of their car, but Cairnes stretched a restraining hand. Despard was kneeling beside Manfred's body, making little brisk movements and muttering and humming to himself; then he stood up and looked consideringly down, holding his hands apart as if he were measuring the body by eye for a coffin.

'Major – Butler, is it? Do you have a revolver? Good. I require your help.' And he jumped down from the tender and set off rapidly along the road.

When Butler caught up with Despard he had already turned off into a broad, well-rutted track that wound through the trees to the left of the road. In a short distance they came to two large wooden huts and a sentry in Anzac uniform, who sprang to attention at the sight of Despard's scarlet tabs.

'I'd like to see your officer-i-c,' said Despard, and was directed to the smaller of the two huts, where a worried-looking lieutenant in gold-rimmed spectacles rose from behind his desk to salute. From inside his uniform jacket, Despard produced a thick wad of papers, selected one and unfolded it, laying it on the desk in front of the lieutenant, who read it, caught his breath, and saluted again without saying a word.

'You've a man here I think I need for interrogation,' said Despard, picking up the paper and replacing it in his pocket.

'Certainly, major,' replied the lieutenant, 'I'll come down to the cage with you.'

A few yards beyond the huts was a clearing in the woods. Here wooden posts had been hammered into the ground, and coils of barbed-wire wound round to make a compound about thirty yards across. Outside, a dozen sentries stood nonchalantly about, their rifles grounded; inside, more than a hundred German prisoners sat morosely in groups, or wandered singly or in pairs, their hands in their greatcoat pockets, their eyes hungry.

Despard gave them a quick glance: 'That's my man,' he said, pointing out a fair-haired private about twenty-four years old, a little shorter than many of his companions. The barbed-wire gate was swung open, and the German infantryman ordered out. Despard briefly signed a receipt and then, with a *'Schnell, schnell,'* he prodded the German in the back with his revolver, and with Butler began a half-run back to the parked cars.

A dreadful realisation had begun to dawn on Butler, but he could not bring himself to say a word. The German was stumbling in the ruts of the track, and Despard urged him on even faster.

At the truck, Despard spoke for the first time to Brown: 'I shall need your help, Captain,' he said, and began at once to strip Manfred of his flying suit. Brown unlaced the black kneeboots, and together they pulled off the breeches and the uniform jacket. As they did so, something dropped to the floor of the tender. It was Manfred's *Pour le Mérite,* its black and silver ribbon broken, which had somehow escaped the notice of the souvenir hunters. Despard picked it up and turned it over to read the name on the back: 'Yes,' he said quietly 'I suppose he'll need this,' and dropped it into the pocket of his jacket. As he began to strip off the grey silk pyjama suit, he brusquely ordered the soldier to strip also, and then to put on Richthofen's clothes. The soldier accepted the order, a slight frown of puzzlement on his brow, but no apprehension in his pale blue eyes.

Despard produced some rough grey blankets from the back seat of his car, and gestured to Brown; together they wrapped Manfred's cold body in them and laid him gently across the floor behind the front seats. The soldier stood, dressed in the torn and bloodstained clothes of a Rittmeister of the German Air Service, watching closely, the slight frown still on his brow.

'Major Butler, Captain Brown,' said Despard, 'I think the Colonel needs you.' Cairnes had remained sitting in the car, his back toward what had been taking place on the road, a brown manila folder open on his knees. As Brown and Butler came up to him, he spoke softly, pointing to one of the typed papers in the folder.

Despard strolled toward them, snapping *'Stillgestanden'* at the soldier as he passed. Then he turned, and saying calmly, 'About here, I think,' he placed his revolver behind the soldier's right armpit and fired once.

The man pitched straight forward into the mud. Brown and Butler swung round in horror, protests half-formed on their lips. Cairnes did not move, apart from an uncontrolled twitching of his shoulders.

'I think I can manage this part myself, thank you gentlemen,' said Despard. He dragged the soldier by his heels, face down in the mud, to the tailboard of the tender, hoisted him up, and laid the body where Manfred had previously lain. 'I'll pick up my sergeant, and get him to send your drivers along,' he added, ran to his car, swung the starting handle, and drove off at high speed.

On the following day Captain Roy Brown, pale, silent and with a flask of brandy in his greatcoat pocket, was posted back to England. A week later he suffered a nervous breakdown, and for three weeks was delirious. He was not returned to combat duty in France. On the afternoon of the same day, the body of Rittmeister Manfred von Richthofen of *Jagdgeschwader* 1, leading German ace, was laid in a simple grave in the cemetery at Bertangles.

'Such a dirty forsaken hole in which to be buried,' said Sergeant John Alexander, who took the official photographs. Three volleys were fired over the grave, and the Last Post was sounded. Next day, a Camel flew low over the airfield at Cappy. The pilot threw down a metal canister with streamers attached, and then made his hedgehopping way back to Poulainville. Inside the canister was Sergeant Alexander's last photograph, and the following message:

To the German Flying Corps
Rittmeister Baron Manfred von Richthofen was killed in
aerial combat on 21 April 1918. He was buried with
full military honours.
From the British Royal Air Force

CHAPTER 2

1-2 May: Neufchatel-en-Bray

THE ROOM was grey. Not the grey of shadows, the lifeless cast of a day of clouds; it was a delicate, dove-like grey, and sunlight from outside seemed to give the walls an undulating motion, as if they were the breast feathers of a giant bird. He could not turn his head, but from the far corner of his eye he was sure he could see a white muslin curtain stirring lightly at an open window. His eyesight seemed as good as ever, but the effect was strange. He felt as if he was lying at the bottom of a deep well, looking up into a world that passed by far above, not knowing or caring that he was there.

He could not move. He could not feel his hands, or his arms; his legs or even his toes. He remembered feeling like this before, in a hospital, somewhere, sometime. What was the name of the place? He could not recall it. Who was he? He did not know.

With the first stirrings of panic, he fought to project his consciousness out into the room; to raise himself bodily out of this deep well and, discovering his surroundings, to discover himself. There were no smells. And then, as he breathed out heavily and suddenly snatched in his breath again, for a brief second there was the close heaviness of iodoform, and the distant sweet reek of ether. He listened: far away he heard an unfamiliar resonant strike of something against wood, like – but not like – the sound of an axeman in the forest; it was followed by the excited exclamations of several voices in a foreign language. Further away still, he heard a girl singing; the sound had a strange metallic thinness, as if it came very quietly through a speaking trumpet, but the words were clear:

Endt uahn dai uihr gonner bilde littel hohm fürtuh
Orchrih offorr omorr
In lahfland furmih endt meigühl

What could it mean? He strained his ears for more, but the song had finished. He heard again the strike of something – but not the ringing steel of an axe – on wood, and the babble of distant voices. But he was tired, too tired. The walls of the well were too slippery, the daylight above was fading . . . he slept.

When he awoke again, someone was leaning over him. He was aware first of a warm plumpness, gently rustling in a fresh white cotton gown that smelt of soap; then of another smell that the soap could not quite overcome. It was the smell of a healthy young girl's flesh, which had been bathed not long before in eau de cologne. Hands were smoothing the pillow behind his head, and two round breasts, between which ran a

34

long line of tiny buttons fastening the front of the gown, were within a hand's breadth of his eyes.

He opened his mouth and, to his own great surprise, spoke: 'Hallo?' The round breasts drew back, the buttons between straining slightly as the girl took a deep, startled breath. He was reminded suddenly of a film – Pola Negri, was it, in *Die Bestie?* – which he had seen on his last visit to . . . (of course) . . . Berlin: of how the photograph had suddenly changed from a close view of a woman's heaving bosom to one that showed her face, her body, and her tightly clasped hands. For now he saw the same thing: a girl of about nineteen, with dark eyes in a round face, and short, curly, dark hair. She wore a long, closely-buttoned, white gown, and he guessed her to be a hospital nurse; although she wore on her head, not a plain white cap, but something more like that of an under-housemaid, with short grey ribbons.

He could say nothing more. Half-perceived memories were rising in his brain like bubbles in a glass of champagne, forming as pinpoints, swelling as they rose, and then vanishing again as they burst at the surface. Words and names came and went – Katie, flame, death, Courtrai, mother, Lothar, Manfred – yes! that was it, my name, Manfred!

And even as the realisation came, the girl made what was almost a curtsey, and said in German: 'Good afternoon, Freiherr von Richthofen. How are you feeling?'

I felt indescribably tired, and yet at the same time exhilarated, liberated. I flexed myself against the rough linen sheet covering my body, and felt my legs move freely, without pain. My toes twitched. I was wearing a short flannel jacket about my shoulders, and I could twist my left arm easily in its sleeve; but my right arm was closely bound across my chest in what I guessed were bandages. I was propped up slightly on pillows so that I could look across the room, and I could see everything.

I could see the delicate grey walls and the weathered woodwork of a similar colour; the white muslin curtains at the long window, and the way they caught the afternoon sunlight and flickered it across the polished floor; the slightly chipped white ironwork of the bed-end, and the woven white cover across my legs, with its worked-in pattern of a large crest in pale blue. I could see the small table beside my bed, with a glass carafe of water and an enamel dish covered with a cloth. The room was

35

small but lofty: it contained nothing but the table, the bed, and my body in that bed. And the girl.

She stood unmoving, her hands clasped in front of her, a look of concern on her face. She was very young, and very pretty, and very solemn. I smiled at her, a smile that seemed to crack my face as though it had been thinly plastered, but she responded immediately, her plump lips opening on regular small, white teeth, and her wine-dark eyes filling · at the same moment with light and with swelling tears.

'Oh, it's so good to see you conscious again, and looking almost like your own self. I've been very worried about · you, you know, but the doctor said you were strong and certain to pull through. Now we must try to get you really well again, as soon as possible.'

'Where am I?' I asked.

'At the British officers' convalescent home, at the Château d'Eawy.'

It was like a blow with a closed fist, jolting the ribs deadly, just below the heart. I was a prisoner. 'But I thought, hearing you speak in German . . . '

'That's why I was brought here to look after you. They wanted to know anything you might say when you were unconscious . . . ' She broke off, blushing, when she saw the expression on my face.

'But you didn't say anything. Not anything important. You called me Katie, once or twice,' she added. Suddenly, it seemed to me, as if she were jealous. 'Is that your wife? They showed me her photograph.'

'Katie?' For a second or two I was puzzled. 'Oh no, I remember,' and as the memories came flooding back to me I smiled again; 'that was another nurse. She looked after me in the hospital at – Courtrai, was it? I remember, they came to photograph us together in the garden of the hospital when I was nearly recovered. She looked rather like you, you know. That was after I was shot down near Wervicq . . . Oh no, she's not my wife – although I think maybe she would like to be!'

From beyond the window there came the sound of striking wood that had disturbed me before, and shouts that I now recognised to be English. I asked the girl:

'What is that?'

'It's only the English officers playing cricket,' she said. And then she became the nurse again, leaning over me – her round breasts almost in reach of my lips – to place her hand on my forehead, smoothing out the bedcover, bustling to the window to twitch the curtains. Talking sweet nonsense all the time and then, suddenly stopping beside the door, making another half-serious curtsey before striding out of the room. In ten minutes she was back, carrying a tray of food: a lightly-boiled egg, delicious bread with butter, and a china mug of tea with milk in it. I ate and drank everything; then she brought a razor, soap, and hot water, and shaved me, not very well but with exquisite tenderness. And when she had finished I brought my left hand from beneath the covers and placed it over both of hers.

'So you are not my little Katie, my *kättchen,*' I said, 'but you must tell me your name, since you know mine.'

'Tatiana.'

'A Russian name?'

'Yes. My mother is Russian. But it's a long story, and I won't tire you with it now. Tomorrow, perhaps. Now you must sleep again.'

The spring day was nearly at an end when I woke once more. I could hear swifts in the evening air, scratching their thin cries as they swept after insects round the eaves of the château. Even before I opened my eyes I was aware of something different in the atmosphere of the room, of something filling up part of the space between my bed and window. The room was filled with a deep sunset blush, and on a low stool sat a man, in a dark blue uniform that I recognised as that of a British naval officer. His cap was raked over one eye, a style that I had seen in newspaper photographs, adopted by the English admiral Beatty, and he was quietly smoking a pipe. His face was turned toward the bed as though he were watching me, but I could not see his eyes because they were hidden by darkly-tinted spectacles. Poised on the stool, he was like a beetle, waiting motionless for some small insect to amble innocently by.

When he saw that I was looking at him, he rose and came to the bedside, standing there slightly bowlegged and staring down at me. 'Good evening. Commander Marlin, British Naval Intelligence. I trust you're feeling somewhat better?' His German was idiomatic, but atrociously accented.

I nodded warily: I knew exactly what to say. 'I am Rittmeister Manfred von Richthofen of the German Air Service – and I do not think I am required to answer any other questions?'

Marlin snorted with laughter. 'My dear Baron, I'm really not here to interrogate you. I assure you that I have absolutely no interest in the dispositions of your *Jagdgeschwader,* your fighting strength, or even the specifications of your latest aircraft.' He tapped the side of his nose with the stem of his pipe. 'On the other hand, I'm sure you'll be pleased to hear that Hauptmann Reinhardt has succeeded you as commander of JG1, as you wished. Though I'm not quite sure how long he'll last: some of your top chaps are talking about a man from *Jasta 27,* an Oberleutnant Göring. No, no, no: my dear Baron, I want to talk to you about entirely different matters.'

I raised myself stiffly as high as I could in the bed. 'Be so good as not to address me as your dear Baron. I do not think that you also have news that my father is dead? *He* is the Baron von Richthofen; I am so far only the – what do you say in English? – the heir apparent, *der rechtmässiger Erbe.* I am the *Freiherr,* what I suppose you would call the Honourable in England.'

Marlin replied ironically: 'I stand corrected, *ehrenwert Freiherr.* I will try not to make the same mistake again. But to me, as to everyone in the British forces, you will always be the Red Baron . . . I see that even this brief conversation is tiring you. I shall not expect you to answer any questions tonight, but I want to put one to you and leave you to think about it. You were at the treaty negotiations between Germany and Russia at Brest-Litovsk in February, I believe?' I stared back coldly: how could he possibly have known that? 'I want you to think very carefully – and I have good reasons for asking this question, and you, believe me, have equally good reasons for answering. Do you know, do you have any reason to suspect, that there might be a secret clause in the treaty governing the safety of the Tsar and his family? – There, you see, a very innocent enquiry; absolutely nothing to do with military matters or the security of Germany. Please think about it.'

I made my stare as hard, and my face as stiff, as I could. 'Commander Marlin, I have absolutely no intention of answering any questions whatsoever. I am a prisoner of war, and I claim the rights of a prisoner of war.'

Marlin had turned to go, but at this he stopped, stared at me through his tinted glasses, and smiled wolfishly. 'Oh, my dear Baron – sorry, beg your pardon: Freiherr – I'm afraid that you're not quite aware of the situation. You see, you are not a prisoner of war; dear me, no. The truth of the matter is, you're dead.' He bent to pick up a khaki-covered folder propped against one of the legs of the stool, opened it, and showed me photographs of my funeral; of the simple coffin on the Crossley tender, of the firing party, in their Australian bush hats, marching with arms reversed, of the four-bladed propeller making a cross above my grave. And finally he showed me a flimsy carbon copy of the message dropped on my airfield at Cappy.

I cannot describe my feelings at that moment: there was relief, of course, that I was alive and not dead and buried; a very eerie sensation at the macabre experience of, as it were, attending my own funeral; and an almost overwhelming desire to burst out in hysterical giggles.

But I put a stern face on it. 'This is ridiculous,' I protested. 'I insist you let my family and the Air Command know the truth. You can report that the body you buried today was wrongly identified; that I came down in the country and you have only just discovered who I am. After all, what can you possibly want with me?'

Marlin shrugged, closed the folder, and started for the door. 'To be honest with you, Freiherr, we've no idea what we want with you. But your family have been told that you're dead, your effects have been returned to them, Reinhardt commands JG1, the Kaiser has sent his telegrams of condolence, the newspapers across the world have published the story, and all Germany has mourned a lost war hero. And you've been in our hands for the past ten days!'

I slept. I was still so weak that it was nearer coma than slumber, and Marlin's visit, and the news he had given me, brought a succession of nightmares from which I could not escape. When I woke I felt lightheaded and broken: my chest throbbed with pain, and the fingers of my right hand, trapped in their bandages, felt numb. I desperately needed to make water. The sound that escaped from my lips was more like a moan than the brisk shout of command that I had intended. But the door opened, and Tatiana was there, and clearly knew exactly what I wanted. The porcelain bedpan, with its printed crest to match the bedcover, was warm; and it seemed to me, in my feverish state, that Tatiana's fingers lingered delicately at their work.

She brought me a mug of sweet English tea, and sat on the edge of the bed watching me carefully as I drank. It was a little after dawn, and the light was cold in the small grey room, reminding me of the morning when I was shot down. I could see the tea trembling in the mug as I held it.

I asked 'Have I really been here for ten days?'

She nodded. 'You were shot right through the chest. It was a very near thing. And there was a bad slash across your groin, from a broken wire, they think.' Her voice shook. 'So close, so very close . . . But we're going to remove your dressings today, and see how you're coming on.'

I laid my empty mug on the bedside table, and reached out my hand toward her. She put her right hand gently into my left. I said. 'You promised to tell me how you came here. A Russian girl in an English hospital. And speaking German.'

'As for that,' said Tatiana, 'you must remember that everybody at the Russian court speaks German, as well as French; because the Tsarina Alexandra is a German princess, you know. From Hesse. My mother was at court: my great-uncle is Duke Nicholas Leuchtenberg. He went to London for the old queen's Diamond Jubilee in 1897, and my mother was amongst his household. She met the Prince of Wales at a ball at Clarence House, and I believe she quite bowled him over. She was very beautiful then, much prettier than I am, and the next day his equerry arrived at her hotel with hundreds of roses and an invitation to attend the Spithead Review. My mother was still on the Isle of Wight, in a villa at Cowes, when she discovered that she was pregnant. Because of the disgrace she couldn't go back to Russia, and I was born in a very strange kind of house called Fort Belvedere, not far from Windsor. I saw my father sometimes when he drove out from the castle, although of course I didn't know then who he was; and twice he came to visit us. It was only after he died, when I was nearly twelve, that

I learnt the truth. So you see, I'm a cousin of King George of England, and of the Tsar of Russia; and, of course, of your Kaiser. But the Tsar is Tsar no more, poor man. Kept a prisoner somewhere, and nobody's quite sure where.'

She stood up, and absently began to smooth out my sheets: a duty that every hospital demanded, though thrones toppled, and nations fought each other to the death, and kings denied their own children.

I was silent. Some people, I suppose, would call this a sad story; but Tatiana herself seemed completely unaffected by it, and it seemed to me that to have such distinguished connections was recompense enough. Then the door opened softly and Marlin, with his peculiar bowlegged gait, slid sideways into the room, waving Tatiana to leave. He seemed excited, in an absent-minded sort of way, and, after the door was closed, he paced up and down the rooms in the brightening light of morning, slapping his hands together behind his back and glancing at me now and again with his round, dark, chafer's eyes.

At last he stopped pacing, and neatly kicked the stool with his boot so that it slid across the polished floor and stopped near the bed. Perching himself on it, he unbuttoned the top pocket of his uniform jacket and took out his shiny briar pipe and a yellow oilskin pouch. With his attention concentrated upon filling the pipe with twists of tobacco that he rubbed between his hands, he began to speak slowly and thoughtfully.

'I asked you last night whether you suspected any secret clause in the peace treaty beteween Germany and Russia that might guarantee the Tsar's safety. I suppose you know that the Tsar and all his family – the Tsarevich, the Tsarina and the four Grand Duchesses – have been prisoners somewhere in Russia for the last fourteen months? Well, I got some rather unexpected news during the night: seems some funny johnnie, who might be one of yours, very nearly managed to spirit the Tsar out of Russia, about ten days ago.'

The pipe was neatly packed. Marlin was silent for several minutes, striking matches, sucking and blowing at the pipe, pressing the mixture into the bowl with his thumb, until he eventually appeared satisfied with the result.

I watched him coolly for some time before I spoke: 'Now

41

I can understand why you asked me about Brest-Litovsk, but I can assure you that I and my brother Lothar were there merely as some sort of side-show, to show the Russians what a German air ace looks like. We only stayed for a day or two before we escaped for some hunting in Bielowiecza; and, although we were called "official observers", we had nothing whatsoever to do with the drafting of the treaty.'

Marlin's pipe had gone out. It took several more matches and a ritual with the detachable mouthpiece before he once more had the smoke billowing from it, and could raise his blank black eyes to stare at me once more.

'There was something else I wanted to ask you,' he began, almost diffidently. 'Know Berlin quite well, I suppose? Of course you do. I never got there, myself, before the war. Wiesbaden, Bad Homburg – but it's not quite the same, is it? Quiet, respectable places, reminded me of Harrogate. But Berlin's different, ain't it? A bit wild, unconventional you might say . . . *exciting*. Where you'd go for a bit of fun that was – well, out of the ordinary?'

I had been awake less than an hour, but this man made me feel exhausted already. I groaned faintly and said nothing, but he persisted.

'Did you ever hear anything about the Green House?'

'Good God,' I replied in some exasperation, 'you are thinking of my father's time, or indeed my grandfather's. It must be nearly fifty years ago that Wilhelm Stieber established that den of vice!'

'Yes,' said Marlin, 'pretty remarkable things went on there, what?' He chuckled. 'Something for everybody, eh? Listen, some chap told me it's going as strong as ever: women wrestling in the mud, dressed as dragoons or nurserymaids or anything you might want, even young lads for them as are that way. And I did hear there used to be one girl, sweet little thing by all accounts, who dressed as a governess.' A few small beads of sweat appeared at his temples. 'In a long, blue serge skirt, and a prim, little blouse all tucks, and a cane in her hand . . . '

I could bear his rambling no longer. 'This has nothing to do with me,' I exclaimed, and I could feel my temper rising and hear the slight tremor in my voice. 'I must ask you once again what you mean to do with me. It's intolerable that you should

42

cause such distress to my mother, and my father and comrades, by letting them believe that I am dead. I insist that you announce that I am alive. You can't keep me here for ever. I am a prisoner of war, and I have rights defined by the Geneva Convention. As soon as I am out of here, and' – my voice faltered – 'in a prison camp, I shall make sure that everybody knows who I am.'

Marlin, who had been sitting sunk in despondency, seemed quite cheered by my outburst. He smiled, although sadly: 'Dear Baron – I know, I know, but that's the name on your file, and it's the way I always think of you – it's not quite so simple, you see. First of all, will anyone believe you, or will they think you just a wounded airman' – and he leaned over and tapped my temple by the old bullet scar – 'with delusions. Secondly, what are your superiors going to make of the fact that you apparently flew deliberately into the Australian sector, and persuaded us to announce that you had been shot down? And thirdly, and this should be enough for now, what about the several thousand French francs you had sewn into the back of your flying jacket?' It was true: I had kept the money there to try to bribe my way back if ever I were brought down behind the British lines. Marlin went on: 'I must confess, we kept you alive because we hoped you would have something to tell us about the treaty, and now that events have overtaken us nobody quite knows what to do with you.' He stood up and moved, crablike, to the door. 'We've got you here, and we'll look after you, but, as far as the big wide world's concerned, Manfred von Richthofen died a hero's death eleven days ago. And you wouldn't like them to think you weren't a hero after all, would you?'

It seemed hours before Tatiana brought my breakfast, and when at last she did I was too distressed to eat more than a few mouthfuls. We were both silent: I was having a terrible tussle with my conscience and my pride, and Tatiana appeared to be seized with some deep emotion that she could scarcely control. After she had taken away the tray, the boiled egg untouched and the bread hardly crumbled, a new visitor entered the room: a tall, grizzled man in the uniform of a major in the RAMC. He spoke only in English, so that I understood nothing of what he said. With Tatiana's help he removed the rolls of bandages from my chest, rolling me brusquely from side to side as he did so, finally turning me nearly on my face to lift the dressing from the wound behind my right armpit. With stiff fingers he tapped and prodded my back and ribs, grunting contentedly to himself. He asked a question, and Tatiana, putting her lips close by my ear, said in German:

'The doctor wants to know when you were born.'

With my voice muffled in the pillow, I replied 'May 2nd, 1892.'

When the doctor was gone, Tatiana gently pulled off the white cotton hospital jacket, and drew back the bed covers. For the first time, I was able to see some of my wounds. The hole in my chest, still brightly red and yellow and surrounded with purple contusions, was puckered and healed over; from my left hip, across my thigh and into my left groin, the long red cicatrice from the lashing wire showed how near my escape had been, not from death but from something infinitely worse. Tatiana brought a white enamel bowl of warm water, towels, a brown sponge and a bar of yellow hospital soap, and carefully washed me all over, her hands shaking a little and her breath coming in tiny gasps. She paid great attention to the scar in my groin and to the flesh nearby – until suddenly the bowl of water was on the floor, and the towels with it, and she was uncontrollably kissing the scar, and sobbing, and shivering, while I could do no more than wind the fingers of my left hand tightly in the curls of her head.

She stopped to take breath, and raised herself to look into my eyes. 'Oh my poor, dear brave boy, my wonderful hero, how proud your mother must be of you, and the Fatherland!'

And now she kissed me on the mouth, whispering all sorts of sweet things. I was weak and unable to move, but suddenly aroused. Tatiana felt the movement beneath her hand and, taking her mouth from mine, began instead to kiss the symbol of my manhood as it began steadily to rise. In a moment she was on the bed, kneeling with one leg each side of my thighs, and raising the skirt of her white gown around her hips. She wore calf-length boots of grey suede with little pearl buttons, white stockings rolled below the knee, and nothing more. Her skin was very white, and against it her pubic hair curled darkly with a glint of red. Holding her skirt high with her left hand, with her right she gently eased me into her. Then, with her dark

44

eyes shining and her nurse's cap touchingly askew upon her curls, she began to move.

I was astounded and bewildered, excited and very proud. Other women had given themselves to me, society women carried away by the glamour of a German war hero, but this was the niece of the Kaiser. Weak as I was, I could do no more than reach out my left hand toward her, but soon I too was caught up in the rhythm as Tatiana, her arms stretched wide, squirmed and panted, seeming to suck me high into her womb – and suddenly the room was full of sunlight, the curtains whirling in the morning air, and a wild bird singing madly beyond the window as if his heart, too, would burst. Tatiana slowed, gasping for breath, and I slowed with her; and then she looked me full in the face, her eyes blazing, and smiled, and said:

'Happy birthday, my darling.'

CHAPTER 3

18 May: Neufchatel/London

AFTER ANOTHER fortnight at the Château d'Eawy, I was without doubt a new man. Tatiana's ardour remained unabated and, as my wound healed, I began to take the initiative in our love-making. I found, however, that I was a prisoner in my room, kept from leaving during the day by a sergeant with a revolver, who sat on a stool in the corridor some yards from my room door, and at night by what appeared to be two Royal Marine sentries with fixed bayonets. So I began taking my first stumbling lessons in English, coached in the fundamental earthier phrases by Tatiana. And I learnt from her the real words of the song that I had heard on a distant gramophone, the first day when I returned to consciousness:

> And one day we're gonna build a little home for two
> Or three or four or more
> In Loveland, for me and my gal . . .

But of what was to become of me I learnt nothing. Marlin
had not returned, although he had taken care to send me all the
cuttings from German and British newspapers that recorded the
heroic end of Freiherr Manfred von Richthofen. The guards
remained in the corridor, the windows, I found, were barred,
and each day it was with increasing embarrassment that I
received from Tatiana, and later handed back to her, the
bedpan covered with its little cloth.

'I am a man,' I protested bitterly to her; 'I am a civilised man
and perfectly fit. I am used to the water closet and to privacy. It
is unfair to treat me like a baby in a nursery.' But Marlin's
orders remained unquestioned, and Tatiana, though a Russian
and in love with me, had been brought up in England.

Then, one bright morning, when the bedpan had been
brought and taken away and I, still dressed in the cheap, bright
blue pyjama suit and white shirt favoured by the hospital, was
looking forward to my daily English lesson ('these are your
hips, these are my thighs, this is my – '), the door burst open to
admit a man in a hurry. He wore a checked Inverness cape, a
tweed suit of a most unhappy shade of green, and a deerstalker
that did not match. Only the large, shiny, tinted spectacles
identified him as Commander Marlin.

'Right! You're leaving here. Quick as you can. I came
straight from Dieppe, and I've got to get you back there by
midday. Oh, sorry my dear Baron: good morning, how are
you? Nurse! ah, Miss – let me see, Fitzalbert? – is the patient
well enough to dress himself? Good. There is a valise in the
corridor, please bring it in. Some suitable civilian attire for you,
Baron – oh Lord, I shall never remember – Freiherr. Yes I
know,' he added wearily, seeing the expression on my face and
stopping the protest rising to my lips: 'You are a German officer
and a gentleman, and the Hague Convention does not permit
you to wear civilian clothes in enemy territory. You can be
arrested by the civil powers, and may be shot as a spy. But, my
dear Freiherr – there, d'you see? – you are no longer Captain
Manfred von Richthofen. He is dead (sorry to have to keep

pointing it out) and these papers that I have here' as he dragged a thick bundle from his inside pocket, extracted one and unfurled it quickly, 'name you as Captain Simon Jones, commissioned in the South Staffordshire Regiment, and seconded until further notice to (ha! so that's what they call them) special duties. Here's your notebook – there, you see, your colonel's signed your secondment – and your travel warrant. I'll put you on your word to keep your mouth shut while we're travelling: we're going to get some mighty funny looks if you start trying to ask for help in German and, besides, nobody's going to understand you.'

I dressed unsteadily, helped by Tatiana, who murmured soothingly to me as she buttoned buttons and laced laces, while Marlin paced up and down in the clear spaces of the small room and laboriously filled and lit his pipe. In a few minutes the late commanding officer of JG1 stood by his bedside in a grey Norfolk suit, brown woollen stockings and bright brown brogues, with a dark Melton greatcoat about his shoulders and a grey tweed cap in his hands. Marlin glanced at me, then scrabbled in the open leather valise.

'Gloves, must have gloves; and a comforter, it's cold on the water. There. Now, Miss – er, Fitzalbert – you too. We shall need you to look after the invalid. Get your travelling bag. You're already signed out with matron.'

Drawn up close by the steps of the château was a Wolseley tourer with its hood up and its engine already throbbing. Officers in blue hospital pyjamas, playing cricket or practising golf strokes on the lawns some distance away, glanced up incuriously. The same gramophone played a new song faintly among the trees: 'Over there, over there, send the word, we'll be heard, over there . . . ' I stood for a few seconds on the top step in the morning sun, staring eastward into the streaked blue sky, hoping that I might see a tiny flight of Fokkers hunting in the upper air, and then, with Tatiana taking my arm, stumbled unwillingly after Marlin down to the car.

The run to Dieppe, past lines of wagons and marching men making their way to the front, over level-crossings where ammunition trains, with one Lewis gun mounted on the engine tender and another on the guard's van by the lookout caboose, held us up for ten minutes at a time, took over two hours. I had my first sight of Americans, with their cowboy hats and their hip-swinging, undisciplined way of marching. Everything that I saw during that racketing, bouncing drive in the dusty gusts of a May morning has remained clearly fixed in my memory throughout my long life, but one sight above all was unforgettable.

Just before we reached Dieppe, in a little town square dominated by an immense town hall, the car was slowed almost to a halt as the driver threaded his way through a large crowd surrounding a military band. All the bandsmen and their conductor, I realised with a start, were negroes. They had the usual military band instruments – trumpets, trombones, clarinets, saxophones, and great tubas like hooded cobras about to strike that I decided must be the famous sousaphones – but their music (although, I must admit, I can scarcely tell one tune from another even when I know it) was unlike anything I had ever heard. Drums rattled and cymbals crashed at completely unexpected moments, trombones cried like mating bulls, saxophones moaned like mourning cows.

The efforts of the driver to force his way through the crowd brought the car very near to the band. The conductor, dressed in a magnificent bandmaster's uniform, stood on a small podium, and a banner that had been draped rather untidily across it read, in gold braid on deep red, 'James Rees Europe & His American Marching Band'. Beside the podium stood a short, thin Jewish-looking man, in American khaki but without a hat. The band came to the end of its piece, and, in the cheers that followed, the short man stepped up onto the podium, accepted the baton and, as the cheers rose louder, stood smiling shyly. As he turned to give the beat to the band, and the same tune burst out that I had heard only two hours before from the gramophone at the château, the car suddenly accelerated away. Marlin swore, and thumped his knee with the fist that held his pipe, scattering glowing cinders across the floor of the car.

'Good Lord! D'you know who that was? Irving what's'isname! the feller that wrote "Alexander's Ragtime Band"!'

Very soon afterwards, we were driving into Dieppe down the tree-lined rue Gambetta, rattling on the cobbles past the buildings hung with tricolours, union jacks, the stars and stripes

48

of America, the red and green of Portugal, and the other flags of the allies, denoting the offices of the RTOs, the billeting officers, signals HQ, commissariats, liaison committees, military police, and all the rest of the bureaucracy of war. The car turned right into the Grande Rue and emerged close to the quay, with the docks spreading out to the right. Here a sentry challenged us nonchalantly, and Marlin produced his bundle of papers and, leaning far out of the car, spoke quietly in the man's ear. The sentry came to attention. The car moved on, and stopped after a few yards at a gangplank that led aboard a grey and salt-stained paddle steamer. Marlin was first out of the car, to show yet again his papers to the sentry at the gangplank's foot, and Tatiana was second, with her medical bag in her hand and a tartan blanket folded over her arm.

'Hurry now,' she whispered to me in German, and then she giggled: *Captain Jones!*

The driver of the car, a silent sergeant in field khaki, brought up the rear with Tatiana's valise and a wickerwork hamper, and in half a minute we were all aboard the vessel. The gangplank was slid away; there were the usual toots of the steam whistle and the shouts of the deck and quayside hands as they released the mooring ropes. Then the steamer, with a great flurry of churned brown water, was making for the harbour mouth.

Over the smart black, white and gold of the Channel packet, the grey paint had been applied in wide untidy sweeps of a huge brush. Shrapnel shields, like vast khaki mattresses, hung down on both sides of the deckhouse, and similar smaller ones were rolled up above the windows of the bridge. Sandbag nests at the bow and stern held Vickers gun crews, and a Lewis was mounted on the roof of the deckhouse abaft the bridge for protection against attacking aircraft. The deck was crowded with stretchers, each bearing a man in bandages, and there was mud and sand everywhere underfoot.

Our little group remained standing silently by the rail as the steamer trudged out between the forts at each side of the harbour entrance. There was a light mist on the water, through which we could see the distant shadow of a destroyer on station, and nearer, where the entrance channel wound out into deeper water between the mines and rusty obstructions of the shallows, a small gunboat patrolled, its after deck piled high with depth

49

charges.

'Care for a spot of tiffin?' said Marlin in English to Tatiana, adding a muttered *'Mittagessen'* for my benefit. A first-class saloon had been reserved for us, its windows shrouded by the shrapnel mattresses and the only light coming from the hooked-open door. The hamper carried by the sergeant contained a cold fowl, some potato salad, two halves of a French loaf and two bottles of Krug '08, rather warm after its morning ride; Marlin persuaded a deckhand to fill a bucket with cold seawater, but the improvement was only slight, and we crouched in the dusty gloom of the saloon, drinking tepid champagne and exchanging brief whispers in German and English, for two hours or more.

Eventually Marlin stood up and addressed me in English, his face twisting below the dark spectacles as he carefully enunciated each word. 'Captain Jones, Miss – er Fitzalbert – tells me that she's been teaching you the lingo for the past two weeks. We arrive in Folkestone in twenty minutes' time, and after that it is essential that we speak only English. I do not expect you to have to speak to me, but I insist that you do whatever I ask you. I'll try to make it as easy as possible for you.'

He led the way out on deck and waved vaguely to the north, where the cliffs of England could be seen rising out of the horizon. Eastward a small flotilla of transports was being escorted to France by a destroyer; westward, thick black smoke along the skyline betrayed the presence of a bigger battleship. The mist had cleared, the swell was light, and the little paddle steamer plodded gamely on for England, home and duty.

Within half an hour we were close under the high white cliffs to the east of Folkestone, moving on an almost westerly course into the bay, to find a berth against the mole. I saw how the downs rose on either side bristling with gun emplacements, and high on the cliff was a confusion of radio masts hung about with wires. Troop transports were moored to the mole, and the length of the breakwater was astir with troops. Heliographs winked, and semaphores above the town jerked spasmodically. In the bay steam pinnaces buzzed busily about.

We landed in the same order in which we had boarded the steamer: Marlin first with the papers, myself and Tatiana together, and the sergeant last with the baggage. Following a single rail track that ran from about halfway along the mole, we walked past engine sheds and the backs of small houses to the station, where a train of dirty brown carriages stood hitched to a panting locomotive. Attached behind the baggage van was a single first-class carriage, shining in the red-brown and gold of the Pullman livery, with paper strips pasted to the windows bearing the single word 'Reserved'. Inside, we found at one end a separate compartment containing four huge swivelling armchairs unholstered in red plush with gold tassels; and here, silently, we installed ourselves.

Ten minutes later, as the train, with whistles, groans, and neck-jarring jerks, began to move slowly out of the station, I was startled to notice that we were not alone in the carriage. At each end, almost identical pairs of figures in dark blue Inverness capes and squarish, narrow-brimmed bowlers were half-visible through the cut glass of the vestibule doors. And halfway down the open portion of the carriage, seated alone at a white-clothed table, a middle-aged man with close-cropped grey hair was staring fixedly at me with bright blue eyes close either side of a bronzed beak of a nose.

'I believe this is your first visit to England, Captain Jones?' said Marlin, making conversation with an obvious effort. I nodded coolly, and glanced at Tatiana beside me. She had said almost nothing since we left the château, and, had it not been for several quick squeezes of the hand, I could have been sure that my fond memories of our passionate lovemaking were nothing but an illusion from my days of delirium. Would I feel once more the grasp of those delicious white thighs against mine, or the hot torrent of her kisses as my hands explored her nakedness? Here in England, I supposed sadly, she would recall her upbringing, her position in life, her honourable blood. And then, as she raised both hands to her head to lift the grey nurse's bonnet from her brown curls, she smiled at me, and hope rose again.

'We call this the Garden of England,' Marlin waved a weary hand, and, turning my eyes to the window for the first time, I saw apple and cherry trees in military ranks stretching to the sunny distance. After the months in the mud of Flanders, and the leaves in the bleak forest of winter Prussia, it was like a view of Paradise. Suddenly, forgetting for a minute the bitterness of

51

my life as a prisoner without a name, I was filled with wild longing and a feeling as though I had been rescued from a deep pit. I was alive and out of the battle, and England was beautiful. Perhaps, when Germany had won the war, I would stay here until I could prove my true identity.

England did not look so beautiful later that afternoon, as the train made its uneven way between the smoke-blackened backs of mean rows of houses in the suburbs of London. The sun was sinking in an angry red bank of cloud, turning the windows into holes of fire, across which our shadows – mine, Marlin's, Tatiana's – rode like the Erl King and his daughters pursuing the train. Here and there the windows were broken, and ruined rafters reared among the jungle of chimneypots where the Gothas and Zeppelins had dropped their bombs. Soon, beyond the roofs, I saw a grey dome that I recognised as St Paul's Cathedral, and a high clocktower that I guessed to be part of the Houses of Parliament.

The train stopped at a wide station above the houses, moved on and stopped again, and then was crossing the Thames between the interlacing girders of an iron bridge. Below a smoky, echoing glass roof it slowed and finally came to rest. The men at each end of the carriage – secret police, I supposed – stepped down to the platform and stood there wearily. The grey-haired man, I was surprised to notice, had already disappeared. Marlin nodded brusquely to his sergeant, who picked up the baggage and led the way out of a side entrance to the station and down steps into a narrow cobbled street that sloped steeply back toward the river. We turned right into an archway below the rail tracks, where ragged beggars lay stretched on sheets of newspaper, and climbed more steps into another similarly cobbled street, which led out in a wide and leafy thoroughfare busy with carts, handsom cabs, and khaki-painted motorcars. Picking his way between the piles of horse manure and torn sheets of paper drifting idly in the evening breeze from the Thames, the sergeant led us across the street to a high modern building. With a slight shiver, I read the notice above the door. Whitehall Court! I had been brought to the very heart of the British government.

From the cool hall of the building we took a small lift, which rose smoothly and silently floor by floor; a notice on its panels announced that it was operated by the London Hydraulic Power Company. There was no one to be seen at any floor, and the building seemed to be only a block of apartments. When the lift stopped at the top floor and Marlin, taking out a key, unlocked one of the facing doors, I was disappointed to find that I was, indeed, entering a well-appointed apartment into which the last rays of the sun were flooding across the roofs opposite. The sitting-room into which we turned from the tiny entrance hall was walled with overflowing bookcases, the contents of which (I later discovered) were largely fakes; the floor space was almost entirely taken up with a huge green leather chesterfield, and between it and the empty fireplace stood a low three-legged table carrying a silver tray with a seltzer siphon, four tumblers, and a cut-glass decanter.

'Please make yourselves at home,' said Marlin, stepping backward out of the room and shutting the door.

We were in one another's arms at once. Tatiana kissed me, hugged me tightly, and kissed me again. The sun began to dip below the opposite roofs, and Marlin could be heard talking on the telephone in the adjoining room. 'My darling,' said Tatiana.

'My darling,' I replied. I realised that the next room, or the one next to that, must be a bedroom, and that only Marlin's presence lay between me and immediate pleasure. I felt Tatiana's body quicken against mine – dear God! was that all she was wearing? I must discover at once – and then Marlin was once more in the room, coughing deprecatingly, drawing down the blinds against the light (or some distant watcher?), and, offering glasses of whisky and soda. We sat in a row on the chesterfield, like three birds on a fence, while Marlin filled and lit his pipe with the customary ritual. We sat silently. I wrestled desperately with reasons for my presence there, but was determined not to ask. Tatiana stared dreamily at a painting above the fireplace, which represented a fallow deer having its throat ripped out by two spotted hounds. And Marlin alternately sucked and lit his pipe.

He had discarded his Inverness cape, but for some perverse reason had kept on his deerstalker. After some twenty minutes he drew a large silver watch from his green waistcoat, nodded, and said, 'Time, I think.' He led the way from the apartment, opened a small door, almost invisible in the corner of the

53

landing, and disclosed a narrow winding staircase. This spiralled its way to an attic floor, where a maze of passages, tiny interconnecting rooms and broom-cupboards brought us to a short flight of steps and a door that opened on to the leads of the roof. Here an iron footbridge crossed the well of the building to the opposite roof. Marlin led the way across, through another door, and into a similar labyrinth of small rooms where typewriters could be heard tapping, telephones tinkling, and soft voices in continual conversation behind a succession of tightly closed doors. Another, longer spiral stair, apparently built in the wall at the corner of a larger staircase, brought us finally out onto a spacious landing, facing a double door on which Marlin knocked lightly before opening it and gesturing us in.

Lit only by the last light of the dying day, the room was in semi-darkness, and against the broad windows everything appeared for a moment in silhouette. Then I was able to distinguish a wide table covered with maps and drawings, models of aircraft and submarines, a row of bottles apparently containing chemical solutions. Another table held half a dozen telephones, and in the darkest corner, behind a vast desk covered with scattered papers and files bound up in pink tape, a man sat writing. He was in his shirtsleeves, while over the back of his swivel chair hung a uniform coat with the braid rings of a naval captain. Hunched over his writing, he was obviously short and thickset, with grey hair half covering his round skull; when he looked up, a bright and piercing eye stared threateningly through a gold-rimmed monocle. On the desk in front of him was a glass inkwell filled with ink of a peculiarly purple colour.

'Sit,' said this person. Tatiana and I founded two rounded club armchairs, while Marlin remained standing just inside the closed doors. There was silence, except for the scratching of the pen as the anonymous captain completed his writing. He signed the paper, I noticed, with a single initial C, put down his pen, and leant back in his chair with a hand on each arm.

'Baron von Richthofen,' he began in English, as Tatiana quietly translated close by my ear: 'I am going to offer you the opportunity to do something for yourself, for Germany, and for humanity.'

'Firstly, as it affects yourself. You have already had it

54

explained to you by – what name do these two young people know you by, 25? Commander Marlin? how very interesting – Commander Marlin, then, that you are now a man without a name. I deeply regret the circumstances that brought this about – an administrative blunder, a little too much zeal,' and he stared accusingly at Marlin – 'but there seems no way, at the moment, in which we can remedy this. I have a crying need for a man with your experience and background, and I hope that you will find it possible to help me. In return, you have my word that, as soon as possible, we will assist you in every way to establish your identity and claim your rightful inheritance.

'Before I go any further, I must ask you whether you'll sign a small piece of paper that I have here.' He shuffled the documents on his desk, and nonchalantly brought out a single typed sheet. 'We are affected in this department by what is called the Official Secrets Act: this piece of paper is an undertaking by you that you will not reveal to any unauthorised person any of the information that I may disclose to you. It's strictly a formality, but my masters insist upon it. You'll appreciate that, as you are not a British subject, it's not really binding; on the other hand, unless you sign it I shall be unable to tell you anything further.'

'Would not my word as an officer and gentleman be enough?' I asked.

'Sorry, old boy, not a chance. Here, all you have to do is put your signature at the bottom.' He pushed forward the pen and the purple ink and I signed, despite my misgivings.

'Right. Now I can put you in the picture. I don't know how much you know about what's been happening in Russia. When the Tsar was deposed, he and all his household were taken to Tsarskoe Selo, and kept virtual prisoners there in the summer palace. So the British government opened negotiations with the Russian Foreign Minister, Milyukov, to allow them to leave for asylum in England. Our man in Stockholm had a word with your ambassador there, and it was agreed that one of our cruisers, under flag of truce, would fetch 'em out from Port Romanov. Cabinet agreed, all the arrangements were made, spring of last year – and then HM put the kibosh on it. Seems he's worried we might get a bolshie revolution here in England, and he got touchy about public opinion. Apparently your

55

Kaiser felt just the same, and in the end Kerensky got cold feet and spirited 'em off somewhere deep in Siberia.

'Then came the revolution, and it took our chaps four or five months to find out where they were. At last Buchanan in Petersburg got word to us that Bruce-Lockhart had discovered that they were being held in a little town called Tobolsk, on the Irtuish river. A clever little letter from their English tutor, Sydney Gibbes, came direct to the King by diplomatic bag, and we all buckled to, trying to work out a way to get 'em away from there. My number one, Colonel Browning, came up with a Norwegian shipping owner who's also Siberian consul, name of Jonas Lied, runs a fleet of steamers on the river Ob, under the flag of the Siberian Steamship & Manufacturing Company. So we roped in Grand Duke Mikhail, and together we persuaded Lied to carry the imperial family as far as Puyko, where we were to have a fast torpedo-boat ready to take 'em through the Kara Sea and round by Novaya Zemlya. Even HM gave his approval for that one. We just had to wait long enough for the ice to melt – and then the Prime Minister started shillyshallying – '

'Bloody Lloyd George!' Marlin burst in. 'All those little Welsh are nothing but damn prevaricators. My father knows 'im, you know. How he ever wriggled his way out of that Maurice letter business last week I shall never understand.'

One cold blue eye flashed in its golden rim, and Marlin subsided, like a balloon with its rip-panel gone. 'Anyhow, the outcome of all this is that the whole scheme's been scuppered. We've known for a month or more that Count Mirbach, your ambassador in Moscow, has been talking to Karakhan, the bolshies' foreign secretary – you'll have met him when you were at the Brest Litovsk negotiations. Then, about three weeks ago, some feller turned up in Tobolsk calling himself Vassily Yakovlev, saying he'd orders to take the Tsar to Moscow at once. We think he was one of your chaps: came a complete cropper, of course. The local what's it called – soviet? – got wind of the business, and the upshot is the Tsar, the Tsarina, and Grand Duchess Maria have been brought out of Siberia to a town called, we think, Ekaterinodar.'

Marlin brought out his pipe and began the complicated manoeuvres of stuffing it with tobacco. 'C' (for so I must call him, and it was many years before I discovered his name to be

Mansfield Cumming) was sitting sideways at his desk with his trousers carefully pulled up at his knees, so that his ankles were almost exposed. As Marlin reached the climax of his operations, 'C' took a match from a box of Swan Vestas before him and reached down, tucking up the bottom edge of his trousers and apparently striking the match on his leg. As he straightened, and waved the flame at Marlin, he slid his gaze to observe my expression, and the ghost of a grin crossed his face. Then he stood up stiffly, stumping his way on an obviously artificial leg to a map hanging over a sort of easel close to my chair.

'Here's southern Russia, the Crimea, the Black Sea, and this part running southward to the Caucasus is called the Kuban, after this river here. There's Ekaterinodar, close to the Reds' front line. Obviously, the original plan was to try to smuggle the Tsar and Tsarina through the lines into the Ukraine, but the situation around Ekaterinodar is so unstable, with the Kuban cossacks rampaging about in all directions, and Denikin's White army along the Don is so riddled with Social Revolutionaries, that we think it would be very unsafe. We can't take a torpedo-boat into the Black Sea, with the Turks holding the straits. Your Kaiser's getting rather anxious about things, and I've had direct orders from the palace here: the King's private secretary, Lord Stamfordham, got on to my chief, Balfour, about it. Here, what do you think of this?'

The sudden change disconcerted me, as I later suspected it was intended to. 'C' had turned to the crowded table and picked up one of the aircraft models, which he was holding out for my approval. It was, I realised with a start, a tiny representation of my own Fokker Dr 1, red as I had ordered it painted. The detail was remarkable, even showing the incomplete obliteration of the cross *pattée* on the sides of the fuselage, where we had replaced it with the Greek cross not many weeks before.

'Did I get it right?' asked 'C' anxiously, and with some slight satisfaction I was able to point out that the inboard struts were not quite at the correct angle. It was only as I handed the delicate little model back that I realised it had been made almost entirely from used matchsticks.

'There's one last hope,' he resumed, holding the aeroplane gently balanced in his fingers. 'If only we could get someone of good enough social standing to be acceptable to the Tsar, preferably a chap that Karakhan would recognise on sight, who could fly an aeroplane into Russia and bring him out.' He lowered himself back into his chair and glared through his monocle: 'Now you, my dear Baron, just about fit the bill.'

And then there was a silence in that room high above Whitehall, a silence so complete that it seemed a physical presence. It was almost dark, and only the gold-rimmed glass of the monocle glinted with the last of the day. I could find nothing to say. I realised that I was too tired even to speak, but still the thoughts tumbled in my head. I suppose my dominant emotion was pride: that I had been saved from the mud of the Australian trenches and brought here to serve not only my Kaiser, but the Tsar of Russia and the King of England – and in serving them, I realised, I would be serving three of Tatiana's relatives. But to expect me to fly into Russia! I had always flown as a hunter, and I knew little of the more subtle arts of aviation. What aircraft could possibly fly deep into Russia; how could I ever find my way; and how could I make myself understood when I landed?

Through the closed windows, from across the roofs of government, came the sound of Big Ben striking eight. The anonymous captain switched on an electric reading lamp on his desk. 'Because this is a matter of the utmost urgency, Tarpaulin here – what? oh very well, Marlin – has authority to get you whatever you need, within reason of course, and he'll keep you *au courant* with developments as they affect you.' He shook hands. 'My dear Miss Fitzalbert, such a pleasure. Your mother's well? I hear she's doing sterling work in comforts. And thank you, 25.'

In the space of a few seconds he had dismissed us, ushered us from the room, and closed the double doors behind us. Marlin, in silence, led the way back through spiral staircases, bridges and mazes of rooms and cupboards to the apartment.

'Well, what did you think of him?' he asked, when at last we were once more sitting on the green chesterfield, fresh glasses of whisky and soda on the table before us, and great plates of cold beef sandwiches from some unknown source. I could say little: my mind was still in turmoil, and my mouth was full of beef.

At last I managed to blurt out: 'How did he lose his leg?'

58

'Dunno,' said Marlin, filling his pipe, 'but it certainly wasn't in any battle. Don't seem to stop his motorcar driving, however; he roars about London in Müller as if he had the whole of the German High Command on his tail.'

'Müller?' My attention was caught by the German name.

Marlin turned almost puce in colour and coughed unhappily, striking matches and puffing for over a minute before he recovered his composure. 'It's the name we gave the car, you see. After one of your chaps. A spy actually. He was being paid regularly by post from Amsterdam, for information he used to send written in invisible ink on packets of newspapers. After we caught him, our chaps went on writing to Amsterdam, and the money kept coming through. So we bought the motorcar with it.'

I laughed without thinking, and then I caught my breath. Poor Müller was the most despicable of men, a spy, yet he had died for his country. And what was I, in my tweed suit, with false papers in the heart of the enemy capital, but a spy like him? Yet, I realised with some concern, I was getting to like these Englishmen, who had so recently been my sworn enemies. They could be devious and ruthless, yet they stood by their own kind; I felt that, if they trusted you, you could trust them equally. Cut off from the comradeship of my fellow fliers, I desperately felt the need to share the confidence of someone, even a Britisher. Should I, could I, do what they asked?

CHAPTER 4

19-23 May: London

I WOKE early, with my arm around Tatiana's naked shoulder, and kissed her gently into life. Behind the blinds the sun was up, poking little fingers of light past cracks and wrinkles so that the flecks of dust danced an aureole about our heads. Tatiana's dark curls spread on the pillow behind her: I raised myself on one elbow and eased my fingers among the curls to turn her face toward me. 'Why?' I said.

I was suddenly seized with bitterness and remorse; contempt, not for the beautiful girl beside me but for myself; and only sorrow for her fallen state. 'Why you?' I said. 'Why does a lovely girl, of such good blood, give herself to me in this way so generously. Isn't a woman's body a sacred thing, to be preserved pure and inviolate for the man she is to marry?'

Her eyes flashed, the lids opened wide, the lashes seeming to bristle like a dog's hackles, and red points of fire sparking in the darkness of the pupils. 'Yes! a woman's body *is* a sacred thing, but it is her own. Or, rather, it is a holy vessel, a Grail, that she carries in the service of the Life Spirit. A woman's body, like that of a man, is hers to do with as she will; hers to give and hers to withhold. Oh yes, for centuries and centuries you men have repressed us, made us into slaves. But once, at the beginning of time, it was the women who made the decisions, women who chose what lovers they would honour with their bodies, and all the world worshipped the Great Mother!

'Then men took over, with their jealous male gods, who taught them violence and brutality in place of women's tenderness and love, logic instead of their divine intuition. Do you remember what it says in the Bible? For we must love one another or die? Love is the only thing that can save this world, not fighting and killing, and it is women who have so much love to give. Oh, you are the first that I have ever loved in this way, but you will not be the last. We are so much wiser than you, my darling!' And she put her arms about me, and kissed me, and soon, contritely, I made love to her again.

After that, as the dusty beams slid sideways and downward into the bedroom, we rose, slipping on silk dressing-gowns that hung conveniently behind the door. In the dining-room a simple breakfast had been laid on the table: a pot of English tea, thin slices of toast with butter and marmalade, a delightful confection that I had not tasted for many years; porridge and a dish of kidneys simmered above a flickering spirit lamp on the sideboard. There was no sign of any servant, but a discreet clatter could be heard in the kitchen across the narrow hall.

Only when we had finished eating, and I was savouring a Sullivan's cigarette which I had found in an onyx box on a side-table, were we interrupted. Marlin eased open the door without knocking, and made his usual sidling entrance. He was dressed again in his naval commander's uniform, and was followed by a dour elderly woman, thickset and short-legged in a vast white apron, who began immediately to clear away the dishes.

He made his usual nonchalant greeting, and then, with his peaked cap tucked under his arm and his hands behind his back, began to pace up and down the room with his rolling bowlegged gait, talking as he went. 'Got a visitor for you in half an hour, Baron, so I expect you'd like to get dressed? My sar'nt has brought a selection of clothes for you; hanging them up in your bedroom at this moment, actually. And we called upon your mother, Miss Fitzalbert – she happened to be away at the time – and brought about half of your wardrobe, so you can have a change from your nurse's uniform.'

I was deeply disappointed with my clothes. With the exception of an elegant evening suit, they were all of unpleasantly coarse tweed. The shirts were vulgarly striped and ill-fitting, and the underwear was of a peculiarly itchy English material apparently called Cardinal Wolsey. In a foul temper, I dressed myself in a brown suit almost identical with the green one that Marlin had worn the day before, a brown-and-white striped shirt with a tie that matched it in bad taste, and (my only pleasure) a finely-polished pair of short black boots by Lobb. Tatiana, on the other hand, looked ravishing in a tabard and skirt of eau-de-nil silk, below which her ankles twinkled enticingly in emerald green shoes.

My visitor arrived on the stroke of ten, and turned out to be the same sharp-eyed silent watcher who had travelled on the train with us from Folkestone to London. Marlin introduced him as Assistant Commissioner Basil Thomson, 'the head of Special Branch' – a description which meant nothing to me at the time. It soon became clear that I meant equally little to Thomson, who spent the next hour talking irritatedly about the unrest in Dublin, the possibility of a police strike during the coming summer ('we're going to be worse off than the Russkies if we don't watch out'), and his differences of opinion with

61

someone he described as 'that self-satisfied Kell.'

Marlin scarcely said a word, and soon Tatiana abandoned her attempts to interpret, so that the fiery conversation became a monologue interspersed with sudden appeals to us for sympathy. It was only at the end of the hour that Thomson fixed his bright eyes on mine and said:

'My advice to you, Baron, is to stay put. You won't be disturbed in this charming apartment, and I've a regular rota of my chaps downstairs to keep unauthorised visitors at bay. But if you were to decide to go out and wander about, I couldn't answer for the consequences. Kell's lads are all over the place, and he shares informers with me; if one of those were to get curious about you and have you picked up, we'd have the devil's own job to get you out of their clutches.' And, with that, he picked up his black bowler hat, shook hands with each of us, and left the room without another word.

I shall never know what instinct it was that made me follow him only a half-minute later, but I found him standing conspiratorially in the tiny hallway, in conversation with another man who was dressed in the same undress uniform, of Inverness cape and narrow, square-crowned bowler, that I had observed worn by Thomson's henchmen the day before, on the train from Folkestone. What amazed me, however, was that, as this second man swung guiltily about to stare me in the face, I found myself confronted, it seemed, by twins: the same close-cropped grey hair and beaky nose, and the same piercing blue eyes.

Thomson seemed suddenly discomfited: he put one hand on his double's arm and the other on the latch of the apartment door, as if he were going to hustle him out without acknowledging me.

'This is one of my men,' he said. 'Constable Thompson. That's Thompson with a "p", actually.'

'To be precise, with a "p",' said the plain-clothes policeman, half extending his hand and then almost fastidiously withdrawing it before I could shake it. At a closer look he was far from identical to his superior: the eyes were shiftier, the teeth yellower, and all his linen faintly stained; his predatory but anxious grin gave him exactly the look of a gun-dog that has been caught raiding the chicken coop. I was conscious of an undefined hostility between us.

'I've just been telling Thompson,' said Thomson ominously, 'that you'll be staying here some time; perhaps a long time.'

'That should be very nice for you than,' Thompson said, with a foxy leer, 'in other words, pleasant. Nobby flat like this, very comfortable; you might say, the lap of luxury. And, I do hear, provided with the very best in the way of companionship. To put it another way – crumpet.'

Fortunately I did not then understand him, or I would have hit him hard. Even Thomson looked almost angry as he continued: 'And I have told Thompson that you will only be leaving this building in the company either of Commander Marlin – as he insists on calling himself – or Colonel Browning.'

'So I don't suppose we'll be seeing much of one another. Still, it's been very interesting meeting you; to be precise, an education. And I'll say farewell – until we meet again, that is.' At which they both nodded brusquely at me, and Thomson turned the latch of the door and led his subordinate out by the elbow.

Marlin whistled under his breath when I told him. 'You weren't supposed to see Thompson,' he said. 'In fact, no one's supposed to see the two of 'em together. Old Basil keeps him hidden away somewhere; only brings him out to use him as a double when something funny's afoot. Deuced shady character, that; wouldn't want to have anything to do with him, meself. But I tell you one thing: it certainly means the Commissioner's damn serious about what might happen to you if you so much as stick your nose out of the front door.'

So I *was* a prisoner: all those veiled threats made that clear. For the rest of the morning I sat silently seething, my brain a battlefield of emotion, while Marlin and Tatiana plotted inaudibly together behind the closed door of the sitting-room. After a light lunch – beef bouillon, some cutlets, and a peach that, Marlin told me, had come from the hot-houses at Kew – I was left alone again to think. But I came no nearer to any decision, and when Tatiana crept in to sit beside me I could only hold her hand, staring blindly through the narrow window and hearing the street sounds rising from so many floors below.

Dusk fell, we ate again in silence, and at last went quietly to bed. I had just fallen into a fitful sleep when I was hurled awake by the roar of a bombardment: a heavy calibre gun was firing, it seemed, almost outside the window. You can imagine that for some seconds I thought myself back on the western front, in the dawn barrage before another abortive push. Then, as other more distant guns opened fire intermittently, I realised than an air raid had begun.

Tatiana, I saw, was already awake, standing at one side of the window with her hand against the frame and silhouetted against the sudden flashes. I joined her, staring into the blue darkness of the early summer night. Like the ribs of a flirt's fan, opening and closing, thin beams of searchlights swept the sky to the east; for a second, one caught the dome of St Paul's, and the golden cross burned in the sky like a sign from heaven. The guns had stopped firing, and in the silence as the blind man's fingers of the light explored the air I heard the distinctive throb of a twin-engined bomber.

I took hold of Tatiana's hand and together we strained out into the night. Suddenly, where two beams crossed and stood still, we saw a brightly shining shape that buzzed and fluttered like a moth outside a lighted window; but even as the guns began firing again it slid sideways and was lost in the dark. And then I heard a sound that I had heard only once or twice before, a sound that on each occasion had filled me with terror – the whistle of falling bombs.

Even as my hand convulsively crushed Tatiana's they struck – exploding about a half-mile away, I judged, on the other side of the river Thames, and a few seconds later flames began to creep up among the narrow crowded roofs. 'Oh, the poor people,' Tatiana whispered to herself, and for a moment I too saw old women trapped by fallen beams as the fire crawled ever nearer, and little girls screaming and young boys desperately determined not to cry. But then my thoughts went out to my brave German comrades, who had crossed the North Sea in the trackless dark, flying low and slow, a sitting target for any gunner who got them in his sights – and at that moment the searchlights found their prey again. The guns burst out, and the little distant moth staggered, recovered, shook its wings, and plunged out of sight, flames already beginning to lick back from the engines and around the cockpits.

'Oh, the poor men,' Tatiana whispered again. And then my mind boiled with emotion as the terror of fire came over me once more: fire in the air, clinging like searing cobwebs about one's body as the aircraft went plunging and twisting down, as one desperately struggled to drag away the goggles from one's blinded eyes; and fire on the ground, roaring and thrusting its way through the shattered homes of men who had long ago left for the front, trusting in the safety of their wives and little children, now broken and wailing, as the flames crept and crept, nearer and nearer . . . I turned from the window, and flung myself on the bed, drawing the sheets over my head and lying there shivering many hours after the night was quiet once more.

In the days that followed I still could not come to any decision. Every evening I repeated the same arguments to myself: I was an officer, and a gentleman of Prussia, and I could make no kind of a bargain with the enemies of my country; but I was also a nonentity, a man who no longer existed, and that very nullity gave me the chance to carry out a mission that transcended all nationalistic restrictions.

During those days, I was like some rare creature in a zoo. Sometimes I was visited, in my lair at the top of Whitehall Court, by anonymous figures who stared, and puffed their pipes, and asked me irrelevant questions in a variety of languages, which Tatiana translated for me as necessary; sometimes I was taken, docile and without a chain, to visit discreet functionaries in discreet offices behind discreetly-drawn blinds. I was not formally introduced to any, but Marlin let me know that I had met, among others, Lord Stamfordham from the Palace, Arthur Balfour, the Foreign Secretary, and Lord Robert Cecil. They did not address a word to me; only Balfour looked directly at me. They stood, carefully separated from me by the width of their well-polished rooms, their hands behind their backs, their voices soft, speaking inscrutably in an English that I scarcely yet could begin to understand. Then I would be led back to my cage, an anonymous tweed-clad figure through the side-streets of Whitehall.

I saw London as I had never imagined it. I had expected rain, and fog, but it seemed to me that the sun shone every day. I remember how dirty the streets were; in the warm air the thick horse droppings stewed and simmered, and the rich stink reminded me of the great stables of our Prussian estates. Everywhere, also, there was a coarse gritty dust; I saw women sweeping the streets, wearing broad-brimmed hats and long canvas aprons, but their efforts only seemed to raise the clouds of dirt, so that we breathed it as we walked. Whitehall was a sea of khaki, navy blue, and the new pale blue of the RAF; hooting cars nosed their way in all directions between the horse-drawn cabs and drays.

As in Berlin, hundreds of middle-aged men and women wore black bands about their arms in memory of sons and husbands who had died at the front: but what surprised me more than anything was the atmosphere of cheerful bravado that prevailed. In Germany I had met only a spirit of desperation: we knew that we still could win the war, and that we had no alternative to winning. We were also told, and we believed, that England and France were finally exhausted; if the spring offensive had succeeded, before the Americans arrived in strength, the war would have been over. But here in London, for the first time, I realised that the war might well be lost.

My impressions were reinforced by a chance encounter one evening – I call it chance, but looking back I suspect that it had been carefully arranged by Marlin. He took me for dinner to the Marlborough Club, a large and comfortable Victorian building almost opposite St James's Palace in Pall Mall, with a bow window over the street where, I was told, King Edward had often sat. We were four at dinner: the other two were the man whom Marlin called his 'chief', Colonel Browning, and Sir Ernest Shackleton, the Antarctic explorer. I must confess that, despite the great respect I had for his exploits, I could not really take to Shackleton; he was a big, bluff man and a hero, but that evening he spoke of nothing but money. He told us of the vast mineral resources of the Antarctic continent, and of the similar treasures that must lie along the northern Russian coast; he told us how he was forming a company 'with a capital of over £1,000,000', to exploit the Russian lands around Murmansk and Archangel; and he tried to persuade me that the first words I should speak to the Tsar – if I were ever successful in reaching him – should be a demand for the mining concessions for this company. Tatiana had not, of course, been allowed to dine with

66

us, and I pretended that my poor grasp of English made it impossible for me to understand what he wanted, while Marlin grinned wolfishly and refused to intervene.

In the dining-room of the Marlborough Club each member sits at his own little table, but the tables are mounted on well-oiled castors, and can be wheeled together to make a group of any necessary size. For some time I had grown increasingly aware that I was being scrutinised by a solitary diner at a neighbouring table. Suddenly (probably, now that I look back on it, following a quiet cue from Browning) he stood up, holding his napkin to his mouth, and signalled a waiter. The little table was wheeled up beside our four, the chair was placed behind it, and the lone diner, bowing very slightly, inquired if he might join us. His name, he told us, was Mr Basil Zaharoff.

What else he had to tell us was drawn from him by what I understand is called in the English music-hall a 'cross-talk act'. Marlin and Browning, with only a little help from Shackleton, appeared to compete with one another in making increasingly outrageous statements, which Mr Zaharoff either confirmed or denied, or smiled at in noncommittal silence. He had fierce grey eyes, and what had once been an immaculate silver imperial, now strangely ragged at the edges; his smile was curiously sweet, but with an underlying menace.

Gradually, Marlin and Browning succeeded in suggesting to me that Zaharoff was a very rich man, an armaments salesman, representing, not only the great British firm of Vickers, but the French firm of Schneider-Creusot, and the Russian Putiloff company, as well as being a close friend of Alfried Krupp! It seemed that he was a citizen of France, and a Greek patriot, and a British secret agent. I was politely sceptical: the old man, though trim and upright, must have been nearly seventy, and I was sure that at this point Marlin and Browning had carried their act too far.

All Zaharoff's urbanity vanished in a second. He sat up stiffly, frowning fiercely, and I would swear that he tossed his head. In a low tone, scarcely opening his lips, he spoke directly to me in perfect German: 'But I assure you, *Captain Jones,* that I have only just returned from Potsdam.'

Browning, in English, took up the act again: 'Is it true, Zaharoff, that you went there in the uniform of a Bulgarian army doctor?' The old man nodded gently, his flash of temper apparently gone, but his reply made me shiver as if he had idly drawn his fingernail shrieking across a sheet of thin glass.

'I paid heavily for that uniform, and the man who sold it died.' His hand went to his beard, and he smiled thinly: 'I fear that Bulgarian doctors are far from meticulous about their *barbure,* and I was forced to disfigure myself with a pair of nail scissors. But it will grow.'

Then he laughed. 'Do you know, the most apprehensive moments of my whole visit to Germany came when I was once more in the train, making for the Swiss frontier? To my horror I noticed that a German officer, sitting opposite me, scarcely ever took his eyes off me. For three solid hours I was obliged to sit there unmoving, with his eyes boring into me. At last, when I could bear it no longer, and the frontier was at hand, I asked him why he was so interested in my appearance. "Herr Doktor," he told me, "I am so sorry to annoy you, but you are exactly like my sister's husband, who is reported missing." You must believe me, I was so relieved that I could have kissed the man on both cheeks!'

'You went, I believe,' said Marlin, 'at the request of both the Little Wizard and the Tiger. What did you find out? Is Germany finished?' I leaned eagerly forward, while Zaharoff, with a conspiratorial glance around, did likewise.

'Germany,' he said 'can hold out another twelvemonth, at least in military terms. But she is rotten at the core, gentlemen! There is a Communist coup brewing in eastern Germany, and a revolution in Hungary. We shall find soviets in Berlin before the summer is out. Zinoviev has said that he expects the red menace to sweep across Europe like the plagues of old, and be in London by the winter, while the Arabs rise in a holy war against British and French imperialism. I told Lloyd George that the only hope for us all lay in an armistice with Germany as soon as possible, and an honourable alliance against the common foe!' His eyes flashed again, his ragged imperial bristled, and Shackleton nearly applauded.

As for myself, I was caught up in the old man's rhetoric. As I have said, I now feel sure that this was no accidental meeting, but at the time I believe that I had at last been given some justification for what I had been asked to do. And later events certainly vindicated any suspicions that I may have entertained of Zaharoff's information: the November risings in Berlin and Munich, Bela Kun's regime in Hungary, the armistice itself, all revealed the authority of what he had to say. I began to feel at last that it was true that Germany was finished, and that the finest thing I could do would be to try to restore the Tsar to his rightful heritage.

For the first time, Zaharoff gave me his full attention. 'I understand on good authority that you are rather more closely connected with flying than your present identity might lead one to suppose?' I glanced cautiously at Browning, who nodded. I nodded too. 'I think I may claim,' said Zaharoff pompously, 'that I was the first man to fly.'

This time I kept my feelings to myself; it was utterly preposterous, but this boast of his was made as calmly as his previous claim to have been in Germany only a week or so before, and that statement had apparently been accepted by both Marlin and Browning. I let an encouraging grin pass over my face.

'You've heard of Sir Hiram Maxim? No? Surely you will know him as the inventor of the Maxim gun? Of course. But this would be more than twenty years ago, when you were scarcely more than a baby. Hiram built a great kite-like machine weighing nearly four tons, with a huge 360 horse-power steam engine to turn its twin propellers. It was to be tested on a railed track, with guide rails running above the wheels so that the machine could not take off. On the day, I persuaded Hiram to let me sit at the controls with him – nobody else dared to go, you know.

'The great steam engine was hissing and bubbling, and when Hiram opened the valve the propellers began to turn faster and faster. Soon the machine was straining against the brakes. Hiram signalled for his men to knock them clear, and then we began to rumble, faster and faster, along the track. The whole structure was straining upward, and suddenly there was a deafening crack, the guide rails twisted and split, and the machine lurched into the air.

'I have been in the most romantic cities of the world, I have experienced war on the battlefield, I have loved many beautiful women – but that moment was the most exciting of my life. I didn't want it ever to end. The steam engine was pumping faster than my heart, the machine was shuddering as if it would break into pieces any second – it was heaven! But Hiram was terrified: we were only inches above the ground but he looked like a man about to be pushed over a high cliff. Without stopping to think, he reached for the valve and wrenched it shut. The machine stood still for an instant in the air, and then it dropped to earth; and as it touched the ground it collapsed upon us like a house of cards. And it never flew again.'

He sighed, and touched his napkin to his temple, almost as if a tear stood in his eye. I had to believe him: I remembered so well my first flight, over Cologne just three years before, the exhilaration of floating through the air, and the sense of loss when the aircraft once more touched down on the flying field. I stood and shook the old man's hand, and, after a few more words, he took his leave with Shackleton at his ear.

I looked at Marlin; he was filling his pipe. 'Can't smoke here, old man,' said Browning in a horrified whisper; they both poured themselves another glass of port and sat together, like rooks on a fence, watching me without a word.

'Very well, gentlemen,' I said 'I'll do what you ask.'

Soon afterward, Browning and Marlin escorted me toward the door. It was then that a young man, in the mess-jacket of some unidentifiable regiment, suddenly rose before me, took my hand, and, in enthusiastic but hesitant German, began to speak to me of the pleasures of flying. I was somewhat confused and quite unsure whether I was supposed to be anyone other than a British infantry officer in mufti, so the conversation was a very one-sided one. It was only after the young man had again shaken my hand, wished me godspeed, and expressed concern about the safety of 'our cousins', that I noticed that my two companions had been standing, Marlin with his bowlegs and Browning with his stiff one, as close to attention as possible throughout the incident. And nobody ever told me whether it was, or was not, the Prince of Wales.

MI-1C
to Prime Minister
MOST SECRET   24 May 1918

'Captain Simon Jones'

We spoke, and agreed that it is essential that Captain Jones should be transported as soon as possible to the Middle East, that a suitable long-range aircraft should be made available for him there, and that he should receive instruction in long-distance flying and navigation.

It seems to me that we can kill, as it were, three birds with one stone: I respectfully submit that we request the provision of one of the Handley Page 0/400s at present undergoing proving tests at Manston, that this be flown to Baghdad, following the route pioneered last year by Squadron Commander K. Savory, and that Captain Jones gain experience at the controls *en route*. Beyond Baghdad, Dunsterforce can provide advance landing and take-off facilities with support from 30 Squadron RAF. Please procure me approval of CIGS and CAS. Request immediate clearance and complete confidence.

As Captain Jones does not speak Russian, and German may be regarded with suspicion in certain areas, it is essential that a Russian-speaker accompany him. He is at present in the care of a young lady who speaks English, German, and Russian with equal facility, and who has been trained by one of my staff in wireless telegraphy and simple ciphering. I appreciate that it is extremely unusual to ask a member of the fair sex to go into the field, and that the ME offers additional hazards, but the matter is of greatest urgency, and she may be of inestimable use when Captain Jones reaches his objective. Indeed, as you know, Miss Fitzalbert can claim close relationship with the imperial prisoners. I am sure that I can count on your utmost discretion in expediting all necessary papers.

I thank you in anticipation of your approval.

CHAPTER 5

*26-29 May: Manston/Villacoublay/Lyon/Frejus/Pisa/
Rome/Naples/Otranto/Salonika*

FLIGHT LIEUTENANT David Copley looked unbelievably young.
He sat on the opposite bench of the dark-green Crossley tender
as it bumped across the grass of Manston airfield away from the
administration huts, and the sudden white flash of his teeth in
the dark showed that he was smiling. I held Tatiana's hand:
even in a leather flying helmet, swallowed up in a flying suit and
thigh-length sheepskin boots, she looked unbearably pretty
as the lights of the quarters dimmed behind us. I had
been with her when she dressed, pulling close-fitting overalls of
chamois over her naked body before I helped her into her bulky
over-garments. During the week that we had spent together in
London, venturing out from the apartment at dusk to stroll by
the river, poring over maps and instructional manuals, and
twice visting the Army & Navy Stores with Marlin to buy
equipment, I knew that not once had she worn stays or drawers.

Now, in the darkest hours before dawn, the tender was
braking beside the spreading shadow of a huge aircraft. It reared
high above us, its twin undercarriages dwarfing the figures who
stood in the glow of a lamp from the trapdoor in its belly. I had
heard of this machine: one had been captured and put on show
at Aldershof, but I had not seen it before. I judged it to be even
bigger than the Gotha G-5, although not as big as the Zeppelin-
Staaken R-6. Marlin was already superintending the loading of
some small blue sacks that chinked attractively, while two
RAF ground crew with rifles stood watchfully nearby. Awaiting
Copley was one other flier, with a map case hanging on a long
strap from his shoulder, while a handful of riggers and mechanics gathered in the darkness beyond the light spilling down.

The parting was brief. Marlin shook hands silently with
Tatiana and myself, while Copley and the other man, with an
inclination of the head and a muttered 'excuse me', disappeared
up the ladder into the bowels of the machine. I followed them
up the ladder and, stooping slightly, along the upward sloping
floor of the aircraft toward the open cockpit, where Copley
was already settling himself into the right-hand seat. A rigger

standing by the left-hand seat, which had been folded up, handed Copley the strap he had just taken from the control column, and then wriggled his way past me, jerking his thumb at the vacant seat. As I hesitated, I heard a light giggle, and, glancing round, saw Tatiana already sitting on a bench below me in the belly of the aircraft, surrounded by baggage of all kinds and with her feet on a pile of the blue sacks. I grinned briefly and then squeezed myself forward beside Copley.

I was sitting nearly twenty feet above the ground, well forward of the wings and engines, and with the head of the second flier slightly below me in the very nose of the machine. To right and left I could see the shadows of two men crouched on each lower wing, one on each side of the engine nacelles. Together they swung on the starting handles, and slowly the four-bladed propellers began to turn; there was a polite explosion, a jerk, and the engines burst throatily into life. Copley eased his throttle lever forward slightly to increase engine speed, twisting a large metal knob on top of it to left and right until the two engines were running evenly, and then he took a large hand torch from a pocket in the fuselage beside him and shone it onto the starboard engine nacelle. I was surprised to see a small row of indicators along the side of the engine: oil pressure and temperature gauges, a revolution counter and an ammeter. They were some ten feet away, and difficult to read as the light from the torch wavered across them.

Copley turned, laid his hand on my arm, swung the light back onto the gauges, held up his thumb, and handed me the torch. Shining the light on the gauges of the port engine, I saw that oil pressure was normal, and water temperature at forty degrees centigrade; I too held up my thumb. For a few seconds Copley ran each engine in turn up to maximum revs, until the whole machine was shuddering against the chocks and the tail began to lift, then he throttled down and waved to the ground crew who stood straining on the straps, and almost immediately I felt the huge machine begin to rumble forward over the grass.

In front of us, a large L-shape of electric lights sprang alive across the field, and from the forward cockpit the front gunner flashed the letter Q in Morse from an Aldis lamp. There was an answering flash in green from an open wooden platform standing on four posts about twelve feet high – I had been told earlier that it was known appropriately as the 'bandstand' – and Copley turned the aircraft onto the long arm of the L with a short burst of full throttle on the port engine. Then he pushed the throttle knob forward as far as it would go, gave the wheel on top of the control column a slight forward movement to raise the tail, and allowed the Handley Page to take herself off, gentling back the wheel and settling into a steady climb as the lights of the airfield disappeared rapidly behind and below.

My first feeling was one of strange isolation from the aircraft. In an Albatros or a Fokker I had been crammed tightly in behind the roaring mass of the engine, the twin Spandaus above the cockpit coaming and the struts and wings cutting off nearly a quarter of my view. Here I was perched in the nose, on a lightly upholstered seat of tubular steel, with the throbbing shadow of a machine stretching far behind me, hardly belonging to the cockpit where I sat. As the speed increased, the noise of the engines seemed to fall away, back toward the ground where Manston was already swallowed up in haze, and I could hear Copley's voice at my shoulder.

'She don't climb like one of your scouts, you know. It'll take half an hour to reach our cruising height at eight thou, and we'll be over the French coast soon after. You've got a watch, haven't you? And a pad? I want you to keep a time and bearing check. Tasker's got a spare compass in the nose cockpit, but most of his navigation will have to be done by ground recognition, and we expect it to get a bit cloudy over the other side.'

I could see the compass in front of Copley: we were flying due west into the wind, which at ground level had been fairly steady at about eight – what did the English call them? knots? not quite the same as miles per hour, but very nearly. The only other instruments in the dimly-lit panel were the airspeed indicator, flickering over the ninety mark, and the altimeter, which now showed 2,000 feet. Take-off had been at 0303 and we had been in the air just six minutes. I noted the figures on my pad, then dragged up the map case from where it hung below my seat.

'I should guess we've made about seven miles in ground distance,' came Copley's voice again, high-pitched as he shouted against the rush of air and the steady rumble of the engines. 'We should be getting near Canterbury. I'm going to turn south now, so I'll give her about six degrees of westing to

74

allow for the wind. We ought to cross the coast halfway between Dover and Folkestone.'

As we climbed, the darkness seemed to fade beneath us. Peering over the cockpit edge, I could see the dark shadows of woods, the pale wandering traces of country roads, and here and there a light left burning in the night. The aircraft settled level on to its new course and, looking the other way, past Copley's shoulder, I thought I could see the street lamps of Canterbury. I also saw, with a start of terror, the cherry red of the starboard engine exhaust manifold and the blue tail of flame that, teased by the wind, seemed to flicker against the wood and fabric of the fuselage. I was about to cry out, in my halting, newly-learnt English, when I realised that this must be normal, that it was only because I had not flown before at night: in daylight the flames would be invisible, no more than the shuddering breath of hot gas that I knew so well.

From the ground ahead of us a thin beam of light suddenly probed the darkness, swinging slowly, flaring off streaks of cloud, blinding us momentarily as it swept across the aircraft. Beside it, another light began to flash in Morse. Copley reached forward, picked up a loaded Very pistol from below the instrument panel, handed it to me, and pointed to a steel tube fitted into the floor of the cockpit, which rose between the two seats.

'Just shoot it down there, will you?' he shouted, and I gingerly inserted the fat barrel into the mouth of the tube and pulled the trigger. Blown sideways by the wind, the flare arced away to port below us in a trail of bright green sparks and drifting white smoke, and the searchlight was abruptly extinguished. 'Colour of the night,' explained Copley. 'Won't need it again. That's the coast defences, and the sun'll be up before we reach the other side of the Channel.'

I entered another row of figures on the pad. Already, the far eastern horizon was glowing pink, and below I could see the white of waves breaking on the shore. The sea seemed to glow with darkness, and then was wiped from view, as if a blind had been drawn across it – we were in cloud. I had flown in cloud hundreds of times before, but always in daylight; there had always been holes and pockets, sudden glimpses of the earth beneath or of the thinner air above, the vapour streaking past had been visible. Here the blackness was suffocating, an almost solid presence made momentarily manifest, as it boiled between Copley and myself in the faint light from the instruments. For ten minutes we throbbed forward, rising with the climb and then sinking suddenly down again, our only indication the oscillating altimeter needle. Then the air began to show bright above us, and we burst out of the cloud into a sky suffused with the first light of dawn. A grey sea of vapour stretched to the east, lit with red from below, while to the west the heavens still were dark as indigo, and set with stars.

A helmeted head appeared by my knees. Tasker had scrambled aft from the nose cockpit. 'Time for tea?' he said. 'I've got a couple of rough star fixes, but they're fading fast, and we'll be on dead reckoning for the next half-hour. I guess we're about mid-Channel right now. What's our height, Copley? Seven and a half? Right, Captain Jones, tea will be served in the bomb bay.'

Crouched so that I would not have to stand up into the slipstream, I folded my seat aside and crept backward down the slight slope into the belly of the aircraft. Tatiana lay fast asleep on the bench, her head pillowed on two valises and her face rosy in the shadow. A haversack hung from a peg below the fuel tanks. Tasker pulled off his gauntlets, blew on his fingers, and took an aluminium Thermos flask from the haversack, unscrewing the cup from its top. We shared the cup of tea, which was sickeningly sweet but still hot, and then Tasker passed a second cup gingerly up to Copley. 'Bloody cold up here,' said Tasker. 'We've been experimenting with electrically heated gloves and boots, but some poor bugger set his foot on fire with a short-circuit. I prefer to manage without.'

He stared belligerently at me. 'You don't say much, I must agree. Jones ain't your real name is it? All right, we've been told not to ask questions. Some Secret Service johnnie I suppose. What are you? Eyetalian? Greek? Rumanian?'

I remembered the briefing I had been given. 'I am Czech,' I began. Tasker's face, in the brightening half-light, showed only puzzlement. 'Our country is part of Austria-Hungary,' I struggled on, 'but we are fighting for our independence, and we have been given permission to serve on the side of the Allies. I am to go to the Middle East to . . . negotiate . . . for . . . for . . . '
Even as Tasker's suspicious expression had begun to soften, my

hard-learned English had failed me.

There was a bellow from the cockpit ahead of us, nearly lost in the noise of the engines, which were much louder where we crouched.

'Lieutenant Tasker! Captain Jones! Where the hell are you when you're needed?' At Tasker's heels, I scrambled to the cockpit, where ripped shreds of fog flew out of the grey wall in front, swirled about Copley's ears, and coalesced again behind him. The roar of the engines seemed to pulse with the movement of the vapour.

'What was your last plot, Jones?' shouted Copley. 'I've been in this stuff since you went aft for tea: it's so continuous that I think the wind must have dropped, and that means I'm steering too far to the west.'

Hunkered on the floor of the cockpit, Tasker and I compared calculations and maps, and at last agreed that our position was somewhere off Cap Gris Nez. The altimeter read 5,500, rather than the planned 8,000, and the machine would not rise. On our present course we were headed down-Channel, and might not make landfall before Fecamp.

Copley altered course SSE, and together we watched the minutes pass, until sudden turbulence, the machine rising and dropping sickeningly and the engines seeming to miss a beat, revealed that we were at last crossing the French coast.

'Better go down and find out where we are,' suggested Tasker, and Copley nodded agreement. The great aircraft leant its nose forward into the murk, and gradually we began to descend through the cloud. Rain flooded the windscreen and whipped against our faces; Tasker ducked below the instrument panel and wriggled his way back to the forward cockpit.

Only the levels in the cockpit rim indicated the trim and angle of descent; we were wrapped in a featureless web of vapour, streaming with our movement. In the low pressure conditions inside the cloud the altimeter was unreliable, but already it was reading uncomfortably low. The rain stood in beads between the rim of Copley's helmet and his goggles; for a moment, I was sure it was sweat. Copley's lips were moving, but nothing that he said could be heard.

I leant sideways beyond the windscreen, stretching my neck out over the cockpit coaming. The rain covered my goggles, and

I wiped frantically at them with my gloved left hand. The cloud below was darker, and for an instant I thought I saw trees and a road, before they were washed away again. I pawed at my goggles again, and saw the ground below us – and then, staring forward, I was suddenly frantically flailing with my right arm in front of Copley's face. The aircraft tilted to starboard, the engines howled as Copley pushed forward the throttle knob and yanked the steering column back, and the pointed steeple of a church rushed past the port wing-tip.

We were only about a hundred feet from the ground, with the rain like smallshot in our faces and the bottom edge of the cloud bubbling just above our heads. The fields of Normandy stretched dismal and empty to the horizon.

'Thanks,' yelled Copley, taking both hands from the control column for a second to wipe down his streaming goggles. He settled the aircraft on an even keel and glanced at his instruments.

'Damn it, Tasker,' he roared, as the lieutenant's pallid face appeared close to his knees. 'you should have seen it first. Where are we anyhow?'

Tasker shrugged, his mouth a round O above his scarf, and then grinned in relief. 'Somewhere in France, dear mother,' he shouted, and ducked beneath the coaming again.

Five minutes later, he identified the unfinished Gothic church of Envermeu as the cloud began to clear above us. Copley put the 0/400 into a gradual climb, and in fifteen minutes we were at 3,000 feet in a sunlit blue sky, with the landscape intermittently visible below. An hour later we came confidently to land on the field at Villacoublay.

At midday we left again, after a silent breakfast in the officers' mess, a bath, and two hours' study of the maps for the next stage of our journey. Tatiana had attracted some curious stares at breakfast, but had spent the rest of the time in the office of the wireless officer, while Tasker had kept an eye on the riggers as they twanged the wires of the 0/400 and saw that the fuel tanks were topped up. In the fine warm May afternoon, with some cirro-cumulus high above us at more than 20,000 feet, we made an easy flight to Lyon in four hours, the patchwork of rural France below, the rising dome of the Massif Central away to starboard. And from Lyon, as the sun was setting, we took off again for Frejus, a small airfield above the coast halfway between Toulon and Nice.

For most of the flight we held a height of about 5,000 feet, following the Rhône valley, where we could still see the dull gleam of the river in the gathering shadows. The moon was high in the southern sky as we bore left, above the wide delta of the Rhône, with the sea just visible some twenty miles to starboard; and half an hour later, in the last light airs of the day, we drifted down through the heavy scents of thyme and mimosa to an L of flaming flares and a landing lit by a single searchlight. Copley yawned, his face drawn in the red of fresh sunburn round the white hollows where his goggles had been.

'Quite a day,' he said. 'Nearly 600 miles in ten hours of flying time. Same again tomorrow, what? Get some shuteye now – and remember, if any of these Frogs try to get talking to you, mum's the word.'

Tatiana explained, giggling when she came to the word 'shuteye'. She was lively and wide awake, having slept more than half the day among the baggage in the belly of the aircraft, squeezing now and again into the cockpit behind me to make excited, schoolgirlish exclamations at the view, or disappearing into the empty rear cockpit to swing the Lewis hopefully about the sky. And now as, exhausted by the long day and feeling the dull ache of my recent wound, I walked with her toward the single hut that had been assigned to us, I was made uncomfortably aware of what she expected of me.

The Riviera night was warm, and as soon as I had climbed down the ladder from the 0/400's belly I had taken off my helmet and gauntlets, and unbuttoned the front of my flying suit as far as I could. And Tatiana's hand was now inside that suit, exploring, teasing, caressing. With a sigh (I must confess it) I resigned myself. Ignoring the single sentry who stood watchfully in the shadows, I closed the door into the hot musty dark, remembering with sudden excitement the tight chamois overalls that were all, within a few seconds, that Tatiana wore.

But it was not a single sentry – as, having slept uneasily and woken early, I discovered when I put my head out of the rear window of the hut to see the sun rising over the sea to the east and smell the Mediterranean blossom high on the air. The hut was surrounded: discreetly, half-hidden by wind-bent thorn trees along the edge of the airfield, armed men covered every approach and every way of escape. No doubt, I thought wryly, they had been told that they were there for my protection. And, as wryly, I realised that indeed they were; there was nowhere I could escape to, and my only chance of ultimate survival lay in the successful and honourable completion of my mission.

By seven, after some strong black coffee and freshly-baked rolls, we were airborne again, straight out over the Ligurian Sea, bound due east for Pisa. The day was fine, the light westerly breeze lifted us along, and soon the twin domes of the Hotel Carlton at Cannes were lost in the coastal haze behind us. Before midday we were in Italy.

The great Handley Page attracted the attention of every man on the field outside Pisa. Almost before it had taxied to a halt a curious circle had formed about it. Although I knew no Italian I could tell their excitement and admiration from the tone of their voices, and amid the chatter I heard the name Caproni repeated many times.

'They're comparing it to the Ca5,' said Tasker's voice at my shoulder. 'Did you hear what happened the other month? Took fourteen newspapermen for a joyride over Rome. All of the sudden, its wings folded up, and that was that.'

We lunched at Pisa on pasta and fruit, slept for an hour, and took off for Rome. Copley insisted that it was about time I took the controls. Used to the screaming revs and quick lift of the Fokker, I made a terrible take-off, dragging the control column back too early before the tail-skid was clear of the ground, over-correcting, feeling the undercarriage thump sickeningly back on to the field, and at last leaving the huge machine to lift itself away, as Copley's hand joined mine gently on the stick. Once in the air, the aircraft seemed to fly itself, climbing steadily although slowly. We circled the Leaning Tower as it cast its strangely tilted shadow north-east beside the great spreading cross of the cathedral, and settled on a course to the south-east, only a thousand feet or so above the Tuscany plain, with the sea blindingly bright under the afternoon sun to starboard. In less than two hours we were over Rome and, with relief and great pride, I brought the machine gently down onto the field near Ostia. Copley patted my shoulder in silent approval. 'Next step's some night flying. We take off again at eleven.'

Tatiana and I took a bath together, in a stone-floored hut

with a tin tub half-full of luke-warm water; standing ankle deep and gently soaping each other, all the dear soft intimate parts, kissing and laughing and pouring clean water over our heads from an enamel jug. Then we made love standing, me with my back against the door and my feet braced on the wet floor, holding Tatiana beneath her buttocks as she wound her legs behind my hips; and then we took another bath, cold now but wonderfully refreshing. We ate at seven, with Copley, Tasker, and a silently thoughtful Italian officer who sat with one hand almost constantly caressing the butt of his Biretta. Then for two hours Tasker and I studied maps and talked of compass bearings and wind speeds.

The take-off was a nightmare. The wind was rising, dragging sideward the flames of the paraffin flares that marked the runway. Gaunt shadows of pines seemed to rise like a picket fence high at the end of the field. I ran the engines up to screaming pitch and set the machine thundering across the grass. The wind seemed to be tugging at the rudder bar, and the aircraft rocked from side to side. The tail was up, but I could not see the ground, or anything like a horizon, and the pines were rushing nearer.

'Now!' shouted Copley beside me and, fighting the over-whelming desire to drag the stick back, I let the machine take over. There was a crunch and a shudder as the undercarriage brushed the topmost fronds of one of the trees, and then we were climbing, seeing the night landscape take shape below us as it had when we first took off from Manston forty-four hours before.

We were in Naples by one in the morning, coming in low over Vesuvius and vaulting suddenly in the pillar of hot breath above the faintly glowing crater. We landed without trouble in a velvet-black night full with the sound of cicadas. I slept the deeply-satisfied sleep of a man who had fought a giant adversary and won, one arm beneath Tatiana's softly curling nape and the other idly between her thighs.

The next day we were in the air for only four hours, crossing the high mountains of the Basilicata to Otranto, the furthest east of all Italian towns. A British cruiser lay at anchor beyond the mole, sporadic black clouds from her smokestacks showing that she was in steam. As soon as we had landed, and brushed off the voluble attentions of the Italian airmen, Tasker set out for the harbour, brusquely explaining that the cruiser would have wireless messages for us.

I had shrugged out of my flying suit and was sitting alone, in the rumpled nondescript tropical gear with which I had been issued, drinking an ice-cold glass of coffee on the verandah of one of the airfield huts, when Copley joined me. He sat on the top step, his knees up high and both arms around them.

'I say,' he said. 'I'm sorry you and Tasker don't seem to have hit it off. He's a good airman, but a bit of a rum cove. He never did take kindly to anyone who isn't English, whether they're on our side or not; he lost both his brothers over the western front last year, and that didn't exactly help matters.'

I did not dare speak. There was one question above all that I could not ask, yet it trembled on my tongue. 'Do you know who shot them down?' I would blurt out – and what would I do, how would I feel, if he answered 'von Richthofen'? For in only three days I had come to like Copley, even to respect Tasker, for all his ill-temper and suspicion of me – a well-founded suspicion, too, if only he knew. And after all the bitter filth of the spring offensive in Flanders, I had rediscovered, flying with these men, some of the chivalry and fellowship that had existed between all fliers when I first took to the air.

'Anyway,' said Copley, 'I, for one, am very glad to have you along with us. I was told not to be inquisitive about you, so I won't ask where you learnt to fly so well. But you certainly handle that great bus as if you'd known her all your life.' I thanked him, and took his hand warmly – and then Tasker came across the field, scowling, and Copley excused himself and joined him, tearing open, as he strolled away, the first of two radio signals that Tasker had brought him.

Tatiana spoke softly behind me. 'Simon, darling.' As my familiarity with English speech increased, I was beginning to detect a charming Russian lilt in her voice. She was also betraying her ancestry in her behaviour: the long flight with nothing to do was boring her, and she had begun to pout – delightfully, of course – and indulge her caprices. While we were in the air she slept for much of the time, and when we landed, weary from the throb of the engines and the rush of the air, she was full of energy and very demanding. I turned in my

82

camp-chair, and saw her standing within the shadow of the hut doorway: she was naked again, and cupping her breasts with her hands so that the full brown nipples were aimed at me like the twin muzzles of an enemy about to rake my defenceless body with withering fire. I looked across the field: Copley and Tasker had disappeared. I must confess, to my shame, that I sighed.

As evening came on the skies clouded over and the sun sank brassily behind the mountains, but the heat did not diminish. We dined early on big bowls of greasy spaghetti and some over-ripe peaches, and Tatiana and I, sated by our earlier love-making, were asleep before ten o'clock, ready to be woken at four for a dawn start.

However, it was nine before the met officer allowed the cloud to be thinning sufficiently for our flight to Salonika. The 0/400 was loaded down with spare parts for the squadrons on the Bulgarian front, the tanks were full, and it was with some misgivings that I studied the map and noted the height of the mountains over which we were to fly. But the skies began to clear as we crossed the straits south-eastward for Corfu, and we flew in bright sunlight on a curved course above the bare brown uplands of the Pindus, with only wisps of vapour streaming from the highest peaks a few hundred feet below us. By two in the afternoon we were bumping our way into the bustle of the Allied landing field in the low country at the head of the Gulf of Thermai. I was at the gateway to the Middle East.

CHAPTER 6

29 May - 2 June: Salonika/Mudros/Suda/Sollum/Helio-polis/Ramleh/Baghdad

IT WAS in Salonika that things first started to go wrong: Tasker got himself drunk. In itself, this would have been something of little importance, had he not done it in an inter-services mess where we were attempting to keep an inconspicuous corner to ourselves. The room was large and cool, with its tiled floor and venetian blinds half closed against the late dusk. We sat in an alcove toward the back, but discovered too late, as it grew darker, that one of the bare light bulbs hanging at infrequent intervals from the low ceiling was suspended just above our heads. To anyone whose attention was drawn from the main room into our alcove, we performed as on a floodlit stage.

Tasker had drunk too freely of the local beer, ordering the steward to bring glass after glass from the bar at the far end of the mess, but he had also eaten well, and it was only the *ouzo* to which he turned after the meal that began to tilt the balance. While we ate he interrogated me suspiciously about my background, my past, and my present mission, and I had found his questions difficult to answer and impossible to evade; Copley had sat quietly embarrassed, occasionally remonstrating weakly, and Tatiana's spirited attempts to intervene for my protection had only served to intensify Tasker's bitterness.

With relief I watched him suddenly leave the table without excuse, and wander, with a momentary stagger, in the direction of the lavatories. As the minutes passed, and he did not reappear, Tatiana, Copley and I began to resume a civilised conversation. But too soon Tasker returned, and with him he brought a smooth-faced, discreetly polite individual, in worn Hungarian uniform without badges or braid, who immediately addressed me in gibberish:

'Ahoj Kamarade! Co tu delas?'

I stared at him aghast. What did it mean? What should I say?

Tasker crowed triumphantly. 'There you are! See! You ain't a bloody Czech! I thought there was something funny about you. Look at this feller!' he shouted, turning to the rest of the mess with his arms raised high: 'Says he's a Czech and he ain't! And *I* can tell he ain't an Englishman; so what the hell do you think he is?'

With Tasker gesticulating before us like a showman at a country fair we were illuminated as on a stage, and for some seconds we sat there motionless as the buzzing room became quiet and everyone turned his attention to the drama. And even as the mess fell silent I saw, a few feet away, a young French airman staring astounded at me. I tried to cover my face with my hand, but I heard his voice begin:

'Mon . . . dieu . . . '

Then Tatiana had sprung to her feet, snatching a glass of *ouzo* from Tasker's fingers, and, first in Russian, then in English, and finally in schoolgirl French, she shouted:

'Here's to victory for the Allies, and God save the King!' She drank off the spirit in one gulp, and dashed the glass in fragments at her feet. All eyes were on me: I could not hesitate. I rose with my glass of port, tossed it down, and copied Tatiana's flamboyant gesture. Pandemonium broke out: the whole mess seemed to rise like a dark wave, there were extravagant cheers and shouts in a dozen languages, and a crash and jangle such as I had never heard before. I like the sound of broken glass; I think sometimes that it is a German national characteristic, at least among the upper classes.

At the height of the uproar I took aim with my fist, and smashed the light bulb above our heads. Then Copley and I grabbed Tasker by his arms and propelled him, protesting feebly, toward the exit, with Tatiana at our heels. We shouldered the astonished Czech aside, and almost fell over the feet of the French airman, and I could not resist the temptation to say to him as we passed in my best British accent: 'Oh I say, old chap, most frightfully sorry.' At which Tatiana reached out her little foot and kicked me in the buttocks.

Outside, far across the field, the looming shadow of the 0/400 dwarfed the shapes of the other bombers beside it. The tents in which we were quartered were close by the aircraft, and so, dragging Tasker, who was now fast asleep, we made our way as inconspicuously as possible to bed.

In the morning, Copley insisted that his orders were that I should have a further medical inspection to make sure that I was fit enough for my mission. Unlike the thinly-garrisoned fields at which we had stopped en route, the city was packed with the forces of the Allies – British, Italians, French and Greeks, as well as all sorts of colonial troops, in their carnival uniforms. It was also less than a hundred miles from the Bulgarian front. I was therefore locked into a car, a closed Rolls Royce, Copley at my side with a revolver belted at his waist, and a British soldier with a rifle in the seat beside the driver. We were driven to the back door of the medical HQ through the recent ruins of a disastrous fire. In the thronging streets I saw Greek *evzones*, in their brief white skirts, *bersaglieri* with their ridiculous brigands' hats, the black *zouaves* of France, Serbians in baggy trousers and fezes – it was like a page from the picture books I had pored over as a child. Bulgarian prisoners of war, easily distinguished by the brightly coloured patches sewn onto the front and back of their filthy ragged uniforms, unloaded supplies from ships along the quays. With Greece now in the war, there seemed little hope for Austria-Hungary in the south-east.

The doctor, a silent Englishman, prodded my wound with his fingertips, struck me smartly with the flat of his hand on the ribs, felt the furrowed bone of my right temple, and curtly pronounced me cured. By the time we returned to the airfield, Tatiana was already ensconced in the belly of the 0/400, Tasker was sulkily nursing his head in the nose cockpit, and everything was ready for take-off.

For the flight over the Aegean, Copley took the controls. Our course lay ESE, down the Gulf of Singitikos, with Mount Athos and its legendary monastery our last sight of the mainland. At sea, two British cruisers and their attendant destroyers, like workers about a queen bee, stood station in the twinkling waves. In two hours, with the coast of the Canakkale peninsula of Turkey shimmering in the eastern haze, we came in low over the island of Lemnos and landed in the uneasy heat among the airships and bombers of Mudros.

We lunched early on stringy stew and took off again after an hour. Copley and Tasker had been silent throughout the meal, and now they both sat constantly turning their heads about the sky. We droned steadily southward, the sea empty below us and metallic in the afternoon light, and the big island of Lesbos like a pork chop in gravy away to port. The bright sun hurt my eyes, even behind the goggles, and I must confess that I was beginning to doze when I felt, rather than heard, Copley mutter a curse beside me. I turned to him, and saw his pointing finger. Below us, and ahead, a two-winged seaplane hawked above the waves.

Tasker was gesturing with his arms, and Copley pulled back the stick and began to turn the Handley Page to starboard. The engines picked up a throatier note, rising in pitch as the aircraft began to climb away into the sun. For five minutes we chugged steadily upward, making for a thin scatter of cloud that was beginning to form at about 9,000 feet. We passed unseen over the seaplane, which continued its skittering flight like a dragonfly over a deep-running trout stream. The tension in the cockpit gradually relaxed, Copley's lips, which had been thin and hard, shaped themselves for a cheerful whistle, and then, glancing back over the cockpit coaming, I saw the seaplane suddenly turn and begin its climb after us.

There was little we could do but continue our ascent, while the smaller aircraft gained steadily on us. As it came nearer I could identify it as a Gotha WD2, with big square black patches on its wings that showed it to be Turkish. I saw the observer standing up in his seat, his head level with the upper wing, where the parabellum swung on its ring mounting. And I saw the first sparks from the muzzle of the gun as he tried his ranging shots. For a minute or two we were still too far away, but we were already dangerously near our ceiling, and Copley was beginning to ease off the stick.

Then I heard the familiar crackling, like cautious footsteps through the mown stalks of a field of grain, out for quail in the fresh of an autumn morning. Looking down and behind I could see the row of holes stitched neatly across the lower port wing.

'Here we go!' shouted Copley, pulling back the stick. The 0/400 seemed to hang still in the air for several seconds and then, as we lost lift, it stalled and dropped sickeningly forward. The engines stuttered and howled while Copley eased the stick forward and then brought it back again. He pushed the stick to the left, kicked his left foot forward on the rudder bar, and brought the aircraft into a lumbering turn to port. I saw the Turkish plane loom up towards us, as Tasker feverishly let off two or three bursts from his twin Lewises, and then we were on an even keel and slowly rising again.

But our turning circle was a large one and the Gotha, although an old design and far slower than the scouts I had flown on the western front, had made a sharp starboard turn and now came straight at us, still firing from below against our belly, where Tatiana lay protected, I hoped, by thin plates of steel. Copley put the Handley Page into another steep bank and slipped sideways down the air – and at that moment I heard a sudden brittle chatter from the gun in our rear cockpit.

My heart rose at the sound. I unclipped my belt, flung the folding seat to one side, and scrambled down the sloping floor of the aircraft, through the bomb bay, and up into the after cockpit where Tatiana, her face rosy with delight, was emptying the drum at the Gotha as it began a turning dive above our tail. I seized a fresh drum as Copley threw the machine into a shuddering split-S turn and the two of us, hurled together about the cockpit like a pair of tango dancers, wrestled to release the old drum and fit the new one. Again the Gotha came at us from below, the bullets whining past our ears, and then it was past, climbing into the eye of the sun. I shouldered Tatiana aside, and got my finger to the trigger of the Lewis.

As my hand touched the gun, I felt the old familiar ice-cold clarity flood my mind once more. My breathing was steady and shallow, my whole consciousness seemed to be extended along the barrel of the Lewis. It swivelled easily and, as the Handley Page bucked and lurched, I found and held the black shape, with its big flat floats, that danced away from me. Without hesitation I squeezed the trigger and held it there, spitting out death for the full five seconds that the magazine allowed me.

It was not silence that followed the last crack of the Lewis: for the first time I became aware of the shattering roar of the twin engines surging about us, and in this sudden flood of sound the Gotha, a lurching shadow against the sun, seemed an unreal dreamlike nothing. It appeared to be turning toward us again, its nose pointing gradually down, and then it tilted back, slipped, and gently twisted, and went sliding down, slowly down the slopes of air, now forward, now back, spinning occasionally, spiralling on its floats like skis, two tiny figures, one still and one frantic, silhouetted in the struts as they cracked and sprang, and the upper wing broke free, floating so gently away. And still the machine went down and down, corkscrewing into the waves with a rush of spume and a bubbling cockade of steam, and all that remained was a scatter of fragments wide across the sea . . .

Tatiana was holding me in her arms, her mouth feverish upon my face. 'We did it! We did it!' But I could say nothing, do nothing, for my head was full of this, my final treason. For I knew that the pilot of the Gotha had been a German airman like myself, a comrade, who had sworn the same oaths of loyalty to the Kaiser and to Germany, and I had killed him. Few of the Turks were pilots, and none would have flown that seaplane as he had done. And then I recalled the events of the previous night, how I had drunk a toast to the victory of the Allies. Now I truly was a man without a country, a mercenary, a plaything of the British; a traitor, and forsworn.

I remember little of the rest of that long day: the hours that passed before we landed at Suda Bay beneath the shimmering mountains of Crete were empty, my meal went uneaten. In a few stammering phrases I had told Tatiana of my horror and shame; but Copley and Tasker, jubilant at our escape, could understand nothing. In the moonlight we made Sollum, and in the noisome Egyptian night I clung to my narrow bed and cursed and shivered in the sticky, mosquito-loud dark.

With the dawn I found some peace, and slept a little. I drank a single cup of black coffee for breakfast, wrapped in the curious silence of my companions, and then we flew low along the coast to Heliopolis, where the Greek columns still stood broken among the gardens of the Nile delta. In our bell tent, its skirts brailed up to afford us the evening breeze from the sea, and its interior thickly draped with mosquito netting, Tatiana tried to comfort me.

'You must not blame yourself, my darling. You were defending me, and all of us, and you had a right to do it. He was trying to kill us, and if he had it would have meant not only our death but the death of some very dear and innocent people – the Tsar and the Tsarina, the Grand Duchesses, and darling little Alexei. You had no choice, dear. At this moment your life is far more important than that of any other German soldier, because only you can save the Tsar.'

'But I have sworn,' I moaned. 'I took a solemn oath upon my honour to serve my country and the Emperor.'

'And so you have and so you shall. You can serve them and all humanity best by rescuing the imperial family. And besides – you don't know for certain that it was a German who flew that seaplane yesterday. It could have been an Austrian, or a Hungarian. Or a Bulgarian,' she added, her pretty face suddenly twisted with disgust so that, involuntarily, I smiled.

'There, that's better; you smiled again, my darling – just for a second, but, oh, how it warmed my heart. Please, please, if you love me just a little, smile once more.' And she smoothed her hand across my short-cropped head, and gazed into my face, and puckered up her lips, and I could not refuse her.

'Oh, you silly men,' she went on, 'why don't you just leave it all to us? We women understand so much more than you men ever will. Oh, you are our strong knights, the sturdy staff to which we cling; but when you fall, it is we who raise you up again.'

I smiled again, I laughed. I could not forgive myself, but Tatiana made me forget my shame. 'How you remind me of my pretty cousin Frieda,' I said, 'the one who married the teacher.'

Next day we flew on, eastward over the Great Bitter Lake, with Suez away to the starboard, and on across the coastal plains that border the north side of the trackless Sinai desert. I am not a religious man, or at least not in the conventional sense, but I had been taught Christianity, and my first sight of the Holy Land, as we bore north over Gaza, brought a strange kind of elation to me. Here Moses had come after forty years of wandering in the wilderness, here Christ had taught, and preached the parable of the good Samaritan – I even imagined myself, for one mad second, some new kind of messenger of mercy. Then I saw the shadow of the O/400, passing over the ground far below like that of the angel of death.

Ramleh lies near the coast, inland some ten miles from Jaffa, and here Allenby had had his advance airfield to support the attack on Jerusalem. Late in the day we droned down in the bright heat, and came to rest among a scatter of Bristol scouts. Australian Flying Corps personnel, bareheaded in the scorching sun, with shirt-sleeves rolled up and shorts flapping about their bright red knees, stood talking to British soldiers in Indian army uniforms and wide pith helmets. Camels roared and spat between the tents, and Arabs, hung about with bullets and with their robes caught up short in their belts and swinging about their calves, skulked in the shadows. We climbed down from the aircraft, the four of us, and, sweating heavily, began to walk across the field to the tents where we expected to find the commanding officer.

Our way was barred by a vast, khaki-painted open Rolls Royce, in the back seat of which sat two Arabs holding hands.

One was a handsome young boy, with dark eyes and curly hair, a thin beard just beginning to form along his jaw. The other, in full white robes and burnous, was an Arab such as I had never seen in any picture book. He was short and red-faced, beardless, and his piercing eyes were grey, electric, almost blue. When he saw us he rose in the back of the car, still clutching the boy with one hand and holding a fly whisk in the other, and spoke in English.

'You've brought me my bomber at last! I've been waiting two months for this! How soon can you be ready? There's five tons of petrol and ammunition to be ferried to El Azraq, and then you can go on to bomb the junction at Deraa.'

Copley, who was leading the way, halted so abruptly that I trod hard on his heels: 'I don't know who you are,' he said icily, and I could almost hear his deliberate suppression of the word *sir*; 'but I can assure you that my orders come direct from Air Staff and are irrevocable. Personally, I'd be dashed glad to have a go at Johnny Turk – if those were my orders. But I must deliver my machine to Baghdad as soon as possible, and I'm not going to be used as a delivery boy for . . . worthy oriental gentlemen!'

A volley of what I took to be Arabic oaths burst from the figure's lips, and, lashing aside the restraining hand of his boy companion, he began to struggle with the handle of the car door. But Copley, erect and without turning his head, led us on between the tents as the voice rose behind us:

'I order you to! I order you to do it at once! I'll have you flogged! No! you'd enjoy that! I could shoot you for mutiny in the field! I'm Colonel Lawrence, and that's *my* aeroplane!'

We had advanced some twenty yards before he was out of the car and beginning to run after us. A group of bedouin had been hunkered in the sparse shade of their camels; at the sound of his voice they had risen warily to their feet, hands on the trigger guards of their rifles – Lee-Enfields, Mausers, even flintlocks with intricate brass inlay along the butts. They were as fine a band of villains as I have ever seen (and I was to see more than a few during the coming weeks in Russia, and in many other parts of the world in later years): tall, and heavily bearded, crossbelted with ammunition, and hung with knives and swords. As Lawrence came after us they moved almost imperceptibly to bar our way, their faces impassive with menace. Tatiana laid her hand upon my arm, and we all stood still.

'I will not be denied!' ranted Lawrence. 'General Allenby promised me bombers, and I'll be buggered' (a fleeting expression of ecstasy crossed his face) 'if I'll have my campaign delayed by a mere airman! Where are your orders? Show me your orders! I'll have them countermanded!'

We were now completely surrounded. At the centre of the circle we stood face to face with Lawrence, whose face was an even brighter red than before, and who was literally shivering with rage. Round us were the bedouin, whispering to each other, some lovingly caressing their knife hilts. And beyond them had formed an outer circle of airmen and soldiers, their faces alight with anticipation.

Copley stood stiffly silent. He could not address a superior officer without calling him sir, and that he would not do now. Lawrence, who was about my own height, stared seething upward at the lieutenant's lanky indifference; he, too, could say no more. We might have remained standing there for hours, even days, caught in a web of obstinacy until we dissolved away in the sweat flooding our flying suits, but the sound of Lawrence's high-pitched voice had attracted attention in the squadron office. An officer in tropical khaki, wearing a broad-brimmed cowboy hat, and with the three rings about his sleeve that showed him to be a major, was crossing the scrubby sand toward us. He saluted in an offhand way and, in that strange cockney-American that I now know as the Australian accent, spoke:

'Trouble here, Colonel Lawrence? Flight Lieutenant Copley, is it? And this, don't tell me, is Captain Jones. Would you gentlemen – and stone me, a sheila! beg your pardon, lady – would you mind all stepping into my office so I can sort it out?'

Five minutes later Lawrence, stonily refusing a warm beer, for which Major Williams had apologised profusely, gathered up his tribesmen from around the tent and strode haughtily off to his car. The sight of Copley's orders, with Trenchard's own signature, and the confirmatory signal that Williams had received from ARFC headquarters, had silenced his protests. I was to meet him again ten years later in very different circumstances – but that is another story.

We spent the rest of the day at Ramleh while the riggers performed their mysteries upon the Handley Page, but Williams insisted that we must leave for Baghdad by midnight.

'It's hot enough here,' he explained to Copley 'but Mespot's like a bloody furnace. Your engines are water-cooled aren't they?' Rolls Royce 350hp V-12 Eagle VIIIs, Copley told him with pride. 'The midday sun'll boil them dry, believe me. Have another beer?' Williams mopped frantically at his face and neck. 'Jeez, I wish I was back in Moonta.'

It was indeed hot. We had changed into tropical kit, but this, too, was soaked in sweat, and the torrid evening breeze from the desert brought swarms of mosquitoes and the tiny vicious sandflies. Only Tatiana, in a sort of boilersuit of lightweight Egyptian cotton, looked cool. She had left far too many of its buttons unfastened, attracting enthusiastic attention in the mess tent, where we fed behind festoons of netting which nevertheless could not keep out the sandflies. Orderlies constantly patrolled the corners of the tent with sprays of Flit, but we were forced to eat only with forks while we swatted with our free hands at the exposed parts of our bodies. It was with great relief that I climbed once more into the aircraft, took the controls, and pointed its great nose to the east.

This time the night take-off gave me no qualms, and we rose steadily toward the high hills of Palestine. We passed over Bethlehem to the south of Jerusalem, Copley firing a red Very light in reply to a questioning signal from the ground, and in the moonlight saw the Dead Sea glinting deep in the cleft of the river Jordan. We swung ENE then, to pass over the lower terrain between the mountains of Ma'an and the Jebel Druz, and began our long haul across the Syrian desert.

The sun rose suddenly, full in my eyes. One minute, the desert was grey and featureless below us, the sky ahead a velvet black in which even the stars seemed swathed – and then the horizon showed, silhouetted like the plunging waves of the deep ocean, against the red of a fire that burned hotter and hotter, lighter and brighter in the space of a few seconds, and the sun leapt into the air. Long shadows stretched across the tawny land, broken and wavering as if seen through water. But soon they shortened, and we could distinguish the great dunes that rolled and swept to the skyline in every direction, only interrupted here and there by the wandering line of a dried up *wadi*.

Imperceptibly, as the sun climbed higher and shifted steadily southward, the ground declined below us. We saw no houses, but once the tiny black smudge of a bedouin encampment, and once a Turkish outpost. Then we saw our first clusters of palms, and, away beyond them, the glittering of Lake Habbaniya and the twin rivers.

Our destination, some twenty miles northeast of Baghdad, was the headquarters of 72 Squadron RAF at Baquba, but we swung south of the city on a sweeping anti-clockwise curve. The land between the rivers glowed green, low-lying and marshy. Narrow channels of bottle-glass water wound between the reeds. Here and there we could see small villages on stilts, dugout canoes threading the waterways. Copley thumped my shoulder and laughed: 'D'you know that's the Garden of Eden down there? Just think of Adam and Eve without any clothes on, and all those mosquitoes buzzin' about!'

As we lumbered our slow circle above Baquba, waiting for a tiny figure at the runway's end to wag us down, we saw a real circus of aircraft types drawn up around the edges of the field, some in the shelter of scanty palms, some half-protected by flimsy canvas screens. I recognised Sopwith Camels, some SPADs, two de Havilland DH4s, several SE5as, and a number of Martinsyde 'Elephants' that had obviously been ransacked for spare parts. And there were a few RE8s, the infamous 'Harry Tates' that I knew so well, for I had shot down eight of them myself over the western front.

We came in slowly over the perimeter markers, nose up, lurching up and down in the surges of hot air that seemed to blast off the hard-baked earth. It was only a hour or so after dawn, yet already the ground temperatures was unbelievable. The ground crews, stripped to the waists of their ill-fitting shorts, wore tropical helmets with broad sweat-stained cloths hanging down the back, and shapeless pads of fabric strapped about their spines. One or two dawdling pilots, obviously just returned from patrol, were in pyjamas. It was so hot that, as we rolled to a stop and the air no longer blew in our faces, a noticeable coolness seemed for a few seconds to wrap us round – until the rolling sweat suddenly burst from every pore, and we gasped for breath.

In spite of the heat, everyone was in a great hurry to get things done, because, as the squadron commander explained to me, while Copley, Tasker, Tatiana and I ate breakfast in the shade of an awning beside his office, 'the weather'll turn quite warm before midday'. This was Major Everidge – 'John Average' to his airmen, I soon discovered – a typically featureless Englishman, with a featureless pepper-and-salt moustache, a featureless briar pipe, and especially featureless knee-length khaki shorts. He was to be our host for the next two days.

After their breakfast Copley and Tasker, their valises bulging with their discarded flying suits, were whisked away to catch a launch for Al-Garbi, where they would take a steamer to Basra to await the next transport for Port Said.

Our farewell was brief: Tasker smiled thinly and shook my hand perfunctorily without a word, but Copley took both my hands in his, gazed earnestly into my eyes, said: 'Look after the old girl now,' waved, and was gone.

For several minutes I thought that he had meant Tatiana. She and I spent the rest of the day prostrated by the heat, unable to eat, and drinking hot soda water, which was all the orderlies could bring us. For much of the day the *shamal* blew, a red-hot wind that brought the sand into every crevice and fold. It came from out of the desert, roaring down into the valley of the two rivers, whose inhabitants regarded it as a welcome relief, but to us it seemed hotter than the stillness of the morning. It was nearly nightfall before we were taken in a Ford transport to British HQ in Baghdad.

From the desert I saw the blue tiles of the mosques rising against an evening sky of equal blueness above the mud-brick houses, the slim minarets pricking the sky, and the great golden dome of Khazimain like a setting sun sinking into the deep green of the date groves. At the outskirts of the city the carcasses of dogs, mules and horses littered the roadside; hundreds of vultures wove overhead or waddled away too gorged to fly; living dog lay in stupor by the corpse of dog half-eaten. The stench of corruption was worse than on the western front.

On Rashid street, with its stone colonnades, and its wrought-iron balustrades writhing against the sun-dry façade, we were led into an adjutant's office, tiled, punkahed and jalousied against the lingering heat of the day. He was a major, crowns corroded into the epaulets of his khaki shirt, his boots unpolished, his breeches crumpled and blotched with sweat. A fat file, mine, lay open on the desk before him, and with weary petulant fingers he flicked through the telegrams it contained.

'Captain Jones, I have what look like hundreds of papers here for you. First of all, I have to give you receipts for what you've brought with you: a Handley Page 0/400 bomber aeroplane, six boxes of Lewis gun ammunition – all empty magazines to be accounted for – and £2,000 in gold sovereigns. Then I have to give it all back to you, and have you sign for it in triplicate, and then I have to make a further three copies for our own records. After that I have to make out requisition papers for you for aviation spirit, and get you to sign another receipt in triplicate. And then General Beach will want to see you.'

Brigadier-General Beach was tall, wiry, middle-aged and twitchy. 'Look here,' he said, 'I've had these instructions straight from CIGS, and I don't want to know more than I have to know. You're flying up to Kazvin, you're to be given anything you think you need, and once you leave Kazvin you're on your own. I'm told you're a very experienced pilot, but even so you're going to require a navigator and co-pilot, so 72 Squadron will lend you one. They've got just the chap for you. And I'm going to let you have one of my politicals – give the feller something to do instead of hanging round the bazaars.'

And that was it. I gave him my best British salute, he dismissed us with a weary wave of the hand, and the adjutant took us to meet Colonel Leachman.

Colonel Leachman was on the ground floor of the building, squatting on the tiles in the cool dark of a room open to the street. He was in Arab robes, his brown and wizened face half hidden, his long skinny legs protruding from the hem of his gown. Behind him a languid young boy occasionally flicked a fly whisk about his head. He had a glass of tea by his right hand, and he was rolling dice with another Arab who squatted similarly opposite him.

He did not rise when we approached, but patted the floor to indicate that we should join him. I lowered myself, rather stiffly because of the still-painful wound in my groin, and Tatiana flung herself down at my side. Our adjutant remained hovering in the background, as adjutants do. Leachman turned his head in my direction, so that one bright eye looked out over a hawk-like nose, and held out his hand: 'Leachman.'

'Jones.'

'Miss Fitzalbert.'

The other Arab coughed: 'Lemme introduce myself,' he said. 'You dunno me, and I dunno you, but I've got a feeling we're going to get on real good. Specially you and me, little lady. Clark's the name, Nobby Clark. Captain Nobby Clark.'

CHAPTER 7

2-4 June: Baghdad – Baquba – Hamadan – Kazvin

ON THE drive back to Baquba, through the warm-bath Mesopot-amian night, I learnt the bare bones of Captain Clark's history; the succeeding month served only to clothe them in a bizarre and rather verminous flesh. A music-hall performer, the son of music-hall performers, he had tried to improve his status by joining a touring light opera company; he had a moderate tenor voice, but the instincts of a knockabout comic. The company, despairing of success in the English provinces, had undertaken a 'continental tour': a backstreet theatre in Monte Carlo, a failing cabaret in Genoa, the opera house in Durazzo. Then fortune seemed to beckon from afar. A telegram from their agent ('sharpest little grafter in Birmingham, old boy') had sent them hurrying down the Adriatic by coastal steamer to Piraeus, where they took ship for India and a season in Simla.

'The principals had cabins – port out, starboard home o' course – but me and the soubrette was below decks, and the chorus had to go steerage, poor buggers.' And in Ooty, decimated by dysentery and disillusioned by the neglect of the British colony, the company had finally collapsed. 'But that's my luck, old boy, destined to be forever among the wines and spirits.'

Clark had spent the next six years in the Indian political service, where his theatrical training in make-up and disguise, and his natural ear for languages, had stood him in good stead. At the outbreak of war, with a vocabulary of Urdu, Hindi, a half-dozen village dialects, and a smattering of Persian, he had been among the first to land with the expeditionary force at Basra. Now, with Leachman, he worked among the bedouin, riding hundreds of miles behind the Turkish lines, gathering intelligence, protecting the British flanks and keeping the Arab's loyalty with discreetly distributed gold sovereigns.

'The Ayrabs think old Leachman's really the British C-in-C; one of 'em insisted he had to be the king of England. 'Ere, take a *shufti* at this' – and he dug into the recesses of his robes and brought out a handful of rather crumpled visiting cards and a box of lucifers. 'You hold these cards while I strike a light.'

He cupped a flaring match in his hands, and by its weak light Tatiana and I saw that the cards, apparently all identical, were covered with Arabic characters. 'Had these printed for British airmen, case they were forced down in the desert, so they could impress the Ayrabs. Not quite sure what it all means meself, except for that bit,' and he pointed to something written large in a flowing script. 'That's the password, the magic name, the Colonel's moniker – *El Idjman!*'

Clark insisted that I should take some of the cards – 'Better safe than sorry, me lad' – and then, settling himself more comfortably against his camel-bag of belongings as the Hupmobile continued its bumping progress: 'So, we're off to visit General Stalky.'

'Stalky?' I echoed.

Clark laughed. 'Major-General L.C. Dunsterville, CB, CSI. The original. But then I suppose you never heard of Rudyard Kipling?'

'Certainly I have heard of Kipling,' I replied stiffly. 'I was told all about him by the English schoolteacher, the one who married my cousin Frieda, Bert Lawrence was his name. Yes, he told me about Rudyard Kipling. I think he was in India also,

98

like yourself?'

'Extraordinary what you chaps pick up,' said Clark. 'Czechs knowin' about Kipling! Who'da thought it? Mind you, though, the best memory act I ever saw was a Czech. Or was he a Pole? Aristotle the Great. He could recite the names of all the England elevens from 1880 to 1904 (which was the last time I saw him) *and* tell you what their battin' averages was. Great act, great act. Memory like a bloody – beggin' your pardon, little lady – elephant.'

Tatiana leant forward eagerly. 'Is it true, Captain Clark – ' ('Nobby, me dear; call me Nobby') – is it true that elephants do really have long memories?'

'Not the only long article about them, believe you me,' said Clark, leering delicately. 'And I often say that the most remarkable thing about them is how they remember which end is which.'

After a night of tense flying and a day of unbearable heat, I was happy to go straight to bed as soon as we arrived at Baquba. Everidge's moral principles had led him to segregate me in a tent away from Tatiana, and I looked forward to my eight hours of undisturbed sleep – but somehow that warm electric body had already become a part of my life, and I must confess that I slept fitfully in her absence. In the morning, after our light breakfast, she took Clark off for an exploration of Baquba town, dressed in a black bedouin gown and mask that he had found for her, and I was summoned to the presence of the squadron commander.

'All right,' he said, 'GHQ have told me what I've got to do for you. You need a co-pilot. And I've got the very chap for the job. Came down out of the hills two or three weeks ago, just after I was posted here, in a Russian uniform, papers all in order, and asked if we would let him fly. You can imagine we were rather doubtful at first, couldn't afford to let some unknown johnny write off one of our few working aircraft; but he's amazing, he can beat any of our chaps into a cocked hat. He's somewhere around, probably in the mess. Corp! Ask that Russki feller to join us, would you?'

The Russian was short, two or three inches below my height, in a faded tunic and breeches with worn gold braid; his hair stood well back from his forehead, brushed out into spikes that matched his pomaded moustache, and he had the biggest nose I have ever seen – not hooked and Semitic, but long and bulbous like a fine stick of the best asparagus.

'Captain Simon Jones,' I said, clicking my heels.

He held out his hand. 'Captain Pavel Tchaikovsky.'

'Tchaikovsky?' I repeated.

'Yes indeed,' he replied with a sad smile. His accent was marked but melodious. 'I must tell you, however, that I am no sugarplum fairy; nor am I a nutcracker; and I am certainly not pathetic.' I confess that Tatiana had to explain this to me later, for I knew nothing of music at that time, and can still scarcely tell one tune from another.

'I'll leave you two together,' said Everidge, 'so Captain Jones can explain what it's all about.' My mind raced. What should I tell? How much could I tell? My mission was a secret between Tatiana, myself, and a few shadowy figures in Whitehall, and I was not authorised to share it with others. But Tchaikovsky was going with us into Russia; back to his homeland, where he was either a wanted man or an agent of the bolsheviks. Dared I trust him? If I didn't trust him I was certainly not going to take him with me.

I was approaching a decision. The longer I left it before telling Tchaikovsky our destination, the greater would be my danger if he were a bolshevik, and the easier it would become for him to dissemble. But if, in these first moments together, I told him straight out what our plans were, I would catch him unawares, and his immediate reaction might give me some clue to his true feelings. I hesitated no longer.

'We are going to fly into Russia and rescue the royal family.' He stared amazed at me for several seconds and then, to my disgust, leapt forward, put his arms about me, and kissed me on both cheeks.

'My dear chap, what a wonderful idea! They are in prison, and we will rescue them. You will show me how to fly that great cathedral of yours, and together we will swoop across the steppes like the eagle that saved Tsarevitch Ivan from the wolves!'

I tried to explain to him that it was not so simple, but he would not listen, dancing about and waving his arms in high excitement. His enthusiasm was so unfeigned that I found it hard to believe that it was not genuine. I decided to consult Tatiana about Tchaikovsky later, but in the meantime I accepted that he was probably on our side, a Tsarist and not a bolshevik. I told him what I could – which was very little.

'The imperial family are in Ekaterinodar?' he asked. 'In the Kuban? Alas, I am from Smolensk and I do not know Georgia and the Caucasus. But we will manage, don't you worry.' He thumped his chest and took up a heroic pose, his hair and moustache bristling and his great nose quivering: 'I, Pavel Tchaikovsky, Captain in his Imperial Majesty's Air Army, will be at your side!' And again he hugged and kissed me. I was relieved when Everidge returned.

The heat was rising rapidly when Tatiana arrived with Clark, exclaiming delightedly over an unattractive piece of ornamental basketwork that she had paid far too much for in the local *souk*. She was even more delighted with Tchaikovsky, kissing him repeatedly and chattering to him in excited Russia, so that I was happy when the temperature drove us to retirement. We spent the rest of the day as the day before, panting in our tents, refreshed by nothing but bottles of hot soda water. After dark we dined in the mess on the nastiest of British bully beef stew and some shrivelled peaches, while the riggers completed their work on the 0/400 in the light of kerosene lamps. Tatiana spent an hour with the wireless officer, and a further half-hour with the sergeant-at-arms, and I took Tchaikovsky into the cockpit of the aircraft and gave him his first lesson at the controls and instruments. Then, under an indigo velvet sky studded with stars, the moon low and gibbous on the horizon, we went to our separate lonely beds and dozed until dawn.

At first light we drank some coffee and took our leave of Everidge, as Tatiana received a heavy little grey box from the sergeant-at-arms. Closely followed by two SE5as who escorted us for a mile or two in curiosity before they swung north for their dawn patrol, we set a course for Kazvin.

We flew north-east for about fifty miles, following the course of the Diala river to Khanakin, which lies at the foot of the Pai Taq pass. Here the crumpled brown hills of Persia rose suddenly from the steamy valley floor, reaching nearly 10,000 feet in twenty miles. Without a map, and with only a rough idea of the course I should take, I followed the road as it wound steeply up the pass and then across the flat-bottomed mountain valleys to Kermanshah.

We had spent forty-eight hours in Baquba and Baghdad; those we had left would be there for months. But the relief we all felt as we climbed steadily into the hills, and saw the first thin green of the alpine meadows, and the rushing streams and water-falls, is impossible to describe. Tatiana began to sing little songs from her childhood, first in English and then in Russian, her head poked up into the cockpit at the level of my thighs. Tchaikovsky, in the co-pilot's seat, joined in in a surprisingly sonorous Russian bass. Clark, in the forward cockpit, could surely have heard nothing of their song, but he glanced hawkily about, scratched his crotch beneath his robes, spat over the side, and then unexpectedly brought out a wooden shepherd's pipe and played a wild obbligato that came thinly back to us in the roar of the engines and the rush of the wind. Even I, tone-deaf and shy, attempted a few grating notes.

From above Kermanshah I still followed the road as it pierced the mountains ahead; flying sometimes only a few hundred feet above the stunted oaks, sometimes almost brushing a wing-tip against a sudden beetling bluff. Ahead, the peak of Kuh-i-alwand loomed above Hamadan, its northern slopes, even in the heat of early summer, still covered in snow.

Although we had set off very early, it had already been very hot at Baquba; but now, as we rose steadily among the mountains, the air grew colder and colder. Clark was muffled in his robes, and Tchaikovsky, in his Russian greatcoat, was warm enough; but Tatiana and I were in our lightest tropical gear. The 0/400 droned on, flying itself, and by judicious wriggling I was able to exchange places with Tchaikovsky and, with a sign to Tatiana, crouched down into the bomb-bay of the aircraft where our warmer clothing was packed into valises.

The heat of Baquba still filled the bomb-bay. Tatiana was out of her cotton boilersuit at once, and in a few seconds I too stood naked. Her mouth moved, but I could hear nothing above the racketing of the engines. I took her in my arms, and felt all my love rise once more. Frenziedly we rolled out a heavy blanket from one of the packs upon the slatted floor, and flung ourselves upon it. Even as Tatiana took me, drawing me in with a supple ripple of infinitely delicate muscles, the aircraft must

102

have found a thermal rising up a rocky spur from the valley floor, for it rose suddenly, thrusting us together. And then it dropped as suddenly, and rose again, dropping and rising in a rhythm that matched our own, as if we flew, not on a rough blanket upon an uneven wooden floor, but drifting in the thin and insubstantial air itself. And as we reached our climax it fell stone-like below us for several hundred feet, leaving us clinging desperately together and shuddering in an ecstasy that seemed to have no end.

Tchaikovsky was roaring some wild horseman's song from the far steppes, but I thought I could detect a quaver of concern in the bravado of his voice: the aircraft must have come close to the craggy ground in that last descent. Tatiana and I delayed dressing as long as possible, murmuring together and touching each other in fond places; then I pulled on a high-necked sweater, breeches and boots, and, leaving Tatiana to snuggle herself naked into her fur-lined flying suit, I scrambled back into the cockpit.

The bright sun burst upon me, the air rushed into my mouth like champagne when the cork first flies arcing across the mess, and your comrades, one with his thumb across the bottle's neck, baptise you with brilliant golden nectar. We were between high walls of rock that rose above us, dry brown scree swooping to meet the tops of scattered birches far below. Waterfalls leapt from the melting snows, and hawks hovered in the wind scarcely an arm's length away. Too soon the top of the pass opened out before us: I exchanged places once more with Tchaikovsky and, swinging eastward on the north side of the mountain, saw Hamadan on the plain below.

The full strength of B Flight, 72 Squadron RAF, was ranged along the side of the field, neatly roped and pegged – five Martinsyde Elephants. A white drogue stood out stiffly in the breeze, and there was a tidy row of brown bell tents. Little piles of rock, some already planted with desert flowers, showed how the ground had been cleared. The field had been levelled by hand, stamped flat by hundreds of labouring Persian feet, and finally compressed by driving motor vans up and down on it. White flags on little sticks marked its boundary, and, gliding in very low and switching off early, to give myself as long a run on the ground as possible, I swept two of these away with my landing wheels and finished up, bumping and shuddering, among uncleared rocks at least fifty yards over the far side. If I were to take off again from this field, the Persian hordes would have to be brought back to do some more work.

Almost before the propellers had stopped turning, the aircraft was set upon by a troop of horsemen on sturdy short-legged hill ponies, who circled us at speed, shouting and waving their guns one-handed in the air. Despite the heat they wore round fur hats, long greatcoats with double crossbelts, and high boots; big white teeth flashed among the luxuriant beards and moustachios. At the sight of them, Tchaikovsky stood up in his seat and started yelling back, and Tatiana, who had squeezed into the cockpit behind him, joined in excitedly. This seemed to provoke a fresh frenzy among the horsemen, who shouted louder than ever, and one or two fired off their guns, not once slowing the speed of their mounts. There was no sign of any RAF ground crew.

'For the love of God!' I exclaimed. 'What are you doing? Stop inciting them. We have no way to protect the aircraft if they come any closer, and if we shoot they will tear us limb from limb. What do they want?' For answer, Tatiana threw her arms round my head, and kissed the top of my flying helmet.

'Cossacks, darling! Russians! My own people!' And she began again to shout and wave at them, big round tears rolling slowly down her cheeks. They were Cossacks indeed: I had seen them on the eastern front at Kalisch, and what I had learnt of them there did not reassure me.

Fortunately an officer now rode up, magnificent in his full-skirted coat, white sheepskin hat, and sword with silver-mounted ivory scabbard. He roared commands at the Cossacks in brisk Russian, reined in his horse below the nose of the aircraft, saluted stiffly, and spoke.

'Hello there, you chaps, and the young lady too. I do hope you had a good flight? Don't worry about my Russkis here: they're all frightfully good fellers, and perfectly friendly. Oh – I'm Major Rowlandson, by the way. Got a telegram to expect you yesterday, actually, but I'm pleased to say you're just in time for lunch, so that's all right.'

We climbed down from the aircraft, and I explained my problems to Rowlandson, pointing out the scattered rocks that lay between the plane and the perimeter of the flying field. Within minutes, appearing almost to spring from the ground as if from the dragon's teeth that Jason sowed, some fifty ragged Persian levies under the command of a single RAF corporal were at work, handing away the rocks in a human chain; and soon after we were mounted on ponies, and making our way with Rowlandson and his chattering, singing, shouting Cossacks toward a distant group of tents on the outskirts of Hamadan town.

After so long, it was an unbelievable pleasure to get a horse between my legs again, to feel the creaking of the saddle and listen to the jingle of the harness. The sun was hot, but at over 6,000 feet the air was intoxicating, and I soon had my mount, a skittish little mare, prancing and curvetting all over the narrow track, to the great amusement and delight of the Russians. One huge grinning fellow cantered up behind me, laid his hand with a noise like a pistol shot on the mare's quarter and, when she bolted forward, challenged me to a race. We reached the tents neck and neck, and reined up panting and delirious with laughter.

Lunch consisted of some stringy pieces of chicken and lamb, grilled in the open over charcoal, and eaten with our fingers. We all crowded into one tent, with only a single thickness of canvas, and the heat of the sun, and the excited bodies standing shoulder to shoulder, soon raised the temperature higher than an oven. Somebody produced a bottle of *arak,* the local firewater, and we all filled glasses and toasted one another in a babel of languages. Fortunately, there was only just enough of the stuff to go round, and then we filled our glasses with tea and toasted each other all over again.

Rowlandson touched my elbow. 'Look here, I'm afraid I shall have to ask you for a lift to Kazvin. I expect you've enough room in that great crate of yours for one more? General Dunsterville is expecting you and myself to dinner – although I must say we weren't warned about the young lady.' He smiled disarmingly at Tatiana. 'I may have to make my excuses before dinner is over, however: Bicherakov has got to get his troops on the move at dawn to secure the road to Enzeli. As liaison officer I must be with him, of course, especially as we're lending him a squadron of the Hussars and a couple of our precious armoured cars. And if we don't get Kuchik Khan and his Jangalis off the bridge at Menjil, we're never going to shift Dunsterforce down to the Caspian and over the waves to Baku.'

'To Baku?' exclaimed Tatiana, turning to speak quickly in Russian to Tchaikovsky, who laughed mirthlessly. 'Isn't Baku in the hands of the Red Army?'

'It certainly is,' said Rowlandson, 'but Johnny Turk is fighting his way down the railway from Tiflis to the Caspian, and we've got to try to stop him. And we think the bolshies in Baku will be deuced glad to get our help.'

Then he told us a little about the 'Hush Hush Army' that was known officially as Dunsterforce. Some two months after the outbreak of the Russian revolution, when it was clear that the Russian army was no longer holding the line between Baghdad and the Caspian that would prevent an attack on India, Dunsterville had been summoned from his command on the Northwest Frontier. He was given a motley band of some 200 volunteers, all of whom claimed to be able to speak a second language – at least one of the South Africans knew a few words of Xhosa, and two of the Canadians spoke Montreal French – a string of Ford vans, and a few armoured cars, and sent, in the depths of winter, through the high Persian passes to reorganise the scattered Russian forces and dispatch, if possible, a British military mission some 400 miles to Tiflis in Georgia.

Fortunately for the success of the expedition, Dunsterville himself was a fine linguist, with an excellent knowledge of Urdu, Punjabi, Pushtu, Persian, French, German, Russian – even Chinese. He had persuaded Bicherakov, who claimed the loyalty – 'to the death!' – of some 10,000 Cossack *partisans,* to delay his withdrawal to Russia. He had dealt deviously with the devious Persians of Kermanshah, Hamadan and Kazvin, and with the even more devious bolsheviks of Enzeli. He had raised levies, sent out punitive patrols and built flying fields, waiting for the force that the Imperial General Staff had promised him and which, Rowlandson told us, was now at last dragging its slow length up the passes from Pai Taq to Hamadan. And in a month's time, if all went well, this force would embark at Enzeli on the Caspian, bound for the defence of Baku and the saving of British India.

But in the meantime the province of Gilan, through which

ran the road to Enzeli, was occupied by some 5,000 Jangalis, raised in revolt by Mirza Kuchik Khan, well supplied with Turkish machine guns and rifles bought from the retreating Russians, and led by a German officer named von Passchen.

I stiffened. Rowlandson, clearly, knew nothing of my background: to him I was just another soldier of fortune, perhaps little more than a mercenary, with a secret role to perform in the Great Game that the British had been playing along their Northwest Frontier for half a century and more. But only a hundred miles away, not more than an hour's flight, a brother officer commanded an effective guerrilla force. Could I, should I, take the aircraft and give myself up to him? It would be all so easy.

With a new British bomber, £2,000 in gold and my prisoners, I would be welcomed like a gift from heaven. But, I realised, Tatiana would be among those prisoners – and, indeed, how could I make my passengers prisoners when I would be piloting the aircraft and Tchaikovsky, navigating, would recognise too soon that I had turned far off my course? I decided not to act precipitately, to fly to Kazvin as expected, and to find out more, if I could, of Dunsterville's plans before escaping.

The sun was already quite low on the mountains to the south-west as we rode back to the flying field. The rocks were cleared, the white perimeter flags had been moved at least a hundred yards, and the ground crew had drawn up the 0/400, nose into the light breeze and with what looked, even to my doubting eye, like sufficient distance for an uneventful take-off. Following my orders – I was rapidly assuming the offhand manner and non-chalant confidence of a genuine Britisher – they climbed up to the engine nacelles and swung them into life, strained on the chock ropes, dragged them clear at exactly the right moment, and stood to one side, waving and cheering, as the great craft lumbered across the flattened earth, shuddered profoundly, and lifted herself slowly into the late afternoon.

I followed the road, which ran north-east toward the Sultan Bulaq pass, which we crossed at about 9,000 feet. Far ahead of us the Elburz rose like a wall between us and the Caspian, with Demavend, to the east, reaching a height of nearly 19,000 feet. But south of the mountains, in the high plateau that now unrolled below us, lay Kazvin, and from there the road ran ever downhill to Menjil, and through the gorge of the river Sefid to the inland sea. We flew in bright sunlight, but the day was fading fast on the earth below, and it was with relief that I saw Tchaikovsky point out the field at Kazvin, where a few paraffin flares flickered feebly along another strip of stamped-out desert. We rolled to a halt before the tents just as the daylight was extinguished like a snuffed candle.

Kasvin was a provincial town trying hard to look like a city. For a place with (so I was told) some 50,000 inhabitants, there was an extraordinary number of flea-ridden inns with such names as Hotel Bristol, the Ritz, the Excelsior – even an Adlon, the smallest and grimiest of all. Between the tiled façades, below the intricately wrought balconies and the sunbleached jalousies, plate-glassed shops thrust themselves forward, the names of their proprietors proclaimed in Persian, Russian and French. In their windows rolls of lightweight suitings crowded pyramids of ladies' white satin high-heeled shoes, and tottering piles of china chamberpots threatened horned phonographs and overstuffed armchairs, all in the light of flaring kerosene lamps. Everywhere there were barbers' shops, crowded with Cossacks, and the streets were thronged with men and women of every nationality – local officials in frock-coats and astrakhan caps, village women in veils, ragged camel drivers, Russian nurses, Greek and Armenian businessmen, and the men of Dunsterforce in their khaki and blue. Our staff car forced its way through, the driver sounding his horn continuously and shouting at the same time at the two-horse flies, the camels and mule-carts, and the processions of porters that seemed to be moving every way at once.

General Dunsterville's HQ was established in a large and comfortable house belonging to the American Baptist missionaries. Tatiana, Tchaikovsky and I were given fairly clean and cool rooms at a modest hotel across the street, while Nobby Clark, with innumerable winks and leers, took himself off to a *tchaparkaneh* by the bazaar. Rowlandson insisted that I should go with him at once to meet the general, who would be holding his last council-of-war with Bicherakov before the Russian left with his men to clear the Menjil road.

The famous Stalky was a tall and broadly-built man, with a trim moustache above his ready smile, and a hearty handshake.

His large tiled room was cooler than the street, but stuffy, the shutters closed and the doors guarded, while the pressure lamps burnt hotly within. Dunsterville and most of his staff were in shirtsleeves, their uniform jackets hung over the backs of their chairs, but the Russians still wore their frogged greatcoats.

The general seemed genuinely glad to see me, glanced quickly through a file of telegrams, obviously concerning myself – 'South Staffords, eh? Got a bunch of the North Staffs lads on their way up from Kermanshah at this moment' – and racily introduced me to the others around the table. Some of the names I still remember, but that was because I met them again during the next few days: Lieutenant-Colonel Mosky, the GSO; Major Dunning, Dunsterville's adjutant; Captain Pope of the 14th Hussars; Major Newcome, a Canadian banker; and Colonel Clutterbuck who, like Rowlandson, was dressed in a striking mixture of British and Cossack uniform, and who sat at the left hand of Bicherakov.

The little Cossack general was about forty years of age, with no beard but a boldly bristling moustache, and two bright, black, boot-button eyes. Later I would see those eyes blazing, twinkling, dulled with pain and fatigue, but at this moment they were fixed unblinkingly upon me in cold suspicion. Bicherakov wore a magnificent greatcoat in black broadcloth, covered from collar to waist in intricate patterns of gold braid, and a high round astrakhan cap; the coat, and even the cap, were crusted here and there with traces of former meals. I could not see his boots as he sat at the table, but later I was to discover that they were cracked and worn down after his many months on the Kermanshah road, and one had lost most of its heel.

To Bicherakov's right sat his lieutenant, Sovlaiev: similarly dressed, but with a full black beard, and seemingly about twice the size of his general. He was even broader than Dunsterville, although some four inches short of his height, and the muscles of his shoulders and upper arms swelled the seams of his greatcoat to a point where gaps and broken threads showed in many places. But in spite of his apparent fierceness, I thought I detected in his face a sort of dogged, but essentially easygoing, fidelity, like that of a well-trained retriever.

'Look here,' said Dunsterville, 'I know you've got your orders, I've had sight of your routing and been told to give you what facilities I can. But one of my chaps has already told me a bit about your aeroplane, what a great big job it is, and I'm sure the word will be all around the bazaars by midnight. What I want to say is, you'd do me the most awfully big favour if you could hang about here a day or two longer, and then fly down to the Menjil bridge and buzz about a bit, give the Jangalis a devil of a fright, what?'

I had little hesitation in agreeing to his request. If I intended to escape, the extra days would give me an opportunity to find out more, and to plan my flight. If, on the other hand, I decided to go through with my mission, there was no longer any Marlin to hustle me onward against my natural inclinations, and I could not see that a few days' delay would be of critical importance; the Tsar and his family were in prison, and would not get out before I reached them. And, as matters turned out, it was extremely fortunate that I did not leave immediately.

But what finally turned the scales for me were Major Dunning's words: 'And I don't know if you're a sportsman, but, if you are, you really oughta stick around here a day or two. We can find you some of the best shootin' you'll get anywhere in the world.'

So we settled for it. At first light, Bicherakov and his troops would set off on the road to Enzeli. And an hour later, when the tail of the column had cleared the north gate of Kazvin, Dunning would mount me on a local pony, provide me with a *charvardar* and a Purdey under-and-over, and send me off, with whoever of the British party were free from their daily duties, to scour the foothills of the Elburz. Then I was dismissed until dinner-time.

We dined two hours later in Dunsterville's private quarters, on the floor above his staffroom. Tatiana was at her most demure: the landlord of the hotel had been so shocked at her flying clothes that she had easily prevailed upon him to send his wife to buy her a local gown, and she came to dinner half-veiled and with a delicate white pump peeping from below her hem. And only I, I hope, suspected that beneath the flimsy silk she was wholly naked. Tchaikovsky was in his Russian uniform, and was greeted ecstatically by Bicherakov and Sovlaiev. Of our little army of fortune, only Clark was missing.

The others at dinner were, naturally, Rowlandson and

110

Clutterbuck, Bicherakov and Sovlaiev; the governor of the town, Midhat-es-Sultaneh, broadly built and plumply jolly; and an intensely silent Persian, named Reza Pahlavi Khan, who sported a thickly bristling moustache and wore a Cossack uniform. As the years have passed, I have never ceased to wonder at how many of those I met on this my first secret mission were to reappear at later stages of my wandering life. I have already mentioned Colonel Lawrence, whose path was to cross mine several times; and Karakhan, the crafty bolshevik, who changed my life more than once; but I would not have believed, that still hot night in Kazvin, that within seven years Reza Khan would crown himself Shah of the Peacock Throne.

The meal, the mess dinner of a scratch expeditionary force in the heart of a famine-racked country, was memorable. First there was caviar: great grey heaps of the finest Beluga, with buckwheat pancakes and soured goats' milk. And Dunning had brought in, the day before, close on a dozen quail, and a handful of their eggs, to provide us, as Dunsterville pointed out to Bicharakov with a wry grin, with a remarkable Quail Marengo, adorned with the grey tails of freshwater crayfish. Reza Khan picked glumly at his food, pointedly pushing the crayfish to one side, while the rest of us expressed our appreciation loudly. Dunsterville drank only *lassi,* a mixture of salted water and yoghurt, but there was a wine from Kazvin itself, sweet yet slightly resinous, that went tolerably well with both the caviar and the quail.

'Chardin said of this wine,' remarked Dunsterville, 'that it was *"le plus violent du monde, et aussi le plus delicieux"*. But then,' he added sadly, 'he also thought the air of Persia so pure that there was no need to cork the wine: just a rose or a carnation in the neck of the bottle was enough to save it from corruption.'

We finished with goats cheese, and newly-picked peaches, and last year's figs in syrup. It was the first good meal I had eaten since leaving London. And that was only ten days ago?

The Russians, except for little Tchaikovsky, who had his fractured English, spoke only their native language. Reza Khan spoke nothing but Persian and a little Russian. I had only German and my painfully-acquired English. Dunsterville dominated the conversation, cracking jokes in Russian, rallying Reza Khan and the governor in their own language, translating for my benefit and that of Rowlandson and Clutterbuck, who at the same time were stiffly trying to draw out Tchaikovsky with all the Russian that they knew. Tatiana prattled on, sometimes in Russian, sometimes in English, occasionally slipping (heavens, was it wise?) into German for my benefit, or flirting privately with Dunsterville in French. I reflected with a secret smile that the Tower of Babel had stood only a day's flight from where we sat.

Rowlandson, as he had feared, was compelled to make his excuses early, with Clutterbuck; but Bicherakov and Sovlaiev seemed set to sit up drinking all night until it was time to join their Cossacks on the road. I was restless, for I was looking forward eagerly to my hunting trip in the morning, and needed as much sleep as possible so that my eye would be sharp and my head clear. Little more than a month before, with my *Jagdgeschwader* on the western front, I had made it a personal rule always to be in bed by ten o'clock, and I had taught myself to stay fast asleep until only a few minutes before the morning patrol was due.

Fortunately for my patience, and for the morale of the Cossack brigade, Reza Khan, who had eaten little and drunk nothing, clearly disapproved of the self-indulgence of the Russians. Glowering morosely in Bicherakov's direction, he spoke rapidly in Persian to the fat governor who, with a look of intense disappointment, promptly rose to his feet and made a little speech of farewell. Reza Khan could scarcely wait for him to finish before he too was on his feet. I took the opportunity to rise hoveringly; and the diplomat Dunsterville, with an apologetic word in one language and a brief exhortation in another, had the Russians on the move in thirty seconds. Tatiana and I swept up little Tchaikovsky, shook hands all round, and within two minutes were clattering across the blue and white tiled floor of the hotel entrance hall.

But if you think that was the end of my evening activities you have paid very little attention to the narrative so far. Throughout dinner, as the polyglot conversation had broken in waves over my head, my eyes had been caught constantly by the tenuous stretch of silk over Tatiana's breasts, the nipples seeming to strain through the loosely-woven fabric, and my mind had been concentrated on the way in which the gown

112

dived between her thighs, as if sucked inward by a desire she scarce could control. And the warped panel door of our hotel room had hardly closed before I had put both my hands to the neck of that gown, and ripped it from her body.

CHAPTER 8

5 June: Kazvin

MY DAY'S hunting was somewhat different from anything that I had expected. At six, still wrapped blissfully in Tatiana's arms, I was wakened by an irregular thumping on the room door that, to my sleep-drugged ear, sounded like the barrage from a battery of *minnenwerfen*. It emanated, I found, from an ancient warped servant clad in a grey wrap, bearing a tray of steaming black coffee and the message that 'English wait downstair.' Fifteen minutes later I had shaved, put on my crumpled tropical khaki, kissed Tatiana, still slumbering rosily, and tottered barefooted to the hotel courtyard.

There I found some half a dozen Britishers, in a strange assortment of uniforms, Persian capes and Arab headgear, with a handful of skittering ponies and a Kurd guide in a felt cap, his beard stained bright orange with henna. The leader of this motley crew was in RAF blue breeches and shirt; his left arm was encased in a tubular leather sleeve on which a falcon, in hood and jesses, sat perched, its blind head turning questingly in the morning light. In his right hand the man held three pairs of riding boots.

He stood about eight inches taller than myself, with bright red hair cut *en brosse,* and his steely blue eyes swivelled downward upon me like the twin beams of a Zeppelin manoeuvring for its mooring mast after a night patrol.

'It's more than ten minutes we've been waiting for ye,' he began without ceremony. 'And ten miles we have to go before we find the game, I'm thinking. Would you be trying one of these pairs of boots? We'd the word from Major Dunning that you'd be needing some, but we had not the size of your feet. And my name,' he added, as he turned away, swinging his long stringy legs straight over a pony's back, 'is Dougal Macdougall.'

The second pair of boots fitted me tolerably well. My pony, a neat little brindled mare, with a high pommelled saddle but no stirrups, was led dancing up to me, and we were off, bells jingling on cheekstraps as we clattered through the early morning streets, past the five-minareted shrine of Zadeh Hussein, and out through the city gate crumbling amid vines and yellow roses.

The road ran north-east, and away in the distance we could see the snows melting on the wall of mountain peaks, like a painted scene in a photographer's studio, above the brown ridges of the lower heights. Widely spaced across the plain, white-walled villages nestled among the only trees; and all around them spread the narrow fields of barley, and the new-broken earth where pairs of black oxen furrowed at the plough. In the morning breeze, the shrill cries of the ploughmen came faintly and intermittently; above us the larks scribbled their slate-pencil songs on the bright blue air.

After a mile or two we took a track to the left, through a desert meadow of rough, browning grass, starred with yellow and lilac-blue flowers. We each, with the exception of Macdougall, carried a shotgun across the saddlebow, and we rode in a silence broken only by the ring of our harness bells, the creak of saddle and girth, the mewing of Macdougall's falcon, and the occasional tuneless whistle of some British officer trying to rival the skylarks' echoing song. Our guide, who answered in the Kurdish dialect to 'The Refuge of Allah', said not a word, but urged us on with sweeps of his broad right arm.

So we rode on across the plain, the track rising over a ridge, then winding down to a thin and straggling watercourse and up again, gradually higher and higher, as the sun rose higher too, and the air blew thinner against our tautening cheeks. After more than an hour, we came up a sharp slope and found ourselves at the edge of a field of desert that stretched away to where the mountain flanks rose suddenly blue above a belt of hazy green. I reined in my pony, and straightened myself in the saddle. The wind was warm, but at the same time it had an inner keenness to it – as you wrap a sabre blade in a fold of your cloak, so that it neither rattles in its scabbard nor glints in the dark. It smelt of mountain herbs, and broken stones, and all the vast emptiness that reached on from where I stared, deep into the further heart of central Asia. The emptiness was so immense that it seemed to surge all around me, and over me and under me, and to be pouring into me, like a calm sea in which I was inexorably drowning.

I took deep breaths; and although I was drowning in that warm, keen, empty air, it seemed I could not drag enough of it down into my craving lungs. But then the spell was broken as one of the Englishmen pointed, exclaiming in a whisper under his breath. We all looked, and saw, about half a mile away over the sand and scree and patches of scrub grass, two birds motionless and watching us. They were the size of large turkeys, standing taller on longer legs, and with slim necks that pecked at the breeze, eyeing us, listening, raised in interrogation like someone trying to catch a chairman's attention. I noticed that Macdougall was very gently unlacing his falcon's hood; then he carefully unhooked the leash from the swivel on the jesses. The falcon, a lanner hen, twitched her head knowingly, her eyes glinting under half-closed lids; she ruffled her feathers slightly, and then, suddenly, was motionless, staring across the desert at her statuesque prey.

'Gentlemen,' said Macdougall 'the first bustard, you agree, is mine?' He did not wait for confirmation, but quietly urged his pony forward in an unobtrusive amble, while the rest of us followed as quietly as we could. We had ridden in this way for no more than a couple of hundred yards when suddenly the two big birds began to run, their long legs skimming the scrub, and their fan-like tails held high. At once, Macdougall swung his left arm forward and up, catapulting the falcon into the air, and immediately after brought his hand back to clap the pony resoundingly on the withers. With a single harsh scream the falcon was gone, her long narrow wings flickering as she raced low across the desert. The two bustard, which had been running

115

side by side, suddenly parted, and for a moment I thought that the falcon, in making up her mind which to follow, had lost them both. But in a fraction of a second she had identified the slower runner and was after it.

Like a hare, the bustard now began to zigzag from side to side – I suddenly remembered the movements of the Camel that I had foolishly chased the day I was brought down – but, as I had done on that fateful day, the falcon easily followed her prey's movements. As she neared the bustard she rose a little higher in the air, and cried her harsh cry once more. Then, as she came within sight of the bustard's eye, the big bird suddenly stopped running, threw itself backward upon its tail so that it could most effectively defend itself with its bill and claws, and puffed up all its neck and breast feathers. But the lanner took a quick climbing circle and dropped, talons forward and cruel beak agape, slipped sideways from the bustard's lungeing neck, swept upward again and struck, easily and fatally, below the gizzard in the big bird's breast, ripping it wide.

We meanwhile, with Macdougall in the lead, had whipped our ponies forward, desperate but unavailing to keep up with the lanner's flight. And as she struck: 'Quick, quick,' cried Macdougall, 'she must not gorge. Our supper it is, not hers.' We reached the kill, and Macdougall fought with his falcon for possession, forcing the leather sleeve upon her with his left arm until he could get the leash attached to the swivel with his right; and then he took her, and gentled her, and fed her bloody pieces from the bustard's breast, as she lifted one foot and rattled her bells at him.

'A houbara bustard, gentlemen,' he told us, 'or should we not say, more properly, Mcqueen's bustard, after the eminent Scottish naturalist who first described it? I doubt you will not object to this bird for your collation, the night?'

After this grand guignol curtain raiser, the rest of the morning's work was almost an anticlimax. I had hunted all sorts of game, from the ducks on my grandmother's pond as a boy, to bison in the forests of Bielowieza during my last leave. I knew the joy of stalking, anticipating the quarry's movement and always being one thought in advance; I knew the excitement of the gun muzzle that always kept ahead of its target, and the squeeze on the trigger that brought the bird tumbling from the

116

sky, the beast sliding forward on its knees. But, even with the best of gun dogs, I had not known the community of trust and companionship that existed between Macdougall and his falcon. And, even faced with the wild corkscrew tusks of a charging boar, I had not experienced such exhilaration as I got in those few minutes when we careered across the desert scrub and watched the calm perfection of the falcon's kill. I rode my pony close to Macdougall, and tried to tell him of my excitement and admiration, but he would not discuss it with me. Not, at least, until I had bagged four brace of quail and another bustard.

'You like to shoot, Captain Jones?' he asked me at last, as we rested in the midday shade of a clump of fig trees. I nodded. 'There is an animal in these hills that would, I'm thinking, satisfy even your taste for hunting. Did you ever shoot tiger, Captain Jones?' His cheeks were high-boned and reddened easily, and his moustache, lighter in colour than his hair, bristled fiercely; but it seemed to me that his blue eyes twinkled somewhere deep in their distance.

'Tiger? But of course not. We have no tigers in – ' I stumbled ' – in Czechoslovakia. But here?'

'Oh aye. I flew to Tehran some weeks by, you ken, and instead of following the road directly I turned a little north, along the flank of the mountains you see ahead there. It was in a little corrie I could find again with my eyes shut that I found him. I was not flying fast – the Martinsyde, I doubt you know, is not a fast machine – and I had the engine well throttled back, following the contours and catching thermals to lift me over the ridges, dreaming a little of the peregrines above Ben Fhada when I was a wee boy. It was the movement that caught my eye: a waving of the long grass, and a bending of a sapling or two. Then the sun struck clear into an open space, and I saw him, pacing grandly forward, a great beast, shaggy and dark with his close-spaced stripes. He paid no more attention to me than he would to a buzzing fly, pausing but a second and turning his head to stare up at me, before he stalked on again, at the same steady pace, into the grass that covered him. . . . And I was thinking,' he fixed me again with his eyes, cool and still like moorland tarns beneath a spring sky, 'that another and I, with rifles apiece and an aeroplane to take us there, could likely hunt

117

him down.'

It was both an invitation and a challenge, neither of which I could refuse. 'Can we get an aeroplane?'

'Oh aye, we can indeed, but I'm thinking we'll need to buy the petrol ourselves; I promise our quartermaster's little eyes would burn in his head with rage if he knew what we were at.'

And so we agreed it. We would fly to Macdougall's corrie, as he called it – a Gaelic word, meaning much the same, I guess, as the English quarry – and there we would hawk about, seeking our quarry (English is a very confusing language). At intervals we would search out an alpine meadow, land, and exchange places, so that both had an equal chance to spot the tiger and take first shot at him. Apart from my essentialness as relief pilot, it dawned upon me that I would be somewhat a passenger on this expedition, for Macdougall clearly intended to arrange everything himself. His corporal would be sent out that evening to buy the petrol, and Macdougall would book himself a dawn patrol that would enable us, at first light, to steal away from our companions and set course for the Elburz.

We rested in the fig trees' shade, lunching on rice pilaf and yoghurt, until the shadows began to lengthen across the desert, and a mule train came down from the hills, bringing rice from the Caspian shore through the mountain passes to the interior. The drivers were Kurds in side-fastened coats of white frieze cloth, with their long straight-stemmed pipes stuck through their coloured sashes. Their beards were all dyed bright red with henna, but cut short in the Moslem fashion; they stared at us from their square open faces, neither hostile nor welcoming, shouted a formal greeting to which one of our party replied in what sounded to be excellent Persian, and passed on, the tiny bells at their mules' hindquarters dwindling gently away into the all-enveloping silence. Behind them, we mounted leisurely, our spoil tied in braces across our saddlebows, and rode contentedly back to Kazvin.

Tatiana was not at the hotel. The *effendi,* said the porter, had called for her before lunch, in his carriage.

'What *effendi?*'

He shrugged. Tchaikovsky, sweating in his room behind closed shutters, could offer no explanation. And suddenly for the first time in six weeks – and what a six weeks! – I was without Tatiana. I felt myself abandoned and alone in this desolate land and, panicking, I did not perhaps act as wisely as I ought.

I should have crossed the road immediately to Dunsterville's headquarters and asked to speak to Major Dunning. With his help I could have had the town and surrounding countryside scoured, Persians questioned, travellers stopped. Instead, I took matters into my own hands.

I went back to our bedroom and, searching briefly, found that small grey box which Tatiana had received from the sergeant-at-arms at Baquba. As I had suspected, it contained two Webley revolvers, complete with lanyards and holsters, and two boxes of rounds. The Webley is not one of my favourite revolvers, nor is a revolver my favourite weapon; at that time I certainly preferred the Mauser C96 automatic, although in later years I was to grow very fond of the Parabellum 08, commonly known as the Luger. Nevertheless, these revolvers were a very useful discovery, and I eagerly loaded them both and buckled them to my belt. Then I set off to look for Nobby Clark.

Already, the shadows were lengthening along the town streets, edged in maroon and lilac; very soon the night would rush upon us from out of the desert, lights would hover behind the jalousies of upper windows, and the air would be full of flickering bats and blundering moths, the scrape of crickets and the sudden song, like water dripping in a well, of the solitary nightingale; and how would I find Clark, or Tatiana, in the dark?

I shouldered my way through the evening crowds. Only last night I had thought them romantic, picturesque, now they seemed to block my way deliberately, jeering in my face, taunting my impatience and concern. The incomprehensible cries of the streets rose all around me, pedlars thrust useless pieces of rubbish beneath my nose, a camel spat at me. I reeled on; in the fitful light of kerosene lamps and naphtha flares, my shadow danced before me, beside me, now ogre-like and vast, now thin as a wraith. My head turned from side to side, my voice choked on the first syllable of her name as I saw her moving in the throng, only to realise that it was not Tatiana . . .
Suddenly I felt my arm seized by a strong hand, and, turning, saw the square face and orange-dyed beard of Macdougall's

119

charvardar, The Refuge of Allah.

In the wildness of my relief I took his shoulders in my hands and spoke to him in German – then, quickly realising my mistake, in English. But he understood neither, staring steadily deep into my eyes and questioning me earnestly in his Kurdish dialect. Then something in my feverish gaze, the sweated anguish of my face, must have communicated itself to him, for he took my elbow brusquely and began to propel me through the crowd. We came to a deep dark lane that plunged through a crumbling archway on the far edge of the *souk,* and stumbled down it. To our right a door stood ajar, a thin light flickering in the cavernous portico within. In the corner of the portico a narrow stair spiralled up to a low arched room whose windows looked out upon a blank brick wall, and in the far end of this room, surrounded by a dark ring of hunkered figures, a man sat singing a wildly nasal song. And the man was Clark.

There was a tall amber glass of tea before him, and before each of his companions; on a small charcoal stove close by stood a large china teapot. By Clark's feet a brass tray held a few small dark cubes of a crumbly but sticky consistency, and as I approached a thin brown hand stretched out to take a cube and pop it into a thin brown mouth. Clark reached the end of his song with a heavily accented line that was obviously obscene, for it provoked a shout of laughter, bowed his head to acknowledge the scattered applause, and only then, slowly, focused his glittering eyes upon me.

At first he spoke slowly, but soon was caught up in the excitement of his own rhetoric. 'Stone me, it's the one and only Captain Simon Jones! O captain of my sole endeavour – my endover sole, perdition catch it! For we are on an experdition, aren't we, Captain? Not a com-perdition, nor yet a got-up petition. We don't go round robbin', or marryin' maids against their will, scarlet with embarrassment – oh my gawd!' And he waved his hands helplessly in the air and collapsed in quivering giggles. I report his speech exactly as he made it, for I understood hardly a word at the time, and little more today. If he had been drinking anything stronger than tea I would have thought him drunk.

The Refuge of Allah drew me into the circle; accepted a glass of tea for himself, and pressed one upon me; took one of the brown cubes for himself, and offered me one. It was not, as I had thought, a sweetmeat: it had a strangely resinous taste and an unexpectedly glue-like consistency. It gave a slight prickle to the back of my tongue and the sides of my palate, but seemed otherwise innocuous. I refused a second.

Clark was singing again. His voice climbed dizzily, quavered, broke into guttural gobbets. As I have said before, I can scarcely tell 'Deutschland über alles' from 'The Blue Danube', and I could only marvel at Clark's skill in holding the attention of his Persian audience with one of their own songs. It was, I suppose, more than a minute before I incredulously recognised some words:

'O, sweet Dardanella, prepare the wedding wine,
There'll be one girl in my harem when you're mine.
We'll build a tent, just like the children of the Orient,
O, sweet Dardanella, my star of love divine.'

As the applause died, Clark stared brightly at me again. 'Dear old Fred Fisher. Written that for me. And – did you know? – one for you too, Captain Jones. Come Josephine in my flying machine – up she goes! And one for you too, you little – you little Turkoman you' – as he fixed on a very dark-skinned figure in front of him – 'How do you like it? If the man in the moon were a coon!' And once more he shook uncontrollably, like a tittering crème caramel. But what are *you* doin' here, young Jones? You do realise, I s'pose, that *I'm* here in what's called incognito, and now you've penetrated my disguise? They all thought I was a genuine bedouin ayrab – didn't you, my fine fellaheen? – until you came in and spoilt it all.'

Every one of the Persians laughed, and so did I. They all seemed very friendly, smiling at me, so I smiled at them. The room was cool after the lingering heat of the streets, and now somebody else was singing. I liked the song, I liked the atmosphere; I was a little thirsty, so I drank some tea, and when The Refuge of Allah passed me the brass tray, I took another of the small brown cubes. A little later, some girls came in and danced – at least I think they danced. I'm sure that girls came in, for when I woke up some time later I had my head in the lap of one of them, and she was stroking my hair. Clark was kneeling at my side.

'Right then, lad, what's it all about? Our friend over there tells me he met you staggerin' about the bazaar, lookin' as if the world had come to an end.' I was sleepy, and somehow Tatiana's disappearance no longer seemed so urgent and so terrifying, but as clearly as I could I told Clark what had happened. He whistled.

'Nasty. And she didn't leave a note or anything? Nasty, very. Sharp's the word, then, just like the toffee. Don't go away.'

I had no desire to go away: I still felt sleepy, and the girl was still stroking my hair, and my previous panic seemed now so unnecessary. I was sure that everything would soon turn out all right.

But then I wasn't so sure. A sudden fear came upon me, like the prick of a hypodermic needle as it slides so smooth and cold beneath the skin. Why was I here, lying on the floor of this brothel (was it a brothel?) when I should even now be searching, searching, for Tatiana? Yet it was comfortable, and this girl, though plump, was pretty . . .

Clark was at my side again. Enquiries had already begun, he told me. He had despatched several of his friends to ask in the bazaar, to talk to the night-watchmen, to interrogate the cab drivers. Very little went on that these men did not know. He had also taken the precaution of sending someone to enquire at the hotel, in case Tatiana had returned. His messenger had found Tchaikovsky racked with dysentery, incapable of taking interest in any movements but his own, but of Tatiana there was no news – and the porter who had seen her go off before lunch could not be found.

My previous lethargy had now vanished, and everything seemed distinct and clear: not only my understanding of the situation, but my surroundings themselves, the pools of light from two or three lamps lying limpid below the shifting fronds of shadow, edged with rainbow droplets, the girls sharply drawn, as in the painting by Ingres that I had seen in Antwerp, one day on leave from my squadron, and Clark's eyes burning, bright and accusing, into mine.

'How could I know that this would occur?' I protested. 'I left her safe at the hotel, with Dunsterville across the street, and Tchaikovsky in the next room. What on earth could have happened to her?'

'Why, she's been abducted, I shouldn't wonder,' said Clark

cheerfully. 'There's a lot o' that goes on, round these parts. Before she knows where she is, find 'erself in some bloke's harem scarum, divil may care 'em . . . Oh, now, don't you fret, young feller-me-lad, we'll find her for you!'

It was nearly an hour later that the first news came. I had spent the time pacing to and fro, sometimes stopping to stare blindly out of the window at the blank wall beyond: I had no idea what to do next. Then a stooped, cross-eyed man slipped into the room and whispered to Clark who, obviously startled, made a swift enigmatic gesture with his left hand that seemed to reduce the messenger to quivering fear. There was a brief exchange of pleas and threats, and then Clark crossed the room to my side.

'Good news and bad news, ol' boy. He's found the hotel porter who saw Tatiana leave this morning. Got some more information out of him. But he's definitely frightened, and there's something a bit funny about this business, though I can't put me finger on it at the moment, as the bishop said, but . . . Did you ever read the *Travels of Marco Polo*?' And indeed I had, although nearly twenty years before. 'You remember the Old Man of the Mountains, Hasan-i-Sabbah? Well, somehow or other, this feller happened to mention the *hashishin.*'

'The *hashishin*?'

'He certainly didn't mean this lot, for a start off,' said Clark, waving his arm widely to encompass the room, the near-silent girls, the scattered Persians quietly singing, giggling or staring blandly into the dark. And then he told me, more than I remembered or ever knew: of the Shia sect, who broke away from orthodox Islam in the seventh century; of the schism that created the Ismailis; and of how Hasan became an Ismaili *da'i* and founded the Nizari sect in 1078; and the stronghold he found, the Eagle's Nest, in the fastness of Alamut, not a hundred miles from Kazvin, where by the subtle use of drugs he enlisted the devotion of many hundred *fidais,* who would kill others or themselves at Hasan's least command – the *hashishin,* the Assassins, those to whom Hasan had revealed the garden of Paradise.

Beware, beware!
His flashing eyes, his floating hair!
Come weave a circle round him thrice:

And close your eyes with holy dread!
For he on honeydew hath fed
And drunk the milk of Paradise!

'Some say,' continued Clark, 'that the Assassins was wiped out by Jenghiz Khan. But that ain't so. There's plenty of Ismailis about still, here in Persia and in India too. In fact – ' but here he was interrupted by another messenger, a diffident boy who stammered, and looked at the ground, and drew patterns in the thin dust with his naked toe. Clark patted him absentmindedly on the head, looking cautiously over his shoulder at me. When he returned, he continued to stare calculatingly at me for some seconds.

'Where was I? Oh yes, the Ismailis. There's an old boy, insists he's the direct descendant of Hasan, lays claim to a tenth of everything every Ismaili earns. They weighed him in diamonds when he was throned! Call him the Aga Khan – the king of kings. I met 'im in India once, at a tent-peggin' do: nice old cove, funny lookin' though, with his pop eyes . . . And that little lad reckons he's seen him in Kazvin, the other day, ridin' in his carriage with the blinds drawn down.

There was nothing I could say, and very little that I understood. But soon it was to become clearer, for a third messenger was able to tell Clark whose carriage it was that had abducted Tatiana from the hotel.

'Right, me lad,' said Clark to me, 'now we know who, when, and where. And I've got a damned good idea why, haven't you? First thing now, let's get you disguised. Your blond hair and blue eyes are a dead giveaway, but if Lawrence could carry it off, so can we.'

CHAPTER 9

6-11 June: Kazvin

THE CLOTHES that Clark found for me were not very clean, and far from prepossessing: a loose pair of striped cotton trousers, which came not more than halfway down my calves, and over them a knee-length grey shirt and a sleeveless jerkin of flea-bitten sheepskin. For my feet he produced a pair of out-at-heel slippers in scuffed crimson leather, while on my head I wore a tight cap of brown felt, round and over which a long tattered scarf was wound, the ends hanging over my shoulders and hiding my hair. With a mixture of mud and coffee grounds we contrived to colour my arms, feet and face so that, at first glance and in a bad light, I could pass for a local inhabitant. My belt and holsters had to be worn, of course, under the long shirt; I could only hope that I would not have to fumble for them in a hurry.

While I dressed, Clark pieced together a patchwork of facts, rumours and hypotheses into a story that gave us hope and a motive for action. Kazvin, in the heart of the country of the Assassins, no doubt still retained a significant residue of Ismailis – if not in the town itself, certainly in the remote parts of the surrounding hills. The carriage that had borne off Tatiana belonged to a very rich man, Buzurg-Umid, who was reputed to be an Ismaili, and who lived a secluded life some twenty miles from Kazvin, in an ancient fortress, the Khak-i-'Ali, perched on a rising spur. As for the Aga Khan, the leader of the Ismailis, he was supposed to be convalescing in Switzerland after treatment for a defective thyroid gland, but he had made no public appearance for many weeks.

'What it looks like to me,' said Clark, 'some'ow or other he got himself out here – perhaps he needed to pick up a diamond or two, something like that – decides to look up his old friend Buzurg-Umid, and then he hears about this very pretty girl in town, and he says to his pal, why don't you see if you can grab her for me? He's always had a very good eye for a woman, I'm told – and a racehorse, come to that.'

The Refuge of Allah offered to find us some ponies and lead us to the Khak-i-'Ali ('If things go on like this, old boy,' whispered Clark, 'I'm goin' to need a few more of your little gold sovereigns') but intimated that he did not expect to be asked to do more than guard the ponies and wait for us. If we intended to intrude upon the lives of local lords, he preferred to know nothing of it.

So, as the first rays of dawn gilded the topmost minarets of Zahed Hussein ('Awake, for morning in the bowl of night hath flung the stone that puts the stars to flight!' chanted Clark in the echoing shadow of the city gate) we rode out on the Tehran road.

Three hours later we took our breakfast – some yoghurt and a handful of dates – in the thin shade of some tamarisk bushes beside a bend in the stony track that wound up toward the gate of Khak-i-'Ali, half a mile away. Downhill from the bend, a ditch, now dry, had been eroded deep by the floodwater of a thousand winter storms, and there we left The Refuge of Allah well hidden, with the ponies and provisions. In the scrub below the track, Clark and I crept forward, the rise of the ground concealing us from the eyes of everyone in the fortress, until at the final bend we could edge ourselves up to take a look at our goal.

The Khak-i-'Ali did not stand high on a rock, nor were its walls precipitous and turreted like those of the castles I had seen in the Schwarzwald and along the Rhine. It squatted massively across a slight promontory that ran out from the higher ground behind, and was only more than one storey high here and there. But the brick walls were strong, battlemented above, with just a few slits in their otherwise unbroken smoothness. There was a single entrance, a great double wooden door, tight shut in a high gate tower; and on the roof of the tower, beside a stubby flagstaff, the morning breeze stirred the white robes of a single sentry.

We crept back into cover. 'Do you really suppose,' I asked Clark, 'that Tatiana is imprisoned there?'

'There's only one way we're goin' to find out, ol' boy. There ain't nobody we can ask, so we'll just have to get in there and see for ourselves. And how the heck we're goin' to manage *that,* beats me for the moment. Can't just go up and knock on the door and say as how we've come to read the gasmeter, now, can we?'

Dejected, we made our way back to our base in the dry ditch. Clark's dark face was twisted in silent puzzlement. And I, though I racked my brains, could think of nothing better than returning to Kazvin, begging Macdougall's aid, and making a parachute descent into the courtyard of the fortress, an exploit I did not relish – I had, of course, been given instruction in the use of the parachute, but had never brought myself to trust it – and one that would not only draw attention to our presence but would make me an easy target for the sentries' guns. If only I had one of those 'helicopters' which, I had been told, the Breguet brothers had built some ten years before!

We lay in the ditch beside The Refuge of Allah as the sun rose higher and higher. It grew ever hotter as we discussed and discarded all sorts of plans for getting into the fortress: lying in wait for the cart that, one day or another, would deliver provisions to the gate, and taking the place of the driver; setting a fire in front of the entrance, and slipping inside in the confusion when the guards came out to extinguish it; making a rope from the ponies' harness, and fashioning a grapnel from the bits, and climbing the wall by night. Oh, we were fools to have left Kazvin without bringing suitable equipment with us.

We ate some yoghurt, and sipped sour water from our skin bottles. It was now very hot. The ponies were thirsty and shifted irritably. 'How shall we water them?' I asked.

'From a well,' replied Clark brusquely, 'we passed one a little way down the track and – ' he stopped suddenly and slapped his forehead. 'By god, lad, I do believe you've got it! A *qanat*!'

He wiped his brow with a corner of his dusty clothing, leaving a grey smear from ear to ear. 'How do they get water in the fort? From a well of course. And where does the water come from and where does it go? Along a *qanat*!' He told me then about the *qanats,* the underground aqueducts of Persia.

In that land where water is so short, they trace the subterranean watercourses, dig tunnels to meet them, and draw off the water for their fields and gardens. These tunnels may be as much as twenty-five miles long, but the way in which they are made is very simple. A well is dug, and from its bottom the *qanat* is burrowed to the source of water. Then a second well is sunk, perhaps nearly a mile away, and the two wells are joined – and so the *qanat* is gradually constructed, and the water led off

127

to wherever it is needed. And all we had to do, Clark suggested, was to climb down one well, wade along the *qanat,* and climb up the next well into the courtyard of the fort. With this decision made, and a plan to follow, we lay back to doze fitfully through the afternoon. But in the event, of course, it was to prove not so simple.

We awoke in the late afternoon having previously decided that we must make our first descent into the *qanat* by daylight, and, on foot, led our ponies back down the track to where Clark had seen the well. Many of these shafts are no more than crumbling holes in the ground, but this one had been reinforced at its lip by oval-shaped sections of baked clay some six feet across, and beside it there was an old timber swing-arm with a rope and wooden bucket for raising water from the depths. First we drew some for the ponies and then, with a box of matches, a small tin canister of olive oil and a piece of string for a wick, I insisted on being first down the well. I judged it best to lower the bucket to the bottom, tie off the rope, and then to climb down hand over hand. Clark would follow me as soon as I reached the bottom safely.

The well was deeper than I had expected. Almost before my head was below the rim the mouldy damp of the depths rose about me, and I was suddenly cold. I went down the rope as fast as I could without burning my hands and my bare feet, but, when I was a little past what I judged to be halfway, the jerking of my body caused the rope to begin to swing from side to side, and soon, try as I might, every movement I made threw me against the rough sides of the shaft. I paused, both to recover my thoughts and to stop the movement of the rope, but as I did so it suddenly dropped sharply for several feet and began to spin me, slowly at first, round in one direction and then back in the other. High above me, the silhouette of Clark's head cut into the oval of light to make a cryptic question mark that twisted wildly to and fro. I was near the bottom when the rope snapped, and I fell with a mighty splash into the underground stream.

Fortunately, my instinctive reaction was to snatch the box of matches from inside the folds of my shirt and hold them high in the air, even as I lay gasping in two feet of icy water. As I struggled to my feet, the echoes still slapping around me, Clark's voice came thin and vibrating down. Yes, I shouted back, I was alive, no bones broken, but very wet. I groped in the black water about my feet and found the bucket: the length of rope attached to it must have been at least thirty feet. There was no hope that Clark could climb down the remaining portion to join me.

I called up to him with the news. There was nothing for it but to set off on my own to explore the *qanat,* while he and The Refuge of Allah went in search of more rope. With a despairing wave he agreed, and the tiny bright oval above my head was suddenly void.

With slippery, shivering fingers I unstoppered the canister of oil, poked in the length of loose string, and then, gripping the canister between my knees, fumbled open the box of matches. Half fell immediately into the water, for the box was upside down. Desperately I turned it over, drew out a matchstick, felt for the head, and struck it against the side of the box. It flared, briefly blue, and went out. The next four would not strike, for the box was damp in my fingers. I felt about me: the stones of the well near my head seemed to be dry. There were only a few sticks left now in the box, and gingerly I took one and struck it on the wall. It burst into flame, flickered agonisingly, and then steadied; a warm yellow glow shuddered in the dark of the well. I held the fire to the oil-soaked string, and thankfully watched it take, the wick sparking and spluttering, and then, with a thick spiral of black smoke, gradually swelling to red, then orange, filling the space about me with an unsteady light.

The water moved sluggishly black about my calves, touched with rippled gold. The rough, loose, sandy stones danced in the faint glow, and a thin shaft of late daylight from above fought with the flame of my torch. In front of me, the stream disappeared reluctantly into a jagged cleft about three feet high and four feet wide, and behind me it emerged from a similar tunnel. Stooping, I waded in with a sigh of resignation.

I had not gone a hundred yards when the light went out: the string wick had slipped inside the neck of the canister. I cursed, and retraced my steps to the foot of the shaft. It took some minutes to get the string out of the canister, then I tore a strip from the hem of my shirt and, wrapping it round the string, was able to wedge it into the neck in such a way that I would be able gradually to pull out the wick as it burned down. By now my eyes had adapted themselves to the dim light, but it took three more matches to light the lamp again, and only two sticks were left. Belatedly, I eased up my felt cap and slipped the box inside: now, at least, I would be able to keep it dry.

The bottom of the *qanat*, washed by many years of running water, was fairly smooth, floored with loose gravel and an occasional larger rock. The roof of the tunnel was uneven, at times, where the bigger rocks had been excavated, giving me room to stand up, and at others compelling me to bend almost to the surface of the water. The air, fortunately, was still and pure, though the damp caused the lamp to burn fitfully. I stumbled forward, steadily dripping, for what I judged to be half an hour and then, shading the flame with my hand, saw a faint glimmer of light down the tunnel ahead of me. A minute later I stretched upright in the bottom of the fortress well and, craning up, saw a crossbeam across its mouth and the thin snake of a rope dangling down to a bucket that hung motionless some thirty feet above my head.

I pinched out the flame of my lamp with my fingers, and stood there, panting slightly. Here at water level the shaft was some six feet across, but above me it narrowed sharply, and if only I could climb some way up I should be able to reach the rope. But on the earth above it was still day: I would have to wait until dark, and at some time while I waited someone would almost certainly come to the well to draw water. I edged myself below the overhang and there, hungry and tired, my feet in the cold water and my clothes slowly oozing dry, crouched alone with my thoughts.

Like a horse, I must have dozed on my feet, for the bucket splashed down suddenly before my face and nearly caused me to cry aloud in surprise. It was much darker now in the well, as the day above died, and the bucket rose and fell again as one of the servants drew water to fill a cistern for the night. Anxiously I watched the bucket come and go; eventually it stopped and, edging out and peering cautiously upward, I realised with despair that it had been withdrawn and that no rope now hung down the well.

At that moment, I nearly retreated. I was exhausted: I had spent most of the previous day and all the morning, with little food and no sleep except for a few snatched half-hours, in the saddle. I had no proof that Tatiana was in the fortress above my head, or anywhere within a hundred miles; I was alone in a soggy hole in the ground, as wretched as any soldier on the western front; and there was no sign of Clark. Without his help, there seemed no way in which I could hope to climb back up the well where I had last said goodbye to him. Perhaps he had deserted me, perhaps I had been left here, buried alive, slowly to rot and wash away.

But there was still a chance that I could escape from the well where I stood, if only I could get up the first few feet. It was now quite dark: directly above, I could see a brilliant star in the velvet blue of the night sky. I did not dare light my lamp again in case someone should chance to glance down the well, so, stretching upward, I groped around the walls above my head. It seemed as if I had already made two circuits of the shaft when my fingers encountered a large rough rock protruding nearly a foot. Getting a firm grip upon it I pulled myself sharply up, scrabbling wildly with my feet against the well sides and muttering a mixture of prayers and curses.

Miraculously, I found myself sitting astride the rock, my face pressed close to the stones above, and my hands between my thighs. From this position I was able to drag myself upright, my fingers dug into the loose walls, and, swinging one leg into the void, eventually discover a second foothold a foot or to above the first. In another minute I had reached the narrower part of the shaft and paused, panting, to consider my next move. It was necessary to get my feet against one side of the shaft and my back against the other, and so, with my hands down behind me to relieve the strain, inch my way upward. I struggled slowly, hearing the dislodged pebbles rattle down and splash far below, fearful that the noise might be noticed by one of the sentries. Several times I slipped back, once falling three or four feet and ripping the skin from my forearms. It only needed a bucket to be thrown down once more, striking me full in the exposed belly and knocking me flailing and helpless, to certain death in the waters of the abyss. But nobody heard the noise I made, and nobody came for more water, and at last I could get my hands to the rim of the well and cling there, peeping fearfully out into the courtyard.

The interior of Khak-i-'Ali was very different from its

outward appearance. The courtyard into which I intended to emerge was an outer court, on to which the main gates opened, but even so it was swept clean and planted with jasmine, almond and roses, whose perfume filled the air. Within the thick walls, rooms opened out like booths, with lights burning inside: a wide whitewashed stable, servants' quarters, a busy kitchen, with rich meat grilling whose tormenting aroma I could smell even above the flowers. Cautiously, I edged my body over the well's rim, and rolled into the shadow of one of the almond trees.

Along one side of the courtyard ran a ramshackle verandah, on which several white-robed figures squatted in the gloom. With my eyes upon them, expecting any moment the pointing finer and shout of discovery, I squirmed slowly between the bushes, making for an archway on the far side that obviously led into a second, inner court. At last, lying in the newly-watered earth beneath a wildly rambling rose, I was able to look through the arch.

It was like looking on to the stage of a theatre. The inner courtyard was tiled all over in blue and white, with raised flowerbeds walled in coloured bricks. In the centre, a languid fountain wavered, its plume a few weak inches of spray: the cistern that fed it was obviously very close at hand. A verandah ran like an arcade all round the walls of the court, and beyond the fountain, standing forward from the principal living quarters of the fortress, was a sort of pavilion. Four fretted columns held up a peeling gilded dome above a floor laid with carpets and overstuffed cushions, among which small lamps burned sweetly. The back of the pavilion was an openwork grille that enclosed, I guessed, the harem, for several small fingers gripped the trellis, and the occasional flash of dark eyes could be seen in the shadows. They were watching, like me, the figures who reclined among the cushions: a plump Persian in a long, loose, embroidered shirt and baggy trousers; a middle-aged man with protruding eyes, in a European suit but with a felt tarboosh on his head; and Tatiana, in a Persian gown of rich blue silk, with a veil of the same colour thrown half across her face.

Even as I watched her, I marvelled at her self-possession. Kidnapped from her hotel – from *my* bed – carried off into captivity to be debauched by this elderly international playboy, destined to be incarcerated for ever, perhaps, in the harem of this desolate place, she could not know that I was close at hand, ready to rescue her. And yet she bravely chatted, smiled, and flirted, keeping her fear and her concern completely hidden from her captors.

Servants brought food: platters of steaming rice and dishes of stew, long skewers of delicately grilled meat and luscious vegetables. They brought them from the kitchen, passing within a foot or two of where I lay among the roses. The aroma of the food as they passed was torture, so that I was forced to gnaw at my filthy knuckles to keep from crying out loud, beseeching a scrap of meat like a beggar at the gate, the beggar that, at that moment, I truly resembled. Indeed, had I known Persian, I swear I would have risked discovery and risen to my knees to ask for food. And all the while Tatiana carried it off so well, eating with well-feigned appetite, chattering, fluttering her eye-lashes, toying so delicately with the emotions of the two men. I could hear nothing of what she or they said, but it seemed to me that Buzurg-Umid – if it were he – spoke no English or French, and that the Aga Khan – if it were he – translated for him.

Close on two hours went by. After the riding, and the wading in the water of the *qanat,* and the climbing up the shaft of the well, my legs felt as if they would never move again. It was not cold in the summer night air, and very gradually, as the talk went on inside the pavilion, and the dishes were cleared away and replaced by a great tray of fruit, by sweetmeats and coffee, my eyelids began to droop, my whole frame to twitch involuntarily, and within minutes I was asleep once more.

It was the petulant stamp of a horse in the stables that awoke me. The stage where I had watched Tatiana's perform-ance was empty, the lights out, the night silent. Stupid fool that I was, I had lost the opportunity of observing where she was locked up for the night. Both courtyards seemed deserted so, miserably, I creaked to my feet, cramped and crippled, and limped forward through the archway.

To the right of the empty pavilion a half-open door led into the back quarters of the fortress, and an ancient retainer lay snoring across the threshold. I stepped gingerly over him, and, to the left, a few yards inside the entrance, saw a low lamp burning in front of a door that was bolted on the outside. My heart leapt: if my guess about the grille at the back of the pavilion had been correct, then this door must surely lead into the harem. I did not hesitate. Drawing back the bolts, I eased the door open a few inches and slipped inside, hoarsely whispering Tatiana's name.

I found myself in a small bare vestibule. It was pitch dark, but some small light came through an openwork screen to my right. The air was filled with a distinctive musky odour, half animal and half cheap perfume. Once before, at the age of twelve or thirteen, I had smelt something rather like it, visiting three girl cousins, and playing hide-and-seek with them among the nursery cupboards of their house outside Breslau. I crept forward, into a wide low room, faintly lit by a flickering lamp, which seemed to be carpeted with dark forms that hissed, snorted and sighed. I whispered Tatiana's name again, and there was a muffled exclamation in the dark, a quick question and answer, an outburst of stifled giggles, and then the lamp was extinguished, and I was taken prisoner by a dozen arms and half as many bodies.

I cannot tell you even a part of what I experienced in the next few minutes. Suppressed laughter bubbled all about me; soft cheeks brushed my unshaven ones and whispered unintelligible enticements in my ear; experienced hands examined me in every part. All my clothes were stripped from me in seconds; only by a miracle I kept my gunbelt, no doubt because its buckles were too stiff for delicate fingers. Persuasive hands took mine and guided them on intimate explorations – I suspect of bodies other than their owner's – and all the time there was a scarcely contained low hubbub of giggles, and murmured exclamations of admiration, and question after question, none of which I could understand.

And then I felt a pair of questing lips, profiting from an excitement I could not quell, take me prisoner as I had never been seized before. My arms were held wide by dim chuckling ghosts, my thighs embraced by hands and legs and shifting breasts, my feet seemed rooted to the floor – and still those lips stroked, and a tongue tentatively touched, as a small child eagerly tastes a stick of sugar candy, and tiny teeth lightly nibbled . . . The spell was broken by a girl, perhaps more intelligent than the rest, or perhaps only envious, who asked me in halting English:

'Why – you – here?'

'I look for girl,' I answered – a reply which, translated, provoked the laughter to a higher pitch. With an immense effort of will, and some physical force, I dragged myself from my restraints. 'English girl?' I added, rather belatedly.

'Oh, *her*,' said my interrogator with scorn. 'You want her? Come.' She took my arm in the gloom and, brushing aside some of her more importunate companions, led me back to the harem door. 'There,' she said, pointing; 'that door at end.'

I took my first and last look at her: a little over five feet tall, rather too plump, but with magnificent dark eyes and an imperious nose. She was naked except for a pair of near-transparent ballooning trousers, and her breasts were very fine, with rich wine-red nipples; but when she realised that I could see her in the thin light of the corridor she screamed faintly, put one hand to her face, and vanished into the darkness behind her.

Very gently, I closed and bolted the harem door. I was now extremely apprehensive: the old servant still slept on the threshold, but I felt sure that the noise in the harem would soon attract the attention of someone, perhaps of the master of the establishment itself, and I was very conscious of how vulnerable I was, standing naked except for two revolvers in the corridor of a house to which I had not been invited. I tried the next door with greater caution that I had tried the last: the experience in some ways had been very pleasant, but I had no desire to go through it again.

This door, however, was unbolted and opened, not into another part of the harem but into one of the guest-rooms of the house. Once again I was compulsively reminded of my childhood: of nursery games at Christmas in the old house, of shadow play with a candle and a stretched sheet – the butterfly, the eagle, the rabbit and the old Turk's head. The wall before me was half lit by a flickering lamp that stood low on the floor beyond a wide divan somewhere to my right, casting a grotesque silhouette that rose and writhed before my eyes. There were knees and thighs lifted high, and the swelling pattern of breasts and nipples, and above them an obese shadow that supported itself on stick-like arms, and a black tumescent shape that thrust forward and down. The air was full with heavy breathing and guttural endearments, and thick with half-known scents.

I swung to the right, my throat tight with apprehension. Spread-eagled on the divan, naked and rosy, was Tatiana with her eyes closed, and above her a fat, old, slobbering Persian, naked as she. In two steps I was at the bed, and had seized his arm below the shoulder, and swung my fist hard to the corner of his jaw, once, twice, three times and let him go, so that he fell, rolling to the floor, and lay there sprawled unconscious.

I dragged Tatiana unresisting from the bed, so that her feet rested on the floor by the old man's head, and shook her until she stood up. I took a pillowcase and stuffed into it whatever I could find lying about, the bed cover and a small rug. I seized her hand, and dragged her from the room. The corridor was still deserted, the door-keeper still asleep, the courtyard beyond the door empty and dark. Still tugging at Tatiana's hand, I made her run across the court, through the arch, to the head of the well. Both naked, with no shoes to our feet, we made little sound, and nobody challenged us.

Then, to this lovely girl still drowsy and scarce recovered from the terror of the assault upon her innocent body, I explained as quickly as possible: I would go down the well first, lowering the bucket to the bottom and making it fast, and then hold the rope steady so that she could follow me. She nodded and smiled sleepily. I threw the stuffed bag of oddments down the well, swung my legs over the rim, and followed it. In a few seconds I was at the bottom and, tilting back my head, whispered, 'Now!'

As I have said, we were both naked. Perhaps it was pride at having succeeded in rescuing her from her abductors, or perhaps it was the stimulation, so far unresolved, that I had experienced at many hands in the darkness of the harem: but, as I waited there at the bottom of the well, my feet in the water and my thighs astride the rope, my hands holding it taut, suddenly I was aroused as I have never been since. Tatiana came down the rope hand over hand, gripping it only now and again with her knees, her silhouette filling the dark above my head. When she was close to me she let the cord slip between her hands, sliding down in front of me with a little sigh, her legs flung wide to balance her each side of the rope . . .

We clung together and laughed and laughed. 'I thought it was all a dream,' she said. 'And such a surprise at the end of it. But where am I? And why?'

I told her how Clark and I had set out to rescue her from her kidnappers, how I had struggled along the *qanat,* how I had climbed the well and waited in the courtyard. I did not mention the harem.

She kissed me thoughtfully: 'And what shall we do now?'

'We dare not wait here any longer, since your disappearance may soon be discovered. But I have lost my only lamp' – I did not tell her where! – 'so we shall have to creep along slowly in the dark, and hope that Clark has found some rope.' I did not add that I began to fear that we would see him no more, and that I did not know how we would ever get out of the *qanat.*

Our bag of clothing was soaked through, so we did not dress, but dragged the bag behind us through the water. We went very slowly, for I had to feel the roof of the tunnel every inch of the way, and even so I bumped my head painfully several times. An hour went by and then, stumbling round a bend in the *qanat,* I caught a first glimmer of light where the tunnel must run out into the well down which I had first lowered myself. The light was reflected off the water, and almost immediately it vanished once again, but I stepped forward more boldly. Tatiana was close behind me, her hand on my shoulder, but the darkness and the cold and the wetness all about us were so depressing that for most of the way we had gone in silence. Suddenly, we came out into the well: I had expected it to be early morning, the first light ricocheting down the shaft to show me the next stage of our escape, but it was still black night, and only the opening out of space before me told me where we were. What, then, was the light that I had seen?

At this moment a mouth about three inches from my ear hissed menacingly in Persian. I swore briefly in German, stepping back in alarm and bumping heavily into Tatiana, who shrieked.

'Ah, I wondered if it might be you,' said Clark. 'Let's 'ave a dekko at you.' He struck a match, and held it to a candle in a small lantern. Tatiana gave another shriek and clutched the sodden pillowcase of clothing to her breasts. 'Now don't you concern yourself about me, little lady,' Clark said. 'I've been in more dressin' rooms than you've had hot dinners. I'll just look

137

the other way – and do meself out of a bit of real pleasure,' he added quietly to himself.

I told him briefly how things had gone since we parted, and he told us how he and The Refuge of Allah had been unable to find any ropes but, wandering in the desert, had come across the next well, which had fallen in so badly that it was easy to climb down on the tumbled stones. And so, with Nobby Clark leading with his feeble candle lantern, and me bringing up the rear with our bag, we set off trudging, heads well down, for nearly another mile along the *qanat*. Dawn was breaking as we scrambled up the fallen well, which lay like a great shell crater to the open sky, and while Clark and The Refuge of Allah went discreetly off to light a fire for breakfast, Tatiana and I emptied the pillowcase of wet remnants and dressed as well as we could.

For my part I had only the bed cover, wrapped loosely about me, and the rug, which I tied about my waist like one of the Scottish 'devils in skirts' whom I had seen being marched prisoner along the roads near Cambrai. Tatiana tore a strip from her hem and wound it about my head as a passable turban, but I must have looked a seedy ruffian.

As I have said, we towed the pillowcase through the water for nearly two miles, and when we emptied it we found several fish among the folds. They were nine or ten inches long, and a dead white in colour. It was their existence without light in the depths of the earth which had affected them in this way, for their eyes were blank as if they were blind. We took them to the fire and grilled them for breakfast. They tasted wonderful.

After we had eaten and drunk, we lay resting for a few minutes before setting off for Kazvin. Tatiana was beside me, and she reached out her hand and laid it on my arm.

'Simon, my dear,' she said, 'I don't quite know how to tell you this. But I wasn't a prisoner there at all. I was an invited guest. I left a letter for you at the hotel – I can't understand why you weren't given it, but perhaps you forgot to tip the porter. And you know,' she said, a teasing frown clouding her face, 'I was really beginning to enjoy myself. I think the Aga Khan is quite a dear old man.'

For most of the next four days I did not speak to her: I sulked, spending much of my time watching the riggers at work on the 0/400. I had missed my tiger hunt with Macdougall, who also sulked. Tchaikovsky, who had been abandoned in the throes of dystentery for two days, had good reason to sulk too, but made matters even worse by being forgiving and solicitous. Tatiana went off on thoroughly unsuitable expeditions to the bazaars with Clark. It was not until Tuesday afternoon that we made it up, and in the evening Dunsterville sent Mosky to request me to make my promised flight to the Menjil bridge, which Bicherakov hoped to storm the following morning.

CHAPTER 10

12 June: Kazvin – Menjil Bridge – Kazvin

BY DAWN the 0/400 was fuelled, trim in every singing wire, and ready to go; and, in two respects, better provided than I could have hoped. As soon as we had landed at Kazvin the week before, the Lewis guns had of course been dismounted and stored in the armoury, together with our bags of golden sovereigns. For nearly an hour, the evening before, I had argued obstinately with Mosky, who had been very insistent that we were not to attack the Jangalis from the air, but merely to 'buzz' them, and who had wanted me to fly unarmed; while I had pointed out that I could not be sure that von Passchen would not have the support of an Albatros or two from the Turkish advanced positions south of Tabriz, and I did not intend to be shot down (and particularly not by men whom I had some intention of joining!). In the end he had agreed, and signed the order releasing my guns and ammunition; and the sergeant at the amoury, with only one entry in his book under my name, had cheerfully given orders for the bags of gold to be loaded as well. To man the guns I had a Cossack lieutenant who

had ridden in during the afternoon with despatches for Dunsterville, and a sergeant observer who knew the course we had to
make for the Menjil bridge. Tchaikovsky naturally flew as my
co-pilot, and Macdougall was to accompany us in a Martinsyde.

I spent most of the night making my fondest farewells to
Tatiana, for I might never see her again. I had still not
determined irrevocably to escape; but I decided that I would
reconnoitre the Jangali positions, land the Cossack as close to
his comrades as possible, order Tchaikovsky to the nose and the
observer to the rear cockpit, so that neither would be too sure
about the course I was taking until it was too late, and, under
pretence of having made a terrible error in navigation, land the
aircraft at a spot close behind the Jangali lines. There I would
hold both men prisoner at the point of my newly-acquired
Webley until help arrived.

When we reached the field it still lay in the purple of night,
although the larks high above were already in sunlight, singing
for another day. Then suddenly they skittered down the breeze,
silent, as even higher, golden in the full morning, an eagle
sailed disdainfully overhead. And when the eagle was gone, the
renewed song of the larks was lost in the roar and clatter of our
engines, as first the 0/400 and then the Martinsyde rose to join
them.

We followed the road, which ran straight north-west across
the plain, rising gradually to cross a narrow saddle about fifteen
miles distant. Beyond the pass, it began to wind steadily
downhill, a grey trace on the brown earth, joined here and there
by the flicker of trickling streams that added gradually to the
flow of the Rud-e-Molla-Ali. With the advancing summer the
water was already failing, but it still ran swiftly deep in its bed of
tumbling stones. Skirting the road, it presented an impassable
obstacle to infantry or cavalry.

Beside the Rud-e-Molla-Ali the road, and our course, turned
due north for another fifteen miles until the Shah Rud, swollen
with the melting snows from the great Throne of Solomon a
hundred miles to the east, drew its thin white foaming line below
us, disappeared beneath the conduits of the village of Pul-i-
Loshan, and re-emerged to the left of the road on its last ten-
mile run to join the Sefid Rud at Menjil. A few minutes later we
passed above the waving Cossack rearguard, bivouacked on a

low bluff to the east, and saw the fields of Menjil ahead, sparsely green about the low houses of the village.

The road below was dark with Cossack squadrons, some of them dismounted, while others ranged the sloping foothills to our right. Directly in front, a low spur ran westward out of the hills, compelling the road to skirt it by a hairpin bend, the broad stony track of the river running close to the left. At the bend stood a low hovel, a *tchaparkaneh,* with a group of men on foot before it, obviously a forward picquet of the Jangalis. Then the fields broadened out on both sides of the road, which ran on to thrust its way between the houses of Menjil. Beyond the village, the mountains hedged in sharply from the right to meet the cliffs that formed the gorge through which the Sefid Rud cut its way to the sea. At the foot of these cliffs the strategic bridge was flung across the river bed in four steel spans. The road ran between the mountains and a small flat-topped hill, a *tel,* which extended about a half mile at right-angles to the road, and completely covered the approach to the bridge. On the top of this hill and on its upper slopes several thousand Jangalis had dug in, the Turkish flag waving over them in two or three places. I could see well-sited machine-gun pits crowded with excited figures, and elsewhere other Jangalis were scuttling to and fro.

We were above the plain at about 500 feet, the morning sun behind us. I led, with Macdougall some 200 feet behind me to my right, and slightly higher, so that he could see me in the cockpit beyond the blind of the 0/400's upper wing. I gave him a sweeping signal with my right arm, and began the run in. I followed the line of the road until we were over the village, and then took a slow lumbering turn, with Macdougall dropping in easily behind my tail, to coast the length of the low hill.

Chaos reigned among the Jangalis. They could have seen few aircraft, and none the size of the Handley Page; they ran in all directions, believing that we were about to bomb them. We swooped lower, no more than 200 feet over their heads, thundering along the ridge, daring them to open fire. There was not a shot. We cleared the hill, swung over the open plain, and turned to make our return sweep. This time they were ready for us. Rifles popped on both sides of our course, a lone bullet ripped a triangular tear in the lower wing, and one clanged plaintively against our steel-plated belly. Someone managed to get the front legs of his machine-gun propped so high on the emplacement parapet that a burst of fire swept perilously close for a second. Macdougall told me later that our Cossack in the rear cockpit had contrived to draw his sword and wave it wildly shouting at the enemy below. Then we were clear of the hill and climbing once more, swinging right around the amphitheatre of the encroaching hills, our purpose accomplished.

I came low over the spur by the *tcharparkaneh,* circled, and found a long flat cultivated field beside the road which looked a possible landing place. I dropped down, running in as fast as I could, the nose well up and my hand on the throttle in case the ground was unsafe. Cossacks on ponies galloped toward us, reared and wheeled away again. The field seemed firm and level beneath the ponies' hooves, so, with my fingers crossed, I pulled the throttle lever back, putting my left hand to the ignition switch and cutting the engines as soon as the undercarriage touched the ground. The 0/400 rumbled, shuddered, slewed and skewed, dragged its tailskid through a tangle of low bushy plants, bounced forcefully several times on all its four wheels, and stopped. Macdougall in his Martinsyde zoomed low, dipped one wing in salute, and was off to report to Dunsterville in Kazvin.

The Cossacks were all about us as soon as the aircraft stopped rolling. The lieutenant came scrambling through from the rear cockpit and spoke excitedly with Tchaikovsky.

'You must go with him,' Tchaikovsky translated: 'you must report to General Bicherakov.' So, leaving my co-pilot and the sergeant to guard the aircraft, I dropped down through the belly trap-door, and, finding a spare pony, was soon cantering off with the lieutenant.

Bicherakov's troops were advancing in a tight mass along the road, jostling together and marching on each other's heels; the field-pieces dragged between them, ponies waiting on the flanks. To the left the river ran in its wide stone-tumbled gully, and across the narrow plain to the right rode the skirmishers and supporting troops of cavalry. Ahead rose the spur round which the road wound from sight. At every second I expected to hear the busy rattle of machine-guns from its slopes, for it dominated our approach, and I rode ready to fling myself from the saddle. But for some inexplicable reason von Passchen had stationed none of his Jangalis there.

The lieutenant and I pushed our way hurriedly through the slow-moving men, who were now almost brought to a halt by the inertia at the head of the column, where Bicherakov and his staff stood in some bewilderment, wondering what the enemy might have in store for them round the corner. No more than a hundred yards away, a tattered Turkish flag waved over the *tchaparkaneh,* where a dozen Persians, hung round with rifles and swords, stood brandishing their fists and shouting ferociously. The lieutenant reined in, dismounted and delivered his report in Russian, and for a moment Bicherakov turned and considered me, eyeing me shrewdly and nodding once. Then he quietly gave an order, and set forward once more.

He strode at the head of his men – the last place I would have expected to find a general – supporting himself, for he had been badly wounded in the legs earlier in the war, on a wondrously carved stick. And I suddenly remembered with affection and sadness the souvenir from the Schwartzwald that I had left behind on Cappy airfield. Despite his injuries he walked well, magnificently upright, his black hair bristling beneath his astrakhan cap; and behind him came his men, undisciplined, crowding together at their own pace, with one or two mounted officers, myself and the lieutenant among them. Still not a shot was fired, though I kept my hand on my Webley in its holster. And so we came face to face with the Jangali picquet.

For what happened next I must rely in part upon what was translated for me later, for I understood no Russian or Persian. Bicherakov spoke quietly, almost pleadingly, to the picquet commander, a wild, unshaven ruffian with huge drooping mustachios, and asked him why he stood there so threateningly. The poor fellow was nonplussed, for he too knew no Russian, but a Cossack officer obligingly translated for him.

The Persian scowled, showed his broken teeth, and shouted, and was interpreted: 'We are here to hold this post to the last drop of our blood!'

Bicherakov paused, turned slowly to look at his men with dramatically raised eyebrows, and then whirled on his toes, his crooked stick raised menacingly in the air, and roared:

'Get out of here, at once, you pigs!'

He needed no interpreter: there were perhaps five seconds of amazed silence, broken only by the grinding of the Cossacks heels on the dirt road behind us, and then the Jangalis turned as one man and fled.

A shout of laughter burst from the ranks; one or two of his men actually reached out and patted their general on the shoulder. Bicherakov limped forward to the *tchaparkaneh* and took a stool in the shade of its narrow verandah, where he could both look down the road ahead across the plain to Menjil and the flat-topped hill held by the main Jangali force, and look back at his steadily advancing column. The narrow bottle-neck between the spur on one side and the river bed on the other delayed the deployment of his troops, and a quarter hour passed before the infantry spearhead had formed up in the open, with the two armoured cars at its head. The Cossack cavalry and the British hussars spread left across the plain against the enemy's right flank, and the Russian gunners were hauling their pieces up onto the crest of the spur. There they found good positions higher than the top of the enemy hill, which, at a range of about two miles, gave them the sort of target artillery-men dream of but very seldom find.

When the dispositions had been completed, and the last orders were being given, we suddenly saw a small mounted troop coming toward us down the road, under a large white flag. Even at a mile, I could recognise the field grey of the man who rode a large dun mare at the troop's centre. Bicherakov rose, and with his staff walked forward until he stood once more at the head of his men, covered by the guns of the leading armoured car. Discreetly, I followed, leaving my pony tethered to one of the posts of the *tchaparkaneh* verandah.

Von Passchen was the worst type of German career officer, running to fat and sweating heavily in the morning sunshine, pompous and humourless, puffed up with dignity, in the uniform of the 4th Brandenburg, with major's bars. He remained mounted as he addressed Bicherakov disdainfully in German. Although he had a disgusting Bavarian accent, it brought a lump to my throat to hear my mother tongue spoken by a compatriot again.

'The Jangalis are, as you can see, very strongly entrenched before you, and the troops at your disposal will not be sufficient to move them from their position. Any attack you may therefore see fit to undertake is doomed to failure and can only result in unnecessary loss of life. Mirza Kuchik Khan therefore empowers me to make the following offer to you. If you will dissociate yourself from the English, he will gladly allow you a free road to Enzeli, for he has always regarded the Russians as his friends and continues to do so; his quarrel is only with the English. Your men may pass down the road, without disarming, in batches of 200 daily and the Jangalis will not molest them. But no Britisher will be allowed to pass.'

I certainly needed no interpreter for this speech, nor did I need one for Bicherakov's reply: he clearly had great difficulty in restraining himself in the face of the man's studied insolence, and the suggestion that he would be prepared to let his men go to an uncertain fate 200 at a time. He spoke icily in Russian for a few seconds, spat on the ground at the feet of von Passchen's horse, and defiantly turned his back, raising his arms and roaring out his orders. The little troop wheeled their horses and clattered away, and hardly had they cleared the field of fire before the guns spoke on the spur above our heads, and we saw the first ranging shots throw up their plumes of dirt against the lower slopes of the Jangali position.

Orders and wild Russian cries rang out on all sides. The cavalry put heels to their horses' flanks; the armoured car drivers let up clutch and stamped foot to accelerator; and the Cossack infantry, shouting madly and whirling their swords, spread out at a run across the flat ground toward Menjil. The guns had found their range, and shells were plunging right among the shallow enemy trenches; clouds of smoke rose from the spur, and cast a fitful shadow where I stood. Impulsively, I grabbed a pair of field-glasses from a Cossack officer standing beside me, and, before the first wave of the attack was halfway toward the flat-topped hill, I could see the Jangalis scrambling from their positions and running down the slopes to reach the bridge, while the armoured cars and their supporting cavalry drove hard to cut them off.

So ended the battle for Menjil Bridge. I could not believe my eyes. More than 5,000 well-armed men, under the command of a German officer, had abandoned their positions. They had deserted machine-guns which would have held up the Cossack advance for many hours and indeed might have prevented the taking of the bridge. And they had done this almost without firing a shot. Major von Passchen escaped, galloping his horse across the bridge only seconds before the armoured cars reached it, and hundred of Jangalis were cut off, killed, wounded, and captured in dispirited bands.

You can imagine my state of mind. I stood at the road's bend, in that sudden glorious silence when the guns cease firing, with all my plans destroyed. Was that scurrying mob the superior force that I had seriously considered escaping to join? How could I throw in my luck with such a cowardly rabble, give up my honourable mission to rescue the Tsar, and condone this ignominious defeat? Well, I had delayed my final decision and now my mind was made up for me.

I remounted my pony and sought out Bicherakov. He was still on foot, well behind his triumphant men who ran every way across the fields shouting with victory, but limping fast to keep up with them, his staff solicitous about him but not daring to offer a hand. Sweat streamed down his face, creased with pain and fatigue, but his eyes were bright. I saluted him stiffly, then leaned down from the saddle to shake his hand, before I turned my mount and galloped back, up the road, round the bend past the *tchaparkaneh,* and on through the rearguard stragglers until I found the 0/400, already dragged round at the end of the ground where I had landed and ready for take-off.

With Tchaikovsky's help I recruited Cossacks to swing over the engines, and man the rocks that we were forced to use as chocks. Crouching low, although our under-wing was well above their heads, they trundled the rocks aside. We bumped, bounced, dangerously tilted a wing-tip close to the ground, recovered, roared desperately as I took the engines up to full revs, and at last lifted off in heavy dignity back up the valley towad Kazvin.

An hour later I was with Dunsterville and Mosky, Tatiana at my side and Tchaikovsky in the background. Macdougall had already delivered his report on the Jangali dispositions, but Dunsterville waited with unconcealed impatience for the outcome of the battle.

'Pon my sainted Sam!' he exclaimed as I entered his room; 'I thought you'd never get here. Come on, now, out with it! How have we done?'

I gave him every detail. As I came to Bicherakov's spurning of von Passchen, and the taking of the bridge, he put his arm about Mosky's shoulders.

'Fids! Fids! Oh fids!' he cried. 'I gloat! Hear me gloat!' and then – a most extraordinary thing – he briefly let loose some kind of strangled alpine yodel: *tu-ra-lu-ra-li-i-ay* – before, blushing scarlet, he restrained himself. 'And how about Kuchik Khan?' he asked. 'Haven't we got him on the Caudine Toasting-fork?'

Then he stopped suddenly, and looked quite crestfallen: 'Oh, if only I'd been there with my camera!' It was true: wherever he went he took with him his big black reflex camera and his boxes of plates. He had told me, the evening before, in a rare, relaxed moment of confidence: 'I've got it all planned, you see. They'll retire me, little doubt about it, soon as this show's over. And what am I goin' to do then? I'm goin' to travel round England, givin' lantern lectures about me adventures – India, China, Persia, Russia. Teach 'em something about the British Empire, what?'

Now was the moment to tell him that I intended to leave for Russia as soon as possible.

'Will you be goin' anywhere near Baku?' asked Mosky eagerly. 'Got to get messages to the vice-consul there, MacDonell; and a letter to Shaumian, the commissar there, if he's still in power. Never know with these bolshie fellers: they all sit round in committee and vote before they'll agree to obey the order to stand at ease.'

I told him that I did not yet know my route; Tatiana had final sealed orders for me which I would open at the hotel. And beside, I added, I must take the shortest possible course, because I was worried about getting further supplies of fuel for the aircraft.

'Then go to Baku, man!' burst out Dunsterville. 'Go to Baku! Bloody stuff comes out of the ground there!'

As soon as we reached our room in the hotel, Tatiana took her modest canvas valise, unstrapped it, and, with a pair of nail scissors, opened one of the inner seams. From within she took a strangely bulky package of brown manila, tied about with pink tape and sealed at every point with red wax marked with the English royal cipher. When she handed it to me I weighed it in

147

my hand for some moments.

My orders were short and precise. I was indeed to fly to Baku, 'with all due dispatch', and from there find the most practicable route round the north-eastern edge of the high Caucasus to Ekaterinodar. After securing the release of the imperial family, 'by whatever means possible', I was to return to Kazvin with them, where arrangements would be made to accommodate them until they could be transferred by road to Baghdad, and so down the Tigris to a waiting cruiser at Abadan. I was to deliver the 0/400 to Baghdad, and there await further orders. The only maps provided for me were some sheets torn from a Baedeker's guide to Russia.

It was the accompanying envelope, again sealed, that had made the package bulky. I thumbed it open and out tumbled a familiar cross of blue and gold, with its black and silver ribbon, and its motto *'Pour le Mérite'*. It was the Blue Max. I turned it over, and there, sure enough, engraved on the back, my own name! There was a folded sheet of paper with it. I opened it up, saw the English royal arms in red, and the simple address, 'Buckingham Palace, London,' and read:

'To the Freiherr Manfred von Richthofen. I am instructed by His Majesty to wish you every success in your daring attempt to rescue the imperial family of Russia, whose present sufferings are constantly in His Majesty's thoughts. It gives His Majesty great pleasure, therefore, to restore to you your country's highest award for gallantry, in the hope that you may find occasion to wear it once more in happier times. (Signed) Hardinge of Penshurst, ADC to HM.'

I was amazed. What extraordinary people these English were. I was their enemy, and yet they treated me with honour, and placed their greatest confidence in me. If I had still felt any temptation to desert them, this generous gesture would have removed all doubts for me. Slowly, I put the Blue Max about my neck with both hands. Tatiana moved toward me, kissed me gravely, and bobbed the ghost of a curtsey. Then she stepped behind me, fixed the ribbon, quickly stripped me of my khaki drill, and we made sweet love once more on the jingling brass bed in the shuttered shafts of the midday sun, my Blue Max pressed hard between her high round breasts.

By six, as the first cooler shadows of the evening came

creeping into the hotel courtyard, Clark had still not been found. The seven men who had been sent to seek him out had scoured the *souk* from end to end. They spoke little or no Persian, of course, and had done hardly more than strut through the bazaar, gently elbowing the inhabitants aside; but it seemed unlikely that he was lurking there. At seven a Ford van took me out to the airfield for a last check, with Tchaikovsky, that the 0/400 was ready. Soon after nine, as night swept in from the east, we were back at the hotel, but still Tatiana had no report on Clark's whereabouts.

We were standing in the hotel hallway, the three of us, anxiously discussing what we should do next, when the confused evening murmur beyond the gate began suddenly to swell. We heard distant angry cries, the nearer slap of bare feet on the street – and then Clark's half-naked figure, glittering with sweat, dusted over here and there, burst into the courtyard.

His eyes were wild, his arms and back bleeding, and he gasped out: 'Fer gawd's sake, you gotter hide me!' We bustled him through the doors of the hotel, but even as we did so the front runners of a furious mob were at the gate.

'The roof! the roof!' exclaimed Tatiana, and we dragged Clark as quickly as we could up the narrow winding stair. At the first landing Tchaikovsky turned bravely:

'I will hold them off,' he explained dramatically, and began a stately descent, twirling his moustache with a grand gesture, as we hurried on up the second flight.

'What have you done?' I asked. 'Oh, she was a lovely girl,' panted Clark; 'told me her husband wouldn't be home for hours. Little vixen! ripped me back to shreds!'

We burst out of the rickety wooden door onto the flat roof of the hotel. From the floor below we could hear the shouts of the pursuing husband and his friends, like hounds upon the scent. Clark ran to the parapet, and looked despairingly around: the nearest roofs were twenty feet away and below.

'The cistern!' cried Tatiana. In the far corner of the roof stood a stone cistern some five feet high. Every evening a wretched child pumped water from the yard below to afford a mean trickle to our washbasin tap. We ran to it, and shouldered Clark into the dark depths; only his lips, nostrils and eyes showed above the water, and as we slid the heavy wooden cover back

149

into place we heard him sigh: 'She 'ad a bum like a ripe water-melon, as the poet truly said . . . '

I hoisted Tatiana bodily on to the cistern's top, and scrambled after her, and I had scarce put my arms around her before the howling Persians were upon us. As calmly and as slowly as I could, I raised myself upon one elbow and stared at them. I was in my British khaki, while Tatiana, dishevelled and breathless from our flight, looked as if I were about to rape her.

'Now then, what do you think you're doing?' I asked, in my most peremptory British accent, and the mob skidded to a halt, rolling their eyes in amazement.

Two or three turned and ran to the parapet, and shouted in surprise, while their leader – the husband, no doubt – growled and barked a question at me in Persian. I knew very well what he asked, but I stared at him, and told him loudly and clearly in English that I didn't understand a word that he said. Someone giggled, another made a remark that evoked a howl of obscene laughter, and then they were all jostling at the stair door, roaring with rage and frustration, and in ten seconds we were alone again. Tatiana was crowing hysterically, her fingers were flying at my trousers, and my hands were as frantically dragging her long skirts above her waist, and then, both mad with laughter, we were at it on the warm, rough wood of the cistern lid, in the blue of the night below the blazing Persian stars, while Clark scrabbled with his nails and rattled with his knuckles a mere inch below us.

At last, all passion spent, we relented, and sliding tousled from the cistern's top we dragged the cover back. Clark rose from the water, dripping miserably, and stood there head and shoulders above the surface, shivering in dejection.

'Thanks,' he said. 'I've got to hand it to you. Very grateful I am, reely, very grateful. You're sure they've gawn? Oh, I never shoulda done it, but she was such a lovely little thing, and very willing. A little peach – and oh! what a pair! But did you 'ave to leave me in this damp so long?' His eyes were sunk into his gaunt face, his sodden hair streaked across his balding head.

Tatiana considered him coolly, as his soiled robes stirred in the water and the blood of his wounds seeped slowly. 'You know, darling,' she said, 'I think I may not want to wash tonight.'

Cautiously we eased the oozing Clark from the tank and led him to our room; down every step of the short flight of stairs he squelched and moaned, complaining that he was laying up rheumatism for his old age, that nobody knew what he had to go through, that he would never have left Baghdad if he had known what he would be reduced to . . . We wrapped him in a blanket and sent for the servant: Clark explained where his baggage had been left, and gave him some money, promising more on his return. Twenty minutes later he was dressed once more, in crumpled khaki from the bottom of his camel bag, and was already beginning to brag again about his latest conquest.

We found Tchaikovsky – 'No, of course I am not hurt. It was very simple, you know? As I went down the stairs I took out a cigarette, and as the mob came rushing up the stairs I stopped their leader and asked him for a light. Of course he had no light, but he politely asked among his friends for one. And by the time my cigarette was lit, I suppose you had Captain Clark well hidden' – and cheerfully we went to supper together in the hotel's stuffy dining-room.

We retired early to bed – Clark had grudgingly been given a tiny room by the hotel's proprietor – and I (for one) slept soundly, though I dreamed many dreams: of fleeing Jangalis and advancing husbands, of Bicherakov, shaking my walking stick at Karl Bodenschatz, while Clark sang 'Take a pair of sparkling eyes', and the Kaiser, naked and strangely like Dunsterville, put the Blue Max about my neck alone on a high roof beneath a dome of blazing stars.

A peevish scratching at our bedroom door, the jangling of the latch, and a sudden sweet aroma of hot coffee, told us that dawn was near. I shaved, Tatiana pouted at the darkly scummy water which ran thinly from the tap; we dressed, strapped up our baggage and crept to the hall, where Clark and Tchaikovsky already stood, talking in undertones to an English van driver. Twenty minutes later we were climbing aboard the 0/400, as the sun threw our long, cold, black shadows in front of us across the airfield.

I got both engines turning sweetly over, had taken a last look round and was about to raise my hand to signal for the ground crew to pull away the chocks, when Macdougall, who was standing beside the runway waiting to wave us goodbye, suddenly cocked his head skyward, semaphored his arms wildly, and pointed to the west. Coming in low above the plain, bright like a bee in the early sun and seemingly aimed straight at us, was a biplane. I recognised it instantly as a DH4: obviously it had flown up from Baghdad with urgent despatches.

Twitching with impatience, I watched the pilot bank it neatly above my head, to bring it bouncing down along the field in front of me. Even as the aircraft reached the far end of the field, turning to one side to taxi back, I gave the signal 'Chocks away!' and set the 0/400 trundling toward Baku. The DH4 slowed some way ahead of us, and a passenger in flying suit and helmet scrambled down from the rear cockpit, to watch us take off and wave us farewell. By now I was accustomed to letting my aircraft fly herself, and, as she lifted in that familiar shuddering movement, I glanced sideways and down at the figure. He had given up running and waving, and stood with his hands on his hips, looking up at us. There was something about the bow-legged stance, and the dark-tinted spectacles, tilted glittering upward in the early light, that seemed familiar.

CHAPTER 11

13 June: Kazvin – Baku

FOR THE first half-hour I followed the course that I had flown the previous morning, above the Rud-e-Molla-Ali to its junction with the Shah Rud, and then down the plains to Menjil, where the Sefid Rud thrust into its narrows. Close on both sides the mountains rose to over 8,000 feet, but between them I traced the gorge, running dark and winding for twenty miles before the hills began to fall away again. Then, dramatically, the landscape changed. Down the northern slopes thick forests spread, the first I had seen for nearly three weeks; and rich meadows; then we flew above Shahr Bijar, and beyond we saw the thin green of the rice fields in the river delta as it spread wider and wider in the low land.

Suddenly Tchaikovsky, who was beside me as navigator, gripped my left shoulder with his right hand and pointed ahead. Beyond the green horizon, half hidden as it was in a morning haze, a shimmering light seemed to be growing brighter every second. Then points of brilliance winked and blinked, and resolved themselves into a play of shining ripples like the skin of a new-caught trout, and Tchaikovsky smiled proudly at me, and cocked his head to stress the joke, and shouted 'Thalassa! Thalassa!'

It was the Caspian Sea, stretching northward in front of us, 700 miles deep into Russia. Yet for all its brightness in the early morning sun, it shone with a dull sullenness: not blue as the Mediterranean had been, but grey rather, like the Baltic, the *Ostsee* where I had been taken, one summer, as a child. We passed high over Resht, and in a few minutes crossed the coast and set a course due north for Baku, blundering steadily on over the water, as the land sank below the sky's rim behind us.

For over an hour we went forward, flying levelly over the great inland sea, which was hidden briefly from us now and then by a thin scattering of cloud. Once or twice we spotted gunboats, fussily busy on the water as they trailed their long black plumes of smoke on the morning air. I handed over the controls to Tchaikovsky and crept back to the rear cockpit, where Tatiana, warm enough in her flying suit and thigh-high boots, had nevertheless chosen to snuggle into a blanket and was nearly asleep. I had been there only a few seconds when the cockpit was suddenly filled with torn shreds of racing fog, and I looked up to see that we were deep in cloud.

With a kiss on Tatiana's nose I turned back, and once with Tchaikovsky I checked our position as well as I could, calculated on the time of our flight since we had passed over Resht and the estimated wind speed and direction I had been given before we left Kazvin. We were nearing Baku, and I guessed that the cloud was building up where the land met the water. I leaned to my right and shouted in Tchaikovsky's ear that it was time for us to begin our descent, and then, routinely, I glanced for the first time at the altimeter. It read less than a hundred feet.

I screamed at Tchaikovsky to reverse my previous order, and then, dragging myself upright into the slipstream, I leaned as far over the side as I could. The cloud was not thick, and glowed brightly about us as the sun rose higher, but I could see nothing below, neither land nor sea. For more than two minutes, while I peered down and racked my brains, Tchaikovsky drove steadily forward on an even keel; but then I put my hand on his shoulder and asked him as calmly as possible (remembering our near escape over Normandy three weeks before) to make a slight descent. He looked at me, shrugged, pointed to the altimeter, smiled ruefully, and gently eased the nose of the 0/400 downward.

The cloud boiled about us; the altimeter needle shuddered down to zero and would have gone further but for its little brass stop; and still there was nothing to be seen – no glimpse of the earth below, no bottom edge of the cloud breaking briefly before it closed again like the eye of a sleeper momentarily shaken from his slumber. I recalled, suddenly, a time three years back when Erich von Holck and I had flown into the black smoke that piled above the burning city of Brest-Litovsk. In the heat of the fires the air had been so thin that we had seemed to drop down like a stone toward the flames beneath. The air so thin . . . and then a thought struck me. I am no mechanic: even in a lifetime of flying my understanding of aircraft has always lagged behind technical developments, and I am as dependent now on the work of the artificers as I was when I first flew; but I know how an altimeter works. It is like a little aneroid barometer – one of those you tap in the hall before you leave for a picnic. It measures the air pressure and so tells you how far above the ground you are; and, because barometric pressure can vary greatly from day to day, before every flight the altimeter must be adjusted to ground zero. At Kazvin the field lay at some 4,000 feet above sea level, but the Caspian is nearly ninety feet below; in the course of our morning flight our ground zero had fallen by about 4,100 feet!

In relief I laughed, startling poor Tchaikovsky; and then I bent toward his ear and quickly explained my theory. He looked

154

doubtful, but continued to let the aircraft slide gently down through the cloud, while we both leant anxiously on the cockpit rim and scanned the blankness simmering around us. And then at last, as the mistiness clears from a window on which you have breathed, so the cloud parted and the land below came slowly sharper into view at what looked to be about 2,000 feet below us.

We were flying above the edge of the coast, where the salt marshes and the delta of the river Kura merge almost imperceptibly with the sea. On the horizon ahead the sharp far eastern ridge of the Bolshoi Kavkaz, the high Caucasus, ran down to Baku. Somehow I would have to find a way through, round or over the mountains, which continued to rise steadily away to our left. At their narrowest, from Tiflis at the head of the Kura valley, they were not much more than a hundred miles across, but at that point they were also at their highest, where Kasbek soars over 18,000 feet into the icy blue. And the Turks were in Tiflis, and all along the railway nearly to the sea.

'Call Tatiana!' shouted Tchaikovsky; 'You must call her at once! That is Mother Russia that lies before us!'

But she was already awake when I found her in the rear cockpit, her rosy face flooded with tears. I put my arm about her shoulders and kissed her gently, and I thought of my own home far away in Silesia. But, to tell the truth, the coast of the Caspian looks no more like Russia – and I, after all, had served for some months on the eastern front – than Silesia, and soon I was puzzling once more over how I was going to find my way to Ekaterinodar.

The land to our left was now curving ahead, and against the foothills of the Caucasus I could see the town of Baku rising from the sea. I kissed Tatiana once more, and then went forward again to consult with Tchaikovsky. Our destination now lay clear before us. From the foot of the mountains a low-lying peninsula slid some twenty miles eastward into the sea, with a scatter of islets off its extremity. Round a bay at the westward end of this peninsula, the town rose in tier on tier like the seats of a theatre. An old and partly-ruined citadel dominated the town on its western side, and below it a massive and Moorish-looking tower reared high into the air. At the end of the bay nearest us, where the ground lay low and a string of salt lakes glittered in the hot haze, we saw the first cluster of oil derricks. They stood in close rows, strangely high and narrow wooden pyramids, and I was reminded once more of the pictures in my nursery reading book, the crowded tepees of the gathered Sioux.

Along the seafront of Baku ran a broad promenade, and Tchaikovsky now banked the 0/400 gently to starboard, so that we flew parallel to the shore of the bay. There were many trading steamers and fishing boats tied up along the quays, and we were low enough to see that we were attracting a great deal of attention. At the eastern end of the quays we passed the railway station, and saw beyond it another town, low and dirty and crowded round a vast sooty factory, looking very much like the gasworks at Potsdam. Later we learned that this was Tchorni Gorod, Black Town, and that the factory was the Nobel oil refinery. Further east along the peninsula lay the so-called Byeli Gorod, or White Town, another refinery establishment: it was not, however, any cleaner.

I was anxious to find a landing place as distant as possible from any town or major village, and yet not too far from Baku for communication. We could now see the whole peninsula below us: the big salt lakes behind the town, the copses of derricks, the railway, the tangle of oil pipes running beside it from the oilfields to the refineries, and the flat and treeless lands further to the east. Straggling across the waste, passing several villages and then coming to an indeterminate end at a very small group of derricks, ran one branch of a single-track railway. I signalled to Tchaikovsky that we would land close by.

In spite of the skill that he had shown in his first flight at Baquba, I had not until now allowed my co-pilot to land the 0/400, and my heart was in my mouth – almost literally, for we seemed to be dropping much too fast – as he brought the huge aircraft down toward a level and featureless tract that stretched before us for a half-mile or more. But he set it neatly upon its wheels and skid as if he had been doing little else for weeks. The ground, though sandy, had a strange soft sponginess to it, and this was fortunate, for we had digging to do.

This was the very first landing we had made without the assistance of a ground crew, or at least of willing hands to hold and moor our aircraft, and we were now entirely dependent upon it for our safety. The name of the town of Baku comes from the ancient Persian *badkube,* a squall, for the north-western winds that prevail in Transcaucasia come suddenly and gustily over the water, and I knew that it was essential to peg down the 0/400 securely. But such a big and heavy craft is not like the Fokker Dr 1, for the most important point to remember in pegging down is that the machine should be raised as near as possible to the flying position, and there was no way in which we could lift the tail to such a height. So the only thing to do was to dig deep, broad trenches for the wheels of the under-carriage. In any event, this was a safer plan: it brought the whole aircraft nearer the ground and also made it impossible for the machine to be blown sideways.

Fortunately, we were provided with all the necessary equipment: two shovels, some pieces of canvas, and all the rope and pegs we could use. Tchaikovsky and I had soon grubbed out deep hollows for the under-carriage, and dragged and trundled the 0/400 into them with the help of Tatiana and Clark, the latter creaking and groaning as loudly as the fuselage itself. Then, from the rings beneath the wing struts, we led out rope fore and aft to deep-driven pegs, leaving just a little slack to allow the aircraft to rock gently. I wrapped canvas round the fuselage in front of the tail, took a couple of turns of rope round it, and pegged them each side; and I also led rope from the tail skid to other pegs. While Tchaikovsky muffled the engines and propellers with additional pieces of canvas to keep out some of the sand and damp, I led another rope from the nose to two pegs in front of the machine. Finally, I strapped the controls, lashed down the elevator control to give as little incidence to the wind as possible, and buttoned the covers over the three cockpits.

By the time we had finished it was an hour or more past midday. We had worked alone on the desolate plain, under the hot sun but cooled by the sighing breeze, while Tatiana and Clark laid out for us a simple lunch of goats cheese, unleavened bread and Kazvin wine. The head of the oil derricks showed distantly on the horizon, and once a railway engine had howled mournfully out of sight, but of Russians there was still no sign. It was only as I stuffed the first piece of cheese and bread thankfully into my mouth that Clark seized my arm and pointed westward, to a growing cloud of dust on the track that ran toward us.

We abandoned our meal, rose to our feet, and tidied ourselves as best we could. Tchaikovsky was in his Russian uniform, from which he had ripped his rank badges and the imperial eagle; Clark had given up his Arab robes for a motley of Cossack clothing – breeches, a short lambskin jacket, a labyrinth of belts and a pair of battered black British boots; I wore my very crumpled khaki drill and a pair of kneeboots with laces; and Tatiana was barefoot in her cotton boilersuit.

The dust cloud came closer, and revealed at its centre a motor car; behind it and around it trotted half a dozen horsemen. The car was a Ford model T, caked in mud; across its bonnet a red flag was tied, two soldiers with rifles and fixed bayonets crouched on either running-board, and five figures were crowded into its seats. It bounced and squawked its way across the rough ground to stop juddering a few yards from us, while the riders made a half-circle at our rear.

A slim man of medium height was helped from the back seat. His hair was long, in wildly curling black locks, and he wore a long frogged Cossack coat of scarlet; his only mark of rank was the leather satchel that he kept clutched beneath his left arm. With four men levelling their rifles behind him, he walked slowly forward, his fierce eyes ranging over us as we stood stiffly in line before him. Then Tchaikovsky stepped toward him, with arms stretched wide; in four quick paces he reached him, flung his arms about him, and kissed him on both cheeks – that nasty Russian habit. Then he took a step back and, before the newcomer had recovered, he spoke.

I heard the names Dunsterville, and Kazvin, and Shaumian. Behind us the horsemen moved closer, their harness creaking and jingling, the ponies snuffling and shuffling the sand. I stood grinning inanely, and Clark scratched his crotch. The Russian still said nothing, only his eyes moving quickly from one to another, but one of his companions – a yellow-looking individual of unmistakable Tartar origins – muttered urgently in his ear. Someone spoke behind me, and was answered angrily by one of the soldiers; and then suddenly all were arguing fiercely, the official turning and shouting, little knots forming

158

and dissolving, arms waving, rifle butts grounded petulantly, the ponies urged from group to another, alternate glares and smiles flashed in our direction . . .

Then Tatiana ran forward, putting her arm about the official's shoulders; the word *tovarich* passed in the air from voice to voice. Tchaikovsky turned back, and took Clark and myself, one by each arm: 'Shake hands,' he hissed, and we shook – hands black with machine oil, and grey with dust, forearms that still crooked rifles, the official's fingers stained with ink. The argument went on, but now it seemed that a vote was to be taken. The official was allowed silence to make an impassioned speech, a soldier replied, Tatiana cried something that brought a relieved shout of laughter, Tchaikovsky spoke briefly with an emotion that caused his moustache to bristle and his eyes – and those of others – to fill with unshed tears. Some cried *niet,* and others *da;* clenched fists were raised, and at last an uneasy decision was reached.

'We must go with them,' said Tatiana.

In a silence of suspicion I was permitted to climb up into the 0/400 to collect my packet of letters; Tatiana already had the messages to McDonell hidden inside her flying suit. In the belly of the aircraft I looked around: piled with our valises were the twenty bags of gold, scarce depleted, and the spare boxes of Lewis ammunition. Two of the Russian soldiers shifted feet apprehensively below. I turned and, standing where I was, roared for Tchaikovsky.

'Jones?' His voice came distantly.

'I'm not coming down from this aircraft if I can't leave Clark to guard it!' I shouted, and dropped the trap-door in the upturned faces of the pair at the foot of the ladder. There was a chaos of voices outside; some booby tried to put a bullet through the floor at my feet, and must have recoiled in amazement as it whined off the steel plating.

'Simon!' It was Tatiana. 'What is it? What do you want?'

'I want to leave Clark here. The Russians can have as many men outside the plane to guard it as they like, but I want Clark inside to stop them climbing in and ransacking it. The three of us will stand hostage for him, and in any case there's little he can do by himself.'

Argument broke out again. I could hear the voices of both

Tatiana and Tchaikovsky, confident, persuasive, never merely pleading, and at last –

'All right, Simon, they agree. Open the trap-door and come down, and Nobby can go up in your place.'

I met Clark on the ladder, and warned him in an urgent whisper not to allow a single Russian into the aircraft; he had sufficient food, water and wine for a day or more, and we expected to return within a few hours.

'A nod's as good as a wink,' he told me. 'In for a penny, in for a pound – a sovereign leastways, if you get me drift. Take care of the pounds, eh – and the puns'll take care of themselves,' he concluded in a disconsolate mutter. Then he nudged me sharply in the ribs, scrambled through the trap-door, dropped it behind him, and a minute later was to be seen in the rear cockpit, nonchalantly polishing the Lewis gun barrel with a handful of cotton waste.

Three of the car's passengers were relieved of their seats; three of the mounted soldiers were detailed to keep guard on the aircraft, and their ponies requisitioned for the passengers to ride back to town. Then Tatiana, Tchaikovsky and I climbed into the Ford with the chief official and his bodyguard. His name, Tchaikovsky told me, was Petrov, and he was, with Shaumian, joint commissar of Baku.

The springs of the Ford were broken, the track on which we rode was deeply pitted and traced with ruts; our journey to the town was like a ride on the back of one of those broncos I was to encounter ten years later in the American rodeos. None dared speak for fear of biting off the tip of the tongue, or at least of bruising a lip. Several times Petrov half turned round in his seat to attempt to begin interrogating us, but each time he had scarcely opened his mouth before he abruptly shut it again, clasping his jaw with one hand while with the other he clung desperately to the handle of the car door. And in the back we three, our arms about each other, bounced up and down in unison.

The track ran gradually toward the south coast of the peninsula; through a small village, silent in the lunchtime sun, past the back of the White Town, and then headlong through the heart of the Black Town, noisy, grimy, reeking of oil. Then we were past the monumental railway station and running, on a properly surfaced road, along the crowded marine promenade, the crumbling town walls to our right. We turned off into the Lalayevski Proyezd, and drew up before the Hotel Europe.

Petrov wiped some of the dust from his spectacles with a red-and-white spotted handkerchief, and turned peremptorily to Tatiana.

'Well, well,' said Tchaikovsky, 'he's inviting us to meet the soviet, and deliver our message in person.'

We all struggled down from the car. Two soldiers slouched at the door shook their fists when they saw Petrov, but it was obviously some sort of salute, for he cheerfully returned the gesture – and so, to my momentary suspicion, did Tchaikovsky.

Entering the hotel was like walking into the tropical bird house of the Berlin zoo. The central court of the building rose three stories to a glass roof, with balconies running around it that gave access to the bedrooms. And the whole of this space, the ground floor, the winding staircases and balconies, was packed with a fluttering, chattering, arm-waving flock of bolsheviks, who vanished and re-appeared between the fronds of an infinity of potted palms. Soldiers lounged on flatulent sofas, their boots kicked to one side, and played cards or threw dice. Busy little men and women, almost indistinguishable in peasant blouses, ran up and down stairs with leather satchels, loose bundles of papers, trays piled high with dirty glasses and half-eaten meals. Committees convened themselves in corners, adjourned immediately on a point of order, and gathered and scattered like drops of oil on running water; bedroom doors burst open, to eject bearded men sucking pipes or cheap black cigars, who shouted furiously into the crowd below and at once disappeared again in a cloud of smoke.

As soon as Petrov appeared he was accosted by four people: a young girl in schoolteacher's clothing and pince-nez put her arm about his shoulders, two men in worn frock coats seized his hands, and an elderly woman in a huge shawl contrived to throw both arms about his knees. Tatiana and Tchaikovsky were both appealed to, and I had my lapels seized by a short and plump, hook-nosed petitioner, in shirt-sleeves and a little beaded cap, who leapt up and down before me and poured out a torrent of pleading.

I pushed him away, but he came at me again, pawing and

clawing. 'What in God's name does he want?' I asked Tchaikovsky, who was himself letting fly with a charge of ks and zs and ys.

'Ha! it was his car that they requisitioned to come and collect us, and now he wants to know is he ever going to get it back?' – and he returned to his own explanations, moustache bristling again, shoulders shrugging, arms waving . . .

Eventually Petrov shook off his petitioners, took the girl by the arm and led us, followed by two of the lesser officials who had ridden in behind, shouldering and elbowing into what had once been the grand salon of the hotel, a place for tango teas and discreet soirées. Undusted chandeliers hung from the smoke-grimed ceiling; the once polished floor, now boot-scarred, creaked beneath our feet; and the mirrors – one of them cracked and starred, apparently by a bullet – reflected a long T-shaped committee table at which men and women sat, slouched, snored, smoked, ate noisily, while one among them, standing, delivered an oration full of pathos and passion.

Around the table, which stood in the centre of the salon, dozens of curious bystanders were listening intently, nudging one another, occasionally breaking into vigorous applause. The crowd parted when we appeared, and places were found for us at the table; Petrov spoke quietly to one of his aides, and in a few seconds we each had before us some vodka in a rather greasy glass, a knob of coarse bread, some pickled herring and a slice of cheese. Meanwhile the speaker continued without pause, except to acknowledge with a nod of the head any approving comments that he heard from among his listeners.

Petrov was seated at the foot of the table, and I was close beside him; directly opposite and the length of the table from us, at the centre of the shorter table set across ours, sat the other commissar. This was Shaumian, a fierce-looking man with black shaggy eyebrows and moustache, and blazing eyes, wearing a striped grey suit with a waistcoat, a high tight collar with a broad loose tie, and a cloth cap. He sat well back in his chair, with his arms braced wide against the table, and shifted his head constantly to follow movements within the room, or to catch the various remarks that were being made. Every now and again he exchanged a stare full of meaning with Petrov, and once as I looked up from my plate he fixed my eyes for a full thirty seconds, wrinkling his nose and baring his teeth in a rabbit-like grimace that was both blank and questioning.

At last the speaker came to his peroration, stretched out both arms to embrace the salon, all Russia, the world, and, mopping his brows with the full cuffs that hung below his coat-sleeves, sat down to cries of mixed approval and opposition. Shaumian held up his hand for silence, and spoke scarcely above a whisper. I heard him name Petrov, and the whole room looked in our direction; I heard the words *angliski* and 'Dunsterville', and a shiver seemed to run the length of the table. Tatiana edged her chair closer to mine, and began to translate in a low voice.

'And who are they, these men and this woman? And where have they come from? From Dunsterville, Major-General Dunsterville, a bourgeois, one of the ruling class, a chief representative of the imperialists. They bring us letters, promising us help against the Turks – but if Dunsterville is to help us, then he must bring his soldiers here. Who knows how many? Hundreds? Thousands? And when the Turks are defeated – as they will be defeated! – will Dunsterville defend us against Denikin and his army of the counter-revolution? Oh no, comrades, he will not. Once they have set foot in Baku, the English will not leave again until they have crushed the people's revolution and restored the forces of capitalism and oppression. I tell you, we have the Red Army, and we do not need these agents-provocateurs among us! Let us send them away, in their great aeroplane, back to where they came from. Or should we look on them as Tsarist spies – and treat them as such?'

I clutched at Tatiana's hand: had we put our heads into the lion's mouth? But almost before Shaumian had ceased speaking, and while the crowd still growled and pointed at us, a soldier rose: he wore the imperial army uniform of a general, but the eagles had been removed and replaced neatly by five-pointed stars in scarlet felt. He was clean, well-brushed, newly-shaven, wearing gleaming white kid gloves – a striking contrast with the unkempt revolutionaries about him. Tchaikovsky whispered to Petrov, received a curt answer, and muttered to me: 'General Duchuchaiev, commander of the defending army.'

'Comrade Shaumian, Comrade Petrov, comrades of this

soviet of soldiers', sailors' and workers' deputies.' His thin, refined mouth seemed hardly able to bring out the words, and the expression on his face was one of vacuous distaste – not merely for the bolsheviks but for all these people below his contempt. The Turks, he said, were denied the use of the Trans-Caucasian railway by the terms of the German treaty with Georgia, but they were advancing fast down the road, and would be in Baku before the end of the month, unless he could find some armoured cars to hold them. While he had no doubt whatsoever of his ability – and that of his brave soldiers, he added grudgingly – to defend Baku and drive the Turks back from the Apsheron peninsula, nevertheless he would be grateful for all the arms and fighting men he could gather, even if they came from the English. Commissar Shaumian had mentioned this huge new aeroplane, for example; surely it was just what was needed to throw bombs at the Turkish advance troops? At least, let Dunsterville's letter be read, before any hasty decision was made.

Yes, came the cry from all around, read the letter! So I took out the oilskin package with its brittle seal, and handed it to Petrov, who broke it open and extracted a thin foolscap envelope, the red lines upon it finely drawn by the best pen of the corporal in the headquarters office. Petrov picked up the knife with which he had just been slicing cheese and slit the envelope along its length; then he took out the few sheets, written in Russian in Dunsterville's own hand, and began to read.

The letter told of the victory over Kuchik Khan at Menjil, and of Bicherakov's march to the sea, to take ship from Enzeli bound for Baku. At this point Shaumian interrupted, rising in the midst of enthusiastic hubbub to hold up his hand and speak loudly and clearly:

'Then we certainly do not need Dunsterville here! What are a few hundred English soldiers if we have Bicherakov and his ten thousand?'

Petrov remained standing, the letter still in his hand, but now a sailor – so far as I could tell, no more than an ordinary seaman – rose as well and drowned out Shaumian with a cheerful shout that was clearly more used to the gale-tossed yard-arm than the deliberations of the soviet.

'We shall defend Baku to the last drop of our blood!' he cried, striding to the end of the room where a map of the town and the surrounding hills hung. And there, for minute after minute, sweeping out lines a mile wide on the map with his broad tar-stained thumb, he harangued us all on the future strategy of the Turks, the proper disposition of the Baku defending army, and the best way in which aircraft could be used in the coming battle. Neither Shaumian nor Petrov – nor, indeed, Duchuchaiev – seemed surprised at this interruption; and the rest of the soviet responded enthusiastically at intervals to the sailor's appeals to their heroism, political acumen and revolutionary fervour.

After some time I could give no more attention to what this man had to say. I signalled to Tatiana to give up her translation and, I have to confess, fell instantly asleep, my head pillowed on my arms across the table, unconscious amid the empty glasses, the remains of herring, and the rinds of cheese.

CHAPTER 12

13-15 June: Baku – near Astrakhan

IT SEEMS that I slept for over an hour. Votes were taken. Should Dunsterville be allowed to come to Baku? The result was inconclusive. Should at least, the receipt of his letter be recorded in the minutes? The result was even more inconclusive. But, in the heat of this intoxicating democratic activity, we were forgotten, and I was awakened by Tchaikovsky shaking my shoulder gently and hissing in my ear: 'Come, quick, we can go now.'

I sat up sharply and looked about me. The room was nearly empty: Petrov, Shaumian and Duchuchaiev had gone, together with the voluble sailor and most of the deputies. Intermittent shouting from behind two gilt and mirrored doors at the end of the saloon indicated that they were still in plenary session. Here and there along the table others slumbered like me, but the crowd of spectators had drifted away, and the declining afternoon sun slid between the half-drawn velvet curtains to light little more than a galaxy of dancing dust.

I felt immensely refreshed. I took Tatiana's hand and urged Tchaikovsky forward: unmistakably Russian, and in a faded Russian uniform, he was certainly the least conspicuous of the three of us, and therefore walked in front. He spoke kindly to the sentries eating watermelon outside the door of the salon, frowned briefly at a lady typewriter who was shrilly berating another in the hotel foyer, and bowed us into the brass-bound revolving door.

Out in the street the sun still burnt fiercely, but a clammy breeze came off the sea, cutting through the strange sweet smell of crude oil that pervaded everywhere.

'I think a walk along the quays could be instructive,' said Tchaikovsky, and we strolled downhill, turning right when we reached the waterfront to continue our walk westward. The promenade was wide and unshaded. The crowd ebbed and flowed upon it: Cossacks, Tatars, Armenians, Persians, parted now and then by a car, or a bicycle, a horse-drawn cab, or a handful of camels. Steamers lay moored to the piers, and two or three gunboats of the Caspian fleet, and between them many small fishing boats with lateen rig.

It was a picturesque scene, and we were strolling slowly along to where the high old tower reared over the waterfront, when a dark young girl came quietly behind us and spoke urgently in Russian.

'Don't stop, don't turn round,' said Tchaikovsky between his teeth. 'Just keep walking, and I'll lead the way. This girl says that it is very important for us to go at once to the British consulate. I think she is telling the truth.'

We turned away from the quay and came, very shortly, to a street where broad, imposing apartment houses faced each other across the cobbles. Over the entrance to one of these buildings jutted a white flag pole, naked now, but beside the doorway a big bold oval plaque, in red and blue enamel, proclaimed this to be the residence of the British vice-consul. Our guide pushed open the door, which swung ajar, spoke ringingly in Russian to an old crone who appeared briefly in a dark alcove and led us quickly up the uneven stairs to a shadowy landing where she thumped heavily at the apartment door for some twenty seconds.

The man who opened the door was dressed in a knicker-bocker suit of pepper-and-salt tweed, not unlike that in which I had first set foot in England a month before. He was no more than my own height, and very lightly built, except for a leonine head with a mass of rich brown hair that waved luxuriantly, and an imperious nose. Our guide spoke quickly, intensely, laid her hand briefly upon his, and was gone, a flicker of shadow on the stairs. The vice-consul addressed us loudly and confidently in Russian, although I thought that even I could detect the English accent. But before he had said more than a few words Tatiana interrupted him, first in Russian and then, realising how unnecessary that was, in English:

'Oh! How terribly silly of me! May we come in? This is Captain Simon Jones, and this, Captain Pavel Tchaikovsky, and we've all come from Kazvin.'

The vice-consul replied in the neatest English I had heard since I left Whitehall, shaking our hands in turn as he did so: 'How very nice to meet you. I'm Randall MacDonell, coinciden-tally (you could say) the twenty-first chief of the clan Glengarry, and for the duration of this emergency, in fact, no longer the vice-consul but a captain in the I Corps. But please come in and make yourselves at home. We have, I fear, very little to offer you in the way of refreshment; my apartment has become a sort of staging-post for refugees, secret agents and conspirators, and it seems they all have to be fed and watered. But we do have some champagne – quite a lot of champagne, to be precise – if you would like a drop. Rather warm, I'm afraid: no ice to chill it, but it's still refreshing, what?'

The apartment was large, and rambled into the dusky distance behind drawn blinds, room after cluttered room. It was very untidy, and the untidiness was of a kind that MacDonell would not have created for himself: ashtrays everywhere stood half full with cigar ends and the singed tubes of brown paper that the Russians call cigarettes; there were plates with the congealed detritus of half a dozen meals, cushions were tumbled aside, and an empty whisky bottle lay along the keyboard of a sagging piano.

'Must apologise for the mess,' MacDonell sighed despairingly. 'My two servants informed me last week that, now the revolution had come, my cleaning will be dealt with in a thoroughly democratic fashion. So far as I can see, this means that now I must do the housework, but still give them their wages and keep. But what about this champagne? Would you like some?'

I looked at the others: Tchaikovsky nodded, Tatiana nodded, I nodded. MacDonell opened a cupboard in the corner of the salon, revealing row upon row of bottles. 'I had General Polovtsov hiding here, disguised as a sick American missionary,' he said, 'and we had to get some of this stuff in to restore him to health.' The champagne exploded into our glasses: it was very warm.

'I suppose,' said MacDonell, 'that you must be a bit surprised that I've taken your arrival so calmly. The point is, I heard all about you two or three hours ago, from Japaridzi, Shaumian's secretary – besides, the whole town was talking, after you flew along the front there, and it didn't take much to put two and two together. You've come from Dunsterville, I suppose? Since Tiflis fell, and poor Pike was shot, my only communication has been with Kazvin and Teheran. All my telegrams are supposed to go *en clair,* of course, but I've got a sympathiser in the wireless station here, and manage to get the odd cipher message through. And by the way, do you have anything for me?'

Tatiana put her nimble hand deep into the front of her cotton suit and brought out a warm and crumpled little package, roundly sealed. 'I'll look at it later,' said MacDonell, delicately.

'Who was the girl who brought us here?' I asked.

'Marie Nikolaievna? She's one of my conspirators,' replied MacDonell. 'The plan, so far as I can make it out, is to get the townspeople to rise against the bolsheviks. But since the Armenians hate the Cossacks, and everybody hates the Tatars, the odds against are pretty long. Down at the Aviation School they've got eight obsolete old seaplanes – Curtisses, they are, I think,' he said, smiling in my direction – 'and when the signal's given the Tsarists will fly over the Fleet and threaten to bomb them if they don't throw in their lot against the reds. Pretty independent lot, the navy, as I expect you know, and I doubt they'll give in to that sort of pressure. Still, the town is full of Tsarist plotters, and they all seem to regard me as their centre of intelligence. They communicate through one of the priests: press a little roll of paper into the chap's hand at Mass, then he slips it to Marie and she brings it to me. Feller came here one day, had a message for me hidden in a secret compartment inside his boot that he said he'd invented for himself – well, he must have worn that boot for weeks, and walked hundreds of miles . . . that was the richest intelligence I ever received.'

I told MacDonell how we had landed to the north-east of the town and left Clark to guard the aeroplane. 'Not much we can do at the moment,' said MacDonell, 'except leave him there to sweat it out. Shaumian and Petrov won't let you out of the town as long as there's any chance you can be useful to them here. And come to that, what *are* you here for?' – and then, as he saw my expression – 'No, no, no, don't tell me, I really don't want to know.'

There came an abrupt knocking at the apartment door: MacDonell excused himself and left the room, closing the door decisively behind him. He returned within five minutes. 'Just as I expected, that was Japaridzi again. Said he knows you're here, and he's very happy to have you stay here, but on no account are you to leave the town; the soviet are still debating the contents of Dunsterville's letter. And that reminds me, if you'll pardon me, that I ought to go and decipher my own despatches.'

When he had left the room once more, I glanced despairingly at my companions. It seemed that I had not acted in the most intelligent way. In deserting my aircraft I was like the captain who abandons his ship; and by leaving Clark behind I had succeeded in dividing my pitifully small force. We were trapped, for the moment, in Baku, with no idea whether or not we could elude the bolsheviks and get back to the 0/400. I walked to the window and looked down into the street: there was little doubt that the nondescript individual who stood in the shadows opposite was watching the entrance to the building. And when, a few minutes later, I found a window in another room that looked out onto a tangle of backyards, I soon spotted another, similar, watcher at the corner of an alley.

So, in the end, we stayed quietly in the vice-consul's apartment, ate a poor meal dominated by watermelon ('All the fruit we can get, old boy, comes in on the steamer from Enzeli') exchanged guarded conversation with three or four shifty characters who drifted in at dinner-time, and eventually found a sofa each on which to doze the sweaty night hours uncomfortably away.

In the morning, MacDonell was visited by his friend Sergei Arsen, an intelligent Armenian lawyer with boot-button black eyes and an air compounded of lugubrious resignation and scarce-controlled excitement – a remarkable combination that apparently came naturally to him. He brought no good news for us: the soviet had still reached no decision, and as for the aeroplane, it was fast becoming a curiosity, and crowds of townspeople were setting off to stand and stare at it. Clark, apparently, was holding his own, but the safety of the aircraft depended upon the soldiers who had been set to guard it – and, remembering what Marlin had told me of the 'souveniring' of my Fokker after I had been shot down, I shuddered in horrified anticipation of what might happen to the 0/400. MacDonell suggested that he should ask Shaumian to post a stronger guard, but I pointed out that this would make it even harder for us to get away when the opportunity presented itself; we would have to put our trust in Clark himself.

The morning dragged by, with no summons from the soviet; we sat on widely spaced chairs, isolated from one another about the rooms of the apartment. For ten minutes or so, Tchaikovsky picked out sad foreign melodies on the piano, then gave up, complaining bitterly that it was badly out of tune. Around noon MacDonell, who had been receiving a stream of surreptitious visitors in his office, made a most extraordinary suggestion: that we should visit a cabaret, and 'take a dram or two'. The idea of a cabaret at midday did not fill me with enthusiasm, Tchaikovsky looked bored, and Tatiana positively shocked. But there was nothing but to follow the vice-consul as he strode down the street, round two or three corners, and into the cellar below the Hotel Bolshay Moskovskaya. We were, of course, tailed all the way by one of our anonymous watchers.

The Moskovskaya cabaret was dark and noisome, but cool after the street. Small tables were set on several levels around –

well, it was neither a stage nor a dance-floor, but rather a tiny arena, a pit for some bear-baiting show. Some of the tables were set in private boxes, with curtains; but all of these were empty, and only some half-dozen others were occupied – mostly by men, in a hodgepodge of military uniforms, drinking with a thin scattering of low-class girls. The most striking of these, who looked like a gypsy and indeed was dressed as one, was in the company of a Cossack lieutenant who, as we entered the cabaret, was gently dribbling champagne from his glass between her breasts. He was fearsomely dressed in a wildly-frogged coat, with an astrakhan cap jammed on his greasy locks, and hung about with cross-belts, swords, and pistols. Even in the gloomy half-light of the cabaret, his dissolute, bloodshot eyes were shaded by a huge pair of tinted spectacles.

Almost as soon as we had sat down at our table he rose from his, the champagne bottle in his hand, and began to wander from group to group, pouring out a drink here and there, shouting a Russian toast and punching with his free hand at any adjacent shoulder. Eventually he reached our table, stumbled, swept the last drops of champagne across our glasses, belched a foul sour stomach full of wind into our faces, and, leaning forward, muttered quietly:

'Good God, Jones, I thought I'd never catch up with you! I must speak to you at once. Follow me to my table in a couple of minutes, will you?' Then he rose to full height on his bandy legs, thrust out his right hand while striking himself full on the chest with the empty bottle in his left, loudly introducing himself: 'Vassilevski!'

Tchaikovsky sprang to his feet with a corresponding cry; Tatiana, suddenly seized with a mischievous sense of the ridiculous, did the same, with a shout of 'Fitzalbert!' And I – for a full thirty seconds I sat stunned, before, fighting down the impulse to exclaim 'Marlin!' and fling myself upon him, I introduced myself similarly. He shook hands all round, staggered back to his gypsy, and ordered another bottle.

I gave him five minutes and then, lurching ever so slightly, made my way to his table. He greeted me vociferously in Russian – a Russian that even I, after only twenty-four hours in the country, could recognise as faintly spurious, with its too-lazy vowels and unnatural stresses – and poured me an overflowing glass of tepid champagne.

'Thank the Lord I've found you at last. There's been a most fearful cock-up in communications, and when I missed you at Kazvin I was afraid I'd lost you for ever.'

I glanced anxiously at his gypsy companion, who was humming a song to herself and beating time with a long, black paper cigarette. 'Don't you worry about her,' said Marlin/ Vassilevski, 'she don't understand English and, besides, she's deaf in that ear – aren't you dear? The fact is,' he continued hastily in an undertone, '*you-know-who* ain't in Ekaterinodar at all. We got word at last from Lockhart – they're in Ekaterin-*burg,* in the Urals.'

It meant little to me. I supposed that, if ever I could get away from Baku, my Baedeker maps would guide me as well to Ekaterinburg as to Ekaterinodar. When all you have is a chart on a scale of one inch to every 400 miles, direction and distances are of small importance.

'My instructions are,' said Marlin, 'that you don't have to go on with this if you don't want to.'

'But what alternative can you offer me? Nothing, I think, but a prison camp and a false identity.'

'True. Still, I'll give you some time to think about it. You're at the consul's, are you? Expect me there for tea. Now give me a kiss and leave me.'

I ignored his invitation, although I knew that nobody around us would expect anything else of me; I shook his hand, and stumbled back to my companions. We drank a final glass, paid our reckoning, and climbed up once more to the hot sun and oil-heavy air of Pratchesnaya street, leaving Marlin slumped back in his chair, running a languid hand over the thighs and rump of his gypsy girl.

It was early evening before he appeared suddenly from the kitchen of MacDonell's apartment: 'Came in the back way, old boy. The bolshies have got a man out there watching your quarters, but I soon distracted his attention, nipped onto the roof of an outhouse, and here I am.'

MacDonell discreetly left me alone in his 'den' with Marlin, and I reported briefly that Tatiana, Tchaikovsky and I had discussed the matter (admittedly in the absence of Clark), and decided that we would pursue the mission we had been given.

'Good chaps,' said Marlin. 'Let's have 'em in, shall we?'

When we were together he told us how he had received the news of the Tsar's true destination in the first days of June, had ascertained by wireless that we were still in Kazvin, and had immediately caught the cross-Channel packet to connect with a train for Paris, Geneva, Milan, Rimini and Bari. From there he had taken a torpedo-boat to Port Said, through the Suez Canal and down the Red Sea to Aden, round and up the Gulf to Abadan. He had caught a transport flight up-river to Baghdad, where he had immediately transferred to a DH4 to fly, by way of Hamadan, hot on our trail, to Kazvin, where he had missed us by little more than a minute. In a last desperate attempt to catch us up, he had then flown to Resht, taken a carriage to Enzeli, bought his way aboard a steamer a day ahead of Bicherakov's advance forces. 'And after that, my friends, finding you in Baku was a piece of cake.'

We sought out MacDonell, and borrowed from him a map of Russia rather larger than the scraps with which I had been supplied, which were, in any case, in the cockpit of the 0/400. Where Ekaterinodar lay less than 500 miles' flight from Baku, Ekaterinburg lay well over 1,000. It would be necessary for me to land at least twice in search of fuel, and the difficulties would be even greater on the way back, with a heavier and very precious load.

'Just let me say it again,' said Marlin. 'If you feel you can't possibly see it through, then HMG will quite understand.' But Tchaikovsky was a Russian and a patriot, and happy to return to his homeland under any pretext; Tatiana was moved both by love for her mother's country and by family feeling; and I had nowhere better to go.

'Well, look here,' said Marlin, 'this war can't go on much longer, you know, and then we'll see if we can't get you back to Germany. In the meantime, I was thinking – just in case, you understand' (I understood only too well) – 'that you might like to write a message to your parents, and then, if by any chance you shouldn't return from Russia, I'll see that they get it after the war.'

I took his advice, and sitting down at MacDonell's desk I composed a letter to my mother and father, and then, just as I was about to seal it, I remembered my Blue Max in the pocket of my jacket. I took it, wrapped the letter about it, slipped both into a Consular Service wrapper, and sealed and addressed it. Marlin opened his Cossack coat to reveal a tight chamois body-belt, already stuffed with packets of all sorts to which he added mine. 'Don't you worry,' he said, buttoning up the coat and patting his midriff, 'I'll see that it's taken good care of.'

There was still no word from the soviet: with a guard on the aeroplane and a watch kept on our every move, they knew that we were prisoners in Baku as effectively as if we had been incarcerated in the town gaol.

'Wait until night,' said Marlin. 'We'll see what we can manage under cover of darkness.' And with a promise to meet us for dinner, he left. 'See you at the cinematograph,' he said.

MacDonell explained. Down by the steamer pier and close to the south-east corner of the Kryepost, the old walled town, a cinematograph theatre stood close to the edge of the water. Above the theatre, a roof-restaurant afforded a splendid view over the Caspian, and it was also the coolest place to dine in the evening. 'Though there's precious little in the way of food,' he admitted, 'and the prices are extremely high.'

Two men in white cotton suits followed us to the cinema, but they remained in the street, and, leaning over the balustrade of the restaurant, we could clearly see them below on the marine promenade. There was no sign of Marlin, and our meal when it came was almost inedible. I have a healthy appetite, but the stale reek of the watery stew, combined with the thick oily Baku air, turned my stomach, and I pushed aside my plate only half finished. Tatiana had eaten none of hers; Tchaikovsky toyed petulantly with his; only MacDonell ate it all, and was eyeing our leavings covetously – when Marlin was suddenly at our side.

'By jove,' he said enviously, 'that looks good. Mind if I have some? – because you three are leaving right away. Down the back stairs, across the quay as quick as a flash, you'll find a boat waiting for you. Off you go!'

A quick handclasp all round, and we followed his instructions. In the gloom at the edge of the water a voice hissed, and we tumbled headlong into a rowing-boat at the foot of the steps. Within seconds we were a hundred yards out on the Caspian, while the men who had followed us stood, impotent shadows against the faint lights of the town.

It was a strangely shaped long boat, very high at the pointed bow and stern and low in the waist, where two fishermen bent to long sweeps that sent us speeding across the water.

'Ask them where they are taking us,' I commanded Tchaikovsky.

'To Tchorni Gorod, the Black Town,' was the reply, but it seemed to me that we were steering almost due south, straight out from the town into the blackness of the night and the low haze that hung over the sea. Then, from the quay we had left only minutes before, I heard the sound of a motor-boat starting up.

The fishermen pulled more frantically at their sweeps, and the engine behind us grew louder, then softer, but thudding gradually nearer as it quartered the waters in our wake. The men aboard the motor-boat switched on a small searchlight, and then we could watch as they hawked backward and forward, closing on us but still ignorant of our precise direction. The sea was calm, with only a slight swell running on our port bow, and the beam of the searchlight cut almost level across the water. Suddenly, by accident rather than skill, it flicked past our boat, swung back, and held us for a quivering second. We had been seen.

I would have sworn that the breeze, such as it was, came with the swell from the south-east, but for several minutes I had been growing increasingly aware of a strengthening of the over-whelming aroma of Baku: sickly sulphurous, greasy-sweet, it now seemed all about us. The beam from the searchlight stabbed us again, the fishermen dragged at their sweeps, the boat seemed to swoop through a suddenly illuminated surf of rising bubbles. One of our rowers ceased his work for a moment, and, groping inside his shirt, struck a match and set fire to a scrap of rag. Even as he hurled this torch astern he bent once more to his sweep, and, as we surged forward again, the surface of the sea behind us burst into blue and yellow flame. The beat of the motor-boat's engine slowed, stuttered, almost ceased. Our boat seemed to spin upon its keel and suddenly was driving north and shoreward; and so we left our pursuers behind us, blindly groping behind a wall of flickering flame, the searchlight swinging to and fro, ever further astern.

One of the fishermen laughed, and spoke to Tatiana. 'He

says it was a great attraction with visitors, before the war. The gas from the wells comes bubbling up out of the sea in several different places, and the fire will burn for an hour or more yet.' Between the slowly sinking flame behind, and the intermittent lamps of the Black Town ahead, our boat sped across the shallow waves, and very soon the gaunt shadows of the wharves loomed up before us.

We were put ashore where a pier ran in carrying a spur of the railway line that would lead us, if we trudged out mile after mile, to the distant waste where we had left the 0/400. We thanked our rescuers and set off, treading the ties, and wondering how long it would be before we were detected and apprehended once more. The line ran inland, and then bore to the right, eastward in the direction we must go. And suddenly there, in the dark, rising silhouetted on the line before us, I saw the machine that could be our salvation.

It was one of those trucks used by engineers to inspect the track: four wheels, with one axle cranked, and a great seesawing double lever to drive it. We scrambled aboard at once, and – after one apprehensive moment when it set off, squealing loudly, back toward the quayside – soon had it labouring steadily along through the narrow dark alleys of the Black Town, past the throbbing pumps of the refinery. At last, as Tchaikovsky and I strained up and down, one at each end of the driving lever, we climbed gradually up the long incline and out into the open desert beyond.

An hour or so after leaving the waterside we came to the end of the line, and knew that we were within a half-mile of the aeroplane. Some way ahead a low light flickered, which we rightly guessed to be the camp-fire of the guards. The night had grown thick and heavy, there were no stars or moon, and this fire was our only guide. About fifty yards apart from each other, we crept forward until we could see the black form of the aircraft dimly against the skyline, and the silhouette of a figure moving before the fire.

The silhouette was erratically circling, staggering slightly, apparently dancing, all alone. As I stole cautiously closer, I realised with a start that it was Clark, a bottle in his hand, a strange faint keening song upon his lips. But where were the guards? And then I saw them, tangled together by the fire's side, motionless, dead to the world. And still Clark went on dancing. I called his name, softly, and he turned, his eyes owl-wide in the light of the flames, his finger to his lips. As we emerged all three from the shadows he stepped forward and flung his arm in an arc toward the slumbering guards:

'Look at them!' he exclaimed. 'Didn't I do well?' and fell at our feet.

We laid Clark beside his victims, stertorously snoring all. For an hour, as the fire died, we laboured at the aircraft, untying the ropes, dragging up the pegs, digging out the sand where it had drifted in front of the wheels of the under-carriage, and laboriously shouldered the great aeroplane out of its furrows and on to the level ground. While Tatiana took brands from the fire and carried them, teasing in the light breeze, to mark out our take-off to windward, Tchaikovsky and I half roused Clark and bundled him, still clutching his bottle, aboard.

Take-off gave us several bad minutes. There were no chocks, only slight hillocks before the under-carriage where the wheels had already begun to sink into the spongy ground. Tchaikovsky and Tatiana had to scramble, one on each side, out along the wing beside the engine to swing the starter handles; then, as I kept the throttles closed as far as possible and the great machine strained at its puny restraints, they had to drop ten or eleven feet from the wing's edge and run for the ladder below the belly. Even as they did so, the first of the guards stirred, raising himself on one elbow and groping for his revolver. Impatiently, I eased the throttle slightly forward, twisting the knob to right and left until the engines settled into an even throb, hearing (I hoped) the belly trap-door dropped into place, and feeling at last the welcome tap of Tchaikovsky's finger on my shoulder to tell me that he and Tatiana were safely aboard. Then I ran the engines quickly up to a satisfying howl, and in seconds the 0/400 was bounding and lurching across the rough ground, lifting herself over the last of the flaring torches and bumbling off into the black, while behind us a wild sparking showed where our guards were desperately firing at the fading flames of our twin exhausts.

I looked at the fuel gauges: if my elementary calculations over MacDonell's map had been correct, we had just enough to reach Astrakhan. I shouted at Tchaikovsky, squeezed into the co-pilot's seat beside me, and he dug out the skimpy page of Baedeker and gave me a course five degrees west of north. The 0/400 blundered on, our only light the faint glow of the instrument panel as I set the aircraft into a slow and steady climb. At 8,000 feet the first swirling threads of cloud glimmered briefly in the cockpit between us, drained away on the slipstream, then thickened steadily all about us. Rising slowly, dropping suddenly in the airpockets within the cloud, staggering drunkenly up again, the aircraft at last emerged into the clear moon-washed upper air, where the stars danced and swung about us.

We flew steadily northward on our compass bearing until sunrise. First came the gradual manifestation of the grey field of cloud below, like the developed negative on a photographic plate as it emerges in the fixing bath, then, like the darkroom lamp, the blood-red ball rising on our starboard bow. It was time to take a look at the earth below, to pick out any landmarks and try to fix our position. The murk rose up about us as I eased the 0/400 down, and we sank unsteadily through the heavy stratocumulus, to slide out into a pale grey dawn. At first there was nothing to be seen but the leaden Caspian; then Tchaikovsky gave a cry and pointed straight ahead, to the far loom of land. Every second brought us nearer, and now below we could see the turgid patterns in the sea, where the great Volga poured out its sediment through a thousand channels. We passed above a sort of pier, some ten miles out from the land, where several ships lay tied up or at anchor nearby. This, said Tchaikovsky, was the Nine Fathom Roads, as close to the shore as the sea-going steamers dared navigate.

We had left the anchorage behind, and Tchaikovsky had just slid forward into the nose cockpit to determine our landfall more accurately, when there came a belching and a groaning and Clark erupted into the cockpit. His face was dull red, streaked with the black of woodsmoke, and beaded with sweat. He seemed to be impregnated with vodka, for his clothing oozed with the stuff and his breath stank worse than the air of Baku. He collapsed into the co-pilot's seat beside me, and grinned shakily.

'Not bad, eh? Fair pulled the wool over them bolshies' eyes, what? Told 'em, I did, now the revolution's 'ere, ever'body equal, get drunk as a lord. As a lord, haha. Not that they understood a word, but they knew what to do with vodka, eh? Knew what to do . . . 'ullo! what's this, then?'

He had his fingers stuck into the steel tube that rose between his seat and mine; the tube through which Copley had had me fire the 'colour of the night' after our take-off from Manston. Clark's face was gazing earnestly into mine, his eyes narrowed in fumbling thought, his breath sweeping over me like the fumes from a still. 'What's this 'ere tube for?' he repeated. And foolishly I told him.

I saw comprehension succeeded by mischievous delight sweep over his features, but I had turned my attention to the nearly empty fuel gauges before me. The green and brown land of the Volga delta now filled the horizon, and Tchaikovsky was gesturing excitedly in the nose, as I felt, rather than saw, Clark fumble about the cockpit beside me. From the corner of my eye I saw him raise the Very pistol, and I turned to protest. But even as I did so he placed its muzzle against the tube and pulled the trigger.

His hand was shaking, the aircraft shuddered in a stray thermal, the pistol was not snugly inside the tube. The flare struck the lip of the tube, knocking the pistol from Clark's hand and past my head off into the empty air, snaked wildly about our feet and then, burrowing into a corner of the cockpit like a demented mole, burst in a ball of fire. In seconds the fuselage was alight, the flames sweeping around my legs as I grappled desperately with the controls, putting the 0/400 down as fast as I knew how toward the marsh, the mud, the wide water, the unknown landing place that still lay so far below.

CHAPTER 13

15-17 June: Volga Delta near Astrakhan

HOW LONG the nightmare lasted I do not know. Some, certainly, was real – the orange flames creeping, flickering forward, slithering silent like a snake distraught, then rocketing suddenly up, as a pheasant does when the brush fire drives in the breeze; the insidious crackle, followed by the fierce full-sap explosions like bursting trees; the choking blackness sweeping all around – but much, much more came swirling up and out from the horror of my past experience, the blind panic of my memory. I tore off my goggles and hurled them from me as we struck the ground. Whether I was flung out on the first impact, fought my way from the inferno, or was finally thrown free by the bursting of the petrol tanks, I shall never know; and my companions knew no more than I. It was many minutes before the darkness began to drain from my brain and, raising myself stiffly on stinging arms, I was able to look about me.

Twenty yards away the 0/400 still burnt fiercely, broken-backed and crumpled, the steel frame groaning and whimpering like a great prehistoric beast in its death throes. Tchaikovsky was near me, kneeling, holding his head in his hands and shaking it from side to side. Clark suddenly was sober: he crouched in a bundle of singed rags, rocking backward and forward with his arms about his knees and his head upon them, moaning 'Oh gawd, what have I done? What have I done?' And Tatiana – beyond the burning plane, revealed momentarily between the billowing smoke clouds, I saw a motionless heap flung down like a broken doll no longer loved.

With a despairing cry I staggered to my feet and half ran, half fell, toward her. As I passed the aircraft a sudden hot breath of hell puffed out and swept off the new-grown hair around the healed wound on my temple, but I scarcely noticed it. I reached Tatiana's side, and flung myself upon her. Her flying suit was cooked black, the leather cracking into cinders as I touched her, and her face was buried in the soggy ground. Fearful, I turned her gently over. Her face, between the flying helmet and the goggles, was black with ash and mud, but I could see no blistering. She was breathing shallowly, and, as I tenderly

180

unstrapped the goggles from her eyes, she slowly opened them and stared wondering at me. Overcome with relief, I held her in my arms and kissed her long, full on the lips.

It was, I suppose, no more than hysterical reaction when, at last taking my loving mouth from hers and stretching back to look her in the face, I burst out in a crow of laughter. For the goggles had kept the smoke and dirt from her eyes, and my kisses had wiped it from her lips, and she looked for all the world like a singer in a minstrel show, ready to rattle a tambourine or strut into a cakewalk.

Now Tchaikovsky and Clark came stumbling toward us, and we took account of one another's injuries. Miraculously they were slight: Tatiana confessed to being bruised but otherwise unhurt, though all the beautiful hair that had curled below her flying helmet was burnt away; and the others had suffered no more than slight burns and grazes. Our clothing, however, was in tatters: black rags clung to us, in some places sticking to the skin, in others seared away to show the naked flesh beneath. Tatiana and I still had our Webley revolvers, the belts all that held the last fragments of flying suits about us; but everything else that we possessed was lost in the inferno.

For the first time I looked about me. We had crashed somewhere in the great fifty-mile delta where the Volga discharges into the Caspian. The 0/400 lay half sunken in the spongy ground, where the flames had blackened all the rough grass and even now were threatening the taller reeds beyond. As far as the eye could see, the land lay flat and featureless, broken only here and there by single scrubby trees and the thicker growth of reeds that indicated a watercourse.

I turned on Clark and cursed him roundly; but he cringed so pitifully, holding his arms above his head as if I were about to strike him, that I was compelled to relent a little.

'But what are we to do now?' I concluded. 'No clothes, no food, no aircraft, no money – no hope!'

Clark brightened visibly as the thought struck him: 'Ah well, now,' he said, 'we might just be all right for spondulicks. When you left me to guard our pile of little sovereigns I spent so long with 'em that, them and me, we got quite intimate. I reckon I could find my way to 'em blindfold.'

'Yes, you damned fool,' I raged, 'but they're lost for ever in this fire you caused!'

'Somewhere in the fire they are,' said Clark, with infuriating slowness, 'but lost – I'm not so sure. Do you know what the melting point of gold is? 1,908 degrees Fahrenheit! Even under the petrol tanks where they were, I'd be doubtful if them sovereigns have melted. And even if they *have* melted – well, gold is gold stiil, all the world over. All we have to do is sit here until the fire's died out and the ashes have cooled, and then dig around a bit. And if by some awful stroke of fate we can't find it, it just so happens that I've got one or two tucked in me boot 'ere. You see,' he concluded shiftily, 'they somehow sort of stuck to me fingers.'

Tchaikovsky laughed, and so did Tatiana. I could hardly be angry with him when it was his criminal instinct that was likely to save our lives. So all we had to do was wait until the fire burned out. And in the meantime? Tatiana was already running toward a tiny stretch of open water that gleamed in the light, to soak from her body the charred remnants of her clothing, and Tchaikovsky was close behind her. Soon we were all four splashing in a brackish pool, gingerly teasing away the tarry scraps from our stinging limbs.

We made a sorry army of fortune when we gathered again to watch the cinders of our aircraft slowly dying. We were all more or less naked, although we had managed to salvage our footwear. Clark was worst off, his scrawny bare frame hunched above bandy legs that ended in a battered pair of black army boots with knotted laces; Tchaikovsky had his Russian knee boots, and enough of his breeches to make a pair of the knickerbockers that the English footballers call 'shorts'; and I, with the holster of the Webley hung low to cover some of my embarrassment, had also my high laced boots. Only Tatiana looked magnificent: with the exception of her gunbelt and her well-singed sheepskin boots she was entirely naked, but she stood there confident and unashamed, her beautiful breasts high with their firm nipples, her hair glinting dark red between her thighs. I was so proud of her then; and Clark and Tchaikovsky were visibly abashed.

The day, though thickly clouded, was hot. The plunge in the pool had refreshed us, but we were all (and especially Clark) thirsty and hungry. There was nothing to do but sit by the smouldering wreckage, waiting for the ashes to cool. We chatted desultorily, but with the heat, and the lack of sleep, and the exhaustion following on the relief at our narrow escape . . .

I awoke with a start to discover that the sun had cleared the clouds on the western horizon, and was already low in the sky. Tatiana lay across my knees, smiling quietly at me; the other two were playing some childish game with their fingers and fists; and the fire was dead.

Tchaikovsky and I were best shod for the search. We broke long staves from an unconsumed part of one wing and, guided by Clark's shouts and his wildly waving arms, we gingerly prodded our way into the still reeking remains. The engines, hideously distorted, lay where they had fallen each side of the fuselage, fragments of shattered propeller sticking up unburnt. Midway between them was where Clark judged the gold to lie, but it was also where the greatest tangle of steel skeleton lay, twisted and black – and the metal was still very hot.

For almost an hour we levered the tubing aside and thrust our staves deep into the smoking ashes, feeling for the loose, heavy, almost liquid movement of a hoard of coins. We found nothing, despite Clark's nearly hysterical orders and directions. Suddenly, with a loud oath, he strode into the wreckage and plunged between us.

''Ow many times do I have to tell you?' he cried in exasperation. 'It's here, right here, just like I said!' And he thrust a hand deep into the cinders. With an even louder oath he pulled it out again, clutching his burnt fingers tight beneath his left armpit, but in the excavation there gleamed, no doubt about it, the tiny glint of gold.

We recovered very nearly all the sovereigns. Some were misshapen by the heat, one or two had fused together, but with care and persistence, as the sun declined, we plucked them from the ashes. But how could we carry them? Clark and I descended upon Tchaikovsky, and despite his scandalised protests, removed his abbreviated breeches. With strips of cloth we closed up the legs, and so had something rather like a saddle-bag which we could fill with the gold and carry between us straddled across a length of steel strut. Then the first mosquitoes arrived, with the cooler air of evening.

To begin with, they were just another small irritation to add to our many woes. We began to walk northward waving our free arms about our heads, slapping at the easily reached parts of our exposed flesh as the greedy beasts settled. But soon, alerted by some kind of insect wireless, they began to swarm in their thousands. The sun was near the horizon: soon it would be dark, and ahead of us the marshes stretched, empty of any shelter.

'Smoke!' gasped Tchaikovsky, taking both his hands from our burden to strike blindly at his face, his chest, his buttocks, 'that is what we must have to keep them at bay.' So there was nothing for it but to turn back, to fan the last glowing cinders of the burnt-out aircraft, and to feed the fire with handfuls of uprooted reeds.

The reeds were dry and made only a little smoke, burning quietly and fiercely. Gathering them, we tore our hands on the stems. Sallying out from our meagre sanctuary to collect them, and soak them briefly in water, we were once more attacked viciously; carrying the bundles back to the fire, we had no hands free with which to defend ourselves. Soon it would be completely dark, and we must pile up our reserves for the night. Clark hit on the idea of twisting small torches for ourselves, which crackled briefly and soon expired, but which gave us brief protection. In between our sorties, we crouched miserably in the wreckage, blackened once more with ash, our eyes streaming with tears.

It was a long night. We dozed in turn, feeding our fire as it died down, fearful of letting it go out, stirred to sudden activity as the smoke changed direction in the light breezes and exposed our flanks to new skirmishers. When the sun at last rose over our near-extinguished embers, we were a sad sight: filthy, unkempt, swollen with bites, our faces streaked where we had wiped our watering eyes with grimy hands. As the swarms retired to their daytime lairs, we stumbled once again into the water and lay there sunk in the ooze.

'We must get away from here as quickly as we can,' I gasped, cupping my hands and letting the water pour down over my hair and face. 'Perhaps we can find a village where you, Tchaikovsky, must try to buy us some food and clothing.' There was nothing to delay us, so we pulled on our boots, and, with the sun before us warming our racked bodies, began our long march out of the delta. We came to a narrow stream, through which we waded thigh-deep, then to another, and to a third, and at last to a fourth that was too wide and therefore too deep to cross. We turned left, following the bank as best we could through the reeds and long grass, struggling on for an hour or more toward the north-west.

Then Tatiana gave a cry and pointed through the reeds across the river. A small flat boat, rather like a punt, was moored to a stake on the far bank. I am a fair swimmer and so, stripping off my boots and gunbelt, I plunged through the reeds and into the water. The current was stronger than I had expected, and it was a long tiring haul before I at last dragged myself, panting, over the stern of the boat. There were no oars or paddles or anything with which to propel it. Sighing desperately, I untied the mooring rope, lowered myself back into the water, and began to kick as strongly as I could upstream. At last, some 200 yards above the point where I had started, I launched the boat out into the current and, using my body as a rudder and trudging desperately with my feet, contrived some minutes later to reach the bank close by where I had first set out.

There we loaded the gold, our boots and guns, into the boat, and then began to repeat the whole manoeuvre; Tatiana, Tchaikovsky and I swimming, wading, manhandling the boat against the stream while Clark ('I never learnt to swim, ol' boy, too busy runnin' errands for me mum') wandered along the bank, shouting encouragement even when he was completely hidden from us by high swathes of reeds. Then, when he and the others were aboard, I once more hung myself from the stern, and, with one eye on my only landmark, the mooring stake across the water, swung and shoved the boat back to where I had first found it.

From beside the stake, a rough track led away through the reeds. We had no need to dry ourselves and dress, and so in a few moments we were on our way: Tchaikovsky in front, with Clark close behind, both grasping the steel strut; then our breeches bag, swinging heavy with gold; then Tatiana, taking her share of the load, and finally myself, cheerfully watching the dimpling of her buttocks as she strode steadily forward.

Ahead of us, the land stretched featureless as before. The sun rose higher in an ever bluer sky, and the day grew hotter. By now we were all desperate with hunger, though those of us who had swum with the boat were at least less thirsty than before. The track wound on, crossing small streams by planks and once, across a wider tributary, a high-backed rickety wooden bridge. At last, near midday, we saw, slowly rearing above the flatlands, the outline of a tumbledown shed.

It was, I suppose, a reed-gatherer's hut, empty and faintly foetid. Here we staggered into the shade and, showering out the sovereigns upon the floor, gave Tchaikovsky back his shorts. Into one of his boots I slipped five of the golden pieces and then, after hearty handshakes, we sent him on his way, watching his short, stocky figure quickly vanish among the reeds. Morose and sweating, still itching from the previous night's bites and scratching at new ones from the marsh ticks, we lay on the floor of the hut and waited.

Hours passed. In the late afternoon Clark, who had been behind the hut to relieve himself, suddenly slid in with his finger to his lips, seized my forearm, and drew me to the door. About 200 yards away a peasant was coming toward the hut; he carried a sack across his shoulder, and his cheerful whistling could be heard louder at every step he took. He wore a big cloth peaked cap, a high-collared shirt covered with bright embroidery, black breeches and felt boots. Little of his face could be seen in the shadow of the cap, except for his proud moustache, which infallibly identified him as Tchaikovsky.

His right hand held the sack, which contained clothes for all of us, some cheese and black bread; in his left hand was a jug of goat's milk. Naked as we were, we nevertheless ate and drank first in our desperation – and Tchaikovsky, though I suspect he had fed already in the village, kindly ate with us as he talked.

'It is only a small village, no more than one church – although there is also a mosque of sorts,' he told us. 'Its name is Staro Kargino. The local headman calls himself commissar, now, of course. I have promised that you will come back with me to speak with him. Indeed, it was only my insistence that we had among us a young lady without clothes, who would be mortally embarrassed if she were seen, that kept him from returning with me – and I do not doubt that it is he whom I can see, peeping from the rushes over there!' He rose, and went to the door, and shouted, and the rushes shook.

'They speak Russian with a dreadful accent here,' he continued, as he sat down again, 'and I think the headman is perhaps half Tatar, but we understand one another. I told him of our dreadful tragedy: how we came in a special high-speed motor-boat from Baku, with important letters from Commissar Petrov, and how the engine of the motor-boat exploded, and we were the only ones to swim ashore.'

'You didn't tell him anything about the aircraft?' asked Tatiana.

Tchaikovsky shrugged: 'Even if I had, he would not have believed me. They are peasants here, they know nothing that they have not seen with their own eyes. But they had heard of Petrov, he is famous in Astrakhan. They sold me the clothes, but they gave me the food, and they will set us upon the road to the city.'

But what would we do in Astrakhan? We were anti-bolshevik agents, without papers of any kind. In the country, among the peasants, we could hope to bluff our way, but in a city we would soon be discovered. In Baku, McDonell had told me of the Chaka, the new bolshevik secret police who had taken over the machinery of the dreaded Okhrana. I had no desire to fall into their clutches.

As we wolfed down the last scraps of bread and cheese, we discussed our future. Was there still any hope of reaching Ekaterinburg and rescuing the Tsar and his family? Tchaikovsky was optimistic: if what Marlin had said were true, and the Czechs held the Trans-Siberian railway, well – we had money enough to buy our way northward until we could make contact with them and perhaps enlist their aid.

'We must not let them take us into Astrakhan, or any big town,' said Tatiana. 'We must buy horses and ride away from here as soon as we can, before the news of our arrival reaches the local soviet. We can't follow the Volga, for that way we will put ourselves into their hands; and we can't go inland, for all the interior is a great salt desert for hundreds of miles – I remember that from the geography my mother taught me. We must go eastward, along the Caspian coast, and find the Ural river, where it empties into the sea, and follow it to the north until we reach the railway.'

Now Tchaikovsky emptied out his sack, and showed us the

clothing he had bought: for Tatiana, a crumpled white blouse, a deep red skirt and an embroidered shawl, with a pair of grey felt boots; a loose shirt in plain grey linen, buttoning on the left shoulder, and baggy trousers of the same material, for Clark, together with a pair of well-worn leather boots; and for me – a faded brown frock-coat with a shabby silk collar, baggy brown breeches, a collarless white flannel shirt, and a peaked cap like his own.

'They sold me their finest clothes,' he explained apologetically.

When we were dressed we looked like a fine party of bolsheviks: three men unshaven, and all four of us bedraggled and stained – even Tatiana's glow of beauty was dimmed by fatigue, and by the streaks of mud that pied her face and arms. Then Tchaikovsky proudly showed us what he had kept hidden at the bottom of his sack: four sturdy belts and four big strong leather wallets to carry on them, which we quickly filled with our hoard of gold, wrapped in a few torn scraps of rag, to silence the chinking. Tatiana picked up the empty sack and jug, and we walked out of the hut into the evening sunshine.

The people's commissar was asleep on his back with his mouth wide open, comfortably stretched on some dry reeds beside the track. He was a tall and heavily-built man, with a broad creased face and narrow Mongolian eyes, dressed in peasant's working clothes. Tchaikovsky gently shook him awake, murmuring to him in Russian and, when he had lumbered drowsily to his feet, introduced us in turn. My name, if I caught it rightly, was Semyon Ivan Ivanovich; Clark was transformed into Ilya Sluzhichi. The wretched man not only shook us by the hand but insisted on kissing us each on both cheeks, pouring out a torrent of incomprehensible good wishes.

Tatiana immediately charmed the peasant, whose own name was Osyp Osypnoy, with her prettily-accented Russian; and the fact that neither Clark nor I could understand a word was explained away, Tchaikovsky told us later, by the information that we were delegates from a proposed people's soviet far away across the Caspian. Clark, I suppose, passed muster, but I must have looked a very unlikely kind of Persian. However, I grinned and nodded whenever the commissar turned to me in the midst of his speech, and shook his hands heartily at the end of it.

As he continued speaking, waving his arms wide at times and frequently turning his face up to address the heavens, we had begun to walk toward his village, and soon it came into view. First the tower of the church, whitewashed and with a bright green onion dome on top; then the thin pencil of the mosque; a succession of low wooden houses, set back some way from the track, with fenced muddy yards before them; and finally the village street, unmetalled, and lined by a dozen or so single-storied buildings, one of them a decrepit inn with a crumbling verandah before it. Here we were herded together by our guide, pushed into a low, dark room full of smoke and the sour-sweet of stale sweat, and made to drink several glasses of a beer called *kvass*, which was no match for our fine German beer – all the while being examined like cattle at the market by the represent-atives of the village. Tatiana, knowing the habits of her country-men, modestly remained by the door; but we three were paraded from one end of the room to the other, quite expecting at any moment to be prodded in the belly, have our teeth examined, or be cut about the hocks by a swishing cane.

Tchaikovsky – God bless him! – made a short but fiery oration, full of shaken fists and the name of Lenin. He was applauded loudly. Clark and I shook him by the hand; we shook the headman by both hands; we shook hands with dozens of people. We were all applauded. The headman summoned a man from the back of the room: a tall, thin dark man with an uncommunicative face. He was the owner of a *telega* in which we could ride part of the way out of the delta, and it was ready, if we wanted to leave. So once more we shook many hands, and struggled out into the last twilight hour of the day.

Our driver would take us some ten *versts* to a rather more important village – with three churches – where we could stay the night at the inn. His *telega,* or mail cart, was a primitive four-wheeled affair, without springs, and with a seat only for himself. The bottom of the cart was strewn with hay, however, and here we threw ourselves for the long jolting ride into the setting sun. There was little to be seen: the cart plunged in the ruts between brackish meadows, occasional rice fields and alder plantations. Huts were dotted here and there, usually on the far side of rough greens where pigs grazed. After more than an hour, in the summer dusk, we arrived at our inn.

It was a surprisingly clean and extensive establishment with a dozen bedrooms, two public rooms, a private parlour, and a broad stableyard. We thanked our driver and paid him off with a whole sovereign, for we had nothing less. We dozed our way through what I was to discover was the usual slow Russian dinner – some thin soup, bread, and then some pork cutlets – and stumbled blindly to our beds.

In the morning, Tchaikovsky went to the stables to enquire where we could buy horses for ourselves, and Tatiana led me to a gunsmith's. Here I bought two ancient fowling-pieces and bags of ammunition. The man showed an unhealthy interest in my Webley, but I paid him well in gold. And two hours later, mounted on shambling, short-legged but sturdy ponies, each of us with a saddlebag of provisions slung before us, we were on our way eastward, following the dusty nomad tracks that we hoped would bring us to the Ural river.

CHAPTER 14

17-29 June: Volga delta – Peski Menteke – Yamankhalin-skaya – Ural'sk – Sarochinskaya

FOR THREE days we rode on to the east, between the shore of the Caspian and the dreadful salt deserts which form the hinterland. The Kirgiz settlements lay thin and desolate, the water was fast drying up and already brackish. Small herds of undernourished camels browsed the low scrub, and the sun shone fourteen hours each day. We wrapped strips of cloth about our faces against the sudden sandstorms, stopped seldom for rest, and slept fitfully each night beside our low fire after a scanty meal of cheese, brittle bread, and sour goat's milk. One day, unspeaking, we rode with a troop of Tatars for some hours before, with a solitary cry and a wave, they turned into the empty sands to the north. On the fourth day our track bore north-east, through the bitter marshlands that lie around the Zhaltyr lake and along the thin waters of the Baksay river as it flows into the shallow valley of the Ural. Low trees grew on the skyline: small clumps and then groves of alders, struggling willows and scrubby oaks. At Yamankhalinskaya, a dry dirty town, we reached the river.

In the grey dusk, when the sun had sunk below the horizon on our left, we surreptitiously skirted the town, and found an anonymous inn on its northern side. We were edgy with dust, which lay thickly not only on all our clothes but everywhere on the skin beneath, unwashed, hungry and saddle-sore. The anonymous innkeeper, surly and grudging, fed us anonymous stew and took our proffered gold piece with great suspicion. For safety, we slept four in one room, Clark and Tchaikovsky in one bed and Tatiana and I in the other. All night the fleas fed unmercifully, but we were grateful for the lumpy mattresses and the grimy quilts, after our comfortless days on the desert's edge. We placed one bed across the door, and the other below the narrow window, and slept with our guns in our hands.

Next morning, Tchaikovsky spoke confidentially with the innkeeper. Four or five days' hard riding lay between us and Ural'sk, the nearest big town. Between, Tchaikovsky told us, the country was only thinly populated, but bands of armed men scoured the land, skirmishing and looting: Red Guards, troops of leaderless Tsarist soldiers, dispossessed kulaks, and opportunist Tatars. We debated finding a steamer to carry us north, but the Ural river winds wildly in its lower reaches, and the current runs strongly for many miles. It would be quicker to continue on horseback, keeping our eyes skinned for the clouds of dust that signalled unwelcome fellow travellers, hiding, when necessary, close to the road.

In the event we were fortunate, and met none of the dangers that the innkeeper had gloomily forecast. We bought fresh food at Kirgiz settlements, exchanging pieces of gold for Russian roubles or bartering for our needs. The road ran flat beside the steamy marshes, but gradually, as we travelled north, the country changed. The trees grew thicker and taller, throwing a welcome dappled shade, and the breeze blew stronger and cooler. Once or twice only we met a cart on the road, a *telega* drawn by a scrawny mare, a farm wagon with two oxen at the yoke. Here and there, where a low bluff rose above the river, there were plantations of tea bushes; rice fields dotted the low valley, guarded by a half-circle of Kirgiz huts.

We rode hard and long, not sparing our horses or ourselves. We made our nightly camps away from the road, screened by thorny bushes and scrubs of alder, and far from any village. We bought our supplies in the mid-hours of the morning, riding together into some small settlement, and conducting our business openly, hoping therefore to attract as little suspicion to our movements as possible. On the evening of the fifth day we came in sight of Ural'sk, a town about the size of Kazvin. It lay on the same bank of the Ural as our road, but we saw it first across the marshes as the river's course twisted from the east. It was a low, mean-looking town, with a single minaret, a few two-storied buildings facing the river, and a scattering of mouldy church domes. We tethered our ponies in a spinney, and dozed together until nightfall.

Just before dark we took a quick meal, lighting a tiny fire to boil some tea. Then we remounted and set our ponies to the north, leaving the few weak lights of the town well to our right. After three or four miles, our ponies stumbling at times into drainage ditches or thrusting withers-high through fields of rice and millet, we came without warning to a railway line. It was a single track, the sleepers pinned straight into the plain without ballast, and the rails uneven. Beside it, rickety poles, silhouetted in the distance against the glow of the sunken sun, held up a looping telegraph wire. I turned excitedly to Tatiana, but she shook her head, a movement I could just detect in the dark:

'No, no, my darling. You know they made me learn all the railways of Russia in the schoolroom? This is the line that runs to Ural'sk from Saratov. They meant one day to continue it to Orenburg, but I fear it may never be built now. We have to go on, north-east, until we reach the line from Samara, another hundred miles or more from here.'

Delicately, our ponies picked their way across the track. And it was as if that railway marked the boundary between one land and another. Beyond the track the ground began to rise steadily for several hundred yards, and then to our amazement we were suddenly riding in grass, the first we had seen (though to begin with, indeed, we could not see it, only hear the sudden change in the ponies' hoofbeats) for many days. The ponies refused to go further, putting their heads down and browsing, crunching, snuffling in excited contentment. So we dismounted again, and for twenty minutes or so let them gather their fill, while we ourselves lay on the ground, and rolled like young children, feeling the fresh green blades tickle our hands and faces.

We rode on again for another hour, bearing slightly to our right, watching the little lights of Ural'sk on the riverside below us fall behind. Then we found a small hollow beside a stream that ran down from the slopes above us in a narrow reed-fringed cutting, and settled ourselves for the night.

It was the larks that woke us: rising all around from their nests, lifting their fragile bodies high into the dawn air on their fluttering wings, quivering with the song that burst from their eager throats. The sun was just thrusting above the horizon, the sky overhead deep ultramarine, a few high scraps of cloud flaming pink and orange. The air was fresh and new as the beginning of time, and I felt wonderfully fit. I glanced at my companions, stirring stiffly – what a pair of dastardly ruffians they looked! Then I heard Tatiana's laugh beside me.

'Oh, Simon! The expression on your face! I know just what you're thinking, and yes – you look every bit as disreputable as they do!'

It was true. Twelve days had passed since last we had shaved: Tchaikovsky already had a fine black bristling Russian beard, Clark's straggled downward, thin but long, and I could feel the blond stubble of my own chin beginning at last to curl. For nearly a week not one of us had washed, and we had no change of clothing. Night after night we had slept fully dressed, wrapped in our saddle blankets, thick with the dust of the road, stained with our own sweat and that of our horses. Suddenly, in this wonderful morning, with the tingling air gusting out of the east, full of the scent of new grass stretching ever onward into farthest China, I knew how filthy I was. And even as the thought came to me, Tatiana flew past me, a twinkling of white flesh, to plunge crowing into the shallow stream.

In a few seconds I was naked too, and leapt in to join her. Tchaikovsky followed, and even Clark stripped to the waist, took off his boots, and waded knee-deep between us to splash his head and shoulders and let the glittering drops run down his thin arms and in among the sparse graying hairs of his chest. We wallowed, scrubbing with our hands at our flesh, watching the grey rolls of dirt float away in the swift running water. Then we waded out, new-born, to dry luxuriantly in the warming breeze. Tatiana was the last one to leave the water:

'I think,' she said primly, 'we know one another well enough by now.' And she sat down as she was to rub her fingers through her dark curly hair, which was already growing full again upon her nape.

I lit a small fire of dried reed stalks, and boiled our morning tea. We breakfasted frugally on dry bread and some hard cheese, shook out the dust of days as well as we could from our crumpled clothing, and dressed again. For twelve days we had said little but the most necessary things to one another, and the habit of silence had grown irksome. It seemed a lifetime since I had held Tatiana's warm flesh against mine, and now I began to wonder if the opportunity would ever come again. Had she tired of me? Had I tired of her? And then, as I watched her pull the worn peasant blouse over her bold breasts, and suddenly saw her smile mischievously at me, sideways through the ringleted hair that fell tumbling across her shoulders, I knew that it was still the same between us, and I was bitterly impatient for a lone bed in a private room, or even a couch of bent grass, there and then on the steppe beneath the wide sky . . .

'Jones! Come! Today we must ride and ride!' It was Tchaikovsky, already mounted, and sawing at the mouth of his shaggy hack in a vain attempt to make it caracole like a school thoroughbred. Clark gathered in the other horses, throwing the saddles one by one over the blankets, buckling the girths, as Tatiana and I swept up the remnants of our food into the saddlebags, and stamped and scattered the ashes of the fire. We rode the ponies gently through the stream and up the easy rise on the far bank, breasting into the full light of the eastern sky, and the grasslands that rolled away to the skyline.

In just that day I grew to love the steppe. I think that a man could easily spend his life – as many indeed do – riding and riding, onward into the rising sun, beneath the high brightness of noonday, and following his lengthening shadow in the last hour of light, without ever being bored. The tight ground drums beneath the cantering hooves; the fresh grass, rippling westward in the steady breeze like a green tide slowly covering the sands of a wide bay, is splashed aside in wavelets by the breath of the horses passing. I know that in winter it can be a desolate place, the earth iron-hard and the air mordant and bitter, but for those three days of June 1918, as we made our way north and east from Ural'sk, we had the finest weather. The sun shone hot, but the air flowed between us like good Rhine wine, cool and sweet and rich with the scent of flowers and crushed herbs. And up from before us as the ponies surged on sprang more game that I had ever seen: rabbits, hares, partridge, pheasant, snipe, wood-cock, and quail. Once, on a low bluff where pine trees stood thickly, we saw in a flash a brown bear raise his head at the sight of our party, pirouette on his toes, and vanish lumbering among the undergrowth; and in the night, as we lay beside the dying embers of our camp-fire, I thought I heard, far away, the cry of a wolf.

To Tchaikovsky, however, the steppe was a desert. On a low rise we halted for a minute to glance back at the land over which we had ridden. He waved his arm widely, a faint expression of disgust on his face: 'Look at it,' he said. 'You could gallop for three days and still be nowhere.'

For three days we did indeed ride, though galloping only when I was overcome with the intoxication of the air, the sun, and the wide blue bowl of the sky. Then, shouting wildly, I kicked my short-legged, shaggy mount from his ambling trot into a sudden, mad, snorting scramble, forcing my companions to follow me as I charged forward like one of the horde of Jenghiz Khan. We encountered nomad caravans from whom we bought cheese, mare's milk and millet flour, and once we tasted *koumis,* the strangely acid, clouded white and brown wine that they brew from the milk. With one of the old fowling-pieces I stalked and shot a fat partridge, which we grilled on sticks above the glowing embers of a fire. And at night, my face and hands taut and tingling from the sun and wind, I put my arms about Tatiana and slept the sleep of pure contentment.

195

With only the sun to guide us, we wandered from our direct route, following the contours and crossing over the few tracks that we met. It was on the morning of the fourth day that, reining in for a few seconds below a slight rise, we heard the sound of guns ahead: the spasmodic rattle of machine-guns, the popping of rifles, and the occasional bang of a field piece. We went forward cautiously, conscious that we were conspicuous on the skyline but unable to tell, in that gently swelling landscape, exactly where the brow before us lay. Then, suddenly, we were at the top of a long straight slope that ran down into a shallow river valley, and there, beside the water, was the railway. And on the line, fronting one another, stood two trains, with men deployed on either side, shooting.

We rode quickly down the slope until we were no longer silhouetted against the sky, and dismounted rapidly. Each train was made up largely of baggage wagons and open goods trucks, with two or three shabby passenger cars and a guard's van; both engines, steaming asthmatically, pushed before them low flat trucks on which field guns were mounted. The gun to our left was bedded in sandbags, which also gave protection to its crew, but the one to our right was enclosed in a sort of casemate of bolted sheet steel. On the front of the casemate, above the gun port, a big red star had been painted. The two engines were about 400 yards apart, and every half-minute or so one would loose a round at the other. They were only 5-pounders, the aim was wild, and the ammunition obviously faulty: they did no damage, the shells falling beside the track and spewing up nothing but a shower of earth and pebbles.

The men to our left were clearly the more experienced and disciplined. On each side of the track they had dragged forward a machine-gun on wheels – a 'Sokolov' I guessed – and thrown out their riflemen in open order in two wide wings, running forward, dropping to the ground to fire and reload, and advancing again. The Red Guards – for that was what those on the right must be – were in disarray, rushing out from the train to fire wildly in all directions, often into the faces of their own friends who were retreating, and shouting and waving their arms in what were obvious tactical disagreements. Even as we watched, their engine belched out a cloud of filthy smoke, gave a despairing toot, and, in a veil of leaking steam, began to trundle backward down the line. Men ran desperately to scramble aboard as it picked up speed, and within a minute it had disappeared from view toward the east, only the sooty cloud above the steppe showing where it had gone.

The victors withdrew in good order to their train, picking up their dead and wounded and gathering in self-congratulatory groups, but I was horrified to see that a small party went among the enemy dead, shooting any wounded survivor, and kicking and bayoneting the lifeless bodies. Later, though I could never excuse it, I came to understand their desperate sense of betrayal, and their loathing for those whom they thought had betrayed them.

'Do you think they are the Czechs?' I asked my companions.

Tchaikovsky shrugged: 'Czechs, White Army, Social Revolutionaries, who knows?'

Clark grinned at me sharply under his gaunt brows: 'Well, if they're Czechs, *you* ought to know. They're your lot, ain't they?' Tatiana laughed, and I – I had forgotten the story that I had been taught so carefully.

'One of us should ride down to speak with them,' said Tchaikovsky. 'Do you wish to go?'

'But if they are not Czechs,' I stammered, 'if they are Russians, I cannot speak with them.'

'Then,' said Tchaikovsky, 'I must go. I think that if they are Czechs they will understand my Russian, and if they are Russians, well – ' he shrugged again ' – I suppose that they are on our side.' So he sprang into the saddle of his mount and, with the reins across his knees and both hands in the air, set off slowly down the slope.

Guiltily, I watched him go. I should have ridden down there, risking the nervous bullet. I had hung back, more in concern for the ultimate safety of my companions than for the question of my own reception at the hands of men who were an unknown quantity to me; but in a few minutes I was to learn that it made little difference.

We heard Tchaikovsky shout when he was still several hundred yards from the train, we saw him covered instantly by half a dozen twitching rifles; and we watched him ride in among the soldiers below, dismount, and begin talking and gesturing. Faces turned to seek us out, far up the slope. We remounted

197

and, like Tchaikovsky, rode down with our hands in the air.

When we were within earshot Tchaikovsky cried out in Russian. 'He says they are Czech legionaries,' translated Tatiana, 'and they are anxious to hear what you want.' She smiled sympathetically at me, but said nothing further, glancing silently at Clark's furrowed face. The first Czechs were about us: honest-looking peasant faces, but sharp and shrewd, receiving us coolly and jabbering away in their meaningless tongue. I rode on, silent still, looking for a senior officer, and found one in breeches and cross-belts, standing with his staff watchfully at his side. I reflected that, as vassals of Austria-Hungary, the Czechs must understand German, and as I dismounted I spoke.

'Good morning. Are you the commanding officer of these excellent fellows? I am Captain Jones. I have come from England, and my companions and I have been travelling many days to find you.'

He stared at me coldly. 'You are not an Englishman: your German is too good.' He spoke my tongue very well, with a slight country twang, not unlike that of my own Silesia. 'I wonder whether you are a released prisoner of war, or perhaps a bolshevik spy. I must request you to surrender your weapons immediately.' Helplessly I turned to my companions and explained; Tchaikovsky protested vigorously in Russian, and Tatiana added her pleas, but the Czech was adamant. I handed over my two revolvers, and the others surrendered their fowling-pieces, and then we were hustled and elbowed forward to the open door of one of the wagons. Its floor was straw strewn, and in the gloom I could see several disconsolate figure huddled in the corner. I felt the prick of a bayonet in my thigh and, taking the hint, scrambled up into the wagon. My companions followed. A soldier with a clanking ring of keys at his belt climbed in after us, produced some chains and padlocks, and in a minute, despite our protests, had us securely manacled by the wrists.

When we were alone, except for the silent doleful figures opposite us, Clark grinned spitefully at me. 'Your friends, eh? The Czechs. Done you right proud. So you ain't really one of them at all. Can't speak the lingo. Then who the hell are you?'

I remembered Tasker in Salonika. There was no diversion I

198

could create here. I glanced at Tatiana for help. She spoke in a low voice. 'No, Captain Clark – Nobby. He is not a Czech, but he is a good man, and he has brought us here, safe and sound, under the orders of the British government, and if you had not been such a damned fool' – and she blushed prettily – 'as to get our aeroplane destroyed, we might have succeeded in our mission by now. We might be flying out of Russia with all the imperial family, instead of being prisoners here!' And suddenly she was sobbing uncontrollably.

With my wrists chained I could do little to comfort her, except reach out my hands together and lay them over hers. Clark was properly discomfited, and Tchaikovsky turned to me:

'I do not know who you are, Captain Jones, but I think it matters little. You were not to know, and I could not warn you, that these Czechs think the bolsheviks and Germans are working together to keep them from fighting for their homeland. They are rightly suspicious of everyone who is not a legionary. It will take a little time, I think, but we will persuade them that we are not their enemies.'

One of the figures opposite growled something in Russian. Tchaikovsky looked at him disdainfully, and spoke a single word. There was silence, broken only by the sound of Tatiana's sobs. Outside, the babble continued, orders were shouted, the engine gave a sharp cough and a sneeze. Our jailer, his rifle slung over his shoulder, climbed aboard again, there came a succession of juddering jerks, and the train began to move, the wagons cannoning and the wheels squealing, backward along the line. Through the open door of the wagon we saw four Czechs riding our captured ponies beside the track.

It was two or three hours later when we pulled into a station: on the single signalman's hut the name was painted in Russian characters which Tchaikovsky read out for me as Sarochinskaya. Here there were more Czechs, bivouacked on both sides of the line, or leaning from the windows of coaches drawn up along a short siding. The train ground to a stop with a mighty clang of buffers that passed from wagon to wagon, and a last exhausted sigh of steam. Eager faces gathered round our wagon doorway, bombarding our guard with a confusion of questions to which he answered in morose monosyllables. After some minutes two pans of tea were handed up into the wagon, with a fistful of battered enamel mugs.

The tea was lukewarm and thin, with a fine sludge of broken leaves swirling in it, but after the long journey in the midday heat it was like nectar to us all. *'Chai! chai!'* exclaimed our fellow prisoners, jostling together to dredge the last drops from their pan. There were four of them, and four of us, but still they stared longingly and enviously as we sipped luxuriously and filled our mugs again. Tchaikovsky, who had ignored all their approaches throughout the train ride, told me that they were Red Guards who had been captured as they patrolled ahead of their armoured train.

Soon afterwards, a party of Czech soldiers with fixed bayonets came and took them from the wagon. Within a few minutes we heard a short, sharp round of firing, and we did not see the bolsheviks again. We were left alone, with only an occasional curious face at the wagon door, until it was near evening, but you may imagine our apprehension. Tatiana and I talked together in low voices, gently, not daring to express what was in each other's mind; Clark and Tchaikovsky sat hunched and silent, staring miserably at the last hours of the day.

Eventually the firing party returned for us, unchained our hands, and let us climb stiffly down to stand in a line, our backs to the train and our faces to the declining sun. I could not even stand with Tatiana, for I was at one end of the line and she, her beautiful frame boldly defiant, at the other. 'Right turn! forward march!' ordered one of the guards in good German, and we were urged onward with rifle butts toward the rear of the train.

I think it was an English writer who said that the prospect of imminent death 'marvellously concentrates the mind'. I have heard others remark, too, how in those last few moments as death approaches one seems able to observe and remember every small detail; and, indeed, I have experienced something of the kind myself, several times in my life. As we walked, stumbling once or twice, the length of the train, I became intensely aware of the extraordinary appearance of the wagons that we passed. Each was obsessively and idiosyncratically decorated with wreaths of flowers and leaves, and on each of the great sliding doors was painted a richly romantic scene – a sentimental exile gazing upon a vision of his homeland, a

200

cottage hearth fondly remembered in every particular, a bold Czech legionary with a red, white and blue flag urging his comrades across a barricade of fallen bolshevik bodies. And then, beyond the wagons, we came to one of the passenger cars, and there we halted

The car was obviously staff headquarters: the rickety tap of an old typewriter could be heard within, and there were two sentries at the steps who accosted everyone who approached – but in a free and easy way that did not seem military to me. One of our escort climbed up onto the rear platform of the car, tapped at the door and went in. A minute later he emerged again, accompanied by a tall, heavily-built man whose uniform, like those of the legionaries around us, bore no marks of rank, but who was obviously an officer of some importance. He put his hands to the rail of the platform and looked us over with a puzzled frown:

'Which of you is the leader?' he asked in a harshly-accented German. I stepped one pace forward in my best parade-ground manner. He nodded briefly, and I was grabbed by the guard and almost lifted bodily on to the train.

The Trans-Siberian railway has a gauge of five feet, which allows for the building of a particularly wide-bodied rolling stock, and when I stepped inside the door of the headquarters car I was amazed at its roominess: it was more like someone's parlour than a coach on a train. There was a worn and torn carpet, a big iron stove, two blowsy armchairs and an office desk, behind which sat a small man in faded field green, a plain little forage cap set seriously on his head. With his deeply-lined intelligent face, hooked nose, protruding ears and shaggy moustache, he looked very like one of the Armenians that I had left behind in Baku a fortnight before.

I clicked my heels as well as I could in my disintegrating Russian boots, saluted meticulously, and announced myself: 'Captain Simon Jones, South Staffordshire Regiment.' I could think of no more plausible alternative. The officer who had followed me in replied: 'This is General Ceček – and I am Colonel Jiri Kosina,' he added, apologetically.

The general stared at me for nearly a minute, his hands wide apart upon the edge of his desk, before he spoke. His German was excellent, but the deep melancholy of his voice gave it a strange monotonous quality.

'Why don't you tell me the truth? because I am convinced that you are not an English officer, and in fact I suggest to you that you are a freed German prisoner-of-war, or perhaps (I don't know) an Austrian, who has escaped, or possibly you were released with the connivance of the bolsheviks for some treacherous purpose of their own – nobody conceivably could trust them, for they are motivated solely by self-interest – and you stole (I, myself, think you stole them, although of course it is always possible that you didn't, that you found some way of coaxing their owner into parting with them fairly voluntarily, or at least with only a little persuasion) these clothes so that you would not immediately be recognised as a German – or an Austrian, who knows? – in the hope that you might be able to pass unchallenged through our lines, and perhaps get back to rejoin your compatriots in the Ukraine, where they seem to be on rather friendly terms at this moment with the bolsheviks, not that that surprises me, everywhere I look betrayal seems to be the order of the day, and we should not be surprised that those who were enemies six months ago should now be in collusion, it is the way of the world as the English playwright Congreve once said, and it suits the Germans, you Germans, very well to be on friendly terms with the bolsheviks, since it frees hundreds of thousands of your troops to be moved to the western front while all the time we are kept here, when we should be fighting in France . . . '

I did not hear him take a breath, but as he paused briefly to consider the awfulness of his fate I spoke. 'General Čeček, upon my honour as an officer, I assure you that I am not an escaped German prisoner-of-war,' (I realised with horror that only the word 'escaped' kept my statement from being a downright lie) 'but a fully-accredited envoy of the British government. And so are my companions.'

'Ah yes, your companions. And who are they?'

'Captain Pavel Tchaikovsky, formerly of the Imperial Russian Flying Service, and Captain Clark, of the British North-West Frontier Force.'

'Oh, so you are *all* captains? Do you know that American saying about there being too many chiefs and not enough Indians? We used to laugh a lot at that. I myself, a few months ago, was only a lieutenant, but now I have been elected general. And Jiri there, he used to be my corporal . . . But who is the lady?'

I explained as best I could about Tatiana, and the aeroplane we had brought from England, and how it had crashed in flames outside Astrakhan, but I judged it unwise to tell Ček of our true mission. He stared steadily at me with his liquid brown eyes as I talked, and then suddenly he cut across me in his slow flat tones:

'I find it impossible to believe this story. You try my credulity too far.'

I shrugged. 'Nevertheless, I assure you that I have told nothing but the truth.'

'And I suppose that your companions will tell the same tale?'

'You are at liberty to interrogate them, one by one. Miss Fitzalbert speaks both German and Russian. Captain Tchaikovsky speaks only Russian and English; Captain Clark, I am afraid speaks only English, Urdu, Hindi, Persian, and a number of dialects, but I am sure that Miss Fitzalbert would be pleased to translate for you.'

He must have heard the disdain in my voice, but he appeared untroubled by it. I was hustled once more from the carriage, with no chance to speak with the others, and stood uneasily by as one by one they were taken before the general. Tchaikovsky was the last to enter Ček's office, leaving the three of us shifting uncomfortably under the eyes of our guards – and ten minutes later, he had still not emerged. It was now nearly dark; we had not eaten, nor had we had any opportunity to relieve ourselves, for more than eight hours, and Tatiana, I could see, was in great discomfort. Then the carriage door burst open, and Tchaikovsky appeared on the rear platform, his hair and moustache seized with a life of their own, and his eyes twinkling.

'Jones! Tatiana! Nobby! Do you know the Laurin & Klement motor car? No? Oh – it is a beautiful car, a dream. And General Ček used to sell them, in Petrograd!'

When we all crowded back into Ček's office the atmosphere was subtly different. He still regarded us with suspicion, but, as he said:

'There seems to be some possibility that your story may be

true, although of course I have no way of corroborating it at the moment, and indeed it is only Captain Tchaikovsky's personal enthusiasm for the Laurin & Klement – a truly magnificent motor car, available in a range of models, of which the type FF, the eight-cylinder model, is particularly outstanding – it was, as I say, Captain Tchaikovsky's familiarity with this motor car (he tells me that his father owned one for several years, and it is possible that I myself sold it to him) that has – temporarily, at least – persuaded me that there may be some substance to your account of your journey here, although I am still not clear as to its true purpose, because all of you have been more than evasive on this matter, and I intend to pursue my interrogations further, but since it appears probable that you are none of you Germans working for the bolsheviks – although I would like to know rather more about you, Captain Jones, than you have so far seen fit to tell me – I will give orders that you are to be allowed to remain at liberty although I must warn you that the sentries will be told to shoot if any of you goes further than the limits of my camp, and now, as I suppose that I must prove to you that any enmity between us is, at least for the moment, removed, I wonder whether you will take a drink with me?'

Colonel Kosina produced six glasses and a bottle of vodka. In pouring the spirit, his attention was momentarily diverted by a distant shout that caused him to turn his head sharply toward the window, and a pool of liquid spread itself across the general's papers. Kosina and Ček leapt at the desk, dragging away documents and dabbing wildly with the cuffs of their uniforms, and in the confusion yet another glass was upset; but at last we all stood to attention, toasted 'Victory! and the downfall of the bolsheviks!' and threw back the fiery spirit in a single gulp. Kosina refilled the glasses, setting the open bottle down on the edge of the desk and desperately lungeing to catch it as it erupted in a stream across the carpet.

I proposed 'General Ček and the Czech Legion!' and again we tossed it back. After our meagre breakfast we had eaten nothing all day, and I began to fear the effects of the liquor on Clark, but Kosina's exploits had nearly emptied the bottle, and Ček, still suspicious and not knowing any good reason why we should be there, did not think it a good moment at which to toast the success of our own endeavours, so we drank no more.

Tatiana spoke: 'General, we have had no change of clothing for a fortnight. Is it possible that you could give us something clean to wear?'

Cecek shrugged widely. 'I have only uniforms: Russian blouses, breeches and boots. Kosina will have some brought to you in your quarters. I am putting you in what was the ladies' waiting-room of this pathetically provincial station. You may eat with the men. Good night.'

Tatiana, and afterwards the rest of us, found some relief in a terrifyingly filthy water-closet. A legionary brought a bucket of water and a pile of uniforms, and, when we had washed and dressed ourselves, Tchaikovsky and Tatiana set off to find food and drink. Clark and I rested for a few minutes on a sticky plush-covered bench beside the cold stove. Clark had begun to snore fitfully, and even my eyes were slowly closing, when our two comrades burst again through the door, and started to perform some kind of jig round and round the waiting-room, eventually seizing me by both hands, dragging me to my feet and planting kisses (both of them – how I deplore this embarrassing Russian habit!) on my cheeks. And all either of them would say, deliriously, was 'Ilya Murometz! Ilya Murometz!'

CHAPTER 15

29-30 June: Sarochinskaya – Kinel

AT LAST, Tchaikovsky took pity on me and explained his excitement. 'We have found an aeroplane! A great and wonderful aeroplane, almost as big, or perhaps bigger, as your 0/400, and better, I think. It was invented by the famous Igor Ivanovich

Sikorsky. It has four engines of more than 600 horsepower, and two wings with a wingspan of thirty-four metres, and a cabin fit for the Tsar! And I, I, Pavel Stepanovich Tchaikovsky, have flown one. At the pilots' school at Kiev, when I was in training!'

Tatiana took up the story. She and Tchaikovsky had fallen in with one of the legionaries who spoke good Russian; it turned out that he had been a mechanic at Gatchina Park, the flying ground close to St Petersburg, before the outbreak of war. He had watched some of the trials of the 'Ilya Murometz' – the aeroplane was named after a hero of Russian mythology – and had later seen it leave on one of the first bombing flights of the war, the raid of 6 March 1915. Quite a number of these aircraft had been made by Sikorsky for the Flying Service, and, some three or four months before we arrived at Sarochinskaya, one had set out from the airfield at Novo Tcherkhask to fly to Moscow. Soon after take-off, however, the pilot had run into a snowstorm and lost his way, and had eventually been forced down, out of fuel, on the outskirts of Kinel, less than 150 miles from Sarochinskaya. And there the aeroplane had remained.

Could we get to Kinel, and could we find the Ilya Murometz and fly it to Ekaterinburg? We argued the question somewhat ineffectually for some time, but came to no conclusions on what we should or should not do. So we set out, all four of us, to find our supper before the night.

It was now dark, but kerosene lamps were burning above the station and along the train. The station stood alone in the steppe, a good half-mile from the village, and comprised only the waiting-room and stationmaster's office, the signal cabin, and a little wooden hut that constantly supplied boiling water for making tea or coffee. Beyond the faint pool of light cast by the lamps, beyond the sidings with their wagons and slumbering locomotives, the Czechs had established their lines of defence; but close by, just at the end of the low brick platform that formed a narrow promenade before our quarters, a field kitchen had been set up. A long line of legionaries stood waiting; we joined them, discovering very soon that they each held a metal plate or mess-tin, while we had nothing. Clark volunteered to find something for each of us, and returned in due course with the tops of two biscuit tins, a saucepan lid and a small barber's bowl, which he insisted upon keeping for himself. We were now so near the head of the line that it was too late to send him in search of forks or spoons, so we were all compelled to eat the meal, a vile mix of floury dumplings and strings of cow's meat, with our fingers. We ate sitting on one of the station benches beside two of the legionaries.

'This cow,' said one to me in German, 'ought to have been pickled in vinegar for a fortnight at least – and so ought the man who bought it.'

The sun had set in a last slow stretch of orange and violet: the kerosene lamps burned flickering in the night breeze, making small areas of umber light that shifted suddenly, throwing the shadows aside like a newcomer elbowing through a crowd. In the dark, somebody brought out a violin, another an accordion; suddenly a song swelled softly about us – not a simple soldier's song, such as I had heard in many messes in the past four years, not a Russian folk-song full of the lingering pathos of a gypsy long gone from his home, nor one of the wild stamping songs of the plains. It was both familiar and infinitely foreign, uncomplicated in its natural structure, but puzzling, with phrases that seemed to last too long and come to an end too soon. Almost tone-deaf as I am, I could recognise it, and in time I would come to identify it as something singularly Czech.

Other songs followed: the whole camp seemed to be singing, each man quietly to himself, in tones that ranged from a sonorous bass to a soaring tenor. Some soldiers near us put their arms about their neighbours' shoulders, and danced a slow stately dance. Tentatively, Tchaikovsky added his deep voice to the others. Tears ran down the face of the legionary nearest us, and Tatiana spoke gently to him in Russian. 'He says,' she explained, 'that this is a very comical song, about a brewer of Pilsen who drowned in his own vat.' The night settled deeply across the steppe, and at last the men were ordered to their beds. We too retired, but for more than an hour I could still hear the sound of singing, like a setting tide upon the beach, coming from the wagons up and down the tracks.

We slept miserably, racked on the narrow waiting-room benches, and it was only a few minutes after dawn when an orderly arrived to take us once more to Ĉeĉek. When we filed into the coach we found only Kosina there. The air was stale with cigarette smoke. Ček's desk was covered with half-drunk cups of coffee, a greasy plate, and tin lids full of cigarette ends, and the colonel was bustlingly engaged in clearing this dertritus from the desk on to a narrow table that ran at right-angles along the wall of the coach. Behind the rows of cups and ashtrays many books, maps and files stood in ranks, and Kosina began delicately to arrange them so that each, though leaning on its neighbour, could be seen.

Ček, with a cup of fresh coffee in one hand and a glass of water in the other, came silently in through the end door, stared soulfully at each of us in turn and, speaking in Czech, handed the cup and glass to Kosina before seating himself behind the desk. His eyes were heavily bagged as if he had sat there most of the night, and at last he spoke:

'I am still far from satisfied with your story, and today I must return to Samara with Colonel Kosina, so, since it is quite obvious that I cannot leave you here in my absence, I must ask you all to come with me.'

I glanced at Tatiana, not daring to say a word. Her eyes were burning, and I knew that we were both thinking the same thought: Kinel lay about halfway between Sarochinskaya and Samara.

The general turned his heavy gaze upon Tchaikovsky; he spoke in Russian, but I heard once again the name of Laurin & Klement. He seemed suddenly to gain in animation, slapped his hand upon the table, and leapt for a small manual at one end of his row of books. He snatched it away in some sort of triumph but, as each book leant upon the one next to it, slowly, but inexorably, like the standing line of dominoes that children set up in the nursery and flick down with a tricky finger, they crashed forward one by one, into the coffee cups, and the ashtrays, sending a turgid brown tide slowly on across the papers on his desk.

Kosina started forward, but he had forgotten the cup and glass which he held, one in each hand, and a sudden spray of coffee and water surged before him as he moved; one of his big flat feet caught in a torn patch of the carpet and, still holding the cup and glass before him like a priest at the altar, he toppled, breathless, across the full width of the desk, into the spreading pool. Ček stood up, the motor manual still in his hand, and stared at the wet stains across his lap. His expression was sunk deeper into melancholy than before, his eyes without hope, and he spoke feelingly like one who delivers a funeral oration:

'It is very fortunate that we Czechs have such a good sense of humour.'

Thirty minutes later we were aboard the train that steamed out of Sarochinskaya. It was short: a small engine pushing a sandbagged flat-car loaded with legionaries and two machine-guns, Ček's coach, and two vans (their name in Russian is *teplushka*) crowded with soldiers, among whom we found a tiny space. The railway lay beside the Samara river, running very slightly downhill as the steppe spread featureless, broken only by a herd of cattle, a field of new grain, or a cluster of low huts. Once we saw a distant detachment of Red cavalry, but they rode away quickly at the sight of the train. Through Buzuluk we trundled, and Borskaya, where we stopped for just ten minutes to take on water.

Some time after midday, we saw the first houses of Kinel begin to show on the horizon. One of the legionaries took me by the elbow, and pointed across the fields that gradually had replaced the open steppe. 'Now, there's a sight for you,' he said in his rustic German. 'Did you ever see such a thing?' Nearly half a mile from the railway stood a tangle of barns and outhouses, making three sides of a square. And in the court-yard that they enclosed, a vague shape without detail and visible only because of the size of its spreading wings, stood an aircraft, a huge biplane.

'Course,' said the soldier, 'it don't go. Ran out o' petrol, they say, and there ain't no more around here, I can tell you. But it makes you think, don't it?'

It certainly did. I caught my companions' attention, gesturing surreptitiously toward the distant buildings. Tchaikovsky made a sharp intake of breath; Clark hummed wildly to himself; and Tatiana's fingernails bit deeply into my hand. There was our goal: could we reach it, and could we get the Ilya Murometz to fly?

A few minutes later, our train pulled into the station of Kinel and stopped with a sudden jerk. Legionaries leapt down to greet comrades gathered on the low platform, or to jostle at the buffet for the few scraps of food on sale. A number of ill-dressed townspeople also stood there, staring blankly at the train, or smiling hopefully, or speaking persuasively to the Czech soldiers. Discreetly, we too climbed down from the train, to stand openly on the platform and talk busily with anyone who would lend half an ear. We were all four in the faded grey-green uniform of the legionaries (our belts and wallets with their gold pieces concealed inside our breeches), and we blended easily with the crowd. Tatiana and Tchaikovsky accosted an elderly peasant woman and began to bargain half-heartedly for a melon; while I, plucking up courage, picked out one of the more respectable-looking citizens and spoke to him in a German heavily afflicted with what I supposed to be a Czech accent: 'So this is Kinel; I look forward, mister, to seeing your beautiful town.'

It was, as far as I could see, glancing uneasily over his shoulder, far from beautiful; a scruffy scattering of houses whose only reason for existence seemed to be that they lay at the junction of two railway lines – that along which we had come, and the main line, which ran from Samara in the west to Tchely-abinsk in the east, where it joined the principal Siberian railway.

The train was now, with hoots, jets of steam and many encouraging shouts, being coaxed onto the main line. Czech legionaries were running to rejoin it, stuffing newly-bought bread and fruit into the open fronts of their tunics. We surged forward with the rest of the people and garrison of Kinel, unobtrusively elbowing our way deeper into the crowd, so that, as the last soldiers were bundled aboard, the engine let out a vast black eruption, and the train began to gather speed on the down run to Samara, we were left behind on the platform, waving wildly and free, for the moment, from our captors.

But we might not be free for long. Already our disappearance could have been discovered: Čeček could order the train to return for us, or at Smyshliaevka, no more than twenty miles away, he could telegraph to Kinel to command our arrest. On the other hand, nobody at Kinel knew what we looked like: we were dressed identically with many of the legionaries around us, and with good luck we might escape detection. Clark nodded to me, I nodded to Tatiana, and as the crowd of townspeople

210

began to drain away from the station toward their homes we moved quietly with them. I glanced at the two or three *izvosh-tchikyi* waiting patiently in the station yard: perhaps one of the dozing drivers would be sufficiently discreet to drive us out to the farm without asking questions or gossiping about us afterward – but Tchaikovsky caught my eye and lightly shook his head.

Already the crowd was thinning and soon we would be conspicuous on the afternoon streets of Kinel. And I was hungry. We passed a small dusty inn: two storeys, a sagging verandah, a half-open door with a cool shadow beyond. Again Tchaikovsky caught my eye, and this time he nodded. We turned back, mounted the two creaking steps to the verandah, and cautiously pushed the door. Inside, the room was empty, with just two scrubbed wooden tables and some high-backed benches.

Tchaikovsky called softly, and a cross-eyed Tatar girl appeared from the kitchen. He spoke to her for a minute or so, she bobbed a slight curtsey, and we were alone again. I flung myself down on one of the benches, and the others joined me.

'I think it would be wise,' said Tchaikovsky, 'if we were to speak together in English. It is the only language that we all understand, and I believe this girl will not be suspicious if we speak it openly. I think perhaps she knows some German, for there are Mennonite colonists not far from here, but I have told her that we are Slovaks from Carpathia, and if I and Tatiana speak good Russian with her she will not think twice about it unless she is interrogated.'

The girl brought us cucumber soup, plates of good cold beef and pickled cucumbers, with glasses of *kvass*. While we ate we discussed our plans, and quickly agreed that we would wait for late afternoon before setting out to walk eastward to find the aeroplane. When we were near the farm, Tatiana, Clark and I would hide close by, while Tchaikovsky went in search of the farmer. From then on, it would be a question of luck.

The *kvass* made us all sleepy, and we dozed the afternoon away with our heads on the table, just like real Russians. The inn was quiet, with only an occasional shrill exclamation and the bang of an empty pan in the kitchen, and the distant clucking of hens in the yard behind the house. At last, it was time to press a

211

gold sovereign into the girl's willing red-scrubbed hand and leave.

The town was silent. We found a lane running in the right direction, which soon became a track, on either side of which green cornfields stretched away beneath the setting sun. Our marching shadows strode out before us, larks sang high in the sky and rabbits bounded away almost from under our feet. In less than an hour we saw farm buildings on the horizon, and a few minutes later we found a narrow path winding into the corn on our right. Here we shook hands with Tchaikovsky, watched him trudge bravely on toward the farm, and then, following our path for some fifty yards, sat ourselves down out of sight of the track.

'Oh my god,' moaned Clark, dragging off his boots and wriggling his bony toes, 'me feet.' These were the first words he had spoken for two or three hours: he had eaten in silence while we discussed our plans, and he had stumbled morosely on with us, scowling to right and left, while Tatiana and I had held hands and smiled fondly at one another, and Tchaikovsky had led the way, whistling some formless Russian air. Now Clark lay upon his back, put his two hands behind his head and, closing his eyes, began to snore noisily.

A cool breath from the north-east began to ripple the young corn. The sun was now so low that we lay in its shadow. My whole body felt gritty, constrained in the ill-fitting uniform, and my head was feverish. I too took off my boots, and then my tunic, and unbuckled my belt. I glanced at Tatiana: her tunic was unbuttoned, and one sly breast peeped coyly from between. I looked at Clark – he was fast asleep – and I looked at Tatiana again. Together we rose softly, walking in single file a hundred yards further down the path, and found a gently swelling bank on which a bed of last year's straw still lay. In seconds my breeches were off, and Tatiana's about her knees, as we felt the air caress our bodies. And then it was our hands as well as the breeze, and our lips were together, our tongues meeting and curling, and the sweet scent of Tatiana's body mingling with the smell of the rich old earth, the warm dead straw, and the thrusting green all about us.

More than two weeks had passed since we last had made love, in Kazvin, on the cistern lid above Clark's head. Then it had

212

been wild and sudden, two crazed young beasts coupling below the staring Persian stars; now we were weary, and slow, even in our urgency, and infinitely gentle. Quail trilled among the corn stalks, a whimbrel whauped its melancholy across the fields, a dog barked far away. When we looked about us again it was dusk.

The dog barked close by. We scrabbled undignified for the clothes that we had flung aside, and crept back to the still sleeping Clark. With a hand over his mouth I shook him gently awake, and quickly together we put on our boots. Seconds later the dog was on us, with no further bark and only a sudden scuffle of paws to warn us: a big black lurching beast with a lolling tongue, which slid to a stop, stared at us balefully, and then began to yelp hysterically, its loose ears tossed back and its eyes rolling red. We stood staring back at it in equal surprise, unable to run, for we had nowhere to go, and with nothing but our bare hands to protect us. From the track we heard a shout and another shout in answer. Had we already been found and recaptured?

But one of the voices was Tchaikovsky's and a few moments later he came stumbling up, followed by a shaggy, shambling fellow who fell upon the dog, and kissed it, and wrestled with it on the ground until it was impossible to tell which was dog and which black-bearded Russian. With a stab of guilt I remembered, for the first time in weeks, my faithful Moritz, the Great Dane who had lived with me, and even flown with me, and now was left forever in the care of the good Bodenschatz.

But Tchaikovsky was bubbling with his news. 'It is very wonderful! The farmer, he is a Tsarist, and I think perhaps he will let us have the Ilya Murometz. Of course, I had to be very discreet: I spoke to him of many things, of the prospects for the harvest, the rising price of cattle, and how bad it is for the herds to have these soldiers fighting all around them, and how far it is to Moscow . . . And then gradually the talk came round to the revolution, and the *moujiks* who have run away, and the foolishness of the bolsheviks in wanting to nationalise the estates. And I have drunk vodka, and eaten smoked sterlet, and all the time you have been waiting out here in the fields, tired and hungry – but what could I do?' He flung wide his arms and rolled his eyes, and Tatiana and I, holding hands, burst out laughing.

'Lead me to it!' exclaimed Clark, clutching at his belly. 'Me stomach thinks me throat's cut. I reckon I could eat almost anything – even caviar, though I never did go for that. It may be all right for the general, but I'm a pretty private person, to put it in a nut, colonel. Besides which, little lady,' he continued, winking at Tatiana, 'the trouble with caviar is, you know only too well where it's bin. *"Caviar emptor"*, my old mum used to say.'

In a short walk we reached the farmhouse. It was a large, rambling building, single-storied, and made almost entirely from pine-logs laid one upon the other. The barns lay behind it, and somewhere there was the Ilya Murometz, but I would have to contain my impatience until later, for there were social duties to be performed.

Our host, forewarned by the hysterically barking dog that dashed madly forward, and then back to wind itself wildly about our feet, was standing on the porch to greet us. He was a lightly-built man, no taller than myself, with a thin intelligent face and close-cropped, almost ginger, hair. He was dressed in peasant fashion: a white bloused shirt of fine cotton, buttoning on the left shoulder, a big belt, and baggy black trousers tucked into unpolished black boots. He spoke only Russian, but his short speech of welcome needed no translator: even I understood when he introduced himself as Stepan Stepanovich Tchubukov. We all shook hands (no kissing, thank god) a bent old woman stood holding the door open, and so we entered the house.

The floorboards of the hall creaked below our feet. On the wall to the right of the entrance door hung a small ikon, with a tiny oil lamp burning before it; otherwise the hall was bare of all furniture except for a bench and a heavy old table. Stepan Stepanovich turned to the left, leading us through a dimly-lit anteroom lined with an assortment of ill-matched chairs and into a vast salon that stretched the width of the house. In the centre of this salon stood a great cubic stove. It was covered with tiles and reminded me of my childhood home: Rococo with red and gilt moulding, the chimney reared up into the dark of the eaves. Round the stove were scattered some half-dozen Bokhara rugs, and beyond them ranged chairs, sofas and low tables, with as many as a dozen oil lamps burning bright. Rising incongruously among the heavy dark chairs stood a grand piano in white and gold, scratched and dusty, and above it hung an unlighted chandelier. The inner sides of the pine-log walls had been plastered, and then covered with French wallpaper in stripes of lilac and green, but the plaster was uneven, and the stripes ran at all angles; here and there, near the tops of the walls, the paper sagged and hung down raggedly. The few windows were revealed by the curtains of brown balding velvet which had been drawn across them.

Stepan Stepanovich gestured round about with a wide sweep of the arm, and spoke again. 'He says that we will eat dinner soon,' translated Tatiana, 'but first he would like us to meet his wife and daughter.' And there was a rustle behind us, and a faint tittering, and two of the most vacuous women I have ever met in my life had entered the room. They were not only vacuous, they were plain, though dressed prettily enough in long white dresses with high collars, which made poor Tatiana, in her crumpled Czech legionary's uniform, look sadly out of place.

We all shook hands again, the wife and daughter giggled, Clark leered at both, Tchaikovsky bowed and made some gallant speech, Tatiana said a few simple words, the bent old woman brought in a tray of tea in tall glasses, and the daughter sat down at the piano to play very badly – even I could tell that. It was a great relief to us all when the salon door was flung open and a squinting manservant – the cowman, I later learnt – shouted that dinner was ready.

Led by our host, who was talking excitedly to Tchaikovsky, we filed once more out of the salon, through the hall and into a dining-room that lay behind it. Clark, who was clearly captivated by both wife and daughter, contrived to get one on each arm, while Tatiana and I followed modestly behind. The dining-room was much smaller than the salon we had left, but accommodated a long table, its varnish badly scratched, on which stood dishes of grilled pork chops, boiled ham, and plain cabbage. At the near end of the room was a long sideboard covered with dishes of smoked and pickled fish, cucumbers and mushrooms in vinegar, and two or three kinds of little pie; there were also four or five bottles of vodka and a platoon of little glasses. Tchaikovsky turned excitedly to Tatiana: '*Zakouski*!' he exclaimed. 'For the first time in months – *Zakouski*!'

I was anxious to get to the meat: I had never taken to the Baltic food that our servants had eaten at home in Silesia. But politeness dictated that we should follow our hosts' example, and so for half an hour or more we sipped vodka, and took titbits in our fingers, standing all the while and making such conversation as we could. Tatiana smiled and babbled on, the wife and daughter simpered at Clark, he shiftily soaking up the vodka and I covertly watching him, while Tchaikovsky and Stepan Stepanovich were deep in a Russian debate.

All the time, the hot food on the table was growing colder, but nobody seemed to care; and when at last we sat down, and filled our plates, the meat was thick with grease, the cabbage limp and clammy. Madame Tchubukov tugged at a bell-pull by the door, and the cowman brought in a jug of *kvass,* half of which he spilled as he tipped it into thick glass tumblers by our plates.

Stepan Stepanovich sat at the head of the table and led the conversation. With four Russian speakers to listen and reply, there was little that Clark or I could say. Now and again Tatiana translated for our benefit, and we nodded and smiled. The room was stuffy, we were all weary after our tramp, and we had drunk far too much vodka.

Our host spoke long and feelingly about his work on the farm, the shortcomings of the peasants, and his love for his country. 'You know, I rise at five o'clock in the morning, and I labour from dawn to night . . . and I see what people are like all around me. One has only to start to do anything to see how few honest, decent folk there are. Sometimes as I lie awake at night I think: O Lord, Thou hast given immense forests, boundless steppes, the widest horizons, and living here we ourselves ought really to be giants!'

I muttered to Tatiana that this was perhaps the right moment to mention the aeroplane; she nodded and addressed our host for some minutes. He looked sharply at me, his eyes close either side of his long thin nose, and then swept his gaze round the table before he spoke.

'The Ilya Murometz is the property of the Tsar,' Tatiana translated. 'He has kept it safe here, even though the bolsheviks came and wanted to take it away. But nobody can take it, because there is no fuel for it. No petrol of any kind nearer than a hundred *versts.*'

Tchaikovsky excitedly asked a question, to which Stepan Stepanovich gloomily replied with a slow shake of the head. Tchaikovsky asked another, and then another, to each of which he received the same answer. His face fallen, he turned to me: 'I fear perhaps we have come all this way to no avail. It seems there is no way of starting the aeroplane.'

So once more our hopes were dashed. I pushed my plate away – I could eat no more. Stepan Stepanovich also put aside his plate, and stood up, speaking. 'But now,' said Tchaikovsky, with a fatalistic shrug, 'he will show it to us.' Dejectedly, Tchaikovsky and I followed our host out of the dining-room, while Clark helped himself to another chop and Tatiana returned to make bright conversation with the ladies of the house. We went through a wide, dark kitchen where the old woman was crouched over a sink by the light of a flickering candle, and out into the thin grey of the midsummer night. From beside the back door Stepan Stepanovich unhooked a lighted hurricane lamp which he held high in the air, casting long darting shadows across the yard as hens scuttled clucking from between our feet.

Two wings of low buildings almost enclosed the yard, and we went through the narrow gap between them. Beyond, the moon was low above the steppe, spreading a yellow glow across the fields and over the sky, against which a heart-stopping great silhouette rose before us. It had a double under-carriage like the 0/400, but did not stand so high from the ground, crouching like a falcon covering its stricken prey. The wings were immense, the upper plane extending well beyond the lower, with great broad ailerons that reminded me of the Albatros: I counted seven pairs of struts each side. There were four slim engines, and the fuselage was completely enclosed, with no open cockpits for pilot or observer. In solemn procession, Stepan Stepanovich swinging his lamp like a censer, we walked silently around the machine: its length was some twenty good paces, and I estimated the upper wingspan at a staggering thirty-five.

I laid my hand upon our host's shoulder. 'It's wonderful!' I said, as Tchaikovsky translated for me. 'May we see the interior?'

Stepan Stepanovich spoke briefly, wearily, and turned away. 'Perhaps tomorrow,' Tchaikovsky explained. 'He says that now it is time for his daughter to play the piano again.'

After another excruciating performance and some more glasses of tea – the Russians, Tchaikovsky and Tatiana included, drank theirs through a lump of rough brown sugar held between their teeth – Stepan Stepanovich at length took up a lamp and led us to our beds. We were to sleep in the *dacha,* a small hut at the side of the farmhouse, with four tiny bedrooms surrounded by a wide verandah. Each room backed onto a corner of a large unlit stove, on top of which stood a pitcher of water and a china bowl. The beds were hard but clean, and I looked forward to a sound refreshing sleep.

But sleep would not come. I turned and turned in the still air, my brain a whirl of thought. I was desolate to have travelled so far, and to have endured so much, only to have all my hopes brought to nothing. Was there no way in which we could get the Ilya Murometz to fly? Was there no way in which we could get petrol? We would need full tanks to reach our destination, and it seemed likely that even after many days of making enquiries, and of travelling all over the region with carts, we would not find enough. We were marooned in the middle of a hostile country, thousands of miles from friends, and now we could not even count on the help of the Czechs to escape from Russia.

The sun was rising, and its earliest rays were creeping through the chinks of the shutters, when the first light came breaking also into my mind. My comrade Werner Voss, who had commanded *Jasta* 10, had possessed a motor-cycle that was as dear to him as his Fokker triplane. Like me in so many ways, he had differed completely in one: he was truly mechanically minded, and spent many hours tinkering with his engines, his hands black with grease. And he had once shown me how his motor-cycle could be run on kerosene.

Could I remember all the details? Did I, or Tchaikovsky, know enough to be able to find the right parts of the aircraft engines and make any necessary modifications? I supposed that kerosene would be fairly easy to obtain in the region, and that Stepan Stepanovich would be able to buy it without attracting undue attention. I seemed to remember that at some point in last night's talk he had told us that he owned two International Harvester tractors, new-fangled machines that his peasants regarded with undisguised hostility. I swung my legs to the floor and opened the door. It was day.

Impatiently I dragged on my breeches and boots, and set off round the verandah to wake Tchaikovsky. I banged at his door for minute after minute before at last, puffy with sleep, he opened it to me.

'There is a chance!' I babbled. 'A chance to get the aeroplane to fly. Quick, quick, you must come with me at once to look at the engines!' As Tchaikovsky withdrew into the dark to dress, Clark's face appeared at the adjoining door.

'I heard that,' he said. 'Bit of a turn up for the book if you can do it, ol' boy. Think you can?'

'It is only an idea,' I told him. 'But it is a trick that Leutnant Voss taught me, and I think it may work. Come with us to see.'

We made our way round the end of the great barn that hid the Ilya Murometz from our view. Labourers were already stirring from their humble quarters, and they stared at us with sullen suspicion but did not speak. The great aeroplane looked even larger in the morning light, and together we walked to the trailing edge of the wide wing. Because the machine stood much lower than the Handley Page the rear of the engines was almost level with my head, and I could see what I had not dared hope to see. Below the upper wing, and immediately above the cabin, were two large torpedo-shaped fuel tanks, which fed separate smaller tanks behind each engine, and from these tanks a maze of narrow copper tubing led to rows of carburettors.

'You see!' I gestured excitedly to my companions. 'We fill the main tank with kerosene, but we cannot start the engines with it, so we must find if there are taps to keep it from flooding into the feed tanks. Then we start the engines, and when they are running hot enough then we can switch them over to kerosene. It worked with Werner's motor-cycle, and perhaps it will work for us!'

'But how do we start the engines?' asked Clark.

I hesitated. 'Werner did it with petrol,' I admitted. 'But he told me that on one occasion he had started the engine with a glassful of brandy.'

Tchaikovsky laughed bitterly. 'Brandy!' he said. 'If we were in Smolensk I could find you the finest cognac, but where will we get it in this god-forsaken province?'

'Well now,' said Clark, with a crooked grin, 'who said we

wanted brandy? It's not quality we need, my friend, it's crudity. It's the alcohol that gets the engine goin', right? And I reckon we had quite a bit of that last night, eh? Seemed to me, that the vodka we was drinking must have been a good hundred proof – and starting an engine's just about what it's fit for.'

I went to seize him enthusiastically by the hand, when his expression told me that someone stood behind me. Turning, I found Stepan Stepanovich staring at me coldly. I took his hand instead, and began to pour out my story again, forgetting that he could understand nothing I said. Tchaikovsky came to my rescue, and, speaking not only with his tongue but with his hands, his shoulders, his eyes and even his eloquent moustache, gradually brought an expression of understanding, amusement and, at last, excitement to our host's face. He shouted something across the yard to a passing peasant, who shortly brought us a stepladder, and one by one we climbed up and into the cabin of the Ilya Murometz.

It was roomy and well-lit by the big square windows each side of the fuselage and the morning light flooding in through the transparent nose. The pilot's seat was well forward, and the controls were dominated by a wheel that was more like the steering-wheel of a motor car than the elegant control column that I was used to. However, the rudder pedals and instruments – such as they were – seemed reasonably familiar. And, as I hoped, protruding into the cabin roof just aft of the pilot's position, were two handcocks obviously designed to cut off the flow of petrol from the main tanks to the engines.

The next six hours passed so slowly, it seemed at times as though Stepan Stepanovich's watch must have stopped. Two wagons were despatched at once to Kinel, loaded with empty barrels. The drivers were given careful instructions, and a judicious number of our golden sovereigns. Then we woke Tatiana, and together ate an excited breakfast. Afterwards, Tchaikovsky and I explored the Ilya Murometz inside and out, exclaiming over the armour plate a full centimetre thick that covered the belly and the sides of the cockpit, investigating all the controls, and testing the tautness of the wire rigging. The aircraft seemed to be in remarkably good trim, and, when we had familiarised ourselves with every part, we asked our host to have it dragged out onto a level meadow that stretched eastward to the skyline. There we laid great logs against the wheels of the under-carriage, and took mooring lines to strong pegs driven deep into the soil. There was nothing more we could do, but still the sun climbed higher in the sky, and no movement showed on the track from Kinel. We were about to resign ourselves to lunch with Madame and Miss Tchubukov when a distant cloud of dust in the west at last heralded the return of the wagons.

The men had done well: they had contrived to gather more than 200 gallons of kerosene, and four glass demijohns of vodka. Now came the job of filling the empty tanks. We had no pump, so it was necessary for men to fill buckets with kerosene, pouring it through the tank spouts by means of funnels. I explained to Stepan Stepanovich how important it was that no kerosene should be allowed to spill onto the cabin roof, but I was very apprehensive about the good sense of the peasants, and I fear that despite all precautions there were several accidents.

Meanwhile, Tchaikovsky and I busied ourselves with filling the small feed tanks. There were, of course, no filler caps on these tanks, but there were pressure-actuated breather valves set into small bolt-on plates that were easily removed. It took us no time to pour in the vodka and replace the plates, and then we had only to wait for the filling of the main tanks to be completed. At last this was done, the filler caps were locked back on, the spilt kerosene was wiped from the fuselage, the wagons were backed away, and I faced my great test.

Forty yards from the aircraft, the peasants and house servants formed a crescent of disbelief. Immediately in front of them stood our host's wife and daughter, their hands clasped in concern, and close to the tail stood Stepan Stepanovich himself, uncertain whether to look apprehensive or to preen himself proprietorially.

I needed Tchaikovsky in the cabin with me to judge the sound of the engines, and so Clark and Tatiana would have to start them – and indeed, if we were ever to escape from Ekaterinburg, this no doubt would be their duty. I explained carefully to them what was to be done and then, with the ignition switches up, we went through the routine. This was not only good practice for them, but it served to draw the vodka through the

221

carburettors and into the cylinders. I began with the port engines: Clark and Tatiana each knelt on the wing beside one of the engines, with the starting handle inserted. 'Ignition off.' I flipped up the switches, and they both swung their handles over. 'Ignition on.' I pretended to switch down, and held up my thumb. 'Contact.' They swung over again and then, as if the engines had really fired, slipped off the trailing edge of the wing and ran round behind the tail to repeat the operation on the starboard engines.

Now it was time to test my theory in practice. Tatiana and Clark returned to their places on the port wing, and this time I flipped the switches down as I held up my thumb. They swung on the starting handles like heroes, there was a second of great silence and then, to my amazement, both engines burst into life. I moved the throttle gently, hearing them stutter and almost fail, then swell into a roar before I brought them back to a steady throbbing. Already Clark and Tatiana were in position on the starboard wing, waving anxiously. Switches down, thumb up: they swung on the starters. Nothing. Feverishly, I went through the routine again. Still nothing. A third time – and then, first one engine coughed, and then the second; they picked up, barked loudly, and at last settled down in concert with the others.

I stared at Tchaikovsky. How long would the vodka last in the feed tanks? How soon would the engines be hot enough to burn the kerosene? In the racket my eyes asked dumb pleading questions, to which he replied with a shrug and a shake of the head, his ears cocked listening to the beat of the four. The heads of Tatiana and Clark appeared at floor level in the cabin doorway. The noise of the engines had eased to a regular thumping, and Tchaikovsky gestured to me to open throttle slightly to port, while at the same moment he reached up and slowly began to open the port handcock. In my mind's eye I could see the kerosene gradually mixing with the vodka, diluting it, cooling its fiery spirit. The port engines caught, one after the other, and clattered, and missed a beat, and then suddenly dense black smoke was pouring from the exhausts, lit with red flickers of flame, and I pushed the throttle further forward and heard the rhythm quicken. Success was within our grasp!

Within half a minute, after a few tense seconds, we had the

starboard engines firing in the same way – and only then did I realise that, if I switched off now, it would be a long and tedious business to drain and clean out the feed tanks and start all over again. I shouted at Tchaikovsky:

'You must explain to Stepan Stepanovich that we have to go now! I dare not stop the engines. Make my apologies and say that we fly in the name of the Tsar!' He jumped from the cabin door, swiftly bundled in Tatiana, and strode off to say farewell to our host. Clark came scrambling in after Tatiana, and peasants, crouching low beneath the wing, came running to drag away the logs from in front of the wheels. Tchaikovsky came bounding back, and I sharply turned the wheel from one side to the other to flutter the ailerons, kicked at the rudder pedals, and pushed the throttles forward. The engines howled, but the Ilya Murometz did not move.

'There's still a mooring rope on the tail!' gasped Tatiana. The aircraft was shuddering terrifyingly, Tchaikovsky was screaming from the open cabin door, and I was just about to cut the engines, when there came a sound like a harp-string breaking, and the aircraft, as if launched from a catapult, shot forward. Within seconds we were careering wildly across the meadow, bumping at every tuft of thick grass, and then, almost without my having made a move, we were airborne and climbing fast. I put the Ilya Murometz into a gentle turn and we circled above the farm, seeing the peasants raising and waving their caps and Stepan Stepanovich in front of them, his hands on his hips and his legs braced wide, and his face turned to the sky, watching us as we levelled up and set course to the north-east in a black cloud of smoke, flying out of his life for ever.

223

CHAPTER 16

30 June – 1 July: Kinel – Ekaterinburg

ALTHOUGH I set a course east of north-east, I had very little idea of where I was headed. We were aloft again, free to fly as we pleased in a new and wonderful aircraft; but we had no food or water, no weapons, and no maps. We could fly for just as long as the kerosene lasted, and then I would have to land, with little hope of getting off again unless I could find proper fuel.

There was a watch hanging beside the dashboard instruments: it had long stopped, but started again when Tchaikovsky wound it, and so we would be able to keep some plot of our flight. While Tchaikovsky began to enter his figures and instrument readings on a scrap of paper, I ordered Clark and Tatiana to search the cabin for anything else that might be useful to us. After nearly ten minutes they were about to give up when Tatiana thrust her fingers into a pocket at the back of my own seat and, with a cry of triumph, drew out a folder of aviation maps. Tchaikovsky fell upon these with joy, and immediately began calculating our course and speed. At intervals he pushed past me to peer out of the forward window and identify some ground feature with a grunt of pleasure.

Being at the controls of the Ilya Murometz was, I think, rather like driving a bus. I sat in a wicker seat that was almost an armchair, without a seatbelt, gently manipulating the great steering-wheel. Behind me stretched the cabin, with more wicker seats, a folding table, and curtains at the windows. There was even a dusty samovar. The feeling of being totally enclosed was a strange one. Even though the four engines were roaring away just outside the windows, it was possible to carry on a conversation without shouting too loudly, and there was no slipstream, so helmet and goggles and fur-lined clothing were unnecessary.

The distance to Ekaterinburg, Tchaikovsky told me after a few minutes of calculation, was some 600 *versts* – a little over 650 kilometres, or about 400 miles. I had the throttles almost fully open, and we were thudding along steadily at about one hundred kilometres per hour on the airspeed gauge. There had been only a light breeze from the east before we had taken off, and I hoped that we might make our destination in some six or

224

seven hours – if the fuel lasted. Meanwhile, there was little to do but calculate our course, and keep a lookout for anything on the ground that would help to fix our position.

Like the 0/400, the Ilya Murometz almost flew itself. Tchaikovsky laid an open map across my knees and pointed out the direction in which I was flying. Ekaterinburg lies on the eastern side of a gap between the southern and the northern parts of the Ural mountain chain. We speak of the Ural mountains – and indeed, between the fiftieth and sixtieth parallels, they are the only high ground between the central Siberian plateau and the hills of Britain – but from the air they are little more than a thin heaping of the earth's debris. The highest point of the range – almost due east from where we took off – rises not much more than 3,000 feet from the surrounding plains, and most of the gentle crests are not more than 3,000 feet above sea level. We were flying easily at about 6,000 on the altimeter, and, since our course lay almost parallel to the far-distant line of the southern range, there was no cause for concern.

About three hours after take-off we passed over the town of Ufa, sunk in the valley of the river Belaya, and saw the Ural foothills rising before us. We were less than a mile above the town and could see the cathedral, surrounded by its park, the governor's house to the east of it, and the railway station to the west. Below us was the main line of the Siberian railway, where we could see two armoured trains slowly steaming eastward: were they Czech or bolshevik? we could not tell. We followed the line as it slowly wriggled its way through a great pine forest toward the gorge of the river Sima, past the town of Asha-Balashov, and on to the spreading ironworks of Miniar. The upland heights, grass and naked rock, rose toward us on either hand. The sun was now behind us, and I could see our shadow threading the shallow gorge, flying steadily forward over the steppe beyond, toward the point on the horizon where the hills dipped down before Ekaterinburg. Behind me, Clark and Tatiana had ceased their conversation, and I thought I heard a steady snore competing with the throb of the engines. Even Tchaikovsky was still and silent, and the blue sky stretched empty before me as the sun dropped lower behind.

Another hour passed. I think that once or twice my own eyes must have closed, my head twitched suddenly upon the pivot of my spine. And then, on the steppe ahead, I saw a scattering of dull blue lakes: there were dozens, filling the view, some huge and many smaller, like uncut sapphires thrown down by a giant hand. I shouted for Tchaikovsky, and he roused himself.

'Too far to the south,' he shouted, after consulting his charts. 'We are above Kyschtyinsky.' I bore up some points to the north. 'More, more!' cried Tchaikovsky. 'We must fly east of north.' A wide forest crept down among the lakes, with small settlements in the clearings. I set our course almost due north, where the hills rose again against the skyline, and glanced at the fuel gauges. They were already low.

Minutes passed, a half hour, and the gauges slipped inexorably toward zero. Then, far to the north-east, I thought I saw a town. Could it be Ekaterinburg? We crept closer, and closer, and then I heard the first cough and stutter in the steady beat of the engines. I altered course slightly to eastward, and heard the stutter again, and saw that both tanks were nearly empty. The town was clearer now, with the railway that ran diagonally north-west to south-east through it, a large lake to the west, and the forest that eased all around. The shadows were longer on the ground, the light beginning slowly to fade, casting amber across the wide landscape.

Suddenly the steady note of the engines changed, and we swung wildly to starboard. One of the engines had failed and the propeller, instead of pulling us through the air, was acting as a brake. I throttled back, correcting my course and beginning to put the aircraft into a gradual downward glide. Tchaikovsky bustled to my side, and stared forward through the transparent nose. I did not bother to look at the fuel gauges, for I knew only too well what they would tell me. The second starboard engine cut out, and the aeroplane began to corkscrew to the right. There was only one thing to be done: I reached forward, put up the ignition switch of the outer port engine, and banked slowly to port. On a single engine, and a fuel gauge that read zero, I began my descent.

At about 500 feet, the last engine died. We were losing speed rapidly, for all four propellers were slowing us. I kept the nose of the aircraft up as much as I dared, knowing that very soon we would reach stalling speed, pitch upward for a brief second, slide gently back, and then plunge uncontrollably to earth. We had passed the town, and the forest stretched broad before us. Then Tchaikovsky gripped my shoulder and pointed: to the left I saw a long clearing, a narrow meadow between the trees. It was now or never. I put the Ilya Murometz into a steep, short dive to gain speed, levelled out just above the treetops, inched the stick forward and went in for a landing. We seemed to drop vertically for twenty feet, hit the ground with a thump that seemed as if it must break every strut in the aircraft, bounced and landed again, and then were rushing forward through the long grass for the trees.

Fortunately the grass was indeed long, burying the wheels of the under-carriage deeply and slowing us fast. A mere twenty yards before the trees one of the wheels hit a hidden obstruction, and we slewed round, grunting and groaning, shuddered sideways, steadied again, and came to a quivering halt. In the cabin behind me, I heard the snoring break off:

''Ullo,' said Clark, 'we've stopped. Are we there?'

I could not move from the controls. I sat shivering, both from relief and from the strain of gripping the wheel in our final descent. Tchaikovsky bristled in every muscle:

'Magnificent!' he cried. 'Magnificent! Captain Jones, I shake you by the hand! I kiss you on both cheeks!' And both of these, to my embarrassment and discomfort, he did.

Tatiana, infinitely more acceptably, brushed her lips gently across my neck and breathed into my ear, while Clark could be heard muttering in a strangled voice that he was 'dyin' for a pee'.

Tchaikovsky opened the cabin door, and one by one we jumped down into the long, green grass. The clearing was surrounded by a thick forest of silver birches, with here and there a taller pine. From where we stood beside the aircraft, it stretched away eastward in the light of the sinking sun. All was quiet.

'First, as quickly as possible,' I said, 'we must hide the aircraft. Someone will have seen us descending, and may come to look for us.' Altogether, we lifted the tail of the Ilya Murometz from the ground. And, straining, we trundled the aircraft as far back into the scrub as we could. But only the last few feet of the fuselage were hidden, and the great wings and the engines loomed out undisguised. Searching the fringes of the forest, we found a number of fallen trees, which we dragged out and stood propped against the front of the wings; then we gathered broken branches and draped them precariously from the upper wing. After an hour of effort, our hands thickly sticky with pine gum, we stood back to look at the result of our labours.

Close to, the form of the Ilya Murometz was still unmistakably obvious. We all set off up the clearing, stopping at intervals to turn and take another look at our handiwork. The aircraft seemed to be dissolving, very gradually, into the trees behind it. We passed, at one side of the clearing, an abandoned mineshaft; it was an insignificant little hole, boarded round at the top of the excavation, covered over with a few rotting planks, and almost lost in the encroaching grass. At the end of the clearing a track came into view; here stood a pair of double pine stumps, and here we turned and looked back apprehensively. Would the aircraft be visible to anyone passing along the track? We, who knew it was there, could still discern it – but we persuaded ourselves that it would be invisible to the unsuspecting passer-by.

'Now, what should we do?' said I to the others. 'The town, Ekaterinburg or no, must lie to the south down this track, and that is where our duty takes us. But we are in enemy territory for sure, and we must move with the utmost caution. I think it would be best if you all stay in hiding here while I scout ahead to spy out the land.'

'But not you,' interjected Tchaikovsky, 'that is certain. You speak no Russian. It is I who will go.'

'No, no!' Tatiana cried. 'A woman is less likely to attract suspicion – and besides, I think I know how to distract any man's attention.'

'If you'll take my advice, ol' boy,' said Clark, 'we oughter stick together, jes' like the ivy on the ol' garden wall. You send a man out reconnoitring by himself, and what happens? Johnny Pathan nabs 'im smartish – and then you dunno where you are, send out another, same thing happens, two men lost and you're none the wiser. I reckon we go quiet an' easy down this track here, keepin' a sharp lookout and listen to front and rear. If we 'ear someone comin', we slide off into the bushes until we can see the cut o' his jib. When we come on a village or anything, that's the time to scout around. And judgin' by the signs in the dust here, there ain't bin anyone along this track today, nor not since a cart went by yesterday afternoon.'

This was a part of Clark I had not known before. He showed us the cartwheel tracks, which were clear and undisturbed by footprints or the tracks of a later cart, and he showed us the horse-droppings, which were dry but still firmly shaped, indicating that they had not been there much more than twenty-four hours. He pointed out where a sapling had been broken by the passing cart, with leaves still green but withered; and, because the hoofprints pointed northward, he deduced that the cart had been going home from the town at the end of the day.

So we took his advice, and, moving quietly together without talking, we set off southward, in the direction of what we hoped would be Ekaterinburg. For more than half an hour we marched steadily forward, the track sandy between the woods of birch and pine, the sun now gone below the skyline but the heavens still bright, as they would be for all of the night, for we were now no more than 600 miles from the Arctic circle, and this was midsummer. We saw nothing and heard nothing until, rounding a bend, we suddenly found ourselves only a few yards from a railway crossing, some sidings, a station platform, and a signal cabin. Cautiously, we backed away to where we were screened from view by scrub. The signalman appeared to be asleep in his cabin, and the two armed guards who sat on one of the station benches were in little better shape.

'No problem,' said Clark, 'We make our way through the woods for a couple o' hundred yards, nip across the line, and Bob's yer uncle.' And that is what we did, although I thought it important to point out to Clark that 'Bob' is not my uncle but my mother's second cousin by marriage. He did not seem to understand.

Beyond the rail crossing the track ran on as before, and we followed it for nearly an hour before we came to a second crossing, this one no more than a few baulks of wood laid between the rails to make a road for carts; it was unguarded. It was strange walking in the midsummer dusk: it was neither dark nor truly light, and it seemed more like the hour before dawn than an evening twilight. There was a greyness to everything, near and far, and above the trees the sky glowed thinly white;

and the woods were full of the noises of both day and night together. About a mile beyond the second crossing the forest suddenly thinned, and we saw to our right the intermittent glow of some kind of factory and, on a rise before us, the few twinkling lights and broken silhouette of a town.

It was now, I supposed, near midnight. We had eaten nothing since breakfast, and there seemed little alternative but to go forward, seek out a place to eat and sleep, and hope for the best. I consulted the others: Clark and Tchaikovsky concurred, and Tatiana told us:

'If we can find the house of the British consul, we should go there. He may even have received messages for us.'

We stepped out as bravely as we could, heads up, looking boldly about us, our faded uniforms the best possible disguise, for they had no insignia and indicated 'Red Guard' as much as 'Czech'. Tchaikovsky began to sing a little Russian song in a quiet voice, and Tatiana put her arm about his shoulders and joined him, so I put my arm about Clark and, close behind the others, we hummed with them as best we might. We passed a few houses, dark and tightly shuttered; we came to a causeway, which crossed a dam between a great lake that stretched blackly away to the right and a wide pond, rippling in the lights from the town, on the left. We passed the factory beside the lake, almost silent and apparently deserted, but tense with the hidden life that factories have at night; and we came, at the southern corner of the pond, to a broad boulevard, high-porticoed façades glimmering in the dusk, and the unmistakable shadow of a huge church.

Here, we met a group of drunken Russians; but Tchaikovsky and Tatiana wished them a cordial '*Dobra notch*', and they stumbled past us with a shout and a grin. They went to the left, along the boulevard beside the pond, so we walked straight forward, up the wide street that faced us. Very soon I was to know it as the Glavni Prospekt. I was surprised at its elegance: although the road was of earth the sidewalks were paved with small stones, there were electric lights at intervals, and the houses and hotels that lined it on both sides were all two-storied and solidly built.

I felt unhealthily conspicuous on this wide and important thoroughfare. Here and there, between houses fronted by tiny gardens imprisoned in high iron railings, narrow lanes ran off into the dark, and I was just about to beg my companions to take one of these when, coming to a corner, on an even wider street, we saw in the half-light, hanging limp from its staff before a house only a few yards to our left, what was undeniably the Union Jack.

I seized Tatiana and Clark each by an elbow, and drew them back down Glavni Prospekt and into the first dark alleyway; Tchaikovsky sauntered after us. 'That is the British consulate,' I whispered. 'And this lane must certainly go past the back of the house. Perhaps we can enter by the back door; it will be more discreet than calling at the front.'

We found the high plank fence that surrounded the backyard of the consulate, and a gate that yielded, creaking, to Clark's hand. The rear of the building staggered down in a succession of roofs and outbuildings, but one strong door looked as if it might lead into the house. I lifted the latch, and pushed gently. The door gave slightly, but some obstruction prevented it from moving. I tried again, a little harder; whatever it was, resisted.

'Give it a good shove,' muttered Clark, putting his hand on mine and pushing strongly.

The door yielded suddenly, so that we both tumbled forward, as, with an affronted scream, a huge black cat catapulted between our legs. At this, a dozen hens burst into raucous clattering and chattering, and several women's voices broke out in cries of fear and lamentation. We stood blinking in a low-ceilinged room lit only by the flames of a kitchen fire; the hens, vaulting suddenly upward like acrobats on a trampoline and descending in a frantic flightless flutter, scattered from our feet across the flagstoned floor; and the women, black dressed and white-aproned, clutched at one another, immobile as three marble figures grouped around a fountain in the Tiergarten.

As Tchaikovsky and Tatiana followed us into the kitchen, these figures let out another shriek, and broke into movement, flapping their aprons about the room at the skittering hens, casting wild glances at the ceiling, and all the time babbling in Russian, to one another and to us. Tatiana said something, and they were once more still – I could think of nothing but one of those peep-shows at a fairground, where you put a pfennig in

231

the slot and the leaden figures whirl about, portraying the last moments of *Til Eulenspiegel* or the assassination of the Archduke Franz-Ferdinand, and then are suddenly frozen in mid-movement as the pfennig runs out – and then, tentatively, one smiled, and then another, and they moved again, this time toward us, their eyes still wary, their hands smoothing down their ruffled aprons.

A door in the far shadows of the room opened and there, in British striped pyjamas and a girdled dressing-gown, with matching slippers, stood the master of the house, Mister Thomas Preston, His Britannic Majesty's vice-consular representative. He was some thirty years of age, tall and sturdily built, with a bluff broad face and straight sandy hair combed to the right. He spoke, in Russian, and was answered by the eldest of the women; but even as she began Tatiana cut across her in English:

'Mr Preston, we have come here from England with the authority of Mr Balfour and of the War Office. We have our instructions, and I was told to request you to give us all the assistance in your power. It is, of course,' she added, 'a very confidential matter.'

Preston blushed: there was no doubt about it; even in the fire-light his face turned a distinctly darker hue. 'Well, isn't that remarkable,' he said. 'I've been half expecting this. There were no telegrams, of course, the telegraph office is in the hands of the bolsheviks; but some of the others have already arrived – oh, don't worry, these women speak only Russian and, besides, they're very loyal. Still, I suppose we'd better go into my office. Can I offer you some refreshment? Yes? and perhaps some tea?'

Preston's office was more like a sparsely-furnished parlour, with scattered chairs and a rococo table in place of a desk; at the front of the house, it had shutters closed and blinds drawn. One of the women brought a tray with bread and cheese, and a samovar, and with full mouths, as soon as the door was closed, we introduced ourselves one by one to Preston. We explained our presence as briefly as possible, giving the rescue of the imperial family as our object, and making no mention of the Ilya Murometz.

'What did you mean when you said that some of the others

had arrived?' I asked him.

'My dear chap, the town is full of secret agents, all of them out to rescue the Tsar. There's an American, Major Homer Slaughter. He's liaison officer with the Czechs under Gajda, but he keeps slipping into town and holing up with the US vice-consul, my friend Henry Palmer. There was a Russian, Pavel Bulygin; the bolsheviks winkled him out a week or two ago, and whisked him into jail. There's supposed to be a German agent on the way – apparently the Kaiser's made another appeal to the bolsheviks to release the Tsar – but of course nobody's going to tell me about him. Then there's a Jap chap, Colonel Kuroki, who says he's the representative for some kind of trade commission. And even the Frogs have got someone here, hiding in the French consulate, though I've no idea who it is.'

I was seized with fury. I had been chosen to rescue the Tsar, I had struggled over thousands of miles to reach this god-forsaken hole in the midst of the Siberian steppes, only to find when I got here that I was just one of a horde of adventurers who had come from all over the world like flies to a honeypot. I had denied my soldier's oath, I had deserted my comrades and consorted with the enemy, persuaded that what I had been asked to attempt was honourable and necessary, that, in fact, I was the only man to do it – and now I found myself no more than a mercenary among mercenaries.

'I'll have to hide you all in my attic,' said Preston, 'until we can decide what to do with you. I've got my wife and son in the house, and I must be very careful. The attic's quite comfy, and from the window you can see the Ipatiev house, where the imperial family are imprisoned.'

Silently fuming, I followed the others up two flights of stairs through the sleeping house, and reached the attic, where Preston indicated some straw-filled mattresses on the floor, blankets, and a low-burning lamp. There was a single curtained window, and we gathered close behind the vice-consul as he drew the curtain and pointed.

We looked out from high on the north side of the British consulate, across the roof of a lower building and a rough wide lane that ran from the main street to our right. The ground before us and to the left sloped gradually down to the big pond, and directly across the lane an impressive townhouse had been built on the slope. It was enclosed by a high double palisade of planks, but I could still see that its frontage on the main street was a grandly erected upper storey, built upon a lower storey that emerged from the slope to open out upon the garden to our left. The windows of the upper storey were whitewashed, and some had gratings lashed across them. It was now nearly sunrise, and the whole building, which was painted white, glimmered in the half-light. The only lamp was burning tiny before a sentry-box at a gate in the outer palisade, and all was silent.

'The family live on the upper floor, and the guards on the ground floor; and other guards live in this building below us,' whispered Preston. 'Sometimes the family are allowed to walk in the garden for a few minutes, but most of their time is spent indoors. They have a valet, a maid, a cook and a doctor, but their only visitors are the bolsheviks; even the priest has been there only once in several weeks. They will be very pleased to be removed from there.'

He wished us all good night, and then he stood at the door and surveyed us, and I thought that he looked in particular at me. 'I told you that I half expected you,' he said. 'But it was really only since this evening. I heard a rumour at teatime that Mister Karakhan, the deputy commissar for foreign affairs in the Moscow government, had arrived in Ekaterinburg. It was hard to believe, no one had seen him . . . And then, some four hours ago, a messenger called here and invited me to go to the Amerikanskaya hotel on Prokovski Prospekt. Beloborodov and Chutskayev were there, the chairman of the Urals regional soviet and his deputy – and another, an intense man with a black beard and watchful, intelligent eyes. I've not met Karakhan, you understand, and only seen a photograph of him once. There was a lot of beating about the bush for an hour or more, and then this man told me – or rather, he managed to suggest to me in a roundabout way – that the bolsheviks were very anxious not to anger the Germans, that the presence of the Tsar in Russia was an embarrassment to everybody, and that I had probably received by now a visitor with a distinct interest in the matter. And ever since you arrived I've been asking myself – how the devil did he know?'

CHAPTER 17

1-6 July: Ekaterinburg

I SLEPT well, for I usually do, and I had missed my previous night's sleep; but I was still in a rage when I awoke in the morning. I had been tricked by the British, lied to, trapped: what was I but a pawn in their Great Game? And now that I was here in Ekaterinburg, what was there for me to do but make the moves that had been decided for me? At least, I determined, I would have nothing to do with any of the other agents. If there were the faintest chance of rescuing the Tsar and his family, I would do it without their help.

One of the maids brought ewers of hot water, bowls and towels, and we were all able to take our first good wash for many days. Stripped to the waist, I sat brooding damply before a mirror, studying my appearance. Two weeks without shaving had given me a fine, curly, blond beard, so that I hardly recognised myself: 'Do you know, darling,' said Tatiana's voice in my ear, 'that beard makes you look positively *jolly*. I almost think I could fall in love with you all over again.'

Breakfast was brought, and we ate ravenously: bowls of curds, honey, black bread, and tea. Beyond the attic window the day shone bright, and I could see the blue sky that spread onward and onward, over the steppes to the arctic ice. As the morning passed I grew increasingly impatient: Preston had told us not to stir from the attic, for he frequently received visits from the bolsheviks, but we had seen nothing of him for many hours, and I was anxious to find some way of reconnoitring the Ipatiev house.

I spent much of the time at the window, but there was little to see at the house across the street. The guard was changed in mid-morning; a woman brought a basket of bread, which she handed in at the gate; and, once, one of the whitewashed windows was opened a few inches and a hand – an imperial hand? – lay upon the sill for a minute or more.

At midday Preston came at last to visit us; he stood just inside the attic door and beckoned me to him. 'It's really rather fishy,' he said in a low voice. 'I don't know what to make of it. I was summoned to the Amerikanskaya again this morning, and saw the same crowd I talked to last night. Not one of 'em looked as if he'd been to bed. The chap I think could be Karakhan asked me again if I weren't expecting a visitor, someone who might be useful to him in his . . . well, predicament was the word he used, as near as I can translate it. Said I need have no fear for my visitor's safety, or indeed for that of the imperial family, if a suitable solution could be found. What do you make of that, eh? Of course, I denied all knowledge of you, and my maids won't talk – too frightened even to leave the house – but what do you think he wants?'

I shrugged, perplexed and a little apprehensive. 'I don't know. They told me in London that the Russians were anxious not to go against any of the conditions of the treaty of Brest-Litovsk, and that it was believed that Karakhan himself had agreed to a secret codicil guaranteeing the safety of the Tsar and his family. But there is no way that he could know I am here, unless – ' and then I remembered that evening at the Marlborough Club, and Marlin, Basil Zaharoff, and Shackleton, and I thought of Count Wilhelm von Mirbach, the German ambassador in Moscow, and of how I had met him once in Berlin before he left for Russia, and considered him a thoroughly devious man . . . I shut my mouth firmly and said nothing more on the subject to Preston. If the British had found some way of informing both my own people and the Russians of my mission and its purpose, and the Russians were in favour, then I must say nothing to prejudice its success.

'I didn't get a chance to ask you last night,' said Preston, 'after all, you were tired and so was I, but how the deuce did you get here?'

'We rode most of the way,' I told him, 'from Astrakhan.' I

had decided to say nothing of the aircraft.

'Yes, from Archangelsk,' he said, nodding wisely. 'Damned good going, that. Must be close on 800 miles. And you rode all the way?'

'Most of the way. We walked the last few miles.' I saw no reason to tell him more than necessary, and if he wanted to believe that we had come from Archangelsk, then I would let him.

'Not like that other chap,' said Preston, musingly.

I felt like seizing him by the throat and shaking him, as one would a teasing child. 'What other chap?'

'Well . . . I'm not quite sure really. I haven't seen him, meself, you understand. Henry Palmer told me he'd heard this feller was in the town. An Englishman of some sort. Came down from Archangelsk like you, a week or so ago. Took the train, though. Disguised himself as a sack-man. Country's full of them these days: fellers riding the train from one district to another – no ticket, of course – just to buy or barter a sackful of grain or flour. The Reds just can't handle 'em.'

'But this Englishman, who is he?' I could feel my rage rising again.

'Can't tell you, me dear feller. As I say, haven't seen him, don't know where he's hidden himself, don't even know if he really exists. May be just a rumour.'

And so he changed the subject: 'Now then, to our muttons. What d'you think we ought to do about this feller over in the Amerikanskaya?'

'Would he come here?'

'Oh, good lord no. He made that pretty clear. I should think only the members of the presidium of the soviet know he's in Ekaterinburg at all, and he's not going to stir out of the hotel. No, I'm afraid he wants you to walk into his parlour.'

So I supposed that I must. Preston agreed that my worn and faded Czech uniform would attract no attention, for there were many ex-soldiers, as well as released prisoners of war, with similar uniforms in the town, although he looked somewhat doubtfully at my blond hair and beard.

'It'll just have to do, I fear,' he said. 'It's an unusual colouring round these parts, but I can't get hold of any dye in a hurry – and, after all, there are other fair-haired chaps about,

237

apart from myself.'

I told my companions what I was about to do. 'I will come with you,' said Tchaikovsly. I protested, but he was unmoved. 'I will follow you as you go to the hotel, to cover your tail, yes? And while you are in the hotel I will keep watch, and make sure that you leave again safely.'

Preston led us downstairs, and peered furtively out through the blinds of his office. 'The deuce of it is, you never know which of these fellows hanging about in the street might be a bolshie spy. They're everywhere. You'd best go by the back gate, the way you came in last night.'

In daylight, Ekaterinburg looked even more prosperous than by night. From Glavni Prospekt we turned into the Voznesensky, where the British consulate faced the Church of the Ascension across the wide boulevard. Fine dominating mansions of two and three storeys rose on either hand and into the distance, where the broad street crossed the river on a bridge adorned with obelisks and ran gently uphill to the distant railway station. I learnt later that the fortunes of Ekaterinburg were founded upon gold, platinum, and emeralds, which were mined nearby in the Urals; and one of the great houses on Voznesensky Prospekt was the former house of the 'Platinum King' – now seized by the bolsheviks as the House of Nationalised Women.

(Apparently it all began just as a joke. Some minor official in Moscow had contrived to have a decree printed, announcing that, following the victory of the proletariat, the nationalisation of the means of production would include the nationalisation of women. But one of the district committees in Ekaterinburg had taken the announcement seriously, and had forced a dozen or so unfortunate women, wives of mine managers and foundry owners, to be gathered together and confined in the empty mansion. Fortunately, most of the bolsheviks, family men with jealous wives, had no further idea of how to deal with the situation. And, although the women, dressed only in scraps of clothing and deprived of most of the necessities of life, were forced to take part in drunken parties at all hours of the day and night, none had so far suffered any serious indignity.)

Following Preston's instructions we turned right out of Glavni Prospekt and found Prokoski Prospekt, where the

Amerikanskaya Hotel reared up in a mélange of French baroque and red-brick classical. Tchaikovsky, who had trailed behind me on the far side of the street, rejoined me as I pushed my way into the crowded hotel hallway, and quietly enquired the way to number three, the room of commissar Yankel Yurovsky. When we had found the room, at the end of a corridor on the first floor, he fell back to the corner of the stairs, where he lounged idly, picking at his fingernails and staring blindly into space.

I rapped loudly and nervously on the bedroom door. A faint rumble of voices ceased, and there was an uneasy quiet in which I heard, from more distant rooms, the crashing of glasses and the thin panting squeal of a ravished girl. I knocked again, and the door sprang open beneath my knuckles revealing a stocky, black-bearded man, with mobile calculating eyes. He stared challengingly at me, and I stared as challengingly back; and we remained so, unmoving for a minute or more, as slowly his eyes moved from my face down to my boots and up again. Then he stood back, holding the door wide, and I stepped forward cautiously into the room.

The air was heavy with stale smoke, sour with sweat and old uneaten food. Thick braided curtains of velvet hung at the windows, where insidious rays of daylight stabbed into the yellow gleam of the electroliers. The brass bed was pushed back into the farthest corner, and in the middle of the room stood a scratched mahogany table of Empire design, surrounded by chairs, and covered with a flotsam of papers, half-empty glasses, greasy plates and a huge overflowing ashtray decorated with a dragon's head. In various chairs and on the bed the presidium of the Urals regional soviet lounged, half-asleep, half-drunk, half-dressed. But at the end of the table, upright, his dark eyes fixed unmoving upon me, sat a man whom I recognised instantly.

Tall and slim, sallow of complexion, with his black hair waving back from his full forehead, and his beard and moustache trimmed neatly. No older than myself, but already a veteran revolutionary and a crafty negotiator, the gold-rimmed eyeglasses betraying the typical intellectual: Lev Mihailovich Karakhan, deputy foreign commissar of the Russian Supreme Soviet.

239

I grinned and held out my hand toward him, but he continued to stare expressionlessly at me. As I came nearer, he raised his open left hand to cover his view of the bearded lower half of my face, narrowed his eyes briefly, and nodded. Only then he stood, relaxing his scrutiny, and at last took my hand:

'Remarkable,' he said in his excellent German, 'when it comes to ingenuity and deception, we still have much to learn from the great western powers. The whole world believes you dead – and I shall not disillusion them, trust me. Well, I am very glad to see you again; and there will be others in this town as glad, I am sure – but we will talk of that in a minute. Come now, you must meet my colleagues.'

The chairman of the presidium: Alexander Beloborodov, huddled on a broken chair, slim and pale, unshaven and racked with fever, his shivering body wound in a cloak in spite of the heat of the room, and his eyes shaded by dark glasses.

The commissar for war: Chaya Goloschokin, on a stool too low for his moderate height, a thoughtful hand still half shading his worn face, with its cold grey eyes above an inquisitional nose and a badly-trimmed imperial.

The commissar for supplies: Pyotr Voikov, light-complexioned and blue-eyed, the table before him covered with sheets of loose paper over which he had been compulsively scribbling.

The commissar for the All-Russian Extraordinary Commission ('Cheka,' explained Karakhan expressionlessly): Pyotr Yermakov, a man with wild revolutionary eyes, a yellow pock-marked face, and shoulder-length, greasy hair into which he constantly thrust one or other of his hands like a clawing comb.

There were others whom I scarcely remember, although later their names made history: Simyon Chutskayev, Beloborodov's deputy; Fedor Syromolotov, and Grigori Safarov – and one with whom I was to spend most of the coming days, the man who had opened the door to me, Yankel Yurovsky. They each received me according to their natures, coldly, shiftily and offhandedly. There was a great deal of muttering in Russian, to which Karakhan replied with his eyes flashing, and then I was offered a rickety stool and we all sat down about the table, fresh glasses of vodka before us.

Since I understood almost nothing of what was said by the others during the meeting, and had to rely solely upon what Karakhan told me in Russian, it would be tedious to attempt to report what went on. I made no contribution to the discussion: I was told what was decided and what I was to do, and there seemed little point in objecting to it.

First, Karakhan told me that the passage of the aircraft had been reported to him during the night, and that he supposed it to be the one in which I hoped to carry the former Tsar and his family out of Russia. I nodded, but said nothing: I did not intend to tell him where it was hidden until I knew more of his plans. And these I now learnt.

Karakhan had to return immediately to Moscow for the fifth gathering of the All-Russian Congress of Soviets; Goloschokin would go with him, and together they would report to Yankel Sverdlov, the chairman of the Central Executive Committee, that arrangements were in hand for the removal of the former Tsar. At present, the Ipatiev house was in the charge of Alexander Avdeyev, a rough and unsympathetic local man who had gathered a mob of his friends about him as guard to the imperial family; but in two or three days' time Yurovsky would be sent, on the orders of the presidium, to arrest Avdeyev and his second-in-command Moshkin, and replace the house guards. Yurovsky had selected a number of ex-prisoners of war, all sworn to secrecy; and I was to join them.

'They're mostly Letts,' said Karakhan, 'who don't even speak to each other, so you need have no worries that they will ask you who you are.' As soon as the takeover was complete, Syromolotov would follow to Moscow to report, and then he and Goloschokin would return with final instructions.

The discussion was long, and at times bitter, but Karakhan succeeded in imposing his will upon the others. He explained that it was necessary for me to be among the house guards so that I could be present at the right moment to travel with the family, but he warned me that I should not attempt to speak with any of them. Then he shook my hand again, and wished me good fortune.

'It is essential that the former Tsar and his family should be removed unharmed from the soil of Russia,' he said. 'Only then can we hope that the great powers will not interfere in the building of our new democratic state. And you have been sent to us, by them, to make it possible. Go now: Yurovsky will send for you at the consul's house when the time is ripe.'

And so I was dismissed: no longer the captain of a great aircraft, the leader of a bold and secret mission, the saviour of an imperial house, but a subordinate, a waiter for instructions, the humblest member of the palace guard. I did not speak to Tchaikovsky, who fell in behind me as I made my way out of the hotel, but I fumed all the way back to the consulate. I ate no lunch, and sulked long into the afternoon. There was nothing I could do, for the plans had been made and the Tsar's safety depended upon them, but I felt entitled to nurse my aggrievement until the moment when success would lie solely in my hands once more.

Tatiana had acquired clothing more suitable than the cast-off uniform of a Czech legionary: the dress of a Red Cross nurse, in which she stood becomingly demure, although I knew that, as always, she was naked beneath. Clark had spent his time in the kitchen, making his first efforts to add Russian to his battery of languages. At teatime, we met Preston's wife and their young son; Mrs Preston played the piano, a long, slow, sad piece, and as it lingered on its dying notes we heard, from far away, the hoot of the train that even then was leaving Ekaterinburg to carry Karakhan and Goloschokin to Moscow.

The sound reminded Preston of another piece of news. 'It seems there's a train, standing in the sidings at the station,' he said, 'stuffed full of German officers pretending to be the Red Cross. Heaven knows which side they're supposed to be on. The bolshies wouldn't dare touch 'em; the Czechs will murder 'em if they get here; but there they are, I'm told, and there they'll stay, if there's any truth in the rumour.'

At least, here was something to do. Tatiana agreed to accompany me, and together we left the consul's house and turned left into the Arsenyevski Prospekt. Crossing the bridge over the sluggish river, with its stumpy obelisks at each end, we climbed the gentle rise to the railway station, where the *izvoshtchikyi* still drowsed the day away waiting for passengers who never came.

Or, rather, passengers who never left the railway. For the station itself was throbbing with life, its single platform crowded with men, women and children, baggage, bedding, bundles of

242

firewood, sellers of vodka and sandwiches; its gloomy restaurant was the local *bourse,* where gilded ikons were exchanged for food, clothing sold for train passes to Perm and Ufa, and information traded for other information. Tatiana and I stepped down on to the track, strolling nonchalantly over to where two or three wagons and shabby carriages had been shunted onto a short spur line. They were certainly occupied, but by a gypsy motley of Red Guards, women and squalling babies. With only a couple of judicious questions Tatiana quickly confirmed that no one had seen any Germans, Red Cross or otherwise, for many weeks.

Back on the station, I ventured idly into the restaurant, as Tatiana dragged a grubby scowling infant from its mother's arms so that she might tickle it, and bounce it up and down, and do all those things that young women seem to want to do with other people's babies. The restaurant was crowded, its ring-stained marble table tops half-hidden under a treasure-trove of household goods over which men and women bartered and fought. In one corner, however, a man sat strangely isolated before a glass of tea. He was dressed in the nondescript half-military jacket and baggy breeches of most of the men around him, yet there was something curiously familiar about him even before he raised his head and fixed me with his bright blue eyes.

I took a half-dozen quick steps to his side, and spoke hardly above a whisper. 'Thompson?'

'That's me. To be precise – it is I.' He looked me up and down, in that insultingly calculating manner of his. 'So you actually managed to get here. I thought we'd managed to pull the wool over your eyes with all that gammon about Ekaterinodar. To put it another way, fooled you.'

So this was Preston's 'other chap'. I could guess how he had arrived in Ekaterinburg before me: a destroyer from Rosyth to some arctic Russian port, perhaps the Archangelsk that Preston had mentioned, and then the journey southward disguised as a sack-man, one of those who travelled about the country buying up whatever food they could find, from station to station, from train to train, without proper papers, day by day as the sun rose behind the birch forest to the east and sank behind the birch forest to the west . . .

'But why are you here?'

243

He showed me his yellowed teeth. 'To keep an eye on you, sunny Jim. To be precise: to scupper your little game. I know there's some that want the old boy spirited away, and that, I hear, includes your own lot. But there's others of us have a better idea: we'd rather see the Russkies hoist with their own petard and bear the consequences. So why don't you throw the towel in now; in other words, give in?'

I swore at him: in German, which was unwise, and in my still fragmentary English, which made him laugh. 'Now, now. I do assure you, I mean it. The old feller won't ever get away from here alive. To put it another way, he'll be dead. And that will be the beginning of the end for our Red friends. You mark my words.'

'But what,' I demanded, 'if I denounced you to the presidium?'

'You wouldn't do that.' He wagged a cautionary finger at me. 'Because, to be precise, remember – I know you for what you are. If Goloschokin learnt your true identity, you'd be up at the Opera House in a starring role afore your feet could touch the ground. Now you'd better scarper before someone overhears us. In other words, go.'

I went. I dragged Tatiana away from her games with the now-gurgling baby and marched her beside me, silent, the length of the Arsenyevski Prospekt, seething at every step. Was this plain-clothes policeman going to thwart me now? Did he think he could just hold up his hand like the 'bobbies' I had seen controlling the traffic in London, and have me obey him? Everything in Ekaterinburg seemed designed to restrict my freedom of action, everyone seemed to be more in control of my fate than I was myself.

Yet I could not imagine that Thompson would be able to interfere without help – and who were his friends? The British, I knew, were devious enough to play the game on both sides, openly sending me to attempt the Tsar's escape, like the decoy duck that floats innocently in the open water, while secretly they aimed their guns from the shelter of the reeds. Was Thompson dealing with a dissident faction of the Urals soviet, who objected to the orders that they had been sent from Moscow, or was there, in the shadows of Ekaterinburg, some other influence at work of which I knew nothing?

Late that evening, as I stared, still raging disconsolately, from the attic window across the Voznesensky Prospekt, I saw a furtive figure come down the far side of the boulevard from the direction of the railway station, and slip into the shadows that surrounded the fine big mansion next door to the House of Nationalised Women. It was almost dark, and the street was wide, and the man – for it was certainly a man – had turned up his coat collar and pulled his cap low over his face. But he somehow looked, to me, like Thompson.

For two days I fretted in Preston's house, squabbling miserably with poor Tatiana, while the sun burned hotter through the attic roof and Clark rehearsed his Russian lessons with Tchaikovsky. On Thursday, 4 July, Yurovsky sent for me, and I reported to the stable-yard of the Amerikanskaya. There I was given a revolver – a Nagant, a Russian version of the original Belgian model, a sort of lightweight Smith & Wesson .38 in appearance – and fell in beside my fellow guards. Eight of them were Letts, stocky morose fellows with set faces, but the ninth was Austrian – Rudolf Lacher, as I later discovered him to be, of the 1st Tyrol rifle regiment. He stared curiously at me, and I stared curiously back.

As we were being marched down to the Ipatiev house, with Yurovsky and his second-in-command Nikulin at our head, Lacher tried to get into conversation with me, but I scowled like the Letts and swore briefly but effectively at him. I have never liked the Austrians, and, besides, their accent is abominable.

We passed the British consulate, and I snatched a glance at the ghost of Tatiana in an upper window; then we trudged round to the left into the lane that ran down beside the Ipatiev house toward the pond, and drew up in a ragged bunch before the sentry-box at the gate. Yurovsky spoke briefly to the sentry, a spotty peasant lad in a leather jerkin, who picked up a field telephone beside him in the box and muttered apprehensively into it. Within two minutes a swarthy swaggering fellow, past his prime and already, so early in the day, clearly the worse for drink, came bustling out from the gate, his deputy like a pale puppy at his heels. These were Avdeyev and Moshkin. Yurovsky deliberately drew a sheet of paper from inside his jacket and read it aloud. Avdeyev shouted furiously, shaking his fists and turning a darker red, but Yurovsky reached forward to take his revolver from its holster at his waist, did the same for Moshkin, and then, with a brief order, sent the two men marching off between two of the Letts, with Nikulin behind them.

As the still shouting and gesticulating figures turned the corner into Voznesensky Prospekt the sentry, overawed, allowed us to enter the compound. It was not so much a fence to imprison the Tsar and his family as a screen to keep any sight of what went on in the Ipatiev house from the curious eyes of passers-by. Within the outer palisade the earth was bare and hard, dotted here and there with the drying turds of a small spaniel, which ran yapping at our feet as we made our way to an open gate in the inner palisade. This wall of planks was some ten feet high, close up against the walls of the house itself, but extending only as far as the lower wooden fence that enclosed the garden at the back of the house.

We entered into the lower floor by what had been the side door; the main entrance to the house, up a steep but imposing flight of steps from Voznesensky Prospekt and into a first-floor antechamber, had been bolted and barred and then closed off by the inner palisade. Across an unswept, muddy hall we followed Yurovsky into a big, low-ceilinged, stinking room that looked out upon the garden through narrow windows. The stink was that of Avdeyev's young guards, who lounged about the room on stained sofas and chairs, surrounded by cigarette ash, half-eaten raw onions, half-drunk glasses of *kvass* and vodka, torn papers, unwashed clothing and rusty rifles. From an inner room, one that faced the street, a near-naked girl looked coyly out before she was dragged back and the door slammed in our faces.

For the first time, I felt a ghost of comradeship with my fellows. We were all soldiers, whatever our training had been, and we came naturally to attention in two (admittedly loose) ranks behind Yurovsky. He produced his paper again, and began to read in a strong, raucous voice. I know, even today, very little Russian, and at that time, of course, I knew none at all, but on the second reading I could begin to guess how it went:

'By order of the Urals regional soviet, democratically convened, I, Alexander Beloborodov, Chairman of the

246

Presidium, etc, etc . . . ' Yurovsky's reading was brief, but as dramatic in its results as anyone could wish. There were growls of mixed bewilderment and rage from the youths; one leapt up shouting and seized his rifle; and Yurovsky slowed and calmly took out his revolver and shot the boy in the foot. Within five minutes we had cleared the guard-room, escorted the young guards – one of them carried by the others and squealing like a scratched pig – to the street, and barred the gate behind them; flushed out two or three half-dressed girls from the lower parts of the house and sent them packing after; and were looking in dismayed disbelief at the squalor that we would have to clear before we had space to sleep and mess.

Yurovsky briskly gave orders in his fragmentary German, which was to become the common means of communication among the guard. Lacher stood sentry at the door by which we had entered; one of the Letts was posted at the foot of a flight of stairs that came down from the door above into a large hall next to the guard-room; and a second went to the far end of a corridor, where a short flight of steps descended from a door opening onto a covered way, between the house and what had formerly been the servants' quarters.

Six of us were left, including Yurovsky, and we tramped up the stairs into an ante-chamber with velvet-covered settees, where a tall, elderly fellow, in peasant's blouse and breeches and with a straggling grey beard, stood wringing his hands anxiously. This, I was to discover, was Alexei Trupp, the Tsar's manservant. He began to ask questions, stumbling and stuttering, but Yurovsky ignored him, opening a door to the right and leading us quickly through a cluttered kitchen where a woman, a man and a boy cringed into the corners at the sight of us, and out into the main hallway of the house. Here broad balustraded steps rose from the barricaded front door, while a second, narrower stairway descended to the floor below; and here three more of the Letts were posted to stand guard. We returned through the kitchen, producing the same flutter as before, and Yurovsky mounted his last guard at the head of the inner staircase. Then, with a brusque nod to me to accompany him, he knocked peremptorily at the closed door that faced us.

There was no reply. The door remained closed. With a brief

247

exclamation, Yurovsky drew out his revolver again, turned the handle, and kicked the door wide. The room beyond was empty. It was obviously a dining-room: a heavy mahogany table with carved legs stood in the centre, surrounded by upright mahogany chairs, their backs inset with canework, and a massive cupboarded dresser ranged the wall beside the door by which we entered. The room was ill-lit by a single glazed door giving onto a narrow terrace above the garden, and a large branched electrolier hung above the table. There were closed doors in the far wall, but to our left, in the fourth corner of the room, was an open doorway, and a man stood, ghostly against the pale hazy light that came from the room behind him.

He spoke, in Russian, in a quiet resigned tone. Yurovsky stalked toward him bulkily, elbowing a chair aside as he eased his way past the dresser, and replied. While I remained where I had entered, I recognised the words 'Tovarich Romanov', and the strange mixture of respect and contempt in which he continued to speak. The Tsar, for it was surely he, replied wearily, and stood aside from the doorway. Yurovsky gestured to me with his head to come forward, and one after the other we entered the main drawing-room of the Ipatiev house.

It was a wide room, stretching across half the frontage on the Voznesensky Prospekt, and divided by a broad open arch. The Tsarina, tall and grave, her hands together at fingers' end, stood facing us from below the arch; beyond her, four young women, caught in their duties of sewing and mending, looked up blue-eyed from their various chairs; on a light reclining cot a boy, tall for his age but thin and pale, raised a weary head. Compared with the dull provincial formality of the dining-room, the salon was untidy but alive. Pictures and mirrors leant slanting forward from the walls in the common Russian manner; oddments of underwear hung drying from cords nailed between them; a straggling green plant pushed ceilingward before one of the whitewashed windows.

The Tsar was beside us. Yurovsky spoke briefly in an undertone, his eyes flicking back to the open door we had left behind us, and then around the silent family. He nodded offhandedly at me, and the Tsar inclined his head without a word. The Tsarina spoke briefly, in Russian but in an accent that reminded me of Preston's; the Tsar smiled at her, but still said nothing. In all, I think no more than fifty words were spoken before Yurovsky turned on his heel and, signalling me to follow, marched stiffnecked out of the salon, through the dining-room, and slammed the farther door behind us.

For hours afterward, he found no opportunity to speak to me. Nikulin, with the men who had taken Avdeyev and Moshkin away, returned within a few minutes, and in small parties we of the guard explored the house. Yurovsky took over a room at the front of the house, between the drawing-room and the upper hallway. Beyond the kitchen we found a small bathroom, with a stone bath, that overlooked the garden, and next to it, at the head of the stairs, was the only lavatory, in filthy condition, with obscene graffiti and revolutionary slogans scrawled on its walls in several languages.

On the lower floor, ransacked storage rooms lay along the street side, and down a few steps a pantry had been built below the bathroom. Now that we had the house to ourselves, only two sentries were necessary, one at the foot of the central stairs and one outside Yurovsky's room. The rest of us spent a noisome hour cleaning out the two rooms in which the former guard had lived. After this it was lunchtime, and a messenger was sent to fetch two billy-cans of thin stew and some black bread from the house of Popov across the lane, where the exterior guards were quartered.

We organised the watch, five on and five off, and with relief I found myself separated from Lacher. Late in the afternoon, as I was dozing uneasily in a battered armchair in the inner guard-room, where thin rays of reflected light eased down from the high windows shadowed by the palisade, Yurovsky sent one of the Letts to call me to him.

His room was dominated by a fine brass bedstead with a torn velvet cover. He sat behind a walnut table covered with papers, his Nagant revolver laid across them. He had removed his jacket, and wore only a stained grey vest, his arms and upper chest thickly covered with curling black hair. He held a glass of tea to his lips, and looked at me over it with his cunning, warm eyes.

His German was so poor that I cannot reproduce it here, but he made his meaning clear enough. Nothing whatsoever was to be done about arranging the escape of the former Tsar and his family until confirmation had been received from Moscow. For the moment I was to consider myself as no more than another member of the house guard, although I might be given limited opportunities to communicate with my companions. But on no account was I to speak with Citizen Romanov, his wife, or their children. I kept my rage to myself – to have come these thousands of miles as the chosen messenger of the British government and, as I now suspected, with the approval of the Kaiser himself, and to find myself finally under the orders of this peasant! – but I determined to seek out the earliest opportunity to disobey him and, with an abrupt nod, went sulkily back to my armchair.

And so began the routine of our days. With the others I mounted guard, eight hours on and eight off, feeding on the foul slops that came from the Popov house, sleeping on a verminous pallet, washing seldom, seeing nothing of the outside world but the blue-white sky beyond the garden fence. I made the grudging acquaintance of Ivan Kharitonov, the Tsar's cook, and of the kitchen boy, Leonid Sednev. Once or twice I spoke to Anna Demidova, the Tsarina's towering maidservant, and to the timid, hand-wringing Dr Botkin, who guarded the health of the Tsarevich Alexei. Every morning two novices from the Ekaterinburg convent, Antonina Trinkina and Maria Krokhaleva, brought eggs and milk to the front gate. Sometimes they were also allowed to bring butter, extra meat or pastries, and everything – or nearly everything, for we had all served in the army! – was handed over to Kharitonov. In the afternoons the Tsar and his daughters walked for fifteen minutes in the bare trampled garden. I kept aloof, for the coarser of the guards took this opportunity to elbow their way close among the Grand Duchesses. Otherwise, I saw the family only on those few occasions when, as I stood my sentry duty in the hallway outside Yurovsky's room, one passed in shamed silence to the lavatory. The door of the little room did not lock, and I made it my concern to ensure that they were not disturbed.

The Tsar, I noted with some surprise, looked remarkably like the English King George, the same trim naval beard and wide moustache, the same level eyes below the high forehead. He wore a khaki shirt and breeches, with an officer's belt, and worn, down-at-heel leather boots. The Tsarina was one of our German princesses, tall and handsome but stern, her hair caught up in two full sweeps each side of her face and drawn into a modest comb behind. The girls, the Grand Duchesses, were all pretty, even after months of imprisonment, their eyes challenging, mischievous and imperious, all in one. Olga, twenty-two years old, was slim and fair-haired, quiet, and most like her father; Tatiana, a year younger, was tall and elegant, rather dark in complexion, haughty and pensive; Maria, thickset and lazy, was the most cheerful; and seventeen-year-old Anastasia, short and plump, was the family comedian. The Tsarevich, young Alexei, was obviously very ill: his father carried him, listless, to the lavatory, his legs bent as if in cramp and small beads of sweat bursting upon his brow.

From the narrow windows of the attics of the Ipatiev house machine-guns covered the approaches, and two of the guards were always posted there. My few brief moments of happiness came when, peering out along the barrel of one of these guns and momentarily imagining myself once more at the controls of a fighter in the upper air, I would suddenly catch a glimpse of Tatiana at her window above the roofs between, waving a small white handkerchief and smiling at my distant startled mooncalf face.

Two days after we moved into the Ipatiev house, curfew was proclaimed from eight in the evening until six the following morning, so there was no opportunity for me to sidle unobserved from the compound to visit Tatiana. But on the third day, I was allowed out to see her.

Yurovsky said very little – indeed, his German allowed him no more – beyond informing me that I had two hours' leave to visit the town. I nodded my farewell to Nikulin, who was lounging at the head of the stairs, marched boldly to the gate, slapped the guard there on the shoulder with a cheerful cry of 'Tovarich!' and stepped out into the street. The weather, as it had been every day, was warm and close beneath a pale blue sky. I thought I heard, far away, the faint dull thud of artillery; for two or three days there had been whispers that the Czechs were closing in on Ekaterinburg. The streets were busy with passing traffic – peasant carts, grinding trucks, all sorts of shabby armed men – yet, at the same time, curiously deserted. It

251

was like a town occupied by an enemy, its life still going on behind shutters and bolted doors, but isolated entirely from the affairs of the soldiers and their officers. I felt as I had felt one day, in garrison in Breslau, when I had gone through the afternoon streets on a visit to the dentist, while my fellow cadets rode at exercise in the woods far beyond the town.

I made my way nonchalantly into Voznesensky Prospekt, past the consulate, idly watching to see who followed me. I strolled into Glavni Prospekt, glanced quickly up and down the boulevard, and ducked into the narrow lane that led me, in a few seconds, to Preston's back door. The kitchen was warm and dark as before, the chickens pecking in and out of the open door, the same three women turning startled, then smiling shyly as I passed quickly through. The house was quiet, and I went precipitately up the stairs to the attic; before the little window, a figure in nurse's habit crouched peering out, then turned with a soft cry and ran wildly into my arms.

For a while there was no talk of anything but love; then Tatiana, gazing tenderly down into my eyes, as she had done that morning when we had first made love, at last could restrain herself no longer. 'Tell me, my darling, what did the Tsar say?'

I had to confess that I had not yet spoken to him, had given no thought to any plan of escape independent of the bolsheviks, did not even believe that the Tsar was aware of my existence. For three days I had lived in the Ipatiev house, learning the routine so that, if there should be a break in that routine, I might be able to take advantage of it; but at the same time, believing all that Karakhan had told me, I had lost sight of my first duty – to try to get the imperial family to safety. So I must speak to the Tsar.

A little later, as we sat, dressed once more but with our arms still about one another, on the hot and rumpled bed, Tchaikovsky and Clark came stamping up the stairs conversing enthusiastically together in Russian. We clasped hands and took stock of each other. Tchaikovsky was almost unchanged, his beard perhaps a little fuller and blacker, his moustache as bravely bristling, his uniform a little shabbier, if that were possible; but Clark was nearly unrecognisable. He had exchanged his uniform for a Russian blouse, with loose-woven baggy trousers and felt boots; his straggling beard had been cut back to a short greying stubble; a floppy cloth cap covered his thinning hair, which hung below, fringing his neck; and from somewhere he had acquired a pair of those steel-rimmed spectacles that marked a party member and active revolutionary. He took a step back, raising his arm in a clenched fist salute, but betrayed himself with a sudden, typical, gap-toothed grin.

'*Zeravstvuite*,' he said, smugly.

There was little time left for discussion, but Tchaikovsky, his nose twitching with pride, gave me a brief summary of the rumours he had heard about the town: of the Social Revolutionary uprisings that, it was whispered, had taken place in several provincial cities; and of the passionate liaison that was developing between Clark and the wife of the manager of the Ekaterinburg opera house.

'Well, you never know,' said Clark with his usual leer, 'I often think, when all this is over, I wouldn't mind treading the boards again . . . '

But most significant of all Tchaikovsky's report was what he had to tell me concerning Thompson. 'Yes,' he said, 'there is no doubt about it. He is quartered in the house across the street. And do you know what house that is?' His eyes grew round with drama. 'The house of the anarchists! Yes, did you not see, this afternoon, how they have raised their black flag above the door?'

'Stone me,' said Clark. 'I reckon your pal Thompson made some pretty funny friends in London. Down Sidney Street, I wouldn't wonder. I always thought those Special Branch boys 'ad a finger in more than one pie at a time.'

We agreed between us to keep as regular a watch on the anarchists' house, and on Thompson, as we could contrive. But how would we communicate? Neither Tchaikovsky nor Clark, nor even Tatiana, could come to the Ipatiev house to ask for me; and I could not be sure when next I would be given leave. We could flash messages to one another by mirrors, but those could be seen by too many people. In the end we settled upon the simplest possible code: while Thompson remained within the house of the anarchists a white handkerchief would be hung at the consul's attic window, but if he was seen to leave my comrades would hang up a blue handkerchief.

253

I kissed Tatiana, and promised that I would find the first opportunity to make myself known to the Tsar; and thinking on this, as I went downstairs with Clark behind me, I was suddenly seized with a ridiculous sense of propriety. My hair was too long and ragged: it must be cut, and my beard trimmed – I would get Kharitonov to do it. Little could be done about my creased and stained uniform, but I could polish my boots, and my buttons. I looked down at those buttons, black from months of neglect, and my heart failed me; but, coming into the kitchen and spying all the necessaries on a nearby shelf, I soon regained my resolution. Preston found me at it ten minutes later: he put his blond head through the door, stared at me, and then laughed uproariously.

'That's it! Captain Jones,' he cried, 'if you can keep your breeks when all about you are losing theirs, and blaming it on you . . . '

Just before curfew I left the house, and set off back to my sordid duties. At the corner of the lane beside the Ipatiev house I paused and turned back to look across the wide boulevard. The mansion next to the House of Nationalised Women stood with all its shutters closed, silent in the early evening. But, drooping from a short ragged pole above the front door, the black flag stirred sluggishly, flapping, like a trooper's heavy cape, in a sudden breath that came from the north, and then falling ominously still once more.

CHAPTER 18

7-14 July: Ekaterinburg

NEXT MORNING, with shiny buttons and boots, and cleaner than I had been for many a day, I at last contrived to speak a few words with the Tsar. It being Sunday a Father Storozhev, with his deacon, came to the Ipatiev house to celebrate mass for the imperial family. I was on sentry duty outside Yurovsky's room; the priest went in there to don his robes, there was a brief exchange of question and answer, and when Storozhev emerged and went into the drawing-room, I nonchalantly sauntered after him.

The room had been arranged for the mass: most of the furniture had been pushed to the walls, leaving a table, covered with a lace bedspread, to serve as an altar. Two or three candles, in battered pewter candlesticks, burnt smokily. The Tsarina and the Tsarevich were seated, but the rest of the family, and their servants, stood in two loose groups just inside the salon door so that I could, with some justification, move them forward a little and close the door behind me.

I could understand nothing of the mass, of course. Sometimes the priest chanted, sometimes the deacon, sometimes they spoke together; once or twice the congregation responded in speech or song, the Tsar's bass voice rumbling below the rest; toward the end of the mass, they suddenly all fell upon their knees. Then it came to an end, and the priests left, and the servants went about their duties, and I shut the salon door behind them, and turned, and found myself face to face with the Tsar.

'Your Imperial Majesty,' I began in German, but the Tsarina interrupted me quietly from across the room:

'Speak to His Majesty in Russian or in English, if you can.'

'I have only a few seconds,' I began again, 'to tell you not to despair. You have good friends in Ekaterinburg, who are working for your escape, and we hope that it will not be very long. I myself have come from England – '

But the Tsar stopped me, holding up his hand and fixing me with his deep sad eyes: 'My young friend, you are just like all the rest. What does Dzerzhinsky call you, agents provocateurs? Please, don't insult my intelligence, bringing me these tales designed to raise our hopes, only to dash them lower.'

'But it is true!' I protested. 'I have been sent from England, and both King George and Kaiser Wilhelm know of it, and there is an aeroplane – ' and then I felt the salon door pushing open behind me, and I stepped back and shouted at the Tsar: 'So, if you wish to go to the lavatory, come!' and together we marched out within an inch of Yurovsky's suspicious face.

There was no further opportunity for conversation, but I thought that the Grand Duchesses looked more cheerful when they passed me on the landing later in the morning. Then, after lunch, the family were allowed out for their daily half-hour in the garden. The day had begun clear, but the sky was now steamily overcast and the air sultry. I was lounging at the garden door, sampling a Russian cigarette that one of the other guards had offered me – a coarse tube of wrapping paper, with a few shreds of tangled tobacco stuffed into its far end – when there came suddenly the unmistakable heavy rattle of a Maxim 10. It was a sound I knew well from my days in the Uhlans: there came the zip and whap of lead, and a spray of splinters flew from the top of the plank fence no more than fifteen yards in front of me.

The Tsar did not hesitate: he gathered the Tsarina to him with one hand and together, like anxious hens, they bustled the Grand Duchesses and the Tsarevich before them into the shelter of the house, the Letts scrambling close behind them while unslinging their rifles.

Where had the shots come from? It was difficult to tell, for the bullets had hit the fence top obliquely, howling off down toward the lake. One of the Letts, his rifle held high across his chest, ran crouching into the garden again and stopped, his head turning and lifting like a stag's in the autumn woods. As he straightened from his crouch – and then, instantly, fell to the ground in instinctive reaction – the Maxim fired again, scattering a whizzing fan of stone chips from the corner of the house with more fence fragments, as it traversed in a wild attempt to reach him.

The imperial family were huddled in the corridor, uncertain what was happening and what was expected of them. With scant ceremony I eased my way through and ran for the stairs that would take me to the attics. Up there at my lookout post – behind the sights of another Maxim 10 – I could scan the whole of Voznesensky Prospekt where it ran before the Ipatiev house to become Arsenyevski Prospekt, the open plaza that surrounded the Church of the Ascension, and the mansions that lined the street on either side. As I stared searchingly at those blank façades reflecting the afternoon light, there came another short burst of fire; and, thinly in the brightness, I saw the random sparks that revealed the machine-gun's position. There was no doubt about it: the shots came from a sand-bagged window above the languid black flag that marked the headquarters of the anarchists.

The Maxim 10 needs a crew of three men: one to aim and fire, one to feed the ammunition belts, which are heaped beside it and can tangle only too easily, and one to superintend the circulation of cooling water. I yelled my loudest for someone to come to my assistance, but there was no response. I tumbled down the stairs again, and found Yurovsky and Nikulin arguing bitterly on the landing outside the rooms into which they had once again herded the Tsar and his family. I told them what I had seen, and asked for two of the Letts to be sent to help me man the gun.

Yurovsky eyed me shrewdly: 'Not you,' he said. 'I will send some others upstairs – but there is no chance that they can put the other machine-gun out of action from here. We will soon deal with these madmen; we will take them from the flank and from the rear.'

But how were we to do that? The whole of the compound between the two palisades lay under the anarchists' fire, the guard at the gate, whom Yurovsky called on the field tele-phone, flatly refused to leave the flimsy shelter of his sentry box, and those in the Popov house were beyond our reach. With a brief excuse to Yurovsky I raced upstairs once more. At the side of the house a small trap-door opened out on to the roof. hidden from the anarchists by the rise of the baroque gable facing the street but in full view of Preston's attic window. As I had hoped, Tatiana was peering apprehensively in my direction and, gesticulating wildly, I got her to bring Tchaikovsky and Clark into view. There followed nearly two minutes of frantic pantomime in which I discovered dramatic talents that, up to that day, I had hardly suspected. Clark, with his thespian's voice, thundered back each part of the message as soon as he and Tchaikovsky had translated it, and at last I signalled that we were agreed.

In the garden of the Ipatiev house, beyond the overhang of the terrace, stood a large upright drum of heavy steel on small rumbling iron wheels, which was used for the occasional removal of night-soil. It was fortunately empty, and had recently been roughly hosed out, but it still stank abominably, and my fellow guards averted their heads and held their noses as we trundled it in through the garden door and across the lobby to the side door of the house. Meanwhile Clark and Tchaikovsky, following my instructions, had commandeered all the washing lines from Preston's backyard, climbed the wall into the back of the Popov house, and explained to the men there what was about to happen. Standing in the shelter of the Popov doorway, Tchaikovsky called across the lane to the sentry at the entrance to our compound, and threw him the ends of two long ropes. Gathering a good length of these to himself, the sentry was then able to crouch in the lee of his hut and bowl the two lines so that they fell at the doorway where I waited.

We tied the ropes to the two stubby handles by which the drum was moved from place to place and then, with a short prayer and holding my tiny ragged scarf to my nostrils, I climbed into the noisome, slimy depths. It was far worse than any stable I had ever helped to clear as a boy, worse even than the pigsties on my uncle's farm. I was reminded of the day on which I took my Great Dane, Moritz, for his first and only flight when, overcome with excitement and apprehension as I put the aircraft into a long slow glide, he had disgraced himself in the cockpit.

There came a jerk as the ropes were pulled: the drum tilted suddenly forward, so that I had to crouch low in the bottom to keep it balanced, and then it began to rumble bumpily as willing arms in the Popov house hauled and strained. The first bullets hit my improvised tank almost immediately. To begin with, the isolated shots banged obliquely into the metal and howled away, but then, as the gunner got his range, came a burst of raking fire that sounded as if the whole of the top of the drum had been ripped open by a gigantic can opener. It was deafening and very frightening, but I smiled grimly to myself, reflecting that, if I were to suffer the same shame as poor Moritz, no one would ever know.

Then the gunner must have shifted his aim, for only stray bullets wailed against the drum, and Tchaikovsky told me later that he had been firing wildly in an attempt to cut the ropes. The drum tottered across the rough ground, stuck, lurched, pitched forward alarmingly, swung rigidly upright, lumbered on again. Suddenly there was a burst of cheering close at hand, and, looking up, I could see the shadow of the Popov eaves. The drum was tipped forward and for a second eager laughing faces appeared staring in at me; then there came the cries of disgust, the coughing and spluttering and holding of noses, and all those faces vanished again. As I crawled out from my refuge, the circle of brave Red Guards retreated before me, and even Clark and Tchaikovsky stood clear.

'Come on!' I cried. 'No time to waste!' We gathered up the ropes, Clark seized two rifles and a bandolier of cartridges from an unresisting guard, and we ran through the house, scrambled over the wall into the lane behind Preston's house, and raced to the corner of Glavni Prospekt. The streets were deserted: it was of course Sunday afternoon, but at the first sound of gunfire all respectable citizens – and more than a few disreputable ones – had closed their shutters and bolted their doors.

Peering round the corner, we took stock of the situation. The anarchists' house was about a hundred yards to our left, almost facing the Ipatiev house, with the high onion-topped tower of the Church of the Ascension rising beyond it. Next to our target was the House of Nationalised Women, a tallish narrow building that was separated from the anarchists' house only by a narrow alleyway, while its roof parapet appeared to be several feet above the other's. We looked at one another and nodded silently. Clark wrinkled up his nose at me and muttered:

'We'd best be quick about it, too, or else they'll ruddy well smell us comin'.'

The Maxim, positioned as it was, would not have a wide arc of fire, and we felt confident that it was, in any case, aimed toward the Ipatiev house. So together we raced across the street and crouched under the cover of the Post Office wall. From there we crept along, past the Club, and visible to an anarchist only if he were to stretch his head a long way out of the window – there came a single burst of fire, but it was directed across the Voznesensky Prospekt, and it seemed obvious that we had not been spotted. We came to the House of Nationalised Women, and did not hesitate: Clark was up the steps and had smashed in the door with his rifle butt in two seconds, and Tchaikovsky and

259

I followed close behind. It was a gloomy house inside, and we saw no women. There were muffled screams and exclamations in the dark from behind curtains and nearly-closed doors, but this may have been as much at the stink I left behind me as at the thunder of our feet upon the stairs.

We reached the attics and, without pause for thought, smashed our way through the tiles on the side of the roof nearest the anarchists. As I had thought, it was no great distance to jump from the stone parapet down on to the roof some four or five feet away; we did not even need the ropes we had brought with us. I went first and landed easily. But it was harder to make the leap carrying a rifle, and poor Tchaikovsky fell forward and hit his nose hard against the roof, while Clark swayed, wobbled, cursed, and at last flung himself into space to land in a heap with a crash that must have echoed through the house below.

I turned for a second to look down into the boulevard below. There was no sign of movement outside the Ipatiev and Popov houses, but with my wider view I could see something that probably the anarchists could not: along Voznesensky Prospekt to the left, a small field gun was being slowly trundled forward by Red Guards crouched behind its steel shield.

Tchaikovsky had already levered open a convenient trapdoor, and hastily we bundled in and crept as quietly as possible across the attic floor. Luck was with us. About a dozen of the anarchists, with their backs toward us, were gathered round the Maxim, jabbering excitedly and peering out of the narrow gap between the sandbags into the street. Clark stayed perched on the stairs to cover us as Tchaikovsky and I burst into the room, and, waving our weapons, soon persuaded them to edge away from the machine-gun and crowd dejectedly by the doorway. There were enquiring shouts from below, and the thud of feet on the stairs, but Tchaikovsky and I contrived to drag the Maxim round quickly to point toward the door; and with this threat in their faces and Clark behind them on the attic stairs the anarchists had little alternative but to surrender. As we gestured them together with our drawn guns I glanced over my shoulder, and was surprised and somewhat alarmed to see, through the narrow window behind me, the field gun suddenly roll into view on the far side of the street outside Preston's house, its muzzle already swinging to point in our direction.

'Quickly!' I urged, 'before we are all blown to pieces!'

We hustled our prisoners down the stairs, disarming them one by one as best we could, and drove them before us out through the front door. The street was silent for perhaps twenty seconds, and then, from behind the gun, from the Ipatiev gateway and from their quarters in the Popov house, Red Guards came running toward us, shouting and cheering. They surrounded the shambling anarchists, jostling, jeering, even punching and kicking at them. I stood apart, unacknowledged – but who would want to come near me in my nauseating condition? – while Clark and Tchaikovsky, with a quick nod and a ghost of a smile, had wisely surrendered their rifles and merged into the crowd of townspeople that was now beginning to gather.

It was then that I realised with a start of concern that Thompson was not among our prisoners. Yurovsky was already bundling them into line, and I saw that all my fellow guards from the Ipatiev house were there. In the excitement of the sudden surrender of the anarchists, they had left the Tsar unguarded and unprotected. And even as the first ripples of fear ran through my mind I looked up toward the attic window of the consul's house, and saw Tatiana frantically waving a blue handkerchief to and fro.

I ran, shouldering through the crowd, which gave way readily at my aromatic approach, and raced for the gateway in the outer palisade. As I had feared, there was no sentry on duty, the compound was deserted, the inner gate and the side door stood gaping open. Once within the house I stopped, panting, to consider my next move. The Ipatiev house was still as I had never known it: no cursing, no coughing and spitting, no trudge of soft boots on the uncarpeted stairs. And then, distantly, I heard a voice speaking, no more than a quiet continuous monotone.

I crept forward with my revolver in my hand, up the stairs towards the Tsar's quarters, and as my head rose above the level of the upper floor, I stayed arrested in mid-movement. The doors to the salon were wide open, and like a group of wax-works the imperial family were posed against the light from the further window. Standing in the doorway with his back to me, a revolver in each hand, stood Thompson.

It was he who was speaking: ' – in a nutshell, your majesties. To put it another way: the Jerries don't want you, they'll be defeated in a month or so, and then you'd be far too much of an embarrassment. We British can manage very well without you, and the Frogs don't care, one way or the other. The worse thing that could happen to the bolshies is for your death to be laid at their door, and that, in a word, is what I'm here for. So, to be precise, I must ask you to compose yourselves as you best know how and prepare to meet – '

Not one of the family had moved a muscle or so much as allowed their eyes to flicker as, moving swiftly in advance of my own betraying stench and thanking providence for my soft-soled Russian boots, I had come up behind him and struck him down with one blow from the butt of my revolver. He crumpled to the floor without another sound, and I was already dragging him by the shoulders to the head of the stairs as the Tsarina, with a faint smile and a whispered 'Thank you', closed the salon doors upon us.

I had to dispose of Thompson, somewhere, somehow, very quickly. I could not shoot him in cold blood, yet he would soon recover consciousness, and, if I were to hand him over to the bolsheviks, he would reveal my true identity to everybody. With a heroic heave I got his sagging carcase over my shoulder and staggered downstairs, through the lobby, and across the compound to the gate. All the guards were still in the Voznesensky Prospekt, revelling in the sight of the discomfited anarchists, but I dared go no further, and in an agony of indecision I propped Thompson's body against the fence.

It was then that I heard in the distance, coming up the lane from the direction of the pond, a familiar but unexpected sound, the bell of the night-soil man. It was still only early evening, the sun nowhere near setting, yet I could see without any doubt, as I peeped round the edge of the fencing, the well-known cart with its abominable burden, creaking up the slope. The driver sat crouched as usual in his rags, occasionally shaking his bell and swearing at his two spavined nags. It was not until the cart drew level with the gateway that I noticed that he wore an unexpectedly familiar pair of dark eyeglasses.

'Marlin?' I cried in amazement and relief.

'Hush!' he hissed, reining in sharply and glancing rapidly to right and left before leaping down to seize my hand. 'Good God,' he muttered, letting go of it again and stepping back 'what in heaven have you been up to? You stink worse than I do. I must say I'm pleased to see you, though. When we didn't get a telegram from Preston, or news of any kind, I reckoned you must have copped a Blighty one. So I bribed my way onto a motor-boat to Astrakhan, then onto a steamer up the Volga, and thought I'd make one last desperate attempt at a rescue. Maybe I'm not needed, however. What's your news?'

As quickly as possible I told him of our situation, and indicated the tumbled body by the gate. 'So I've arrived in time, after all. Our old friend Thompson, eh? Can't leave the feller here, whatever he's done – after all the chap is British! Come on now, give me a hand.'

And so we bundled the still unconscious policeman in among the slopping buckets and cans of the cart, and Marlin climbed up once more. I could see that the crowd in front of the anarchists' house was already beginning to break up, and one or two guards were turning idly to stroll back to their duties, but Marlin still lent down conspiratorially from his seat.

'Look here,' he whispered, 'I've heard all about this House of Nationalised Women. What's it like, eh? Have they got any governesses in there?' Some of my companions of the guard were scarce more than ten yards away, swaggering to their deserted posts. Despairing, I slapped the nearer horse stingingly across its hind quarters. It let out a shriek, eyes rolling white in its head, and the cart shot forward, weaving, bouncing, and groaning down the rough lane, pitching Marlin back on top of Thompson in the spilling swill, and disappeared in a cloud of dust, and a stench that almost eclipsed my own.

For a further week there were no developments and, thankfully, no news of Marlin or Thompson. Nikulin found me a ragged, but clean, shirt and breeches to replace my filthy uniform, although I was forced to keep my fetid boots; and Yurovsky, who had taken full credit for the bloodless capture of the anarchists, made jovial remarks about sewer rats and *Scheisshunden,* which my circumstances compelled me to ignore.

Beyond relaxing the lofty blankness of his expression slightly when he saw me, the Tsar made no further recognition of my part in saving the lives of the entire family; clearly he still regarded me as a bolshevik, his jailer, and one of his potential executioners.

On the following Sunday – Bastille Day in France, I reminded myself – Father Storozhev came again to celebrate mass, but I had no opportunity to intervene. After lunch, Yurovsky and Nikulin were suddenly summoned to the Amerikanskaya, and a little later rumour reached me, by way of a lout who came ambling across from the Popov house, that Goloschokin and Syromolotov had returned from Moscow. They had brought with them sensational news: a week before, Count von Mirbach had been shot dead in the German embassy by two Social Revolutionaries.

CHAPTER 19

14-17 July: Ekaterinburg – and away!

IT WAS early evening when Yurovsky and Nikulin returned to the Ipatiev house, and within a few minutes Yurovsky sent for me.

'So, you have heard? Mirbach is assassinated; Comrade Sverdlov told Comrade Syromolotov that the Germans wanted to invade Moscow; and now nothing, absolutely nothing, must happen to the former Tsar and his wife. But then there are the Czechs, those traitors to their class! They are fighting us all along the railway, and we cannot hold them. Unless Trotsky can send us more men quickly, Ekaterinburg will be surrounded within two or three days. My prisoners must not fall into their hands, so I ask you to carry out your plans as quickly as possible. Your friends hiding at the consul's house – I will get them papers, and they must show us how to prepare the aero-plane.'

I thought quickly. I still did not trust him, and I had not told him where the Ilya Murometz was concealed. To get it refuelled I would have to reveal its hiding-place – and then how could I be sure that my companions and I would be allowed to fly away in it?

'My friends must guard the aircraft,' I said. 'You must give them weapons. They are here to rescue the former Tsar, and they will not leave without him, have no fear. But if the Czechs should find the aeroplane . . .'

He scowled, and folded his arms across his chest, and stamped quietly about his room for some minutes, but at last he agreed. 'We will arrange this now,' he said. 'In one hour we go to the consul's house, with Commissar Voikov and Commissar Yermakov. Your friends will be taken to the place where you have hidden the aeroplane, and they will stay there, with some Red Guards, to guard it while Voikov requisitions the fuel for you. If they go in the night few people will see them, now we have curfew. But your lady friend – oh yes, we know that she is there also – she will remain in Preston's house until it is time for you to leave Ekaterinburg.'

He dismissed me curtly, and soon afterward Nikulin was despatched to arrange the meeting. The evening was hot and tense, with summer lightning spreading white above a high thin sheet of cloud, and it was impossible to tell whether the regular distant rumble was the growl of thunder over the steppe or the sound of the Czech guns creeping ever closer to the town. All were uneasy, moving restlessly about the house and speaking infrequently in whispers. Some of the Letts had bottles of vodka, and when (tinkling faintly in the drawing-room above) we heard one of the Grand Duchesses at the piano, they began sullenly to shout out the revolutionary songs – 'Let's forget the old regime' and 'You fell as a victim in the struggle'. I was glad at last to escape with Yurovsky into the evening street, lit no longer by electric lights but only by the low glow of the western horizon and the almost continual ghostly flashes of lightning.

Preston's 'office' was densely crowded when we all assembled there: Voikov accompanied by Yermakov, his complexion even more sallow and his long hair greasier than before; Clark and Tchaikovsky, apprehensive, for Preston could not tell them why they had been summoned; Yurovsky and myself. Preston was jumpy and irritable as he showed us in:

'See here, old man,' he said, 'what on earth have you done with all my washing lines?' He and Tatiana were pointedly excluded from the meeting. The shutters were closed and the blinds down, and a single oil lamp burned low in the thick air.

Our business was rapidly concluded. I reassured my companions as best I could, told Voikov that I needed at least 150 gallons of gasoline, and repeated my insistence that Clark and Tchaikovsky should be armed. There was further argument about this, Yurovsky taking one side and Yermakov the other, and Voikov playing intermediary between them, but the point was at last conceded. Beyond the shutters we heard a truck arrive outside the house, and wait with its engine throbbing unsteadily. As we passed the hall, I caught no more than a glimpse of Tatiana, a grey shadow at the turn in the stairs, and managed only a brief, but (I hoped) reassuring, wave of my hand before the door shut firmly behind us and we were in the street once more.

Four guards lounged in the back of the truck, and I watched with misgivings as my friends were hoisted up; but they were handed rifles, and, as the truck pulled jerkily away, down the slope toward the pond and the causeway that led to the forest, I heard Clark burst out, in his fine tenor voice, with a bold song. The words echoed back in the heavy night as Yurovsky and I returned to the Ipatiev house: 'When told that they would all be shot, unless they left the service, that hero hesitated not, so wonderful his nerve is, he sent his resignation in, the first of all the corps-o . . . ' – the last note dying into the distance like the howl of a prairie dog.

How matters fared with them, I heard much later from Clark. They found the Ilya Murometz safe, still concealed behind its screen of branches, and spent the rest of the night bivouacked beside it. In the morning the guards, exclaiming delightedly at the size of the wonderful aircraft, helped to drag it free, and then Tchaikovsky, checking meticulously through the controls, discovered that the batteries were discharged and badly corroded. The truck was dispatched for Yermakov, who returned bringing with him a man from the Verkh-Isetsk factory named Dr Arkipov, a furtively jovial man, with gold-rimmed pince-nez swinging on a black ribbon. It was agreed that new batteries must be found, and Arkipov was given the task of requisitioning them, filling them with sulphuric acid, and making sure that they were fully charged. Away went the truck again, to return in due course with the first load of gasoline in a motley collection of cans and glass carboys. Tchaikovsky began to superintend the flushing of the fuel tanks and the cleaning out of the carburettors. The fuel arrived very slowly, and two days passed before Voikov had found anything like the quantity I had requested. And every hour the Czech guns sounded nearer.

Shut up in the Ipatiev house, I was consumed with impatience. Yurovsky would tell me nothing of the progress in the woods, and for most of the day was away in conference with the presidium of the soviet. I did my guard duty, for there was no alternative, and twice was able to signal briefly to Tatiana at her attic window. I would have shouted to her, for she was not fifty yards away, but I dared not draw the attention of the exterior guards to her presence. And I found no opportunity to assure the imperial family that their liberation was at hand.

That day, Monday, the kitchen boy was sent out of the house to live with the exterior guards, and four women were drafted in by the local labour union to sweep the floors, not only in our guard-rooms but upstairs as well. We were ordered to help them by gathering all the refuse we could find and dumping it in the garden, behind a small locked shed that contained the family's meagre baggage. It was as if Yurovsky had decided to leave the house as clean and tidy as possible when we left it. There was unrest in the air, and the morose Letts drank heavily, and Lacher with them. I had avoided him as much as possible, but he pursued me still with questions I would not answer, and now he began to taunt me whenever we passed in the corridors of the house, calling me 'little mister mystery man' in his nasty Austrian accent. I was glad to get away from him to take my turn beside the machine-guns in the attic.

So Monday passed away, and the summer dusk crept in, and all the time the guns rumbled, and from the attic window I could see bedraggled, weary cavalry ride through the town, many of them wounded, and stumbling infantry – if those ragged undisciplined bandits were worthy of the name. Off duty, I dozed, but even I could not sleep well, and round my bed the Letts still drank, sang incoherently, and argued through the night.

On Tuesday at dawn the two nuns brought their usual morning milk, and a basket of fifty eggs, which we ordered Kharitonov to cook for the guard. He made omelettes, tough and watery, but the finest food I had eaten for two weeks. At midday, Yurovsky called all the guard to stand to: he addressed us in his fragmentary German, telling us that the time had come for particular vigilance, ordering that we should speak no more than necessary to the exterior guards, and, at the end, it seemed that he gave me a special, lingering look. In the afternoon all the family, with the exception of the Tsarevich, walked for a half-hour in the garden; and at six in the evening they ate their dinner, closed away in their private apartments.

At seven, Yurovsky summoned the commander of the exterior guard: Pavel Medvedev, about thirty years old, tall and sturdy, with a thick, unruly, ginger moustache. He was a former factory worker, with an eager ingratiating manner, and he willingly carried out Yurovsky's order to collect all revolvers from his men. There were twelve guards in all, most of them making a kind of informal sentry-go beyond the palisade, and Medvedev brought the revolvers and piled them on Yurovsky's desk. As for the interior guard, we, too, were all prowling about like tigers at the zoo, but armed every one; sober or drunk – several of the Letts were staggering wildly, and, one, I noticed, laughed briefly – we were all equipped with a Nagant revolver on the hip, while some carried one, or even two, old rifles (Männlichers or Mausers) slung heavily across the shoulders. The air in the Ipatiev house was thick, yellow, greasy: the electricity was again switched off, and the few oil lamps burnt fitfully; the corridors were full of the reek of tobacco, unwashed bodies, and cheap vodka; and through it all we stalked, each one alone, eyeing all others in suspicion and dread, while the thud of the guns in the night came ever nearer, and Medvedev, stumbling at every corner, drank drink for drink with Lacher.

An hour before midnight Yermakov arrived. To my great

relief he brought with him Tatiana, pale and silent in her Red Cross weeds, who took a chair beside the foot of the staircase and did not dare catch my eye. Shortly after, some half-dozen of us were ordered from the house, to open a gap in the planked fence of the compound, and let in a truck and a motor car. As we returned to the house I found Yermakov by the guardroom door. I asked him impulsively, 'Is it tonight?' but he stared coldly at me, with a silent shrug.

At about midnight, Yurovsky went upstairs and roused the family and servants. Bursting through the dining-room, he went first to wake Anna Demidova, and then, by way of the room where the four Grand Duchesses slept, to the bedroom that looked out upon the corner of Voznesensky Prospekt, occupied by the Tsar, the Tsarina, and the Tsarevich Alexeï. Stumbling back into the drawing-room in the unlit gloom, he tumbled Dr Botkin from his sofa to the floor, and finally roared into the kitchen to bring Trupp and Kharitonov from their perches on the stove.

I had followed half behind him as he made his tour, and was at his shoulder as he took the first step down the staircase to the lower floor once more. He turned suddenly, his face a few inches below mine, and I saw eyes full of contained passion:

'Well,' he said tightly and bitterly, 'are you satisfied? Does it go according to plan?' And then, turning again, he blundered quickly down, shouting for some men to get the family's baggage from the garden shed and load it into the motor car.

Nearly an hour had passed before the imperial family emerged from their quarters. The Tsar came first, staggering slightly as he bore the thin frame of the Tsarevich; then the Grand Duchess Anastasia, carrying the little dog Jemmy. The Tsarina came slowly behind, followed by her other daughters. All wore dark skirts and jackets, with rather crumpled blouses, close-fitting hats and loose scarves, and the Tsarina had a long grey overcoat across her shoulders. After these came Anna Demidova, carrying two cushions, and Dr Botkin, creased and tousled and scarcely awake. The humble Trupp and Kharitonov, grey and anxious, followed from the kitchen.

They came out into the hallway by Yurovsky's room, where I snapped fiercely to attention at the sight of them. The Tsar inclined his head slightly, fixing me momentarily with his soft glance; the Tsarina passed by, head high, and the Grand Duchesses eyed me curiously. The whole party tailed past as if on a communal visit to the lavatory, and plunged down the narrow back stairs. But those stairs, which we of the guard had seldom used, led only to the storerooms below the entrance hall, or out of a side-door into the covered way that connected with the former servants' quarters. Through that door the Tsar was compelled to lead his train, and back into the house by a further door, while I, foreseeing their course, had rattled quickly down the inside staircase, past Tatiana – who rose and curtsied low as the Tsar appeared again – to ensure that the drunken Letts observed some kind of respect when the family approached.

Yurovsky, Yermakov, myself and Lacher – who, for all his drunkenness was still an Austrian soldier and knew his duty – ushered the family and their servants through the outer guard-room, into the lower hallway where I had first entered the Ipatiev house, and then, to the left, into a waiting-room. The room was empty, the walls papered in stripes but otherwise bare, and the ceiling barrel-vaulted. Yurovsky shouted: some chairs were brought, the Tsarina sat on one, and the Tsar upon the second, supporting the Tsarevich, who rested across a third. Demidova placed one of the cushions she carried behind the Tsarina's back; then she and the rest ranged themselves behind the chairs, as if posing for a group photograph. From the hallway we all stared through the open doors at this strangely formal party.

The Tsar turned the Tsarevich slightly so that he could sit alone, rose, and beckoned modestly to me. Yurovsky and Yermakov together pushed me forward into the already crowded room, and I walked with the Tsar as he moved toward the Tsarina, where she sat close to the wall by the shuttered window. Trupp and Kharitonov held wildly fluttering oil lamps, which threw our shadows gesticulating against the wall and up into the arch of the ceiling.

The Tsar spoke softly in English, close by the Tsarina, his head bent forward but twisted oddly to one side so that he could observe me beneath his brows:

'So this is what it comes to, your great plan? Our cousins have finally washed their hands, and we are to be executed here, in this sordid cellar?'

'No, no, your majesty,' I stammered. 'I assure you, all will be well. I have been promised – '

He smiled, calmly and disparagingly, and, taking the stub of a pencil from the pocket of his uniform shirt, he wrote upon the wall beside him, turning two or three times to watch my changing expression. It was a couplet from a poem by Heine that I knew only too well:

> *Belsatsar ward in selbiger Nacht*
> *Von seinen Knechten umgebracht.*

'And Belsazar was, that same night, by his own servants put to death'. And I shuddered and wondered at the calm humour that, at such a moment, could make a pun upon the name of Bels*atsar*.

I was about to speak again when one of the Lett guards, blundering drunkenly forward, seized the Tsarevich roughly by the shoulder as if to shake him. Seeing the movement from the corner of my eye, and hearing the thick words bursting from his throat, I spun on my heel in time to see Dr Botkin reach forward in remonstrance; but even as I turned the Tsar plunged past me. I stumbled to one side and almost fell, and luckily so, for the Lett, swinging upon the Tsar and unslinging his rifle in one movement, thrust forward and pinned him against the wall behind the Tsarina, the bayonet going through his shoulder like a pin through a captured butterfly.

All the women screamed, Trupp and Kharitonov dropped to their knees, still holding their lamps so that ghastly shadow-play swept up high above our heads, and another of the drunken guards, seeing Botkin still swaying forward, pulled out his revolver and fired full five times into the doctor's body. The Lett who had struck the Tsar pulled back his bayonet and was about to rush upon him again when I, almost unthinking, drew my revolver and shot him dead. He fell, knocking me to the floor, drenching me with his blood, and, as I struggled from beneath his weight, I heard more shots ring out.

One lamp was extinguished, the other lay flaring in a spilt pool of oil; everybody was shouting or sobbing; the Tsar, one hand to his spouting shoulder, leaned heavily upon the Tsarina; and the Tsarevich, struck by a flailing rifle butt or a rain of fists, was stretched upon the floor. Yurovsky was beside me, his revolver waving high, screaming orders in Russian and broken

German, a second Lett dead at his feet and the remainder, hollow-eyed, jammed cowering in the doorway. Through the ruck came Medvedev, babbling insanely, elbowing, kicking at everything in his way, as the little dog ran squealing about and the girls huddled weeping and stretching out helpless arms toward their father.

I felt a hand seize my elbow, and swung round to see Yermakov. 'For the love of God, help me get them out of here,' he cried. I turned to Yurovsky and together with our revolvers we drove the guards back to make a passage. Tatiana came pushing through, and ran to the Tsar, who had now collapsed into the Tsarina's chair. I took Medvedev by the neck and hurled him from the room.

'A stretcher,' said Tatiana, 'we must have a stretcher!' And one of the Letts, more sober than the rest, cried out:

'The sleigh! The shafts from the sleigh in the yard!'

While Tatiana took one of the Grand Duchesses' scarves and with the Tsarina made a pad to stem the Tsar's bleeding, some of the guards fetched the shafts of the sleigh, and a grey army blanket, and Lacher found some cord, and clumsily we made a crude stretcher. There was now a deathly silence, broken only by Demidova's uncontrolled sobbing, the heavy panting of the Tsar, and the shuffling of the boots of the guards. Even the wretched lapdog was quiet. The air was thick with powder fumes and the smoke of the lamps, and the hot sweet smell of blood and death.

Without ceremony Yermakov shepherded the survivors from the room, while Yurovsky and I, with some interference from the Tsarina, lifted the Tsar on to the stretcher and followed them. Out in the compound, one or two wary faces of the exterior guard peered from the shadows, but the night was quiet. Three of the Grand Duchesses, and the maid, were crowded on the back of the truck; we slid the Tsar's stretcher aboard and hoisted the Tsarina after him, as Yermakov clambered up beside the driver and gave him the order to move. I looked round wildly for Tatiana and saw her with the Grand Duchess Anastasia in the back seat of the motor car, the sagging shape of the Tsarevich held between them. The car's engine was running, and it was already turning to follow the truck out of the gateway as I ran breathlessly forward and flung myself on to the baggage beside the driver.

He was one of the exterior guards, whom I recognised: a stocky, middle-aged man named Lyukhanov, with a spotty face. He drove fast but erratically, swerving close behind the flapping tailboard of the truck in the summer half-light, down the lane to the Iset Embankment, left to the corner of Glavni Prospekt by the district courthouse, then right along the causeway between the two lakes toward the forest. It was now near dawn, and the road ahead stretched, clearly marked by the dust of the truck before us, straight into the trees.

We hit the first level-crossing too fast, lungeing and springing madly across the tree trunks laid between the rails, evoking a cry of pain from the Tsarevich and a sudden English oath from Tatiana. Then we were roaring on again, swaying in the ruts of the track, the springs of the car groaning as Lyukhanov tried to catch up with the truck.

After three or four miles we came round a bend between the trees to see, a few hundred yards ahead, the signal cabin of Ekaterinburg Station No 2. There were some wagons in a siding, and Yermakov's truck had stopped beside them: a crowd of Red Guards stood around, and I could see figures climbing down from the truck and being urged toward the train.

Lyukhanov slowed the car gradually, and stopped a few yards from the group, just as the Tsar's stretcher was lifted down. Yermakov stepped forward, and spoke commandingly.

'He says the family are not to go with us. They are being taken on the train!' exclaimed Tatiana.

There was no time to think, to hesitate, to argue: 'Tell the driver to drive on,' I urged her, and, as she spoke rapidly and fiercely to Lyukhanov, I drew my revolver and thrust it against his ribs. With a terrified exclamation he let in the clutch, missed Yermakov by an inch, and roared forward across the railway track. There were furious shouts, and, as we careered up the road, a scatter of rifle shots, but we were soon clear.

'Faster! faster! faster!' I cried at Lyukhanov in English and German, and Tatiana and Anastasia added their pleas in Russian. It would be but a minute before Yermakov filled his truck with riflemen and set off in pursuit.

In ten minutes we came to the clearing, the morning light flooding the sky. Clark and Tchaikovsky, and the men with them, were awake but moving drowsily as the car skittered across the dew-drenched grass. A ladder leaned against the upper wing of the Ilya Murometz where the tanks had been filled, and a small pile of cans stood still waiting to be emptied. The car slewed to a stop beside them, and I sprang out. There was no time to explain.

'Will she go?' I asked Tchaikovsky, and he shrugged his shoulders calmly:

'Let us hope so.'

Tatiana and Anastasia carried the Tsarevich to the door of the aircraft and helped him in. He was bleeding freely from numerous cuts, and his hands and forearms were puffily purple as if they had been crushed beneath a heavy chest. Crude chocks fashioned from pine logs lay before the wheels of the Ilya Murometz and I asked Tchaikovsky: 'Have you told these men what to do?' He nodded, and I send him running to climb into the cabin of the aircraft with Anastasia, while I reminded Clark and Tatiana of their duties in starting the engines. Clark was up on the wing beside one engine in a second, but Tatiana scrambled desperately in her nurse's dress before, with the same English oath, she put both hands to her skirt and ripped it bodily from her waist.

Tchaikovsky was standing beside the controls as I slid into the pilot's seat. 'The gauges are full, the batteries are charged,' he said. 'Now let us pray.' I glanced out at the window to port: Clark and Tatiana were at their posts. I nodded, and they swung together on the starting handles; down with the ignition switches, up with the thumb, and they swung again. With scarcely a moment's hesitation, both engines fired. Now for the starboard engines – and this was no time for end-of-the-reel suspense, such as I had seen in the *kinos* off the Kurfürsten-damm, on a carefree Berlin leave. Indeed, Tchaikovsky had done his work well, and again both engines fired at first swing.

As Clark and Tatiana dropped from the wing, and as I eased the throttle forward to feel the engines pick up speed, the truck appeared far away at the end of the clearing. But the men at our chocks were too fascinated by the sight of Tatiana's bare buttocks to notice its arrival, and the roar of our engines covered the sound of shouting. Glancing aft, I saw my two companions scramble through the cabin door: 'The chocks! the chocks away!' I screamed, and Clark leant out into the slipstream shouting and gesticulating. I felt the jerk, the sudden lurch forward, and the Ilya Muromets was rolling through the thick grass toward the truck, faster and steadily faster, bouncing and shuddering, howling in every joint, and at last, as I dragged the wheel back, taking the air almost in the faces of Yermakov's men. They fired on us as we came near, and as we rose over them Clark opened one of the cabin windows and fired back, but all the shots went wide. As I banked to starboard I saw one of the gasoline cans on the ground explode, and then the whole dump, and while we slowly climbed toward the south-west we could see the black column of smoke rising where the car and all the imperial baggage were consumed in one great pyre.

Ekaterinburg lay to port in the dawn sunlight, the twin lakes gleaming and the whole town laid out as a map of my past fortnight: the Ipatiev house with its double palisade, the vice-consulate beside it, the pretentious façade of the Amerikanskaya hotel . . . I was weary, and far from triumphant: only heaven – and the bolsheviks – knew whether the Tsar was still alive, and what would become of the Tsarina and her three other daughters. I had managed to rescue but two of the family, with nearly 2,000 miles to fly before they would be safe. And then the Tsarevich began to scream.

Tchaikovsky turned to see what was happening, but I ordered him to take the controls, and myself went aft. The boy lay in a pool of blood on the floor of the cabin, his head in his sister's lap, and Clark and Tatiana on each side of him, gently restraining his limbs as he arched and kicked. His face was drenched in sweat and yellow like that of a corpse, except for spreading purple stains about his mouth as if he had been eating bilberries, and heavy dark bruises round his eyes. He tried bravely to contain his cries, but he was clearly in great pain and delirious as well. Anastasia was distraught, tears streaming down her face as she stroked the boy's hair, and then, as she spoke incoherently in Russian, Tatiana let out a sudden cry: 'Haemophilia!'

'Oh my gawd!' exclaimed Clark, 'is the poor little bloke a bleeder? There's not much we can do for him here, then. Every one of them bruises must be bleeding away inside, and as for these cuts – what do you think, little lady?'

Tatiana could offer no more comfort than Clark. The Tsarevich was weakening fast, and his screams bubbled only occasionally in his throat.

'We must land and find a doctor,' I said. 'But we must go south, until we are away from the bolsheviks, and hope that we can find one still loyal to the Tsar. I dare not land for at least an hour, or we will be delivering the boy back into the hands of the murderers.'

I told Tchaikovsky to alter course for the south-east, to where the Czechs held the railway, and so we drove desperately on, as the sun rose ever higher, and the forest unrolled before us, and the cries and sobs in the cabin behind grew gradually quieter. At last the forest gave way to the rolling grassland of the steppes, and I saw, clear on the plain before us, the thin trace of the railway line, and close by it a tiny village. I took the controls again then, easing the throttles slowly and coming down as gently as I knew how. The Ilya Murometz slid and staggered in the green grass, rolling on and on until at last it came to a stop. I had already switched off the engines, and as the great aircraft came to rest I became aware of the oppressive silence within the cabin. Clark came to my shoulder and spoke hardly above a whisper. 'The little chap's dead,' he said.

Tatiana and Tchaikovsky were both in tears. Anastasia was silent, but her eyes were wild, and she appeared unaware of her surroundings. I opened the cabin door, and gently set her down on the ground, where she began to pick idly at the grass blades. The boy was not a pretty sight, bloody and broken, his fists clenched and his limbs twisted in final agony.

There was nothing to do but bury him, there and then, on the wild and wonderful steppe, returned to the rich soil of his Mother Russia. Clark and I broke up one of the chairs from the aeroplane's cabin, and with these and our hands we dug a grave, deep enough to resist the scrabbling paws of the winter wolves. We laid the Tsarevich on the ground beside the aircraft, and then, for he had no further need of them, we stripped him of his breeches and boots and gave them to Tatiana. Tchaikovsky had gone wandering off, and now returned with a wide bunch of wild flowers, purple and white and yellow. And all the while Anastasia sat quiet, her blue eyes blind as the sky.

The sun shone, and the high larks sang uncaring, and we

lifted the thin body, light as a tiny child's, and lowered the heir to all the Russias into his grave. Tchaikovsky stood with his head held high, and sang in his thrilling deep voice, a long and tragic Russian hymn. Clark took a handful of the soil we had dug, scattering it over the body, and muttering 'Ashes to ashes, dust to dust, God rest his poor little soul.' And Tatiana, Tchaikovsky and I did likewise, and stood a minute silently praying. Then we filled in the grave, beating the earth down firmly, and Tchaikovsky scattered his flowers upon it. We could not mark it with a cross, for we feared that some inquisitive peasant would see it, and dig there to discover who was buried.

And still Anastasia had not moved, although she seemed to watch us with her empty eyes. But when Tatiana went to her, and spoke gentlingly, and tried to raise her and lead her back to the aircraft, she broke away, wailing, and flung herself upon the grave. We left her to her grief and walked, we four companions who had been through so much together, a little way across the steppe. We could not stay much longer, I argued, we must get Anastasia to safety.

'She will not go,' said Tchaikovsky, 'her mind is gone, and she only knows that she must stay here and mourn her brother – and perhaps her father and her mother and her sisters too, who can tell? Besides, here she is just a poor Russian girl; nobody knows her and she cannot betray herself. I am here too, and this is Russia, my native land, and she is the daughter of the Tsar. I will stay with her, and we will find a kindly family to look after us, for I have gold to pay for food and lodging. And when she is calmer, and her grief is less, in a month or two perhaps, then I will seek out help and take her to a place of refuge. Who knows? perhaps the Reds will be defeated, and she can rejoin those of her family who are still alive.'

Tatiana took my arm and led me aside. 'Do not argue with him,' she said. 'His mind is made up. It is for the best. He is home again in Russia, and he has a duty to the imperial family. And oh, my darling,' and she looked full at me, her dark eyes flooded again with tears, 'it is time for me, too, to say goodbye. I have thought of this for two whole weeks, alone in the consul's house away from you. This is my country, my people, my destiny is here, and I must part from you,' and she flung herself upon my breast, her arms tight about mine.

'Then I too will stay here with you,' I cried, desperate in my sudden grief.

'No, no, you cannot; you are under orders. You must take Nobby, and get back to England and tell them all that has happened in Ekaterinburg. You have to regain your name, and find your family again. Do you remember what I told you, that morning in London – is it only a few weeks ago? I told you of how much love I have to give, and today it is Russia that must take it all. There will be happier times, and perhaps we shall meet again. But now, my darling, go quickly with this one last kiss – and when you get to London, find my mother and tell her what I have done.'

We stood together, teased by the soft breezes of the broad steppe, the infinite arches of the sky stretching high above. I do not know whether we were there for a minute or many hours, I only know that the ache in my breast would not ease, even when I wept. At last Tatiana gently pushed me away, and I stumbled back toward the aircraft. Blindly I scrambled aboard, feeling, not seeing or hearing, that Nobby Clark was quietly impelling me. He led me to the pilot's seat and, when I was seated, put his hand on mine and guided it to the controls. Unbelieving, I heard the four engines roar into life and then, as the mist began to clear before my eyes and I instinctively took hold of the wheel and pushed the throttles up, I saw through the transparent nose of the aeroplane the steppe grass running faster and faster toward me. Without thought I drew the wheel down and the Ilya Murometz took off with its familiar curtseying dip, the engines howled louder and we went up to meet the sky.

I turned the aircraft in a tight bank round and round, higher and higher, seeing the three figures on the plain below grow ever smaller: the Grand Duchess Anastasia flung wide among the strewn flowers on her brother's grave, Tchaikovsky erect and wildly waving farewell, and Tatiana, still as a stone in her nurse's blouse and the breeches of the Tsarevich, her hands held tight at her waist, and her lovely face turned up to the heavens, full in the bright of day.

Slowly across the steppe toward them, I could see a peasant driving his cart. It seemed to me that he was smoking a pipe, and as I turned away to the south the sun flashed suddenly upon a pair of dark spectacles . . .

POSTSCRIPT

I can now confess that when I wrote *The Red Baron Lives!*
inspired by the discovery of a single mis-routed file in the
Public Record Office, I knew very little about my hero, and
absolutely nothing of his fate. The PRO file that had first
excited my imagination closed with a laconic minute, dated 31
August 1918 and handwritten in a characteristic violet ink: 'In
view of the rumours then current in Ekaterinburg,' wrote C,
'my man appears to have gone rogue.' To this was attached the
copy of a note to the administrator of the Secret Service Fund
instructing him that all credits in the name of Captain Simon
Jones should be immediately cancelled.

And there the trail went cold. Even if, somewhere, there were
other secret files with the same code-name 'Baron', there was no
way in which I could get to see them in my lifetime. Rather half-
heartedly, I admit, I pursued my researches into family papers
and contemporary writings, and eventually made an encouraging discovery: a brief indiscretion among the letters of Frieda
von Richthofen made it clear that her cousin was still alive in
1924, and indeed spent the winter of that year in Mexico with
Frieda and D.H. Lawrence. This was tantalising but of little
help, for search as I might in the correspondence of Mabel
Dodge, of Lawrence himself, in Dorothy Brett's *A Friendship,*
and in *Not I, but the Wind,* I could find no further reference.
Then, quite by accident, came the third and most fruitful of my

lucky breaks. A casual remark by my old colleague Mrs M-J. Lancaster, a passing mention in Sefton Delmer's *Counterfeit Spy,* an unintentional hint from my friend Ellic Howe, an apparently unrelated reference in Sir John Masterman's *Double Cross System,* two obscure footnotes in Ronald Lewin's *Ultra Goes to War* – these clues and some weeks of ferreting took me at last to an old people's home within sight of the main runway at RAF Abingdon. And there a sprightly 89-year-old, answering to the name of Freddy Baron, greeted me.

When I told him my name, and reminded him of the proofs of this book that I had sent to him, he smiled, the cool blue eyes warming briefly. 'I was expecting your visit,' he told me. But despite all my efforts I could not persuade him to admit to me that he was the Baron von Richthofen. He was prepared to tell me much about his adventures over the years, and from his more oblique references I was able to follow up some of my own researches in the darker corners of Intelligence history. When it came to his origins, however, he would not be drawn, muttering that he was very old, that it was all a long time ago, and, in any case, of little interest. There is no way in which I can prove that Freddy Baron, some of whose picaresque adventures form the body of the present volume, is the Freiherr von Richthofen who disappeared in Russia in 1918, but I hold to my own convictions, and eagerly await the publication of further documents to support them.

Select Bibliography

Aucleres, Dominique: *Anastasia Qui etes-vous?* 1962
Baedeker, Carl: *Russia,* 1914
Baerlein, Henry: *The March of the Seventy Thousand,* 1926
Becvar, Gustav: *The Lost Legion,* 1939
Bradley, John: *Civil War in Russia,* 1975
Burrows, William: *Richthofen,* 1970
Carisella & Ryan: *Who Killed the Red Baron?* 1969
Carr, E.H.: *The Bolshevik Revolution,* 1950
Cutlack, F.M.: *Official History of Australia in the War of 1914-18, Vol. VIII,* 1923
Dassel, Felix: *Grossfürstin Anastasia Lebt,* 1926
Dukes, Sir Paul: *Secret Agent ST 25,* 1938
Dunsterville, Maj.-Gen. L.C.: *The Adventures of Dunsterforce,* 1920
Flight Commander, A: *Practical Flying,* 1918
Gibbons, Floyd: *The Red Knight of Germany,* 1927
Gilliard, Pierre: *Tragique Destin de Nicolas II,* 1921
Green, Martin: *The von Richthofen Sisters,* 1974
Jones, H.A.: *The War in the Air,* 1935
Kiernan, R.H: *Lawrence of Arabia,* 1935
Krug von Nidda, Roland: *I, Anastasia,* 1959
Lawrence, T.E.: *The Seven Pillars of Wisdom,* 1926
Lockhart, R.H.B.: *Memoirs of a British Agent,* 1932
McCormick, Donald: *Pedlar of Death,* 1965

MacDonell, Ae. Randall: *And Nothing Long,* 1934

Moberly, Brig.-Gen. F.J.: *History of the Great War – the Campaign in Mesopotamia,* 1927

Neumann, Robert: *Zaharoff the Armaments King,* 1938

Nowarra & Brown: *Von Richthofen and the Flying Circus,* 1959

Preston, Thomas: *Before the Curtain,* 1950

Rathlef-Keilmann, Harriet von: *Anastasia,* 1929

Richthofen, Manfred von: *Die Rote Kampfflieger,* 1917

Summers, Anthony & Mangold, Tom: *The File on the Tsar,* 1976

Tennant, Lt-Col. J.E.: *In the Clouds above Baghdad,* 1920

Thomson, Basil: *Queer People,* 1922

Titler, Dale: *The Day the Red Baron Died,* 1973

Tuohy, Frank: *Crater of Mars,* 1929

Ulanoff, Stanley (ed.): *The Red Baron,* 1969

Zdziarski & Dmitriev-Mamonov: *Guide to the Great Siberian Railway,* 1900

FALSE FLAGS
by Noel Hynd

'. . . some sort of false flag job. It means someone is made to look like he's working for one country when actually he's in the employ of another.'

Bill Mason, ex-CIA, survivor of a Chinese prison, contemplating an empty future . . .

Robert Lassiter, the man who taught Mason everything he knows, the man who now urgently needs his help . . .

Six silicon chips, tiny micro-circuits that could mean everything or nothing, found in a London flat. They are the triggers in a devil's game of life and death and betrayal . . .

NEW ENGLISH LIBRARY

Book Tokens

**Give them
the pleasure of choosing**

Book Tokens can be bought
and exchanged at most
bookshops in Great Britain
and Ireland.

NEL BESTSELLERS

T51277	'THE NUMBER OF THE BEAST'	*Robert Heinlein*	£2.25
T50777	STRANGER IN A STRANGE LAND	*Robert Heinlein*	£1.75
T51382	FAIR WARNING	*Simpson & Burger*	£1.75
T52478	CAPTAIN BLOOD	*Michael Blodgett*	£1.75
T50246	THE TOP OF THE HILL	*Irwin Shaw*	£1.95
T49620	RICH MAN, POOR MAN	*Irwin Shaw*	£1.60
T51609	MAYDAY	*Thomas H. Block*	£1.75
T54071	MATCHING PAIR	*George G. Gilman*	£1.50
T45773	CLAIRE RAYNER'S LIFEGUIDE		£2.50
T53709	PUBLIC MURDERS	*Bill Granger*	£1.75
T53679	THE PREGNANT WOMAN'S BEAUTY BOOK	*Gloria Natale*	£1.25
T49817	MEMORIES OF ANOTHER DAY	*Harold Robbins*	£1.95
T50807	79 PARK AVENUE	*Harold Robbins*	£1.75
T50149	THE INHERITORS	*Harold Robbins*	£1.75
T53231	THE DARK	*James Herbert*	£1.50
T43245	THE FOG	*James Herbert*	£1.50
T53296	THE RATS	*James Herbert*	£1.50
T45528	THE STAND	*Stephen King*	£1.75
T50874	CARRIE	*Stephen King*	£1.50
T51722	DUNE	*Frank Herbert*	£1.75
T51552	DEVIL'S GUARD	*Robert Elford*	£1.50
T52575	THE MIXED BLESSING	*Helen Van Slyke*	£1.75
T38602	THE APOCALYPSE	*Jeffrey Konvitz*	95p

NEL P.O. BOX 11, FALMOUTH TR10 9EN, CORNWALL

Postage Charge:

U.K. Customers 45p for the first book plus 20p for the second book and 14p for each additional book ordered to a maximum charge of £1.63.

B.F.P.O. & EIRE Customers 45p for the first book plus 20p for the second book and 14p for the next 7 books; thereafter 8p per book.

Overseas Customers 75p for the first book and 21p per copy for each additional book.

Please send cheque or postal order (no currency).

Name ....

Address ....

....

Title ....

While every effort is made to keep prices steady, it is sometimes necessary to increase prices at short notice. New English Library reserve the right to show on covers and charge new retail prices which may differ from those advertised in the text or elsewhere.(7)